Misbeliever

by Éanna Cullen

Throw into hell every stubborn
<u>misbeliever!</u> - Who forbids good, a
transgressor, a doubter! who sets other
gods with God - and throw him, ye
twain, into fierce torment!
(Holy Quran Qaf: Qaf, English
translation by E.H. Palmer)

ISBN 978-1-84753-573-3

<u>A Note:</u>

Take your chances with this novel and learn something about yourself, and not a little of life.

Below you will read about how I almost died and about how I came to be privileged with life; in order of importance to the story.

I have been able to write a book and that is enough for me.

I saw the demon and have proof that he was real.

Believe it if you like, but enjoy the journey,

Jacob Terry (misbeliever)

Recollections 1

Obsequium funeris ~ Decus

At a funeral it is completely possible to look both pathetic and noble at the same time. In fact, it serves as an unexceptional rule.

In a field full of crosses, the rain soaking and the wind whipping, the best clothes of all were muddy and dishevelled. In situations such as this self inflicted gender-programming sets the faces of the men to hard and the faces of the women to soft and tear stained.

Today's gathering was typical to these policies of behaviour. They cared about their mortality in a way they could never allow during their normal explainable weekday mornings. In this case however, the mourners also cared about other things, interested parties; Reporters.

Outside the Cemetery gates these squinting creatures stand in wait with cameras and pads, with lists of names and targets. They braved the rain and the soggy discomfort, because being there meant a lot of things.

Jacob felt his head, running his fingers through the gel and rainwater. Why the hell had he dolled himself up so? Now his forehead was getting sticky and it was only a matter of time until he forget himself and wiped an eye with the sticky fingers he'd just cover in fashionable glue. There were hundreds of leeches here today and Jacob hated the whole thing, the whole stupid cemetery service show. What was it for? Who was it for? It was indeed a show and nothing more. He was sure of that.

Jacob felt the grinding fist strangling his stomach. He felt that he was no better than any one of these scrambling attention seekers. He did not believe in this sort of ceremony and yet, he was here, for vanity.

The previous morning he'd arrived at his Dublin home tipped his taxi driver and entered the cold empty apartment flicking automatically at his answering machine as he passed it in the hall. The squeaking voice message from his PR watchdog Janice had very nearly knocked him off his feet, such dreadful news it reported.

'Hi Jacob, welcome back; only one message today. That Italian writer... eh, Candelli croaked it yesterday evening. You'd better go to the funeral... looks like you're the big cheese now, eh!'
'Yeah sure,' said Jacob, answering the machine. He couldn't be dead. It couldn't be true.

But Daniel Candelli was dead indeed. Dead! Dead! Dead! Candelli was a good friend to Jacob and much more than the "Pompous old pain in the arse" Jacob had always called him. Hero; would have been a better description.

Daniel Candelli was a writer too. Actually, he was the only real writer of the two. Daniel wrote books that sold millions of copies, as did Jacob. Yet he also received a regular dose of plaudits and awards, while Jacob received none.
A few years ago Candelli had even received a lifetime achievement award from Noble's Gunpowder Company. And, it was not long after its presentation that he had disappeared.
It had been three years at least. Off the face of the earth wouldn't have been an accurate term, mind you, Candelli was around somewhere. But the Italian did disappear out of Jacob's world, a world of book signings, launches, and movie premiers. In empty cocktails parties with empty heads making empty

conversation, he was nowhere to be found. Of the many disappointingly fruitless dinners with unpleasantly narcissistic whiners, Candelli attended none. Jacob could say he hadn't really noticed but there had been extra sales, which meant money and Jacob always noticed money. And without a Candelli novel in three years a host of other writers typed frantically to fill the void.

In the Cemetery of the Most Holy Saint Peter amongst the hills of suburban Rome, the Padre invoked the Latin lines. They were well-rehearsed and spoken as such for hundreds of years.

Jacob thought about them as he always did. Who made them up? Ashes to ashes etc... Who actually sat down and worked it out, Jesus? Jacob never read the bible but he was pretty sure that Jesus didn't actually write any of it himself. So, somebody else must have.

Daniel always took care to tell Jacob how much he liked him. Jacob used to say that he would hate the old man if he weren't such a good cook. They had a bantering relationship. Mostly because Jacob couldn't have any other sort of relationship with another man and luckily Candelli knew this and treated Jacob as an old retired schoolteacher might cajole a former favourite pupil.

But Jacob did hate the man too, in a way. Daniel was better than he and Jacob knew it. Not just as a writer, that was blatantly obvious, but as a man too. The Italian author wrote from the heart, or seemed to, which was much more potent. Jacob wrote from between the legs, spitting his attitude at people, selling more books with his energy than with his talent. He even managed once or twice to get his horrifically unphotogenic face into movies based on his bland thrillers. He was young and he wrote for himself, fitting perfectly into his own fantasies. While the movies made from Candelli's work were timeless epics frequently associated with the golden grimace of a certain blind statuette.

Still Jacob loved, had loved, the elderly scholar. Daniel understood the power they had. No matter which of them was the more talented, the Italian understood the reason they were as popular as they were.

People believed them, believed in them. In fiction or in non-fiction, the people who read their respective books believed what they read for as long as it took to tell a story. And, whether the writing style was smooth and perfectly executed or just thrown onto the page. When you read their work, you believed it. Not many writers could lay claim to literary charisma like it. That was something special, something they shared. It drew them together and bonded them. Now Daniel Candelli, the one that had fully realised their talent was dead.

Dead, and gone, well not technically gone, unless the coffin was empty he was right down their in front of them, in a needlessly expensive box, going off.

Daniel's sister, Maria Candelli was looking at Jacob across the void. She Daniels Jacobs age but extremely pretty all the same. Was it wrong to think of her as he now did, younger, naked and sweating? This was a funeral after all and God could resent his lack of respect. Or maybe he would understand the basic animal nature he'd programmed into his arrogant monkeys.

Daniel used say that Jacob could marry Maria as soon as he became a real writer. Jacob used to say she was ugly and smelly and he'd never let a Candelli into his house unescorted. This was true, if she entered his house, Jacob would surely be following closely after, panting like a hound.

There were a dozen or so people encircling Daniel's muddied hole. A publisher, A couple of relatives, his ex-wife avec daughter Madeleine, a very tasty young Venetian girl, only ten years younger than him and making eyes at the millionaire she saw across her father's sodden box. Jacob looked down into the grave. Candelli was in there, in his box, probably getting soaked too. Jacob wondered if the funeral directors had put hair gel in the Italian's expired curls.

Jacob was still staring at the mucky wood when he noticed the movement of the funeral party as they headed towards the cameras, duty fulfilled and with headshots in mind. Jacob hurried after for the same reason.

There was a group of clergymen hanging around behind the hearse at the bottom of the hill by the gate. Like corner boys in a schoolyard waiting for the bell to ring they stood waiting for him as he trailed after the other revellers. The comparison made him smile. Then, as he grew closer, Jacob likened them to a group of old experimental trees crossed with human DNA. One, two, three… eight of them stood there in total. Eight priests, or bishops, whatever they were, Jacob wasn't known for his religious trivia. They should wear strips like in the army.

Their collars reminded him of Daniel again - it was his funeral - and that last telephone call three days ago.

'Howdy Dan,' Jacob had answered, 'what's your damage?' Jacob was stoned, watching Star Trek Voyager and stealing character ideas.

'Don't do it' Daniel rasped, 'don't let him come back.'

'Of course not,' Jacob replied smiling. 'Never would I ever let him come back,' unfortunately his sluggish mind realised the tone of Candelli's voice too late, stupid.

'Dan… Daniel?' he asked awakened by the wavering in the other's voice, but the line was dead. Lots of things were dead now. Ideas.

The octo-clergical circle closed around Jacob as he exited the hallowed grounds. He began mentally compiling a list of adverbs for funeral use.

- Deadly, falsely, sexily, youthfully, finally, tightly, and pitifully - Also
- Terminally, murderously, depressingly, darkly, muddily and sadly -

The copse of clergy took turns shaking him by the hand and all eight congratulated him on 'your last piece of work'. Jacob had no idea priests were allowed to read books like "Blood Suckers". He was happy however when the first three rubbed their hands uncomfortably after he shook them.

How many priests does it take to wipe the hair gel from a wet man's hand? Hilarious, he thought, one more adverb, you're on thirteen.

'Peacefully,' He said.

'Excuse me?' asked the nearest grey willow.

'I'm sorry,' Jacob told the priest, 'I'm a little preoccupied today,' He shifted from one foot to the other uneasy under sixteen pious eyes.

'Of course of course, young Jacob,' this one spoke again with an Irish accent. The leader, Jacob thought, or a chosen friendly voice.

'It's a terrible day for literature.'

'Yeah sure,' Jacob said. 'Listen, em?'

'Archbishop Dillon.'

'Fr Dillon, I'm really knackered… tired. I just want to go back to the hotel you know? Have a think and all that?' He looked for an opening in the Holy Circle. There didn't seem to be one.

For a moment Jacob was reminded of Red Rover, a game he used to play when he was a boy and wondered who the weak link in this chain was and what sort of reaction he'd receive if he burst unceremoniously through their ranks and dashed off down the road. It would really be sweet if the priests forgot themselves and gave chase and after being caught Jacob ended up at the bottom of a Catholic pile-up. Catholic pile-up, the reference led to a group of revolting images.

Concentrate.

Fr Dillon placed a hand on Jacob's arm as he snapped back into reality. The old man had tiny pupils even in this dim light. He looked like a real concentrator or maybe it was just colour blindness.

'I think you should stay in Rome a little longer, my boy' he said raising his hand and sweeping it around in a wide arc, Jacob waited for a bull to dash by. 'There is so much to see in Rome. So much to do.'

'I don't think so sir… Father. I'm not really up for…,' Jacob began but stopped in shock as the old priest squared up to him. Toe to toe, eye to eye.

'But the Vatican boy, surely you can't miss that,' then he tightened his claws on Jacobs arm and widened his eyes to whisper, 'especially when you could meet the New Pope eh? In person?' Dillon lowered his eyebrows one at a time and Jacob considered both the "invitation" and the old man's facial dexterity.

Over the boughs of the holy forest he could see the Candellis were climbing into their cars. Maria looked so beautiful and excited by the weather. He really wanted to see her soon. She must feel distraught to be smiling so bravely.

'OK,' he told Fr Dillon, 'but tomorrow yeah?'

Recollections 2

Damn it

The wonderful and elegant Maria Candelli. That's how Jacob had always labelled her in his mind. There was no other way to describe the woman. He could have called her beautiful but that would have been a fib. Beauty is a look, a setting, an arrangement of bones, or a matter of taste. Maria was a sixty-year-old woman that could draw the attention of every man in her vicinity, not with looks, but with her power. That was more than beauty. That was... What? Charisma is a very male word. So it was with elegance alone that she could be described.

There she was in the centre of the room, actually she stood by the large bay windows but to Jacob she was always the centre, no matter how worn out the phrase may seem. Around Maria the funeral party churned. There were plenty of people there, but less than six that cared a mite about Daniel or his family, who themselves accounted for many of the indifferent. The Italian writer's own wife -number three- was only there to find out what was in the will. A will, which Jacob knew -if Daniel Candelli could ever have been fully believed- left everything he owned to the homeless of Rome, to which he often claimed that, he was a member.

Not a penny to his wife, 'That woman has far too many problems,' Daniel had told him, although Jacob was sure that his fortune would have been welcome nonetheless.

Nothing for his Daughter, 'Her father will no doubt provide for her. She cannot be mine, she is far too skinny'

And, nothing for Maria, his sister and confidant, 'I would not want to have them pawing at Mari, not if I can prevent it. And anyway she would only give it to them!'

11

Jacob had a lot of ideas about what people, Candelli included, should do with their money and many of them included giving it to him. But, he had to say that he would be surprised if Candelli hadn't left them something. Or more likely, he'd left them with the promise of something. Yes, that would be more the old man's style. Get them scrambling over one another, make fools out of them, keep them busy. The thought made Jacob smile to himself. The bastard had probably arranged some sort of treasure hunt, like one of those awfully dire American movies made so that everyone could praise the fun loving side of capitalism. The smile on Jacob's face turned into a sneer when he admitted to himself that he would hunt down those clues as avidly as anyone.

'You're going to be bitter without him Jacob,' said Maria, appearing at Jacob's ear jolting him astir.

'You're very sneaky today,' Said Jacob, his face warming to her, 'is that you funeral sneakiness?' he looked down at his drink, a shy little boy around such a Queen, no Empress, Queen always made him think of cousin Billy with his wild blue eyes and his dazzling heels.

'Really Jacob, you think you're funny,' said Maria. 'Why don't you stop acting like a child, eh?' Jacob just laughed and Maria joined in. She linked her arm round his and leaned against him. 'Go on Jacob,' She said with a conspiratorial lean of her head.

'Oh no, I'm not in the mood.'

'Oh, my boy, please. It reminds me of such wonderful fun the three of us had. Please!' Maria begged, knowing that Jacob was only waiting for her to ask him the correct number of times before doing what was one of his favourite things.

'Ok,' he said, 'who will I do,' Maria laughed in very unladylike way and the masculine version of the word queen raised its stubbly head again in Jacob's mind.

'Do them, no, those ones. Yes, the Agent and Madeleine, oh do!'

'Very well Maria, for you, anything,' Jacob cleared his throat and began to narrate:

'Jacob turned to where Daniel's agent Hertz, a suspiciously pleasant man, was defacing a fine crystal goblet filled with expensive wine, merely by allowing his bulbous strawberry chapped lips to come into regular contact with it. He was drinking in between laughs and between laughs he was drinking. Hertz was using the wine to disguise how uncomfortable he felt in the presence of a recently dead man's daughter, and his rushed gulping belied his obvious distaste at having to listen to the shallow little wretch giggle and succeed with small talk, less than an hour after her father had been dropped in the mud. Perhaps I've misjudged him, I thought as I turned back to Maria who, as was usual in my company, was attempting to empty her own glass for an excuse to avoid my rapist wit and untrimmed nasal hair.'

Maria thought this was hilarious. If eyes could dance, which they can't, Maria bright blues would have been fluttering through Flamenco with purpose and skill. A woman who could laugh like that and yet seem so mysterious and elegant, that was Maria.

'Oh Jacob you are so good at narrating,' said Maria between wholehearted peals.

'Oh, not half as good as Daniel. Do you remember the time he called the conductor of the, oh, where was that again?'

'Prague.'

'Oh yes Prague!' Jacob laughed, 'When Dan goes: Ok boys, now remember to play what ever you like, the audience is full of Americans. I'm going to sleep, if you see me pissing myself, crescendo and exeunt all!'

'And all just before the first movement!' added Maria.

13

The two of them laughed again and it was like another party at another time, but like memories of such times, the humour just faded away and the two of them were left with the recollection of it and how it could never be again. The room was full of people, but it was Daniel's room, and it was empty of him and as such it was empty of everything.

'Fuck this,' said Jacob, the scene becoming too much for him to bear.

'Jacob!'

'No really Maria, fuck it. I have to go; I can't stay here, with these…' Jacob showed her the room, 'these mourners, Ha, mourners!" Maria gripped his armed tightly.

'Don't leave,' she said. She was brimming with tears.

'I have to. I'm so sorry'

'No, I mean, don't leave Rome, not yet,' Jacob grew worried, Maria was whispering and her usually chic expression was lost for a second and the worry on her face belied her age. 'I need to talk to you,' she told him, 'It's important.'

'Absolutely,' he agreed, 'I'm staying at the…'

'Eden,' said Maria her smile returning, 'as always Jacob, you are spoiling yourself,' Jacob shone back at her.

'I'll wait for your call,' Jacob said and kissed her lightly on the cheek.

It was then that Jacob left Daniel Candelli's old house and he was glad to escape. His skin was crawling. Not just as a result of being in close proximity to the jostling bastards inside the villa, but seeing Maria look so worried had thrown him off balance too. Her brother's death was the obvious reason for this, but Jacob was fearful that it was not the only one.

After driving back from the Candelli villa near Tivoli, an area that always gave him pause, Jacob found that he'd been too preoccupied to even notice the view of the Roman countryside.

Where as before he used to stop near Hadrian's Villa and go for a walk, maybe even smoke a joint, now he was so full of anger that he was back in Ludovisi before he knew where he was. Damn it and he could have used a smoke about now too. Jacob parked the rental car and hop-footed across the road as a white Renault sped by, barely missing him. Bloody Italians, their driving was atrocious. Oh well, he could have a smoke in his room, where he would probably be able to forget the day, for a little while

***

Rajette laughed as he made a u-turn in the middle of the Via Vittorio, causing the supposedly reckless Italians to shout out in disgust. Lives were threatened and the undersides of chins were flicked with distaste, which the Arab thought was really quite funny.

Rajette imagined himself getting out of the car, right there in the middle of the cross roads and showing them how their idle threats were carried out. He envisioned breaking the driver's window of the nearest road-raging Italian and dragging them out onto the road. He wouldn't even shoot them, no, he would beat them to death with something inoffensive like his mobile. Actually no, those things break easily and he was expecting a call, his shoe perhaps. Now, that would be an insult.

It was a pleasing daydream, but there was, as always, work to be done, urges to be resisted.

The white Renault pulled up across the road from the front entrance to the Eden hotel. Rajette's mobile phone rang and he pressed the speaker button on his car kit. It didn't work. When he finally did hear something through the speakers, it was the engaged tone.

'Zarba!' Rajette swore fumbling with the phone. After some seconds of techno phobic panic he managed to set the stupid thing up correctly and return the call. There was no answer and Rajette hung up and waited, and the phone rang again. Carefully the little man squinted forward and pressed the little green picture of a telephone.

'Hello?' he tried.

'Having trouble with your phone I see,' the voice was male, American, and amused.

'No sir, a… policia was passing,' Rajette hated to look stupid in front of people, especially when they were paying him.

'I see,' said the voice, he did, 'how are things going?' Rajette felt that he had sufficiently escaped embarrassment to continue the conversation.

'I'm outside the hotel, he is inside,' Speak shortly, he thought, it is more professional. Don't sound angry, or murderous, even if you are.

'Good. Follow him and tell me everything. Goodbye,' Kanith, Rajette thought, ordering him around like a child, how dare he.

'Hello?' he said, wary of making an audible mistake. There was a click and the engaged tone filled the car once more. 'Kanith!' Rajette swore aloud this time, 'you speak to me like that again Amerikan, I kill your mother,' the flat tone emitted by the phone seemed unperturbed by this. For months now he'd been sitting and watching. Always sitting on his ass like a monkey, an Israeli could do it. It made him furious, but he forced it down.

Work to do; urges to be resisted

Rajette cut off the phone and settled back into the driver's seat. Yes, he was being treated like a monkey, but he was being paid like a Prince. He'd also made an American connection, which was worth more than his fee. And if he did his job well, Rajette would be sure to make more.

16

Rajette looked more closely at Hotel Eden's entrance; he'd been looking all along, unconsciously, the way a person can walk to work without even thinking about the route. He was a professional, even if sometimes the urges got the better of him. It wasn't as though the white boy had seen him as he careered past, the fender almost touching the Irish man. It was just a bit of fun after all, something to amuse him while he watched and waited. The end, which was the part Rajette, enjoyed the most.

The end was never boring.

The proactive defences of nature

Approximately two thousand two hundred and two miles, three thousand five hundred and forty five kilometres, or one thousand nine hundred and fourteen Nautical Miles from away from Italy, Rome to be specific, Julien De Fois was feeling guilty.

It would take at least another five or six hours for the Cascades to dry up but he was already dreading the backlash from the locals. He could blame a lot of things for his betrayal of the Bobos and the Lobis and since twelve o'clock yesterday afternoon he'd tried them all on.

Excuse number one:
What am I supposed to do in such a situation? The people of the area need the jobs that the manganese mine can produce. Don't they?

Answer: No.

Number two:
It is not my fault. Since the fall of Sankara, Burkina Faso has fallen back into the old governmental ways of West Africa. Her ministers are rich. All government officials are forced to turn to corruption to survive. I have resisted it for so long (aside from the Mercedes last year)? If blame is sought, shouldn't we blame Compaoré who overthrew Sankara and pushed the entire country into decline?

Answer: Again no. And, if any of his constituents were close by and available for comment, they may have added. It's your fault, you traitor.

Excuse number three was Julien's most pitiful. It had something to do with the percentage of deaths related to contaminated water in the Banfora region over the last fifteen years. There had been twelve, but you get the message by now.

Julien De Fois had betrayed his people and there was just enough honour in the little rodent's soul to make the knowledge of it unbearable to him.

As a local government official, Julien was not exactly voted for per se. He was officially voted into office, but there was never any need for the people to actually go to the polls. The government saved them from the inconvenience of it and were sure that the people were glad that they did.

As a government official Julien's task was to see to the welfare of his constituents where their concerns coincided with those of the governing party of course. This left him a lot of time on his hands; time that he spent talking to developers and other powerful businessmen, chatting and enjoying their money.

These were interesting people to a small-minded man like Julien, the type of people that built factories on previously under-mined seams of magnesium; the same people that would need workers when the factory was built, and, oh, by the way, they were also the type of people who might very well ask certain questions of their local government official.

Questions like: Where is the nearest river?

And: Couldn't it be nearer?

The answer was of course: Yes, for a fee. There is a river not too far away. It's not terribly important to the locals either, you know. And it certainly doesn't have a three hundred foot, tourist-attracting Cascades feeding from it or anything. Honest.

So, at twelve o'clock on the day before this one, Julien De Fois had signed the correct forms to have the river diverted and his personal fortune inflated. Today the diggers had already moved in and an old quarry through which the river had been running southwards would soon undergo a change of personality. It would have its southern end blocked and its western wall demolished in that order. And, hey presto, just like that, the poor starving factory would have its river and justice would be done, for three and half stupid reasons.

It was a heart-warming time in Julien's life and it was no wonder that the emotion of it would soon prove too much for him. In a week's time, harangued and destitute, homeless and unloved, Julien De Fois would kill himself. The people of his district may have been poor and uneducated, but they believed in magic. And, more importantly, so did he. But that is something you'll be hearing about later.

So, what has any of this got to do with Rome or Jacob Terry?

Tons

Recollections 3

Big Deal

On Via Ludovisi in Rome, in the executive suite of the Hotel Eden, Jacob was mulling. He enjoyed a good mull. He sat on his balcony drinking scotch and thinking, or rather trying no to, which was easy. Jacob had spent many hours of his life not thinking, he was sure everybody did it. Obviously there *were* thoughts being thought, but they were inconsequential and able to think about themselves, leaving the brain free to shut down and blow dust over the memories of old friends and their absent futures.

Currently thoughts of whiskey were happening in Jacob's mind, completely free of his control and as dull as a Shepherd's social skills. He was thinking about Scotch and why he was drinking it.

Why indeed? It wasn't nice to drink, it didn't smell nice, so why? In movies and books, in bar and parties all over the world people were doing it. Again why?

Coolness, the thoughts decided amongst themselves. That was it. Scotch had a Steve McQueen-ness about it. Adults drank it and children wanted to. When you were younger, the thoughts told Jacob, you used to think that scotch would taste like chocolate. I did, Jacob answered, taking up his own cognitive duties once more.

He'd gotten it wrong of course, about the whiskey. When he'd tasted it for the first time in a friend's house in the middle of the night, the stuff had made him wretch. It was so bitter and galling. Again and again he tried to drink it, steeling his gullet in front of friends and smiling wryly as it went down his throat, pretending that it didn't burn him, showing everyone how cool he was. Oh Yeah.

How many other people had done the same, and not just with whiskey, with everything. Who didn't spend their childhoods aspiring to be something that wasn't real, copying something enough times only to find that the skills they prized so highly, the nonchalance, the indifference, were alienating them from each other.

Until you find yourself alone, your best friend having just died, drinking a drink that you never enjoyed.

Jacob shook his head. That's what he got for taking part in your his thoughts. He stood up and stretched, the thoughts of impending depression were depressing him. He needed a change of scene, to get out of Rome. This was Daniel's home, not his. It was a pity that such a beautiful place could conjure up such negativity, but there you go, Jacob was all about the negativity lately. At the end of his stretch he bellowed out the yawn that belonged to it. It was so loud it made him laugh and stagger a little. He was drunk, good. Jacob reached for his glass of single malted imitation but found that he'd misjudged the distance from hand to eye and simply turned it over on the tabletop. The liquid splashed out of the glass and the table was such that the whiskey formed into drops upon its surface and didn't soak in.

For more than a few moments Jacob watched the droplets move in the breeze like little translucent brown beetles. One of them was much bigger than the rest and whenever smaller ones blew near, they seemed to get sucked in. It was as if the Whiskey had its own liquid gravity and the other parts of its alcoholic self would return to the mother load. Homeopaths believe in the memory of water, although it seems unlikely. But if it does, then Whiskey would too, wouldn't it? Isn't everything in the universe either moving away from or heading back towards its origin. That would mean that everything had a sort of universal memory. Didn't it? Maybe the Pope knew. Or perhaps the Pope was too new to know yet. Jacob decided to ask him anyway.

Getting back to the spilled Whiskey, Jacob felt that, unlike the alcoholic lives of human, the liquid seemed it would never fall apart. How could it? Jacob's aimless drunken thoughts had taken over again.

'That's better,' said the thoughts as he reached for the bottle, 'Let us take care of everything.'

***

The New Pope indeed. All Jacob could think of when he thought of his Papalness was the Emperor from Star Wars. That often happened to him and, he expected, to a lot of other people. Whenever he heard the word "famous", Jacob pictured a red carpet and cameras flashing. When he saw a limo with a sunroof he thought of the movie "Big". At some point his mind had linked words and phrases to certain images in his memory, and now, whether by ingrained logic or, and he suspected this of his own, the mind was too damn lazy to update the images. Maybe the mind was like Microsoft, you just take it the way you get it, after all, what choice did you have?

'Mr Terry?' said the priest with the white goatee. 'Are you listening?'

'Absolutely,' Jacob lied, but the man, whose name Jacob had immediately forgotten was not convinced, so Jacob tried to convince him. 'You were saying that Rome was much more than the spiritual and cultural capital of Italy. It is the capital of the Catholic world. Of, em, Christendom, and so on. That if everything that has happened in this city were written in one book, it would take a century to write…' Jacob trailed off.

'What?' said the priest with the white goatee, 'I said nothing like that?'

'Oh,' Said Jacob, he could have sworn the man had said something about that sort of thing. 'Bad guess?' he tried, but it didn't help. The man facing him in the back of the Limo with the "Big" sunroof, was now annoyed and not showing any signs of impending good humour.

The car had arrived to collect him first thing that morning while Jacob was loosing an argument with the bastard behind his eyes. The Bastard, his headache, was being far too stubborn. Even now in the back of the Vatican courtesy car after being spoiled with several painkillers, the Bastard kept piping up. What about me? It said, don't you forget about me!

The bedside phone had woken the two of them, the Bastard and him, with the shrillest of rings. Greeeeeeeeeaaannnnn, Greeeeeeeeeaaannnnn! It harassed, until they'd had to get up. It was probably for the best though. Jacob had been in need of some air, and something -aside from alcohol- to keep his mind off the real reason why he was in Rome.

Hoping that he was right Jacob had taken the lift down to the lobby and noticed as soon as he emerged there that the Earth's orbit had decayed drastically during the night. The sun was now virtually on top of him and it burned the eyes right out of his sockets, figuratively speaking.

Christ! Jacob had thought, but there wasn't much he could have done then. He was up and out, and not the type to go backwards. This only left him, unfortunately, with forwards.

Resigned to his faith Jacob had paused momentarily at the front desk to leave a message for Maria, before walking out onto the street into the blinding light. Out there in the glare, stood a white stretch Limo, the door was open and a collared man with a white goatee was beckoning to him.

Stretch Limo. Did people still say that? They were all stretch, weren't they? It was then that Jacob had realised it was going to be one of those mornings where he wouldn't be able to control his own thoughts. And, although he was used to his spells of confused madness, the only way he could ever control them was by sitting down and getting some writing done. Well, that wasn't going to happen today, he was just going to have to make the best of the situation.

So Jacob had decided to take his confusion and his Bastard and get into the waiting car, out of the blazing sun. He could recover when he got back at lunchtime, if he hadn't been pan-fried in the sun first.

So there he was in the Limo, pretending to pay attention, Jacob, his Bastard and an increasingly tetchy clergyman.

'Mr Terry?' Said the priest with the grey goatee... Claudio was it? 'Are you listening?' Jacob resolved to keep focused from now on.

'Please,' he said, 'don't mind me, I am listening,' Claudio or whatever his name was looked at Jacob with great doubt before continuing. As he did so an expression of resignation replaced the peevish pinched look that had been on the priest's previous face. It was as if he was thinking, 'who cares if he listens or not, the quicker I get rid of this fool, the longer I'll have this Limo to myself. And then I can put my head out the sunroof and....'

'So,' Claudio began, interrupting Jacob again, 'there is a reason you were invited to come and see the Pope today,' Jacob tried to nod, but the Bastard told him that nodding was not so good.

'Apart from actually seeing the New Pope, you mean?' Jacob said. Claudio laughed to himself.

'Yes, apart from that. You see,' and now he leaned forward taking Jacob's hand and stroking it as though he were a sick child, 'the Church needs you Jacob Terry. She needs something from you. Something only you can give' Claudio leaned back and Jacob rescued his hand.

25

'You?' Jacob asked, 'aren't "the Church", are you? If you know what I mean?' alluding to the other's hand stroking. 'Because, if you are, I'm not really into, you know... that. You know what I'm saying?'

'Very funny,' said Claudio, giving Jacob a no-nonsense look.

'Sorry,' said Jacob. Claudio reached inside his shirt and brought out a bejewelled crucifix the size of a CD that hung about his neck.

'Do you know what this is?'

'Yes,' said Jacob, wanting to say, "Oohh fancy" but sensing that something bigger than his petty jesting was about to occur.

'This,' said Claudio, grasping Christ by the feet and shaking him in Jacob's face, 'is the reason for all of this. The Lord is the reason for everything,' Jacob nodded again, but this time the Bastard didn't respond, things were getting interesting.

'What about God?' Jacob asked, aware that he was expected to do so, but curious all the same.

'God?' Claudio smiled, 'God was here already. Long before the Catholics and the Islamic, the Jews and the Hindus, God was around in one way or the other. But he was only an idea then. A hope. A prayer. When the Lord came down from heaven he changed the shape of our faith,' Again Claudio shook the Crucifix. 'To this shape, his shape, the shape of man himself. Then they all started to have messiahs. The Lama, Mohammad, it became fashionable to have a manifestation of God, on which belief could be focused. Like the Egyptians and the Aztecs they saw that the power of their religions grew exponentially when a being of flesh was made the incarnate of God himself.'

Claudio's voice strained with emotion. Here was a quiver in his voice when he tried to continue, but the words escaped him. Once, twice, he attempted to resume before he found them again.

'I have always been certain that all of these other messiahs were nothing more than the clever marketing that they seemed to be. Because I knew the Lord and I have dedicated my life to understanding his words and the words spoken about him,' Claudio stopped then. The priest looked tired to Jacob who watched him as he slumped into his seat. Was it an act? Jacob thought not.

'And now?' Jacob asked. The priest with the white goatee looked up at him.

'Now, the story is incomplete. I studied for years the books of the Bible only to find that it was incomplete. Oh, I knew that it had been edited, reworded to suit people to whom it was being taught. But I did not know that there were pieces missing. Important pieces.'

'Pieces missing?' Jacob asked, 'There are *pieces* missing from the Bible? Like what?' He wanted to know.

'During Jesus life, the Romans ruled Judea yes?'

'Yeah,' If the life of Brian was anything to go by, Jacob knew this to be true, 'And?'

'Many of the young Hebrews were forced into service.'

'So…?'

'So, I have read accounts in the last two years that speak of a young Judean soldier in the Roman army. How he became a leader, that he was cunning, ruthless, a killer. The accounts speak of him murdering and raping along with his Roman counterparts…'

'No way, you're bullshitting me,' said Jacob, 'there's no way, no way,' Claudio smirked.

'In the beginning I thought, so what! Some man following Jesus' description, it means nothing.'

'So, come on, is it nothing?' Jacob really wanted to know now.

'That's where you come in,' said Claudio.

'I don't follow you,' said Jacob.

'It must be true because they want your help to write them in.'

'Them what?'

'The missing pieces! They, the holy Church want you to help them write the missing parts back into the Bible. It will be an astounding work. You have been chosen to explain the *why* of it. Why Jesus did the things he did. Why the knowledge was kept away from God's people for so long.'

'And?' asked Jacob, 'why was it? Or, more importantly, why bother to tell them about it now? Surely it's too late?'

'Well it's very complicated,' Claudio began, 'you see, freedom of information and growing interest in…'

'Oh fuck off!' Jacob told him, 'freedom of information, yeah right. Why, really? If all of this is true, then tell me why it has to be done?' Claudio thought for a moment before answering, it was obvious that he had reached the end of the information that he was supposed to impart, but he did answer.

'There is a man,' Claudio said. 'A man who knows…'

'But!'

'Shh… Not only does this man know, but also he has proof. If the Church don't try and beat him to it, he will tell the world, unless we give in to his demands.'

'Demands? What does he want, money? Come on, surely the Church has enough money to buy off a million guys who know?'

'Oh yes Mr Terry, '

'Jacob.'

'Jacob, you will soon see if you take this job, how much money the Church has. But this man does not want money.'

'What does he want?' asked Jacob. What could be more important than the mountains of money the Catholic Church could surely provide?'

'He wants to live forever,' said Claudio. Jacob was more than a little disappointed with the answer.

'What? He wants to go to heaven, is that fuckin it? Can't he just go to fucking confession or something?' Claudio shook his head.

'Can you believe that I asked the same question when I heard what he wanted. Exactly the same question?'

'Word for word?' Jacob asked.

'Especially *some* words!' Claudio said as his voice crackling with a regretful and bitter humour. 'But then they told me what he really wants,' Claudio took Jacob's hand again and leaned forward. This time the sentiment was not out of place. Now that Jacob knew what the man must have been thinking when he had first begun to speak, it seemed apt and conspiratorial.

'Jacob,' said Claudio, 'Yes he wants to live forever, but not in heaven. He wants to do it here. To rise from the dead like Jesus and be immortal.'

'Here?'

'Yes here.'

'And he thinks that the church can give him that?'

'He is not… a good man,' said Claudio leaving out *some* words and releasing Jacob's hand once more. 'He believes that the church has lied about the details of the Lord's resurrection and he wants us to share it with him. Of course, the church knows nothing of this, so you see why we have to continue along a different course.'

'Yes,' said Jacob. 'I see,' but he wasn't sure if he did. It was then that Jacob noticed the car hadn't moved for some time. 'Where are we?' he asked.

'Outside your hotel,' said Claudio.

'So we're not going to…?'

'No,' Said Claudio. Jacob nodded to himself. 'No Pope today,' he said to himself.

It was a lot to take in. The whole story was huge and completely ridiculous. One thing was certain. This week was definitely one for the scrap heap.

'The accounts are kept separate from each other, you will get some of them here, but the rest you will have to collect yourself. It is no longer important to keep them apart. Now that this man has gotten proof of their existence,' Jacob was shocked; he had somehow glossed over what his role was to be in this farce.

'Hey wait there,' he said, 'I never agreed to anything!'

'Of course, of course,' Claudio placated him, 'we will contact you tomorrow morning before you leave. I am sure you will have your answer then,' the priest ushered Jacob to the door that had been opened from the outside, allowing the nearing fireball of the sun to assail Jacob's waning state once more.

'Ok,' said Jacob, knowing that his answer would be a firm, no. He stood out of the car and the priest closed the door behind him. Jacob was turning to leave when he heard the window opening. Claudio stuck his hand out and Jacob shook it.

'Thank you Jacob, for listening at least,' said the priest as the engine roared. The driver, who must have opened the door, was back in his seat and the engine was gunning hard.

'Thank you, Claudio,' Jacob called as the Limo moved off and was swallowed by the hungry Roman traffic.

'Claudio?' mouthed the priest as window was wound up.

'Damn it!' said Jacob at the roadside, 'I could have sworn it was Claudio.'

It hardly mattered now anyway. He would meet Maria for lunch later, go out for a cure tonight, and tomorrow he would be gone, back home to Ireland. Or maybe somewhere further? Whatever he did, it wasn't going to involve him writing some PR booklet for the Catholic Church.

Jesus Christ murdering people, men who wanted to be reincarnated as themselves? Somebody else could have them. What Jacob needed now was a really greasy salty plate of fried food and a cup of tea. It was too bright out today. Perhaps he could go somewhere dark, but the only types of places that were dark at this time of day were strip clubs. Could he get a fry in a strip club?

Jacob wandered off, thinking about greased strippers and whether the two would be available together. He didn't notice Rajette as he fell into step with him a regulation thirty yards back down the road, nor did he notice that the little Palestinian man was fingering what could only have been a gun in his jacket pocket.

Well, you wouldn't would you?

Recollections 4

In the interest of coherence

By the time his lunch appointment with Maria came around,
Jacob was in a much more positive and stable mindset. The Sun's
apocalyptic advance towards the Earth seemed to have been
cancelled and instead the benevolent amber ball was smiling
down upon him, rather than searing the flesh from his crumbling
radioactive bones.

Yes, Jacob was in a great mood now. And, although he
had satisfied his grease requirements earlier in a nearby,
disappointingly moral café, Jacob was starving for a bit of lunch.
It seemed to him that over the last couple of hours he had gained
much needed perspective. Daniel Candelli was dead and that
was shit, but he had no control over it now. Some guy was
supposedly blackmailing the church, which was also sort of, but
not as, shit. The fact that he'd been offered the bizarre task of
beating the blackmailer to the punch was both unbelievable and
unwelcome, but Jacob had no control over that either.

Sitting in La Terazza, the roof garden restaurant of the
Eden hotel, Jacob looked out over the Roman rooftops, and
found peace in his latest summation that, yes, a lot of things
were shit, and no, he had no control over them. So, why worry?
It was a beautiful day, his head was clear once more, and he was
going to have to deal with everything whether he wanted to or
not.

That decided, Jacob picked up his menu and his new
mood spoke to him. Order what you like boy, it said, it's on me.

This was pleasing, because not only did the menu look
really fancy with its little velvet rope and tassel; it was also full of
things that he loved to eat. Cannelloni, gnocchi, Calzone and to a
lesser extent risotto, all his favourite Italian foods, and yes, they

really did taste better in Italy. Maybe it was physiological, or maybe it was the tomatoes? The atmosphere probably leant a hand too. Whatever it was, Jacob was in love with it. It felt good to recapture something of his liking for Rome. Only yesterday he'd been afraid that he could never come back again without feeling great sadness and regret. It really was amazing what food can do for you.

There were of course other reasons to come back to Italy and the most important one of these was walking towards him across the rooftop at that very moment.

Maria was not herself, Jacob could see that immediately. He rose to greet her. She gave him a wan smile and a peck on the cheek but seemed more interested in the view than in Jacob.

'Maria,' Jacob asked, 'are you alright?' She sat down and fidgeted something that he had never seen her do before.

'Oh Jacob,' said Maria, 'everything is so wrong,' She picked up her napkin and hid her face with it. Was she sobbing?

'Maria,' Jacob said, trying to be stern as he pulled the cloth from her grasp, 'what…' He stopped in mid sentence. She looked so frightened, what could possibly have happened?

'Maria?' he asked again, softly this time, 'tell me,' she sniffed and took herself to hand.

'I can't,' she told him, 'not really. I can never tell you really, because I don't understand it.'

'Don't understand what?' Jacob looked at her trying with his eyes to force the answer from her. It had the opposite effect and Maria broke down again. It almost seemed to him that she was someone else, not the woman he knew. This was Maria Candelli, the sister of his best friend and mentor Daniel. She was elegant and charming, intelligent and strong. This was not the same person at all.

So again, Jacob could feel his mood descend to the depths of yesterday.

'Oh Jacob,' Maria said suddenly and with a burst of rebellious energy. 'Don't do it Jacob. Just leave. Whatever it is they ask of you, refuse. Leave!'

'Listen Maria,' he began, but Maria was already rising to go. 'Wait,' He said. Maria reached into her handbag and brought out a small book, looking around frantically as she did so.

'Daniel was going to give this book to you on your birthday, he posted it back from the trip he was on, just before he died,' she said handing it to him, 'it's full of short stories about honour. Oh Jacob, he said it was exactly what you needed,' Maria patted Jacob's hand as he took the book from her. 'You're a good man, Jacob. You pretend you aren't, but you are,' a tear slid slowly down her cheek as she turned away and Jacob, felt a surge of horrible frustration. He wanted to stop her, make her stay and explain. He wanted to say something. But, for once in his wisecracking smart-alecky life, he couldn't push a single word out of his stupid mouth. Speechless. So this was how it felt.

'Please,' he whimpered moments later, but by then Maria was gone and left Jacob feeling more confused than ever.

This morning after he'd gotten out of the Church Limo Jacob would have readily put his hands above his head and admitted. Yes, I am officially confused. But now after what Maria had been trying to tell him, failed to tell him, his mental state that morning was akin to spiritual enlightenment when compared to how he now felt.

Jacob turned his attention to the street so that he could catch a glimpse of Maria again before she got into her car, but this only served to make things worse. Jacob's heart flinched away horribly in his chest from what he saw on the footpath below.

Outside the restaurant waiting at Maria's car were two men in black. Jacob cursed his constant vanity. Why did he always leave his glasses behind whenever he went out? The faces below were frustratingly blurred, but even so, he felt that the initial shock of recognition he'd felt had been right on the money. Dead on.

One of the men was largely built and Jacob couldn't place him, but the other was a much smaller, much older man, unmistakably grey and willowy. Down there on the street, intercepting Maria as she left the hotel was Archbishop Dillon, the leader of the Octo-clergical circle Jacob had encountered at Daniel's funeral.

Jacob watched the two men as they guided Maria into the car, the larger man climbing in with her. This was of some relief to Jacob. He couldn't explain it, but he somehow preferred the hulk to the scrawny Dillon anyway. The Archbishop's presence frightened Jacob. It meant that all of the events of the last two days were connected somehow, and couldn't be ignored. Not any more.

Fr. Dillon turned his attention upwards from Maria's car as it drove away. He looked up at Jacob and held his gaze. He didn't smile or sneer, or squint or nod, no. There was no expression on the old cleric's face at all. He simply looked up so that Jacob could see him clearly. It was a dumb statement of fact.

Yes it is I, Dillon's presence told him. Work it out.

After that the Archbishop walked off out of sight down the street, as though he were strolling carefree to church on a Sunday morning and Jacob was left half-standing and looking out over the restaurant wall at the empty street below.

Oh my god, he thought, what the hell is going on?

As he sat back down he noticed the book that Maria had brought him. It was typical of Daniel… had been typical of Daniel to buy a present for someone, either for a birthday or for Christmas, long before it was needed. Jacob's birthday wasn't for another two months, but he guessed that Daniel had planned to read the book himself before giving it to him. That way the two of them could have heated arguments about its content.

The old bastard

Stories of Nobility and Honour, the book was called. And, inside the cover Daniel had written an inscription:

For Jacob, I just thought you would like to know what you are missing. Daniel.

Jacob smiled at this.
    'Asshole,' he said aloud.

***

In the white Renault Rajette watched the day unfold upon Jacob like an anvil hidden in a bed sheet. Everything seemed to be happening according to plan as far as he could see. Unfortunately for Rajette, this meant that there was no chance of a little action. Jacob was being easily led and as yet didn't need any knuckled reminders. The writer was also quite safe and unharmed, meaning the Black and Whites didn't warrant a pasting either. How boring.
    That evening the hired Palestinian pinch followed Jacob out to a bar and watched with pleasure as the young man's face displayed the pain and obvious personal anguish that he must have been feeling. It wasn't as good as actually beating the hell

out of him, but Rajette reasoned that as long as someone was suffering then the day wasn't a complete loss.

Rajette left the bar at quarter to twelve and headed back to his car outside the hotel. It was beginning to smell like cheese and unfiltered cigarettes, which was comforting. As he suspected Rajette had returned just in time to see a light being turned off in Jacob's room, the Black and Whites were at work again, perfect. As soon as Jacob was asleep he would go up there and take a look at what they had left behind. Then he would have tomorrow's destination. Rajette leaned back to wait.

At twelve forty, bang on time, Jacob came rolling around the corner and up the street. Rajette had known that it would be twelve forty because the bar they'd been in was closed at twelve and Jacob, in his state would be shown the door by twelve thirty. After that the three minute walk would then take at least fifteen minutes.

It took a couple of practice runs but Jacob managed to mount the front steps to the hotel and manoeuvre himself through the lobby doors, which were held open by Christopher who worked as a night porter and was used to this sort of behaviour from the excessive and the wealthy.

Five minutes later Jacob was mostly in bed and soundly asleep, fully clothed and snoring. He had almost been on his hands and knees in the hallway as he tried to put his key card into the little slot in the door. Fortunately the porter had been following at a respectable distance. And, after giving the distinguished guest a deferential number of attempts at opening the door, Christopher picked up both card and owner and did it for him, helping himself to a generous tip from the wallet that Jacob had thrown at him saying.

'I think it's in there, off ya go, work away, mumble, mumble,' And Jacob was asleep.

Now, Christopher wasn't a bad guy. He didn't steal any cards or anything. He didn't even take all the money. He only took some of it. Well, most of it actually, but he left enough for a taxi to the airport. Not a bad guy at all.

After leaving the room Christopher walked down the hallway, head down, counting his money. A dozen steps on and he came to a complete stop as he felt something press against his bowed head. From Christopher's perspective all that he could see was an expensive looking shoe and a pile of recently dropped money, covering presumably, another expensive looking shoe.

'Don't move,' said a voice, 'I have a gun against your head.'

'Ok,' said Christopher shaking. It wasn't that he was a coward. There was a gun at his head, or so he'd been told. That sort of thing would make a lot of people wet themselves.

'That's disgusting,' Rajette informed the porter, his nose wrinkled with distaste. 'Do you have a key card for the door?' he asked, nudging Christopher's head with the muzzle of his gun.

'Wha?' Christopher squeaked. Rajette spun the porter around and marched him up the hall to Jacob's room.

'Open it,' said Rajette. Christopher didn't for even a brief moment harbour any ideas of refusal and immediately took out his master key-card to open the door. Rajette was a little disappointed at this but he supposed that it could be taken as a compliment, so that's how he took it.

Using Christopher as a doorstop Rajette entered the room and straight away found what he was looking for. On Jacob's bedside locker there was an envelope and a leather wallet of papers. Rajette ripped open the envelope and read the letter inside. It had a check attached. He straightened the letter out and placed it on the table. And, taking his mobile phone from his pocket he took a picture of it. It took him a couple of tries before he was sure that he had a readable picture of it but the flash was bright enough and the penmanship wasn't too flamboyant. Then Rajette took an envelope of his own from his breast pocket and folded the note and the cheque into it whilst putting the ripped envelope and his phone back into his pocket. Everything was now in order.

Rajette left the room stopping only to whisper in Christopher's ear.

'Go and pick up your money,' He said and strode towards the stairs. There was no need to threaten the porter for silence. Rajette knew the type, just a normal guy. He wouldn't tell a soul. Even if the thought did cross the porter's mind, he had his money and his embarrassment to think about. Better to just forget the whole thing had happened, that was the easy way and normal guys always took it.

Rajette left the hotel and crossed the street to his car. After sending the picture by email and calling Marshall to confirm his orders, Rajette was off to the airport. He felt good that this part of the process was over. There was no doubt now that the writer would take the job. He had little choice now after the little show the Black and Whites had put on for him.

The most professional way to follow someone was to find out where they were going and then get there first. This meant that the pursuer could familiarise the lay of the land and plan his strategy before the target even arrives. This was straight out of the FBI textbooks and Rajette was a big fan of the FBI. Not the real FBI no. The movie FBI now, they were the business, "Hands on your fuckin head!" and all that jazz.

Anyway, all the "lay of the land" rubbish hardly mattered in this instance, because Rajette knew everything there was to know about their destination.

The Palestinian was going home.

Finally, he thought, some real food.

***

In the morning Jacob was surprised to find that his hangover
was nowhere near as punishing as it had been the day before. It
was quite possible though that he was still drunk, so he decided
not to make any assumptions just yet. Waiting in the back of his
mind, Jacob knew, were dark thoughts that were jostling for his
attention but he resisted them for as long as possible in order to
make himself a cup of coffee and turn on the television. Jacob
always put on the television when he wasn't writing, even when
he had no intention of watching it. He was prone to loneliness
and it made him feel like he was connected to the world.

Jacob's blissful ignorance however was quickly stamped
out by the presence of an envelope and a large leather folder on
his bedside table. He couldn't remember seeing it the night
before, but then again, he couldn't remember seeing much of
anything after eleven o'clock.

He opened the envelope and read the letter.

Mr Terry,

*Enclosed is a cheque, which you will find is most generous. Thank you
so much for your assistance in this matter. Below is the address and
phone number of a prominent church scribe by the name of Darit
Richeloe. He has been informed of your visit and will have the relevant
papers ready for your collection.*

*In the folder you will find copies of the information and notes
compiled by Fr. Alexander De'Angelo with whom you spoke
yesterday…*

'Alexander,' Jacob said aloud, he'd been way off. The rest of the letter was an address in Jerusalem of all places. So that's where he was going? He didn't seem to have any other option. The decision had to be made, and with Maria in mind, Jacob made it.

It was then that Jacob decided to play the fool. The priests, he told himself, were merely friends of the Candelli family who were helping Maria through a difficult time. Daniel's sister was obviously distraught at his loss and could not been taken seriously in such a state. The lie actually made Jacob feel better. The falseness of his logic was classic.

He picked up the cheque and stared at it. He even got a pen and paper from his bag and wrote the figure down upon it. It was a huge fat number that pleased him greatly.

Well, Jacob thought, if he was going to fool himself for anything, it may as well be for a big dirty pile of money. He might not agree or even understand what he was taking upon himself, but one thing was for sure.

He was getting paid.

***

Coherence, meaning and other worthwhile aims

People are always talking about finding meaning in their lives. What a load of rubbish. Everything has meaning.

In every week there are seven days, and in each of them there are twenty-four hours. In every hour there are sixty minutes and in each the same number of seconds.

Inside every single second there are probably lots of other measurements of time with names like nanoseconds or milliseconds. And, someone with the capacity and know-how to do so has broken down these too, into even smaller dot and blips of existential measurement.

It really is amazing that the human brain can even fathom such ideas. But what is even more amazing is this:

All the time, regardless of the unit chosen to quantify it, the universe is doing something. *We* are doing something, going somewhere, growing, dying, feeling, rotting, expanding, ingesting, reacting, excreting, and making lists. In every version of time, every second, every hour, every fortnight, all the bank holiday weekends, during summer holidays, surgery opening hours and commercial breaks, we are thinking, and we are living.

If you can't find meaning in that, then there probably isn't any to be found anywhere. Not even on eBay.

***

A week later Jacob was thinking his own thoughts about meaning. He too was wondering about whether he could find meaning or whether it was supposed to find him. He was on a plane again, leaving Israel for Africa. The last seven days had been full of events that were full of meaning for Jacob. Unfortunately, he wasn't sure what they meant.

Africa? How did he get to this stage? Where were his choices? He couldn't remember making any at all recently. All he knew now was that he was afraid and lonely and had more to lose than ever. But he denied himself the truth of it. He wouldn't back out now, he would never back out. Instead he would pretend that at any moment he *could* back out. Just give them back their money and walk away. Hell, he could give them back twice what he had been paid, that was all he had to do. And, then he could go and find Becky, and they could be together.

It wasn't that simple, not any more. It was only a week after Rome and already it was too late to stop. He was hooked, and he was decided. No matter what the outcome.

Jacob would come to regret that decision. It would break his heart. But for now he pretended that it wouldn't, that it couldn't. He even fooled himself into thinking that he was not being used.

Who is the Head Man here? Jacob asked himself as he watched the little plane on his TV screen move slowly closer to Ghana. Jacob Terry; that's who. He was one hundred percent in-charge of the situation, like always. He could handle it all. Weird scribes, little druggies with guns, losing his only friend and mentor. Yeah, he could handle.

Jacob leaned back into his long hall flight and thought. What else could possibly happen to him after this last week in Israel?

After all, hadn't enough happened to him already?

Recollections 5

Turn over your doubts

Turn over your doubts and spread your arms apart.
Submit and be saved by the light in his heart,
And your soul will be once more, a joyous place.

<u>Israel: One week later…</u>
It was midmorning in Jerusalem and the call to prayer was once again creating an atmosphere of otherworldliness as it reverberated around the old city. It was also the day before Jacob was to set off for Ghana. He was sat for the second time on the other side of Richeloe's desk and wondering how it came to be that he was now taking orders from the old man. He'd always sworn that he would never work for anybody but himself. In fact, he was sure that that was one of the most important parts of being a writer.

He was to leave immediately for Africa, West Africa in fact or Ghana to be precise.

It seemed unlikely that the Church would keep such sensitive material in Africa. As Jacob had witnessed the day before, Richeloe kept the papers in his charge under such complicated restriction it was more than a little odd to hear that similar material had been placed in the hands of some African librarian.

Jacob was no racist, he didn't think so anyway, but he was pretty sure that all these African countries were corrupt and dangerous. Narrow minded maybe but definitely not a racist.

It didn't make sense. Why Ghana? It was a serious question. So Jacob asked it, if not in expectation of a coherent answer then, at least with the hope of looking vaguely intelligent.

When Richeloe answered it was as usual, hazy and sermonised, the man obviously accustomed to preaching.

'You have no understanding,' he told Jacob, 'of the simple honour bequeathed upon the African Christian.'

'Bequeathed?' asked Jacob, now there was a word that should have gone down with the Titanic.

'And!' Richeloe interrupted with a tired schoolteacher's harshness. 'The key is not why, young man. The key is where,' Jacob rolled his eyes but listened all the same. Richeloe continued as though he hadn't noticed the slight so Jacob began spinning his pencil between his fingers as annoyingly as possible. It wasn't enough and the Scribe continued with his speech unaffected.

'A clever location can be as effective, nay, more effective than locks or metals doors,' Richeloe continued, 'because, though combinations and chains may be cracked, a secret my young friend, is sacred,' Jacob missed a spin and the pencil dropped on the table. He reached for it again and Richeloe paused to grip Jacob's hand over the dark hard desk. The Scribe's face tightened as he leaned forwards. His expression turned churlish and the coiled cunning that lay beneath the surface was suddenly revealed. Cunning that now hovered only a few inches from Jacob's barely contained surprise.

'You will keep this secret too, young Jacob,' the expression never changed. 'You will not crack,'

Jacob gulped. Did Richeloe know about the Americans, or was it a test? No, he couldn't know. What would the old man do if he found out that some of the documents that he had handed over to Jacob only yesterday were now in the possession of a third party? Could they hurt him, or harm Maria? Jacob recalled the sensation of having a gun held to his back, and the memory assured him of how serious all of this really was. The moment of tension passed, however and it seemed that Jacob had gotten away with his betrayal so far.

'Well?' asked Richeloe the amiable softness returning, the frightening grimace receding. 'You understand, yes?'

'Yeah sure,' Jacob nodded weakly freeing his hand from the others grasp. The white pressure mark remained for a moment, his fingers tingling for a few seconds longer. The old man's body was weak, but his spirit was solid and fervent enough to supply him with great strength. Jacob could feel the sweat dampening his back.

'When do I leave?' He asked with a feeble smile. What have I gotten myself into? He thought. Richeloe rose and went to the door opening it.

'Well, off you go,' He said, 'I'll send a boy round to your hostel with your flight details. You leave tomorrow,' Jacob had little choice but to take his cue and leave.

'Oh Jacob,' Richeloe added as Jacob tried not to rush through the doorway, 'you will take care of the documents I have given you. They are worth a great deal,' Jacob was at eye level with Richeloe and he was sure he saw, for a moment, a twinkle of acknowledgement in the scribe's. Surely he didn't know.

'Absolutely,' Jacob answered without a flinch or delay. Well, he thought, may as well be hung for a sheep as a lamb, eh?

***

Ghana…

Two days after leaving Israel Jacob set foot in the airless terminal building of Kotoka Airport in Accra, Ghana. He still felt uncomfortable about his lying to the old scribe, bet what else he could have said.

'Actually Richeloe, I only have a few of those scrolls left. I gave the rest to an American guy with a gun, you know how it is?'

Jacob stopped worrying for a moment and paused to catch his breath. There were butterflies in his stomach engineering a hurricane in his chest and the heat was making him feint. It was seven o'clock on Saturday morning and he felt so alone. He wanted to see Becky's face, or at least to hear her squeaky little voice giggling at his crap jokes and cheering him with her own.

The Airport was an Airport and nothing more. A sluggish queue, a brief moment of panic over his misplaced passport and he was free of it. His mood was darkening. Becky was in London now and there was no time difference between them, it seemed like a hundred years since he's left her in Tel Aviv and a thousand since they'd met only a week before. He couldn't call her at this hour. He would sound desperate and uncool. Sleep, if it came, would have to do him for now.

Outside in the early light Jacob found that getting a taxi in Accra was never going to be a problem. Dozens of taxi drivers accosted him as soon as the automatic doors whooshed open. They shouted prices at him and tried to lead him away. He caught himself about to snap at one of the black men talking loudly, shouting prices in his ear. Calm yourself Jacob; he ordered himself, this is probably worth a lot to them.

'Let me see, how much? Twenty five thousand, twenty thousand?' He hadn't thought to learn the exchange rate and he was loath to take out his lonely planet to see whether he was getting robbed or not. Jacob decided to trust his judgement and picked a bearded driver with a pleasant smile, as the other drivers had neither. Jacob knew he was a useless judge of character so a little blind luck was his only option.

Tee hee, he thought.

After negotiating the car park Jacob's driver led him down the main airport road to where his taxi awaited. Climbing into the front of the rickety yellow and brown painted car Jacob quizzed his new African friend about decent hotels in the embassy district. He was ready for bed but later he was thinking of taking advantage of the trip and visiting some other countries in West Africa. That plus laziness caused him to choose accommodation near the embassies of Mali and Burkina Faso, so as to avoid any unnecessary walking. Jacob had seen the name Timbuktu on the map and couldn't believe his luck. Was it a real place? He couldn't wait to be half way there. He let out a huge yawn and began thinking again of a nice soft bed. After sleep, he could do things.

'Not too expensive of course,' He told the taxi driver who didn't respond. 'Any suggestions?' he tried again. George the pleasantly bearded Taxi man had three.

'Hotel California' Jacob exclaimed at the second. That would do perfectly. Pleased with the idea he settled back and thought for a moment of the writings that were left in his carry-on bag and his mood slumped once more. The things that were written on those pages!

So far he'd read about Jesus as a soldier. He'd learned that Jesus name was actually Joshua and, on the corner of a boorish account of a suspicious arson, that Jesus, sorry… Joshua was punished for by the village elders, he'd found a spot of blood, or ketchup. No, it was definitely blood. It gave him a shock to realise it, but he felt an unwelcome idea building slowly in the part of his head that he usually gave the most freedom.

He flinched away from the disturbing thoughts and he refocused himself on Jesus, sorry… Joshua. How could he spin Joshua's service in the army? After reading it, it seemed logical that the Pre-Lord had served his time in the local militia. The

Romans were ruling the country at the time and they demanded that a certain amount of young men be forced into the service, if only to free up centurions for more important front line duties. Concentrating Jacob began to spin the idea around. He could write about some great epiphany on the eve of Joshua's first battle, though the records showed him surviving at least three. Such a revelation could easily have caused Joshua to rethink a military career, but what?

The taxi entered the city of Accra as Jacob stared out into space and the clay secondary roads flicked by under his blinded gaze. The car jerked suddenly and Jacob was shaken free from his hazy storyline visualisations.

Then he saw it, Accra. It was right in front of his eyes and he had been letting it go by!

The dirt road they were currently on had rickety stalls set up along on either side for as far as the sun would allow his eyes to see. The stalls were full of... everything. There were people carrying massive silver bowls on their heads, filled with bundles of cloth or stacks of fruit, handheld stereos and handkerchiefs. Women with children on their backs wrapped tightly in coloured fabric, their large behinds serving as a shelf, big enough for the child to ride comfortably in sleep or look out sideways at the crowd. While stopped at a Junction one such child with only a ribbon to belie her gender, gawked at Jacob with wide eyes from her perch behind a woman he supposed was her mother. Jacob smiled at her and the child burst into tears and turned quickly away, and then he noticed his reflection in the window. He was so damn white! It must have been a big shock to the child living in such a black place.

Here it was, Africa.

The streets were a shock to the system. Where were the buildings? Was this entire city comprised of shack like shops and dirt roads? It was so poor looking.

But he shouldn't think like that. This was a different world, there was no point being a total snob about it, and turning up his nose at a city he knew nothing about, at a culture he hadn't even begun to understand.

Keep your mind open, he told himself and sank back into the leopard skin upholstery. He was in Africa and it was the only positive side effect to this mysterious adventure, but he had little time to enjoy it. He had to think of Joshua and the book he was already beginning to hate. And he hadn't yet written a word.

So Joshua didn't stay with the military? How would he write the Lord out of that? Not cowardice of course, but a memory of an Aramathean playmate from the same region where Joshua would soon be battling. Yes, that would do. Rebellion rather than cowardice that was the way to go.

Would that be enough for Richeloe and the Archbishops? No, he guessed that it would not be, but the real problem was that he wasn't sure what would. There were too many records conflicting with each other. Most likely he would have to include all of Joshua's war records and give reasonable explanation for the Lord's murderous past. And, what of the scrolls he had handed over to the American? What secrets did they hold that he would now never discover?

Corner cutting already, he thought. That was no way to write a book.

***

The Taxi stopped alongside a massive stack of rubble between two buildings. Here stood, - figuratively speaking- the now closed, Hotel California.

'It looks deserted,' Jacob stated, pointing to the empty space. 'Is this it George?' he added, anger rising. 'Am I supposed to get a fucking room in there?' A bird landed on the demolished hotel and cawed at him. Jacob suddenly felt the need to kill something. The bird, however, was a mere innocent.

'No' George answered. Nothing about the driver belied his possible surprise. He just sat there waiting for Jacob as if the white man had just climbed in.

'Did you know?' he asked, but George said nothing. 'Hey, you fuckin asshole! Did you know this place was… gone?'

'Yes'

'Then why?' Jacob was shocked. 'Are you stupid?' Jacob asked him. George turned around, looking upset now.

'Eh! Why you say that?' he asked 'I wan-ted to go to a Ho-tel" Jacob mouthed, 'to sleeeep in!' George looked deeply hurt now. 'Take me to an open Hotel now!' Jacob raged 'Hurry,'

Jacob fell back into his seat. 'Un-fucking believable,' He mumbled through clenched Jaws.

Relax.

George took off, grumbling and beeping his horn somewhat randomly at the other cars on the road, mostly Taxis, as he went. Jacob imagined it a code.

'Beep-beep-tourist-coming-through-beep' Or maybe it was, 'I'm-a-big-beep-bearded-idiot-beep-beep-beep!' Jacob was peeved and as they drove through Accra spent the next ten minutes grievously injuring his new Ghanaian friend with imaginary pitchforks.

Eventually the Taxi stopped outside the actually photogenic 'Lemon Lodge' on the decidedly fruitless Mango Tree Avenue. It was in a district called Asylum Down and when Jacob read the address in his guidebook it made him smile. Perfect, he thought.

George helped Jacob out with his bags. Jacob's large rucksack, a veteran from his backpacking days, was very heavy and it surprised the driver who stumbled under the weight. Grinning, Jacob steeled himself and took the bag off him hefting it onto his back, sharing the bulk evenly over his frame and pretending that it weighed him down no more than schoolbag would. Then Jacob handed the Ghanaian his smaller knapsack and noticed the annoyed look on George's face. In the "lobby", a room that was neither outside nor in, Jacob took the bag back from him.

'Twenty thousand?' he asked doubtfully, knowing that George would probably demand double that for his round trip here.

'Oh no, now,' began the bearded weirdo.

'Forget about Hotel California,' Jacob ordered. 'I'll pay you from the Airport to here.'

'Fifty thousand' George tried - you had to admire that gall of the man-

'I won't pay more than twenty five' Jacob argued only for the sake of it, he was tiring of this tourist's pretence but was far too stubborn to just let it go, as far as he was concerned, tourists always pay more, and it was probably the equivalent of a quid, but it's wrong to rip people off, full stop.

Jacob paid forty-six in the end.

George was guilty, Jacob decided, and shouldn't get away with it.

Inside Jacob found four Africans standing at the desk. He asked each one in turn for single room for three days. After a long silence one of them called out something to the air and received a short answer from a deep male voice. Jacob asked again.

'Can I get a single room for three days?' he asked and once more the four Ghanaians just look at him. Jacob felt his blood begin to shoot around his body as his heart picked up its pace. He growled quietly under his breath and focused on the oldest male, asking again.

The man tsk'd him and said something wearily to the youngest, a boy really. The boy humpf'd and moaned before the oldest man spoke again roughly and he sloped out through the door behind the counter. There was an excruciating pause before Jacob began to shout. - The words "Stupid" and "Fuck" featured continuously-

The slackers began to laugh as the boy returned with another man, stopping Jacobs ranting immediately. This one was huge and fat, with greying hair. Even before he spoke the others were scampering off out the front door. He shouted after them and Jacob felt like shouting "Yeah!" in agreement.

'Now sir,' said the man. 'You would like a room?'

'Yes,' said Jacob. 'Yes I would.'

Jacob paid the man up front. Three days should be enough, he thought. He could relax here a while and get adjusted before going to the beach. Then was due in Kumasi on Thursday. But first He would have a rest and then he would write a little, if he could.

'Is your first time in Ghana?' asked the fat man behind the counter.

'Yeah,' Said Jacob.

'You will enjoy it yes,' He was told. Jacob thought about Daniel and Maria, and about Joshua and Becky.

'I doubt it,' Jacob said and began climbing the stairs to his room.

***

Take a step back in time, a week to be exact. Back to Jacob's first day in Israel and meet Becky for the first time, and witness another beginning, of which in life there are so many, but none as important as this one, because there is little that is more important than love.

Recollections 6

Israel and love, the two happening together

When he first landed in Israel Jacob received a message on his phone telling him to meet the first scribe in Jerusalem in five days time. What he would do in the meantime, he wondered.

Think. That was all he could do. Think and wait. These being two things that he was definitely not in the mood to do, Jacob decided to stay in Tel-Aviv and try and have a bit of fun. He'd been there before. He knew bars.

Jacob's accommodation in Tel-Aviv was simple at best. He'd stayed once before, in this very hostel, on Dizengoff Square, a much poorer man. At the time he had shared a room with a group of Korean pocket rifflers and had to stow his belongings in a locker. He wanted to see if the place was the same and if so, had his perspective changed? In other words, could he still live like that? Over the years since the dawn of Jacob's success he'd allowed himself to be pampered and his preferences had become concrete and necessary, which may have ruined his willingness to take adventure over discomfort.

But now that he was there he felt he could handle it, so far anyway. And, disastrous career choices aside, this pleased him.

Immediately after arriving, Jacob took to the showers. Ten minutes later as he brushed his teeth in the communal bathroom he realised that it was the same room he'd stood in five years earlier, staring at his empty self and not realising at the time that his dreams were much more than that, and about to be realised. Things were going to happen for him sooner than he thought, he would write a book. And anyone will tell you, a book, can change your life.

After sprucing himself Jacob thought of food. Oh yes, this was the best part of travelling. Every country had its own marvellous flavours and foods. This was Israel, which meant: Falafel. Jacob loved it and found it hard to explain why. Once, to a close friend, he had tried this analogy.

Sometimes you walk up to a bar in a nightclub and stand there, waiting to be served. A beer for your boredom is always better than standing there outside of the fun, waiting for your friends to come back or watching them enjoy themselves on the dance-floor.

Not making any friends and not having the courage to fail at the feet of some cute girl or other, you retreat to the bar. Sometimes, though rarely, someone interesting, walks up and waits to get served too, joining you while you stand there, trying to get the only barman's attention as he serves one customer at a time, head down and in no hurry. Even more rarely, instead of the awkwardness or paranoia that can grip you in such a situation, especially when it's a member of the opposite sex. For once you manage to react with wit and ease. For a moment, you are cool.

'Hey,' she says.

'Hey yourself,' you answer.

'Nice T-shirt,' she tells you.

'Not as nice as mine ha ha!' you respond. You are hilarious, no?

To your amazement, she laughs too, and properly. Congratulations, you just hit it off, no hassles. The rest is easy, for the moment anyway. For the rest of the night the two of you are amazingly polite and cheerful. You love this song. She thinks you're funny. Everything is perfect and for a moment you think that it could be so for ever. Or maybe you're both just really drunk. Whatever the reason, you click and it feels just great.

Well, it was like that with Jacob and Falafel… It was mmmwonderful! Since the first tentative taste-testing moments five years ago he'd positively pined for it. Jacob had tried to get it everywhere in Ireland, but hadn't been able to. Well he had found it all right, but it just didn't taste right. There is a reason that Irish people don't eat it, because in Ireland, it is muck.

But here it was again, Falafel, everywhere he looked. On the street corners, in the rubbish even. Big yum and tasty, like that girl in the club, it was smashing.

Although it is worth making the point that usually, when someone comes up behind you at the bar, they manage to get served before you, and that's just annoying.

***

Outside the hostel on Dizengoff Square Jacob munched on his Falafel kebab and savoured the experience. It was just how he remembered it. Better even.

Although the take-away was busy he had no trouble finding a seat outside, sitting with the wind playing in his fine hair he began to drift away with the gathering rumble of overheard voices. At the end of the week he had an appointment to meet this Richeloe character and begin researching his new book. For now though, there was only the warm luscious sun and the white sauce rolling down his fingers to drip onto his paper plate below. It was…

'Excuse me,' a shrill Australian lilt interrupted the thought, 'can I ask you to move up a bit?' It was, excuse me.

'Sure,' Jacob answered giving the girl, just a little younger than he, a quick glance or appraisal. She had ruined his moment, but he wasn't sure that it would stay ruined.

'Excellent' he muttered to himself. She was a fine looking little thing, a blonde "surfer girl". He remembered his old classification from his days in Oz. There were six types of Australian girl, ranging from the lowest: 'Ming rat' to...

'Sorry?' she asked, he hurried to find the place where he had exited reality.

'Oh... Excellent' said Jacob wondering if he should turn on the charm.

'Why excellent?' her blue eyes squinted when she smiled. There were little sun wrinkles in the corners. Maybe she smiled a lot that would explain them too.

'Well' he said taking the opportunity, 'I said it because it is not very often that a beautiful girl just sits down beside you in the middle of your Falafel,' He gazed at her wide eyed, to let her see that he was being completely honest.

'Beautiful eh?' she looked Jacob up and down gauging him, a trait he felt of every pretty girl who can pick and choose.

'Thanks' she exclaimed, making Jacob jump a little at her eagerness.

'My name is Becky' she offered him her hand. Should he kiss it? No, that would be too much smarm. He shook it heartily instead.

'You here with friends?' Jacob asked. A little blunt, but honest, he'd just remembered he was crap at chatting up girls. And not remembering that was the key to success.

'No, I've just finished in a Kibbutz and I'm spending the next couple of days here to chill out, you know?' she smiled again. Actually, she'd been smiling. Her smile simply became more personal.

'I know what you mean' Jacob agreed, "I'm staying a couple of days myself'

'You're Irish yeah? Your accent is cool,' Wow, he thought. No wonder the Irish are so patriotic when abroad. It suited them.

'Maybe we can go for a beer when we're finished here?' he said. 'I mean, if you want?' He felt that that was a bit fast but he really wanted to. He really, really wanted to.

'Sure,' Becky smiled happily, turning to her kebab and looking hungry. Jacob watched with interest as she opened the wrapper. Little white dots of garlic sauce appeared on her fingertips as she did so.

And what was inside? Falafel, yes! He was in Love.

***

That was how Jacob and Becky met. Back in the Lemon Lodge, Jacob still felt the happiness that their meeting had given him. He felt a renewed vigour for the task ahead. If it was the only good that came out of this, then at least he had found Becky. Anything was worth that. Wasn't it?

He had to focus now though. Getting something actually written was the main objective even if it was unlikely he could include the tale of his Tel-Aviv love affair whilst writing such a basically religious volume. But getting words down on paper was what he needed to do and what he'd been doing since he began as a writer. Something, anything, get it down. He hadn't felt he had anything important to say before this. Now he had his big chance and he didn't know where to start.

Rummaging through the papers in his carry-on bag Jacob hoped to come across something inspiring, a beginning of some sort. Jacob quickly scanned the stack of tightly written and descriptive eyewitness accounts until he came across a small brown book. It was the book that Maria Candelli had given him in Rome.

Jacob flicked it open and ran his finger down the contents. One story, the third, was a short story by Saki. He remembered

Daniel preaching about Saki's simple stories and how he'd become hooked on them himself. It was called *The Image of the Lost Soul* and he hadn't read it before.

Jacob sat down on the bed and started to read.

***

Saki – The Image of the Lost Soul

There were a number of carved stone figures placed at intervals along the parapets of the old Cathedral; some of them represented angels, others kings and bishops, and nearly all were in attitudes pious exaltation and composure. But one figure, low down on the cold north side of the building, had neither crown, mitre, not nimbus, and its face was hard and bitter and downcast; it must be a *demon*, declared the fat blue pigeons that roosted and sunned themselves all day on the ledges of the parapet; but the old belfry jackdaw, who was an authority on ecclesiastical architecture, said it was a lost soul. And there the matter rested.

One autumn day there fluttered on to the Cathedral roof a slender, sweet-voiced bird that had wandered away from the bare fields and thinning hedgerows in search of a winter roosting-place. It tried to rest its tired feet under the shade of a great angel-wing or to nestle in the sculptured folds of a kingly robe, but the fat pigeons hustled it away from wherever it settled, and the noisy sparrow *folk* drove it off the ledges. No respectable bird sang with so much feeling, they cheeped one to another, and the wanderer had to move on.

Only the effigy of the Lost Soul offered a place of refuge. The pigeons did not consider it safe to perch on a projection that leaned so much out of the perpendicular, and was, besides, too much in the shadow. The figure did not cross its hands in the

63

pious attitude of the other graven dignitaries, but its arms were folded as in defiance *and* their angle made a *snug* resting-place for the little bird. Every evening it crept trustfully into its corner against the stone breast of the image, and the darkling eyes seemed to keep watch over its slumbers. The lonely bird grew to love its lonely protector, and during the day it would sit from time to time on some rain shoot or other abutment and trill forth its sweetest music in grateful thanks for its nightly shelter. And, it may have been the work of wind and weather, or some other influence, *but* the wild drawn face seemed gradually to lose some of its hardness and unhappiness. Every day, through the long monotonous hours, the song of his little guest would come up in snatches to the lonely watcher, and at evening, when the vesper-bell was ringing and the great grey bats slid out of their hiding-places in the belfry roof, the bright-eyed bird would return, twitter a few sleepy notes, and nestle into the arms that were waiting for him. Those were happy days for the Dark Image. Only the great bell of the Cathedral rang out daily its mocking message, "After joy . . . sorrow."

~

The folk in the verger's lodge noticed a little brown bird flitting about the Cathedral precincts, and admired its beautiful singing. "But it is a pity," said they, "that all that warbling should be lost and wasted far out of hearing up on the parapet." They were poor, but they understood the principles of political economy. So they caught the bird and put it in a little wicker cage outside the lodge door.

That night the little songster was missing from its accustomed haunt, and the Dark Image knew more than ever the bitterness of loneliness. Perhaps his little friend had been killed by a prowling cat or hurt by a stone. Perhaps . . . perhaps he had flown elsewhere. But when morning came there floated up to him, through the noise and bustle of the Cathedral world, a faint heart-aching message from *the prisoner* in the wicker cage far below. And every day, at high noon, when the fat pigeons were stupefied into silence after their midday meal and the sparrows were washing themselves in the street-puddles, the song of the little bird came up to the parapets a song of hunger and longing and hopelessness, a cry that could never be answered. The pigeons remarked, between mealtimes, that the figure leaned forward more than ever out of the perpendicular.

One day no song came up from the little wicker cage. It was the coldest day of the winter, and the pigeons and sparrows on the Cathedral roof looked anxiously on all sides for the scraps of food, which they were dependent on in hard weather.

"Have the lodge-folk thrown out anything on to the dust-heap?" inquired one pigeon of another, which was peering over the edge of the north parapet.

"Only a little dead bird," was the answer.

There was a crackling sound in the night on the Cathedral roof and a noise as of *falling* masonry. The belfry jackdaw said the frost was affecting the fabric, and as he had experienced many frosts it must have been so. In the morning it was seen that the Figure of the Lost Soul had toppled from its cornice and lay now in a *broken* mass on the dust heap outside the verger's lodge.

"It is just as well," cooed the fat pigeons, after they had peered at the matter for some minutes; "now we shall have a nice angel put up there. Certainly they will put an angel there.

"After joy . . . sorrow," *rang out the great bell.*

***

Jacob stared at the pages for a long while. Like so many Saki stories Jacob felt that he would probably have given it a different name, but which, he did not know. Jacob was becoming increasingly suspicious that he didn't know much of anything at all, like what was the point in those italicised words? Jacob counted them. Fifteen. He read them in order.

65

'Jesus,' Jacob dropped the book on the floor. He was shocked. The words actually made sense when read in order. Now he felt profoundly confused, another weirdness to add to the quickly expanding list of oddities. There had to be an answer to all of it, some of which were already forming gin his mind. Answers of a nefarious nature, and ones he was not ready to recognise yet. He needed to do something simple now, and the memory of eating falafel in Jerusalem had made him hungry. He had to go outside for some food.

And, maybe some fresh air would make the hairs on the back of his neck sit down again. The words were obviously a note left for him in the text. It was impossible that they were merely a random mistake. It was a message all right, possibly a warning. He didn't want to read them yet they clawed at his eyes and he looked down at the book again. He grabbed a pencil and wrote them down on a piece of paper.

Demon folk pious and snug but the prisoner falling broken rang out the great bell.

He decided to leave. Paranoia was ok when you could convince yourself that there was no one after you, but all of this was proof to the contrary. Even then Jacob wasn't able to believe what was happening to him. So, he just continued on as normal, and went out for his tea. He left the room wondering what sort of food he could get his hands on in Ghana's Capital. There was only one way to find out. Actually there were two ways, but there was no chance of an Internet connection here. He grabbed his shirt and his flick knife and headed for the door, stopping only long enough to grab those fifteen words and put them in his wallet.

He had a brief vision of himself actually gobbling them up, shoving them in his mouth, and trying to swallow them. Yet he couldn't and he began to choke and retch as the word "Demon" became lodged in his throat. In the vision he put his hand into his mouth to retrieve the fifteen words. They came out one by one attached to each other on a chain of saliva, there were sounds of laughing in his ears and the pounding of another's heart, slow and faltering, vibrated in hi imagination. Jacob looked down again and the words were back on the page. He put them into his wallet and shivered. Then he left.

***

Outside The Lemon Lodge white and orange taxicabs made their way carefully along the furrowed muddy road. Lower down at ground level where the street must have looked more like vast wet wasteland, a lizard bravely attempted to cross the street among the cars and peoples feet. His reward would be a large hunk of stale bread sitting out in the open only a few yards from the door of the Lodge. Skittering back and forward he slopped and splashed his way across, making it miraculously to opposite side where his prize awaited his success. There was a little scaly surge of pride and much dancing about in triumph.

Then lizard only picked at the bread, not sure if he would even be able to eat it. There were lots of things he couldn't eat; the city was a collage of plastic and tin. His tiny head shot up and craned around, his attention caught by the arrival of a car blocking his return to the nest. As the car came closer the lizard scarpered up onto the steps of the Lodge, and from his vantage point he rose up and pressed his chest up and down furiously. He had by now, already forgotten his way home.

A black Mercedes pulled over and parked with one of its wheels occupying the space the lizard had only just vacated. The darting cold-blooded creature had managed to avoid it only narrowly.

Inside the car Rajette settled down to wait. He felt uncomfortable here. He always did in the black countries. The people were even harder to understand than the white whites and the facilities were poor and disagreeable. At time like these Rajette always found that he could ease his discomfort by thinking of his wife and his goals. He wore her ring on his finger and he liked to picture her in compromising positions, pleading with him for mercy as he pounded her, the pattern of the ring, a dog, being impressed all over her body. He hated the women immensely, but he would never leave her and because he loved her so much more than he could ever describe, because she could understand him. Rajette was not the type to meet girls easily. He was too blunt, too hard. It would take a very special sort of woman to find him desirable.

Rajette and his wife

Rajette used to beat his wife with incredible force. Their marriage was a furious collection of bruised muscles and screaming arguments. She feared him and he found her deliciously ungrateful for the life of luxury he allowed her to lead. They belonged to each other.

Years ago when Rajette was nothing more than a local hoodlum, they came across each other on the streets of Jericho. He'd been busy in an alleyway with one of his master's shy creditors, negotiating full payment with his fists and venting his frustration with every thump and punch, another decent evening in Latrel's underground strip-club ruined. If he was going to have to give up his fun for some tight-fisted scum, Rajette felt more than justified in pounding every single moment out of him.

From the mouth of the alley Dirla watched him the entire time. Although he was concentrating hard, Rajette did notice her but continued on. Eyes had way of breaking through to him. Pupils staring making his skin crawl, he hated it. Whenever somebody looked the little Arab in the eye he wanted to show him or her who they were really looking at. Bring them to the show as he called it, the beating, punching, and kicking show. He wanted to show them that here was a man who would destroy all of his enemies, big and small, with the same gusto and if some woman wanted to watch from the street while he did so; then let her.

Like a Neanderthal's mating ritual, Rajette began to show off for the woman. He spun kicks into his victim's bloody face and threw the unfortunate man around the alley like a bundle of dry sticks. At one point he was sure he heard a cheer and she definitely gasped with pleasure a number of times.

When it was over he turned to her and saw that she was smiling. It was the happiest moment of his life. She knew what he was, and she wanted in.

At that moment Jacob walked from the main door of the Lemon Lodge and onto the roadside. He stood there for a moment leafing through his guidebook, obviously deciding in which direction he would go. Rajette watched the white boy realise that the door to the Lodge hadn't swung closed. What did he expect? He was in Africa now.

Jacob walked back to the door and unwedged it from the uneven concrete step pausing to allow a lizard to streak inside. The Irish man looked soft to Rajette. He would never survive in Palestine this writing boy Jacob. He was weak and undisciplined.

Rajette had received many orders from a great many people over the years and had never failed to carry them out. But this, he felt was a joke assignment, with only one highlight. If the white boy so much as stumbled in the wrong direction, Rajette had permission to kill him. He had permission from two sources in fact.

He watched Jacob close over the door, turn and walk down the street and after quick apprehension Rajette decided not bother to follow him. He wouldn't be going very far.

**

Not a Fan of the food.

Jacob sat at the side of the road outside a chop bar a couple of streets from the Lemon lodge. Even sitting there eating he could feel how much hopelessly he missed Becky. He thought of the days he'd spent in Tel-Aviv with her. Could he ever find that again? Why did romance novelists say things like that? Find it again, something lost, love hiding somewhere? Could he ever relive those two days? Those were slightly better words, but the answer was still no.

In truth, love sometimes did get lost. There were always reasons to move on. "Gotta go do's," that took him away from love and towards opportunity. One day he hoped he could make the big sacrifice. Throw everything down, take her in his arms, and damn the consequences, but not now, not in the middle of this. This book and the mystery that surrounded it were burrowing in deep. And no, it wasn't one of his heart stopping thrillers but he was stuck on it just the same, even more so now that he felt there was something going on underneath that he didn't yet understand.

Sometimes he did dream about finding that perfect woman, but usually he dreamt about himself and the things that he would do. The feats he would accomplish. Or, he would dream of finding a lot of perfect women, all at the same time.

He looked down at the bowl in his hand. His Fufu was getting cold. Good, he thought. His first taste of African cuisine was beginning to sicken him. The sloppy lump in his bowl looked more like a ball of plaster or dehydrated cauliflower than a main-course but it tasted worse than either ever could. The ground was reddish-yellow dirt and there were plastic bags of all sizes camouflaged in the dust. The street was quiet and it lulled him.

He thought of their last day, his and Becky's. He was looking in the mirror of her hostels communal bathroom mirror, brushing his teeth. Her head appeared over his shoulder, he smiled, lighting up the picture in his mind. It instantly made him feel sad and lonely. Another picture in reflective glass, there, only as long as the moment, and always replaced, sometimes by another face, but usually by a wall or some other nothing.

He remembered this from his old backpacking days in the not too distant past, always leaving someone behind and always going away somewhere else.

Memories of different countries and breathtaking sights were coloured with sadness and regret. A good friend lost in Australia, a lover lost in Berlin. And now Becky was left behind in too uncertain oblivion? When would the magic wear away, how long did they have before it was too late?

Maybe he shouldn't let it go again this time. Maybe he couldn't. His heart leapt as the Batman theme tune burst forward from his shirt pocket. 'Becky?' He thought, rummaging for his mobile. The screen simply said call' and he answered quickly.

'Hello?'

'Hello Jacob, how are you, my fine young writer eh?' Fantastic, it was Richeloe. Had there been some sarcasm in there, hidden cleverly between the words "fine" and "young"?

'Oh, eh grand,' Jacob answered, 'You?'

'Are you there yet?' Richeloe's voice annoyed him simply because it wasn't hers.

'Yes, yes, I'm in Accra now, eating some muck or other,' Jacob wasn't in the mood to talk to the ambiguous old scribe now. 'What's the story?' he asked.

'There has been a delay my friend' Richeloe's voice scrambled on the airwaves for a moment. Jacob strained to hear it.

'... Ready ...days'.

'What?'

'Will not be ready for you for a few days.'

'What won't?' Jacob asked though he knew very well. 'Who won't?'

'What?'

'The keeper in Kumasi will not be able to see you until Thursday' Richeloe snipped. It was easier to play games when the scary grey cleric was hundreds of miles away.

'Fine' said Jacob 'crap' he thought.

'Will you amuse yourself until then?' Richeloe made it sound seedy, like Jacob was liable to run out and buy a hundred weight of porn once given the opportunity. 'Yes sure I've got plenty of writing to do,' Jacob said and thought for a moment. 'I may go to the seaside actually,' He added.

'Good good,' Richeloe responded. 'Call me on Thursday morning, I'll tell you where to go.'

'I'll tell *you* where to…' but Jacob was robbed of the retort. The phone was dead. Maybe the old man must have had seen it coming.

Taking out his guidebook Jacob opened it on Ghana and leafed past the Accra pages and onto 'Cape Coast'. It sounded good. He envisioned for a moment about a vampire from Cape Coast and wondered was there a joke there. He decided there wasn't.

He handed back his bowl to the woman in the chop bar trying to ignore her baleful look as she noticed how full it was.

'Kwasi Broni,' she chided, 'you don't like our food, ah?' She laughed happily and scraped out his full bowl back into the cauldron that stood upon a glowing Coal-pot at the side of the road. He hoped the white man's eating habits didn't amuse all Ghanaians that much.

'It's the texture. I'm not really used to it,' He apologised. 'It tasted fine though,' He assured her and walked away. Fine was a pleasant word for crap at the moment.

Not wanting to return to his empty room yet, Jacob wandered down two mad roads that lay "parallel" to the hotel. Jacob watched a young boy washing outside a group of wooden shacks and wondered what 'Broni' meant. He'd heard it a dozen times in the last half an hour and he guessed that it must mean American, Tourist, or maybe even white man. It was probably the latter. Well, it was better than a kick in the face, as his uncle used to say.

The boy's mother pummelled him with a towel, rubbing him down vigorously. Jacob smiled at her when she looked up and noticed him.

'Kwasi?' she said and hurried the boy inside.

'Kwasi indeed,' Jacob muttered turning to leave. He paused then, a recollection stopping him where he was

'Thursday!' he said aloud. He'd booked the hostel until then because he was supposed to be in Kumasi on Thursday. That was the plan all along, wasn't it? He wondered at the real reason for Richeloe's useless phone call. Was it absentmindedness on Richeloe's part? No, there was something else. The old man was very well organised, so what then?

Forget it, he thought. Who cares what tricks some old priest was up to? He should just keep his mind on the book and away from conspiracies. Then he realised. If Richeloe was telling him something he already knew then it mustn't have been for him to hear. Someone else was listening. Was his phone tapped?

'Yeah, that's what it is. You're being followed' He told himself sarcastically. He would have laughed at that any other time. He shivered instead. It was possible.

73

Jacob returned to his hotel room and lay down on his bed, watching fan as it shook dangerously above him. He wondered where Becky might be now. Probably out on the razz enjoying a beer somewhere, with some other guy. He pictured her standing at a bar waiting to be served, with some guy cracking onto her.

That's enough; he thought, time for bed and time for dream, hints of meaning, or just cognitive filing. The cabinets were full of sheep tonight and he began to set them free, one by one, two, three, four, five…

***

Although the earth is surrounded with satellites and information is whizzing through the air from mobile to mobile and from dish to dish. Most communication, the internet, the cable television, dial up, dial in, and landline calls, still requires the aid of a piece of wire. Granted, the wires are not big fat copper ones any more, they are optical or alkali, or fashioned from a seagulls eyebrow, or something. Whatever. The point is that broken down conversations, between people, and computers are being propelled around the worlds inside little wires which in turn are included in bunches of cable. Things called routers and diallers and junction boxes everywhere are managing to relay information about everything about us, from an ointment ordered to counter that embarrassing little problem, to the ingredients for a homemade bomb or bong, depending on your preference.

If you could just pick just a wire and listen, or see, how many pieces of information were flitting up and down it, and then look again and see the information that is currently passing by. You would have a window into the world of information. And, no that's not what a computer is; a computer has its own little rules and operating systems that get in the way of total and unadulterated, world information viewing.

So anyway, you have this connection, and you can listen to any conversation you want. What would you listen to? There's a lot of choices aren't there. But let's just say that you've decided to listen into international phone calls, especially the ones that involve the story we are concerned with here. What can you hear now?

'Hello?'

'….'

'Hello?'

'Hellllo, I am here, who is this?'

'It's me sir.'

'Yes?'

'Yes sir, it is me, Marshal'

'I KNOW WHO YOU ARE. IDIO!'

'Sorry sir.'

'….'

'I'm very sorry sir. I just thought you would like to here the latest?'

'….'

'Sir?'

'Yes then, tell?'

'The third is on its way to you.'

'And the fourth, where is it?'

'We are in the process…'

'Process!'

'Sir, it thought you only needed the third for now, to start…'

'Start! I want to finishhhhhh.'

'Sorry sir, very sorry, we will have it as soon as possible…'

'….'

'Sooner, sir.'

'Good. I need the fourth or all efforts are wasted.'

'Yes sir.'

'….'

'Sir?'

'Yes?'
'The Italian…'
'Yes?'
'Well, the muscle…'
'Yes?'
'He said the Italian, told him that.'
'That?'
'That you wanted the… the four pieces to em… to em, come back sir'
'Is it your business what I do, American?'
'No sir,'
'No, it is not.'
-CLICK- -click-

Recollections 7

A blue ring and aura

In his dreams, Jacob was waiting to meet Becky in Italy by the marina of Trieste. He was sitting on a bollard and there was a bluish tint to the air.

'You're late,' Jacob smiled as his Australian love approached from the great square. Jacob had been sitting on a Bollard drinking beer, watching Italians act like Italians do as they streamed from the town heading south and along the water's edge. The men were showing off and gesturing wildly while the women were laughing fashionably. Becky came closer and shushed him with her finger on his lips. She gauged him with a look and then she spoke with sadness in her voice.

'You're not happy,' Becky stated, reaching out to hold his hand.

'No,' Jacob realised he wasn't. 'Let's go,' he said standing, heading back for the square against the current of the rushing crowd, 'we should try and find a good place.'

'No, this way Jacob,' Becky led him along the waterfront. 'Always go this way,' she said, pointing at a far off something to which the crowd were all travelling. Jacob followed her along the waterfront, watching the other people as they flowed around them. He noticed then that the people in the crowd were not all Italians. Some men were in Muslim dress and some women in Saris, but they were all walking the same way.

'What's going on here?' Jacob asked Becky, and the different passing happy faces charged him with a peaceful energy.

'I don't know' Becky smiled. Jacob asked the question again of the people around him.

'I don't know' said a walker, smiling as he went.

Jacob turned to look behind them. There were millions of people heading this way and they all seemed happy enough. The relief of the herd and the joy of belonging filled the mass of bodies with ecstatic rushes of well being. Jacob realised he'd been travelling in the wrong direction before.

'OK' said Jacob deciding, 'this way it is.'

***

Waking in the early morning Jacob was all too aware that he had been dreaming. The sheets of the bed were gathered down to his feet, wrinkled and battered looking and the mattress was scratching his face and chest as he lay face down in warmth of the new day. On no, it was tomorrow already.

Jacob remembered only the basic details of his dream and wondered whether it was a sign that he should call Becky who would surely be in England now.

He wanted badly to be able to tell her of his assignment but although he had not signed any contract of secrecy, the presence of guns and buckets of money meant that confidentiality was certainly implied.

Lying prone on the bad mattress Jacob realised how much the contents of his first information pickup in Jerusalem had badly unsettled him. It shouldn't have. He had no interest in religion, no real interest anyway. Being brought up a Catholic in Ireland had allowed a healthy dose of religious mistrust to soak in. Religious institutions were built on lies and money and the proof was now sitting in his knapsack in sealed airtight packages, some of it anyway.

So why should the truth unsettle him? Obviously, the world would be better off knowing it. Jacob's job was to spin that truth into a comprehensive official interpretation. That wasn't a bad thing, was it? He was going to leave the Catholic Church in a position of righteousness and not collapse, regardless of the facts, so yes, it probably was. But why should he care? A few weeks ago he wouldn't have and change is a terrible thing.

A wall gecko scrambled over the door as Jacob rose. He went into the shower room only to realise that the shower had no pressure or heat. It took him by surprise for a moment and he yelped girlishly. Soon he would realise that having a shower in Ghana was a luxury that he would not experience too often and he should have appreciated clean water coming from above while he still had access to it.

After cleaning and dressing, Jacob sat at the dresser to write once more. He put Becky and her swallowing eyes right out of his mind. He certainly didn't even spare a thought for the contents of his wallet. Not one thought.

Instead he picked up a bunch of papers at random and set to work. The pile he'd chosen were notes by an unknown author translated into English headed:

"Joshua our Lord – aged 19 approx."

Jacob read them:

Joshua travels to the Red Sea to where Sinai is today, he was accompanied by four of his closest friends, three of which he had served with in the Legion of the armies of Rome, based in Terrill where Haifa is today.

A female called Orit also accompanied him there. In the scrolls of Janehel, second Aquarius in Caesarium, located in the heart of what is presently known as Israel's Gazza strip, the water engineer wrote to his centurion about the group after he was awoken by a disturbance in the night.

Janehel speculated that Joshua and Orit were engaged sexually and further proof in the diaries of the travelling preacher Deredilum from Neapolis informs us that he and

Janehel found the girl dead outside the Aquarius' rooms the morning after the incident.

After carrying the body to a nearby Inn Deredilum was informed that a Roman Soldier's conscript named Janehel -here the name Joshua had been overwritten- had left the day before with the girl and that three soldiers and one poorly clothed man had left the two at the Inn two days before, bound for Sinai.

Jacob stopped his reading.

He was unsure what he could do with this information other than leave it out entirely. And that had already been done.

Someone had already done his research for him. Deredilum had mentioned the name of the soldier with whom Orit had left the Inn and this account allowed Jacob to cast doubt on Janehel's earlier letter by placing him as murderer, thus leaving Joshua free of blame. He began reading again.

Note: It is doubtful though that Janehel could have killed the girl. Janehel was Roman and had no need to kill the girl himself. He could easily have had the girl killed and no one would have bothered him.

The previous researcher's note didn't fill Jacob with confidence. Damn! This was going to be impossible. He was going to have to think it out and find a different angle.

Jacob rose and decided to go and get some breakfast. It seemed to him that all he was doing lately, was eating, sleeping and reading. Even so he had a real gue on him for eggs and toast and wondered if he could find such a thing on Mango Tree Avenue or in Ghana for that matter?

Sparing a thought for the integrity of the scrolls, Jacob placed the first translation he had been reading back into its airtight plastic packages. Two accounts was all that he'd read and already he was trying to divert the blame for murder and trying to explain why Christ had been in the army in the first place. The young Jew was going to be a handful.

Jacob left the room feeling not unlike a lawyer leaving his client to cogitate a strategy. The wrongness of it wasn't lost on him either. Every step of the way there was going to be doubts and lies. It didn't matter though. He was a fiction writer being asked to go heavy on the fiction. The only problem being that people knew that his books were fiction. This however, was people's faith, their beliefs. What would Becky say if she knew what he was doing? It was so strange, being in love. Where did it come from? It just happened, blammo! It was there.

***

In Tel-Aviv amidst the strangeness of the wary, Becky and Jacob had conspired to fall in love. That first night they went to a bar where they grinned and joked along to the music of a little Arab man named Majar singing his heart out in perfect English.

    After the show the man joined them and they laughed to hear that although he was Arabic to the core, the maggots in that core were actually Irish, which still didn't explain the perfect English.

    Majar told them that he was from Galway. Later on he told them again he was from Galway and that he was living in Israel for the time being, waiting for a visa so he could return to India. Everything else about the man was so out of the ordinary that Jacob decided it must all be true.

It was one of those idyllic nights where cheeks ache from laughter and a pregnant pause is always fertilised. In a dreamlike way they drank into the night every moment they spent together seemed to out do the last for ease and fun and happiness. It was a bit soppy too, but neither of them really cared.

After the bar closed, Becky and Jacob took a slow stroll down to the Mediterranean Sea only a couple of hundred yards away, refusing an invitation from the Irish musician to go on a party hunt.

They were more interested in each other than in Majar. Even with him being from Ireland and no matter how many times he was from Galway.

Jacob was the type of person who used to watch with interest as those dreamy looking couples smooched around in self-appreciation. He noticed that they occupied a space in the crowd reserved for the blessed and were oblivious to a large amount of resentful stares from strangers and friends alike.

Why was it that some people resented happiness in others? Usually he was a bit jealous himself, but jealous of their happiness and not of them having it. For once Jacob felt that he was part of such a perfect couple and it felt fantastic.

Becky and Jacob reached the beach and stepped off the path and into the sand. After a few minutes of polite moonlit walking and point-avoiding awkwardness, the two finally hopped on each other. In the sand, down by the heavily polluted Mediterranean shore they only barely resisting the urge to have sex there on the beach.

It would surely have been too tacky for their first time, they decided. Becky decided.

Ten minutes later back in Becky's dorm-room, Jacob was tiptoeing around rucksacks and flip-flops trying not to wake the other girls asleep all around him. One was snoring gently and another was reading a book with a flashlight. When he saw that one of the girls was awake, Jacob realised there was no chance of any monkey business tonight. Becky, on the other hand, had different ideas. Hooray.

'I'm tired,' she said feigning a yawn.

'Asleep on my feet,' she confirmed, winking at him as she climbed onto the top bunk across from the reader.

'Fair enough,' Jacob said taking her lead 'straight to sleep for me too,' It was so cheesy that the two of them were giggling under their breath, a difficult manoeuvre if you've ever tried it, it is probably louder than an outright laughing fit and much more noticeable.

Jacob climbed onto the top bunk with Becky and shed his clothes down to his boxer shorts, elbowing Becky in the jaw as he did so.

'Oh shit, I'm sorry!' he whispered, trying not to laugh.

'Real smooth,' Becky replied. He leaned forward and kissed it better. 'Yeah,' she said, 'real smooth.'

Unlike him Becky stripped completely and Jacob felt like a prude but recovered quickly by whipping his shorts off and tossing them across the room. He was sure he heard them rip a little. Not knowing what to do next in the confines of the narrow bed Jacob just lay back and let her sit astride him. They stopped then to let the initial noise of their mounting the bunk to fade away and heard a brief sniff in the dark as the girl with the torch put her book down and suddenly the light was extinguished.

As Jacob's eyes grew accustomed to the light he noticed that there was a dull cobalt light coming in through the curtain beside Becky. The day was being born outside through the mist from the sea and a blue streetlight gave her a glowing outline as she rose above him.

Jacob

83

She was amazing, sitting there naked on his legs her eyes closed with a small perfect smile that excited him so. He lifted his hand up to touch her face as gently as he could. He stroked her cheek with his fingertips and her eyes opened, only slightly.

Then she raised her own hand and covered his as it passed, her smile was bigger now.

Still there was no sound from either of them on the top bunk. Jacob could almost hear the reader listening in embarrassed curiosity across the darkness of the room. It excited him.

Becky pulled Jacob's hand down off her face and arched her back, closing her eyes again. Jacob moved his fingers down her neck bringing his other hand up to copy his left as he moved towards her chest. They were just the breasts that Jacob had hoped to see on her. He was no fan of massive boobs, no. Jacob liked them round and shapely but small enough to almost cup completely with his long fingered hands. As corny as it sounded to him, he knew she was a vision of everything he ever found exciting and attractive.

Trusting to the moment he began to let go and enjoy her. Oh, how he enjoyed her.

Becky

Becky felt Jacob's hand moving gently across her chest. If he did it just a little harder. She pushed his hands towards her and he roughened his grip. Perfect, she thought. He was looking up at her enraptured. The expression on his face as he gazed along her body sent a shiver through her.

Becky enjoyed the sensation for a while letting her body tingle as she thought of what would come next. She felt only a brief moment of doubt before she gave up completely and leaned forward to kiss him…

Jacob looked up, startled and a little abashed at the waiter. He was sitting in the only a semi-normal looking cafe in the neighbourhood, three streets from the Lemon Lodge. The waiter, a tall gangly man laughed at him.

'Hey, you are sleeping!' he said.

'Yeah,'

'Would you like some food?' asked the waiter.

Jacob wasn't sure what he'd just been doing, but it seemed far from sleeping. It was like he'd just blacked. He was getting cracked over that girl.

'Shit,' He said, he didn't like the idea of making a fool of himself over a woman.

'Eh? Would you like some food?' Asked the waiter again, looking confused.

Jacob asked for his breakfast and the man took his order quickly, but the eggs and toast took an eternity to arrive.

He had drifted off again trying to pick up the memory where he left off trying to envision that first night again. It was so vivid that when Jacob closed his eyes he could feel her hand on him. Then the eggs arrived and the whites were running.

'What the hell is this?' Jacob enquired to a blank stare.

'How does it take twenty minutes to undercook a boiled egg?' The waiter leaned forward and inspected the plate.

'If you eat them you will be sick,' he stated helpfully.

'Yes'

'Mmmm'

'Well?' The waiter was puzzled but soon realised his role in the exchange.

'I will take them back?' he asked.

'Yes,' said Jacob, 'please do,' and as an afterthought he changed his order to scrambled eggs and settled down again for the long wait.

Suspiciously the scrambled eggs arrived in only a couple of minutes accompanied by his coffee and toast this time.

Jacob narrowed his eyes 'Are you playing a trick on me?' he joked. The waiter just nervously backed away and left Jacob without a reply. Jacob would have to adjust his sense of humour here if he wanted to get along with these people.

'Yeah,' he said aloud, 'cos you're not funny boy.'

It was all about Life really, that's all.

There once was a man who needn't yet be named, who compared himself to God - with a capital G. Not in a metaphysical way though, no. This man compared himself to God under a much more base and self-gratifying premise.

You see, this man saw himself to be powerful, like God. He saw that he was somewhat misunderstood and misused, again like God. And, he found that he was sometimes despised and cursed by people for reasons beyond his facility to care, which he felt also allied him to the big G.

All that being said, the comparisons were not really bothering this man too much, as a matter of fact, they suited him fine. It was the differences that he couldn't stomach. The main one being that this man, like all others, found himself to be a mortal one, and as such very unlike the G he so otherly resembled.

He was not immortal, nor was he likely to be. He would not live forever. He would die. He would expire. Fade away. Rot.

After years spent searching -years that would have served him better spent living- our friend, or little g, uncovered a vast and terrible secret, terrible to some anyway and awful too, in the bad sense. But not to g. To our man g it was a beautiful thing to behold. It meant that he could finally pool his massive resources into serving this one last aim: To destroy that final difference between the G and he.

Time was getting short, running out, and spending not biding, flying not watching the pot and this man had a great and horrible fear of it. This man was an old man, and old men die. A lot.

Recollections 8

A Sunburst Lizard

As Jacob ate his breakfast and dreaming of riding/making love to Becky, inside his room in the Lemon lodge, a lizard with a sunburst of colour brightening its forward quarters was scampering along the windowed wall. For a moment a lone wall Gecko stood defiant in his path and a vertical confrontation took place. The Sunburst lizard insulted by its miniature brethren's petulance immediately began to do threatening press-ups to show his superiority and also to distract the gecko before pouncing.

The wall Gecko responded quickly when her larger cousin commenced his attack sprinting frantically down the wall onto the floor, heading for the door, but the Sunburst Lizard was cold on her tail.

The tiny luminescent gecko swerved left, then right, and then left again. The speed of the exchange and Sunburst's utilisation of his evolutionary advantages could fool the observer into thinking it was only a single eight-legged lizard they saw, dashing across the floor. The pursuit was so close, so hot that it also made the smaller chased gecko look as though she was like a reptilian tug boat, towing its brethren so accurately were its tiny twists reproduced.

Gecko straightened her flight and made for the crack under the door realising instinctively that this was where she should be headed and that weaving would only serve to tighten the Sunburst's control of the chase. This strategy, if it could be claimed as such, was successful. The tiny prey escaped her pursuer with an equally tiny scraping and scrambling sound as she raced through the crack through which the larger aggressor could never fit. A tiny insect audience would have applauded were it present, and maybe it did, but probably no.

Foiled but full of confidence the Sunburst executed another brace of his territorial push-ups to warn the tiny upstart not to consider returning from exile in the corridor beyond. When he finished, Sunburst looked around at his new surroundings, he may have been confused.

Now at a loss and far away in position and memory from the wall where it began the chase, Sunburst began to cast darting glances about him. Like uncountable legions of small reptiles or rodents before him, Sunburst wondered what had happened to his surroundings.

The surface was smooth under his belly and the air had changed.

We could ask ourselves if he know that he was now indoors. Did he realise what "indoors" meant? Sunburst, unaffected by the philosophy of it, began to scout around after a target for his intentions.

Scurry, scurry and stop. Nothing. Scurry, turn, focus, scurry, nothing of any interest there either. The room was cold. Sunburst began to submit to the delicious chill, becoming a victim of Jacob's preoccupied mind. The ceiling fan had been left on and the frigid air made it difficult for sunburst to ignore his biology.

Scurry, scurry, he found a warm place. The cold was beginning to shut his body down, like the night; the room was demanding that sunburst should stay as still as possible. He was not a nocturnal breed of lizard.

He had eaten. He was warm. He would stay there, for now at least.

There was a rustling in the empty room as Sunburst's little claws scrambled over the clothing in Jacob's rucksack. The sound became increasingly muffled and then stopped completely. The lizard's body shut down almost completely and he drifted off to sleep.

***

On his first night in Israel Jacob lay awake and restless. In his Jerusalem hostel room listening to the tannoyed sound of the sacred ritual reverberate around the old city. The call to prayer was so full of mystery that Jacob always felt like he should be falling on his knees and joining in the worship. This thought was usually accompanied by many thoughts about his expensive trousers and the unwanted damage that prostration would impose on their imported fibres.

Jacob bit his nails in the darkness. He was nervous about his first meeting with Richeloe. In many ways he wished he'd left the country with Becky. But what then of Maria and the part of him that was dying to know what would happen next?

It had been a difficult day for him, leaving Becky in Tel-Aviv to come to Jerusalem. Jacob felt sadness and relief. The relief that now he could really sink his teeth into this mysterious project and sadness for the loss of such a perfect moment of romance.

Jacob's leaving Tel-Aviv would forever ensure the romance would remain just that, perfect. So there was no real reason to be sad and he was sure that in a few days the memory of Becky would fade like all the others before her. He was in Jerusalem now to meet the Church's scribe Richeloe and the thought of it made Jacob sweat with anticipation. That, and the fact it was thirty-five degrees, in the shade.

Now though, Jacob had a moment of worry. His assignment was about to begin. A first encounter with the secrets manufactured by the Catholic Church and Editorial powers nearly fifteen hundred years old. The thriller writer of today was about to re-commit the sins of the past by leading the Lord's flock, even further astray. It disturbed him for some reason and he felt new beads spring up on his neck. Was it fear? It was the heat again, probably.

Well hot or not, Jacob did feel uneasy. He hadn't thought about it like that before. The business of religion was someone else's business. This was a book project. He had the basic story; everybody in the world had it, from A to Z. Jesus was an open book, a very popular one. A life filled with miracles and temptations, suffering and joyous rapture, and what else? What sort of mysteries if any, still remained? The official story was so amazing Jacob found it hard to imagine what could have been left out.

His job was to create an unabridged version of the most popular story ever told and keep the outcome, the gist and the focus, the same as before. Worship was to continue.

Jacob's mind was fully awake now, damn it. He rose from his bed thinking as he did so that it was a real pity he couldn't re-write the night and allow his sleep to continue unbroken.

Jacob left his hostel room, decided that Nicotine was the answer and headed up onto the hostel roof where the budget travellers snored on cots in a shed that housed twenty. The warren of the old city was silent except for the Muslims call. In the buildings that loomed over the streets below, almost tunnels they were so narrow, the People of Allah faced roughly east and spoke again to their prophet Mohammed. Be praised, they said, and Jacob wondered who had edited the Quran, if anyone had.

To his left not more than two hundred metres away behind the Western Wall, the prophet had descended from the heavens to save his people. The golden "Dome of the rock" built on that spot rose above the city in gaudy recognition of the event.

Jacob thought about it. How could it be an accident that the site of the prophet's appearance could overlap the location of the "Holiest of Holy's"? The concentration of God's spirit lost to the Hebrews when the temple surrounding it was destroyed. Now only a single wall was left for them to pray to. It was called the Wailing Wall and named the Western Wall. He'd been to see it that afternoon. There were deep grooves between each stone where the Jews left prayers and thanks to God. They'd made him wear one of those skullcaps made out of paper. Why the back of his head would insult anybody was a mystery to him, but he'd felt more respectful doing it. There was also an urge to say, "Oish" after a Mel Brooks fashion.

The Wailing Wall was a sad place, a whole people's desperation and hope on one, and on the other; Hundreds of happily snapping tourists with sarongs covering their unrighteous naked flesh, blind to their innocent invasion upon the holiest spot in Judaism. Tramping on history.

Certainly this was a centre of the earth? Jacob thought. Maybe deep in the earth below this point Shiva was running? Although if her many-armedness was in fact in the centre of the world then she was directly below every point, wasn't she? It didn't really bother Jacob whether Batman was there too; he believed in them the same. It was merely interesting to notice what a hotbed the region, the city, was and always had been.

Man began, some say, on the Savannah of Northern Africa when the world was a different shape, size consistency, flavour. Christians and others have stated that this was wrong and God created man on the seventh day. Yet the location of the Holy Land on the northernmost verge of Africa could not be a coincidence. Come on. Animals don't have souls, so say the overly religious. What gives man the monopoly on souls?

Lighting his cigarette Jacob put aside his minds impossible urge, to solve the earth's ancient mysteries and then and decided instead to picture his old dog Sammy. He could see the terrier catching a bird as it swooped through the back garden. It was a spring day and the exceptional canine presented it to the house by leaving it on the back doorstep, and you thought only cats did that.

Then they say that animals don't have souls. Jacob was sure that he'd heard a logical argument to support the theory, but could not remember a word of it. How could Sammy not have had a soul? Jacob was sure he'd seen it more than once, but once in particular.

One day while Jacob sat depressed on the floor of the garden shed. Sammy trotted up to him and inquired of Jacob's sadness moving his little head to one side, not just curious but worried. Jacob hadn't spoken to the Jack Russell that day because he'd been crying and he was, even then, too proud to reveal the quaver in his voice, even to the dog. Sammy leaned slowly up, licked the tears from Jacob's check, and began to whine, he understood his masters pain, sensed it, shared it even. And this animal had no soul?

Again, Jacob was back to the big questions.

It was this wondrous place. Simple thought was impossible here. He needed to rest his mind, to think of women and chocolate or money, something easy and shallow to release his troubled thoughts from this heavy brooding.

But Jerusalem was such an awesome place, so tiny yet it housed such huge layers of civilisation and savagery. Man, if thoughts did come in trains, these were laden with freight. He had to lighten up.

'And I'm not even stoned,' he said aloud, a mistake he didn't notice at the time.

'Oh no?' a voice enquired from behind him. Jacob spun around.

'What?' he replied, he hadn't heard this man approaching.

'You want to get stones?' The man was Arabic definitely, he had a friendly smile, Jacob thought. He didn't bother to correct the man either. After all, he was looking to get stones.

'Yeah sure, you have some weed?' Jacob asked the man. If he were going to tackle the cosmos tonight, he would feel better with a rolled excuse in his hand. Besides, it had been a week since he'd had a good smoke.

'They're in my bag, downstairs,' said the man who smiled and turned away. He said 'in' like an Australian would say "Ian" with a twitch of the cheek. 'Come on,' the little man added and trotted down the steps.

'Why not,' Jacob shrugged and followed the Good Samaritan downward, his second mistake.

Jacob followed the man to the ground and realised as he did that there had been no introductions.

'Hey,' he whisper-hissed at the little Arab in the hall, 'what's your name man?'

'Shh!' said the man picking up a bag in the reception area and opening the front door. He left the building quietly, pausing only long enough to beckon Jacob on.

Outside the little man grabbed Jacob's hand and shook it with vigour.

'Rajette,' said the man with a big-toothed friendly grin alarmingly halving the front of his head. The fakeness of it was lost on Jacob.

'Jacob,' said Jacob, beginning to get *that* feeling.

'Let us find somewhere to have a smoke, yes?' Rajette asked holding up a piece of brown paper folded into a donut shape. Jacob recognised this as the normal way grass was wrapped here, little bank bags not being in plentiful supply. It was a good deal too.

'Ok but..,' Jacob began to point out that the roof of the hostel would have been perfect for their needs, but his little Arab friend was already gone around the bend in the narrow market street.

Jacob then made his third and most grievous misjudgement of the night. He followed Rajette again and in doing so he committed his very near future to the adventure presented by the little man, and his marijuana.

'Hey!' called Jacob, rushing to catch his partner in crime, 'slow down,' but the little man kept moving, his pace just too quick for Jacob to match walking, instead he found himself ambling awkwardly along, not quite running, not quite walking. It was an uncomfortable half jog, and quite ungainly.

Body language is important. When your body is vulnerable so are you. Jacob stuttered on unwise and unready, and never saw what was coming. If he had been watching, been more in control, he would have noticed that Rajette's stride was purposeful and measured. Their meeting had been no coincidence.

As a rule Jacob didn't run unless he was playing football. When he had found fame after his first book three years ago, Jacob had immediately found out about reporters and running in public could be an absolute disaster.

After the film premier of his first book "Parrots of Power" Jacob walked out of the cinema a good ten yards behind some Tom Cruise type who was playing the lead. Tom-ish who was talking to a gaggle of pressmen and women about the movie and its coming success also deigned to mention in the self-effacing style of the popular actors that Jacob was the writer/screenwriter for the movie.

'Hey Jake,' Tom-ish called to introduce him to the mob. Jacob being far too eager to join the counterfeit star found himself half-jogging forwards with no regard for his surroundings.

The memory sickened him.

A TV Crew had just passed between him and his target audience, leaving a tail of wires and cables for him to trip over, which he did.

Down he went, only managing to keep his feet under him by staggering forward his body moving faster than his desperately scrambling legs. He reached out to steady himself on the nearest person, who turned out to be a model, a Giselle-type, who'd starred as the mute muse for a tortured artist.

The model was wearing a designer, nothing, held on by some sort of double-sided tape that any normal sweaty humanoid would find impossible to keep inside of, forget about walking about and carelessly pirouetting for the cameras. However a model's genetic advantages must include the talent to shut off the sweat glands. So it was down to Jacob who accidentally, he was *almost* sure, to strip her or the outfit in his futile attempt to keep his balance. They both went down in a flurry of flesh and flash photography.

Of course the Press was delighted. A "naked model" embarrassed by a "drunken Irish writer." Oh God, the embarrassment! Jacob nearly committed suicide in his hotel room an hour later. What saved him from doing so was a phone call he received from the Giselle-type's publicist. He'd had an idea, a bloody good one.

Within a half-hour the two arrived at the after show party arm in arm smiling and conspiring. At one stage Giselle-type even nibbled his ear!

'Ha ha' said the Cruise as they entered, 'I knew you were only having us on.'

After that the rest of the party laughed too, one table full of mad and drunken actors actually applauded. Actors will look for any chance to make applause. Jacob and the Giselle laughed it off too, co-conspirators, saved by good PR.

Later that night when Jacob really was the "drunken writer", Tom Cruise-ish winked at him and whispered in his ear.

'Good recovery,' he said and it had been. But Jacob had learned his lesson and from that day on, he never again ran in public.

But here he was, trotting after Rajette in a swoon instead of keeping a wary eye on where he was going as his path grew darker through the old city's corridors.

He finally caught up with the little Arab at the door of a square grey building that could have been in a different country, it was so different from his hostel. They were in the Jewish quarter now and everything was a world of difference. Rajette stopped suddenly and Jacob overtook him for a second, before stopping and looking up at the high grey walls that stood in front of him.

'This is a Jewish building,' Jacob said, realising they had left the Arab quarter far behind. This didn't seem like the best place to have a sneaky smoke.

'Inside,' said Rajette in an American accent. Jacob also felt a push from behind and another American voice added 'Hurry'.

'Shit,' said Jacob entering the building.

*

'Hello Mr. Terry,' said a tall American standing in the hall of Jacob's trap. 'I hope my associate's methods were not too underhanded bringing you here to meet me,' the man added. He sounded like he was giving directions, except he was giving the wrong ones, just for spite.

'Associate?' Jacob asked, 'you must have me confused with someone else. I was looking for my dog,' Jacob leaned forward and began to whistle patting his lap as he called, 'Here Crusher, here boy, where did he go?' then he pretended to look around the room, 'He mustn't have come in here at all. Well I won't trouble you gentlemen any longer,' said Jacob straightening up, 'Here crusher, here boy!' He turned to leave, hoping that there would be a couple of seconds of confusion, which would allow him access to the street where might make a run for it. There wasn't.

'Now, now, you're not going anywhere,' said Rajette in his newly acquired American accent and with his even more recently acquired firearm.

'A gun?' He'd never seen a gun before, not in real life. It looked… pointy. His heart clutched and his stomach shifted. Don't be a coward, he told himself, not sure what he was supposed to be.

'I don't know what you guys want,' Jacob said, 'but I'm sure I will be very helpful without that,' he added, motioning towards the pointy revolver.

For the moment Rajette looked at his "Associate" who nodded slightly. The gun was lowered and Jacob would have sighed with relief if he hadn't just had a gun to his back.

'I'm sure you will be very helpful,' said the tall American from the lobby, 'If you'll just step in here,' now he gestured towards an open door, revealing a small sitting room, 'my colleague will put his weapon away completely,'

Jacob moved to comply and Rajette or whoever he was put the gun back in his jacket. He entered the room still unsettled, uneasy and unhappily confused. The couch was very comfortable though and there was a bowl of fruit with Pitaya's in it. Jacob remembered tasting one, years before. They were very tasty indeed, but he didn't think that there would be a chance to try one.

'Now Jacob Terry, my name is Mr. Marshall and I have a few questions to ask you,' Mr Marshall sat across the room while Rajette closed the door behind them.

'Hello' said Jacob, helplessly.

Mr. Marshall was wearing a grey suit with nice lines, shiny shoes and a little golden clip on his purple tie. The clip had a red sword on it which rung a bell with Jacob but he wasn't able to remember just then why he recognised it.

'Mr. Terry,' Mr. Marshall began.

'Jacob,' Jacob interrupted automatically, Marshall only smiled crookedly at this.

'Jacob. Are you a Catholic?' Jacob considered this. How would he answer? Honestly.

'Sort of,' he answered, 'my family is,' He didn't like where this was going; religion was not a good conversational subject with guns present.

'More specifically, Mr. Terry, have you become more interested in religion lately?'

'Just now, yes,' Jacob answered. It was true. The situation had caused him to think of God. Mr. Marshall was not pleased with this response and his eyes narrowed.

'You tryin to be funny? Cos you're not funny boy.'

'Just tell me what you want?' Jacob pleaded with sincerity. Ten minutes ago he was going to get stoned; now he was in the clutches of some suit wearing lunatic, who obviously wanted to know something about Jacob's new book project. Jacob had no intention of keeping any secrets.

'I know what you are doing here,' Mr. Marshall said, 'and I will not stop you continuing your research.'

'I'm not sure I know what..,' Jacob began but noticed Rajette's hand moving into his jacket again, 'Ok,' he admitted 'what do you want to know?' Mr. Marshall grinned.

'Good,' he said, 'a quick learner,' He handed Jacob an envelope; it was small and felt familiar to his hands.

'A cheque?' Jacob asked. This was another unexpected turn.

'You will write this book and hand it over to your "previous" employers only, and I really mean only, after we have taken any of the materiel that we think necessary. Any scrolls, notes, accounts… anything they give you, we want to see it first. Before even you, look at it,' Mr. Marshall sat back into his leather chair. 'Does that sound ok to you?'

'And, "we" are?' Jacob risked.

'We,' said Mr. Marshall, 'are paying you 200,000 euro Mr. Terry, so don't worry too much about it. Rajette will stay in contact with you so you can deliver the information to us,' From over Marshall's shoulder Rajette grinned at him, he was a creepy looking man now that his earlier, obviously false joviality, had completely disappeared.

Jacob sat back, not bothering to open the envelope. He didn't care what was in it. He just wanted to play out this encounter and get the hell away from here.

'What do you say?' asked Mr. Marshall.

There wasn't much he could say. So he agreed. He made arrangement to leave any he received from Richeloe in his room the following night and to go out for at least an hour while

Rajette made a visit. Only after this was Jacob to look at the writings. And, he wouldn't. It was more than his life was worth.

***

The next morning in Ghana when Jacob arose from his scratchy mattress, he found that he was feeling more positive than the previous day. Today he would be leaving Accra and he was a relieved. After only one day in the capital he'd climbed into bed feeling rigid and nervous with nightmares posing sleep-destroying questions during the night.

How serious were those Americans? They had guns and that was serious enough for him. The scribe Richeloe was mystery too and the two threats together caused a large and incomprehensible idea to form in Jacob's mind. Pathways were being built and written clues led to motive but actions spoke louder than both. He'd been intercepted before his first meeting with Richeloe; the Americans knew where he was going. The message that was hidden amongst the words of a celebrated long-dead storyteller smacked of another, only recently deceased. If Daniel was still alive Jacob could have called him and asked his advice. What would he do in these circumstances? Daniel wouldn't stand for such underhandedness. He would get out of the whole deal, turn his back and leave promises made in ignorance and fear. But it must have been Daniel that left that message for him in the book of short stories. Why? There were no others, Jacob had checked.

Jacob washed himself and put on a ratty pair of shorts he'd included in his rushed packing. He couldn't get out of this, not now, when he knew so little, with all the unknowns gnawed at him until he was dying to, had to know, the whole story. No, he would not get out, not yet. He probably couldn't.

Jacob had no idea what sort of power the Church could wield against him in exchange for his silence or to pressure him into service but he'd seen a gun pointed at him and he had was certain that they had threatened Maria's life. That gun could have gone off and ended his life right there with the American watching him writhe on the floor, his darkest blood oozing out of whatever hole the little Arab had made in him. The same could happen to Maria and he could not let her go through that alone.

Besides, he was too much of a coward to get out of this now, but he could get out of this room, out of this city where he beginning to feel so vulnerable. He would go to the ocean and try to put the pieces together there with the massive body of the water breathing in front of him. You could turn your back on the sea and face the land with all its lies and promises. You could trust it to ignore you in times when the world would not. It was bigger than everything but the planet itself, so "I have much more important things to do" and stronger than anything Jacob could imagine. When you believe in so little…

Rooting through the pockets of his old shorts Jacob found and old Irish five pound note and tried to remember when he'd last worn them. It must have been before the euro at any rate. Five or six years ago it was worth a lot more to him than is was now. He used to think that money would solve all of his problems. And, for a while it had.

'Money money, money,' he had once half joked. 'Give it all to me now. I want to count it and buy expensive electrical gizmos,' Jacob scrunched up the old note and threw it on the floor, sneering at the note, as it lay there useless and out of date.

'You don't even care, do you?' he asked the five. Jacob picked up his bags and opened the door, trying to leave in a dramatic flourish, but one of his bags pushed it closed again and he was forced to shuffle out without a smidgeon of grace. Downstairs he would have to explain to the owner why he was leaving. Or, more likely he would spend twenty minutes explaining it to some hanger-on who had nothing to do with the hostel. Smiling, Jacob pictured the encounter.

'Oh, why are you leaving?' the proprietor would surely ask.

'I'm frightened,' Jacob would say.

'Eh?'

'Well you see,' says Jacob, 'and this is where it gets more complicated. I'm in the middle of writing a religious book about Jesus.'

'Jesus?'

'Actually he was really called Joshua. Anyway, I'm becoming increasing concerned for my life and I think…' Here Jacob would pause for effect. 'That if I continue finding all I am likely to discover, I may be killed by a little Arabic man with a shiny black revolver,' the owner's eyes would now be glazed and he would be nodding.

'On the other hand, if I don't continue on my course I will never forgive myself, will never understand what I've gotten into, or I may be killed by a little Arab man with a shiny black revolver. I'll never be able to walk down the street again without thinking, what's the point of all this, if I don't know everything? Why bother going home when I won't know what I'm going home to?' The owner would suddenly brighten and answer intelligently.

'Oh, are you going home?' To which Jacob would reply with a very cool, 'Hardly.'

However when Jacob reached the Hostel desk with this imaginary narrative still playing on the movie screen of his mind, there was nobody there. So he just left.

When at last he reached it, Jacob found that Accra's central Circle bus station was a pain in the arse his one big rucksack became the epicentre of a pandemonium people-quake as it was promptly taken from the boot of his Taxi and whisked away, without his constant, off through the crowds of hawkers trying to get him into one rickety paint deprived bus or another. They tugged at him and called him Whiteman but Jacob only saw red as his bag disappeared from view.

He drew his flick knife. It had a pitiful little blade and couldn't cut the ears off a jelly baby, but it did flick into view with a loud metallic clack! which made it a crowd pleaser. Jacob accosted the bag thief as he tried to put the liberated luggage on the roof of a formerly blue Leyland coach. The man cried in panic saying that he was working on this bus and was only carrying Jacob's bag so he wouldn't have to. His bus was an air-conditioned bus with, very very much comfortable seats, only 25,000 Cedis, all the way to Cape coast.

Jacob started to shout but stopped himself; he could feel foam in the corners of his mouth. This wasn't like him. Thinking about his ambush in Jerusalem was causing his rage to build and boil up inside of him. At least he was angry now, earlier he'd just been frightened. But whipping out a knife like that just wasn't cool. These were just people, and he was like a bar of gold thrown into a poorhouse. But that was a thought that Jacob wasn't having yet. 'Put it down' Jacob roared flicking his knife closed to the relief of the Ghanaians surrounding him. The blade didn't close completely though, its point poked out from the handle disappointingly like an unconvincing erection. The many bus drivers and the general bus station community forgot about the knife directly and continued trying to sell him ice cream, water, biscuits, mints, chewing gum, plantain chips, nuts of all types, yam, donut balls and fried fish. There were so many people jogging around working off the trade from the buses Jacob saw them for a moment like tiny fish living off the great whales of the ocean. The buses and their customers needed the worker fish for food and water, old sandwiches and fake

"Durafel" batteries and the fish needed the buses to survive the cold harsh climate of the big city as it ebbed around them, ignoring them though it was they who gave it life.

The Africans pushed right up to him invading his space, but giving his bag, newly returned to his side, a comically wide berth. Jacob and his Taxi driver inspected three buses and picked out one with comfortable seats, but no air-con. It was 30,000 Cedis and Jacob wondered for a moment whether he should go and find the victim of his earlier blade wielding, but he was far too stubborn for that.

He gave his driver a dash, ensured his gear was stowed safely and boarded the bus with a notebook, a minidisk player and a fan-ice, the ice cream being Jacob's preference to the fried fish on sale all around him. The "fish" was easily identifiable by its horrendous odour and when it came in to view he could see that the charred marine remains looked cruelly tortured. The fish lay sideways on top of each other atop an African head. Their little pointed teeth were bared in agony and their very bones were fried into edibility. No waste, no taste.

Jacob sucked on his bag of ice cream for a moment before reality swooped in. He'd taken out a knife and flashed it about, like some sort of... God! What an asshole thing to do.

***

Messengers

In between ages and systems of belief the human soul has always had a thirst for understanding. There is a constant need for meaning and spiritual translation that the constant struggle of normal life cannot supply.

Therefore explanation and interpretation must come from somewhere else, somewhere outside the self, a wondrous translation of God's will, showing us the true meaning behind the divine obscurity. The question is, where does if come from, or to be more precise, from whom?

After twenty minutes of waiting the bus –with comfortable seats, but no air-con, shook free from the chokehold of the city and Jacob felt that he could relax. He leaned back in his seat and listened to the Electric 6 as they blared his thoughts away. A peace and quiet of sorts was finally his.

Then the preacher started.

It wasn't that Jacob had any real problem with preachers. It was more that he had a problem with lack of choice. It was with being forced to listen that he disagreed. The tall white suited black man stood up bible in hand as the bus left the city and began to harangue the passengers with the will of God. Oh God!
Even with his minidisk up full Jacob could not escape the garbled words of our Lord that were flowing around him. What was worse, the people around him were joining in! Jacob's fellow passengers were arguing theological points of ambiguity with the man. Brandishing their own bibles and obviously quoting versus from the book of whomever, section ninety-nine paragraph one million they revealed their own personal slant on the lies that they held in their hands. Jacob felt guilty as he watched and listened, turning his Walkman off as the Ghanaians gestured and articulated. Did they know what a load of bullshit they were peddling, believing? Jacob was spellbound. He gaped around the bus in misbelief. God didn't say this; it was somebody else. A mere man wrote it. Apparently an Italian name Mark was the main contributor, and even then no one can be sure.

Would his re-written interpretation become common enough to be the basis for religious beliefs? The Church obviously thought so, or they would have found another was to counteract the whistleblower.

Only a few weeks ago Jacob would have thought that very cool indeed, but now it was an idea from which he recoiled. In a couple of years time there could be a man on a battered old bus travelling the roads of Africa, South America or anywhere in the developing world, quoting from his book, the book of lies he was about to write.

'Fuck that,' He said aloud. The whole bus turned to look at Jacob and the preacher approached.

'You have something to say-o?' asked the three-pieced preacher. Jacob sat up and coughed in embarrassment.

'Alleluia?' he tried aloud and the people around him nodded in agreement.

'Alleluia,' they cried.

***

Money was good, Jacob knew. Since he began to amass large sums of it he'd become very happy indeed. He certainly didn't miss not having any. The waiting for payday, sitting in front of terrestrial television dreaming of a bar of chocolate, an ice cream or a big fat steak. 'Living of the clippings of tin' his Da said it was called.

It was crap, having no money. Never being able to do everything you wanted to.

Since his first book and the subsequent film it had been big-money-love-city for Jacob. Up until two years ago Jacob had coasted along with a fat wallet, basking on the rocks of financial security and tanning in the limelight. He'd become green skinned.

Then the rich cake he was eating became a Black Forest gateaux with a little too much chocolate and a mite too much sugar. Now it was covered with crusty yellow cream that soured his gross oversized slice. His metaphors were weakening and turning out like similar without direction. Meaning, being so much harder to find, impossible even, since the day Da died.

Since becoming a big earner, Jacob had forced his Dad to accept dozens of gifts. He was the newly wealthy son dying to show off his gaudy happiness. Jacob always tried not to injure his Father's pride by splashing his cash around too much and for a long time and he thought he'd succeeded, but the cars always sat unused and dusty. The expensive exercise machines lay in mint condition still in their original packaging in an old shed out the back of his Da's farmhouse.

Not so long ago Jacob had been standing in that empty place, looking out across the fields surrounding the farmhouse in the Vale of Avoca. In these fields he had often watched his Da as he pottered amongst the weeds and weeded around the flowerpots. Seeing out through the huge bay windows Jacob was proud that he hadn't been allowed to put his money into any of it. Da had bought it all himself from the proceeds of their city house. All Jacob had done was to buy a gimmicky little tractor and a nice fountain. He'd also clad the driveway in cobbled marble. It was meant to be a shinning road to his Father's new home, but in the winter cars had to park by the roadside, the surface being too slick and the incline too sharp to navigate safely.

The farm remained a beautiful sight regardless of that present doubling as a death trap. It was the home Jacob's Da would have for the rest of his long healthy life, which turned out not to be so long, or healthy. Short in fact. Painfully short.

By the time his father had withered away the fields had become unruly, overgrown and ugly. There were no more strawberries growing fenced-in away from the dog. No herbs or berry bushes to be seen at the end of the lawn. The grass was tall and trees were diseased looking with. Untended flowers outgrown by hogweed and the entire property looked dead and empty. In a year the fields had produced naught but tears. Da was dead now, and his only son Jacob, like the grounds, was suffering his wake. For the last two years Jacob spent a lot of his time with his only real friend, a fellow writer. Someone he'd always looked up to.

Daniel Candelli had known, as did Jacob, that during this period he was playing the role of Father to the young Irish man. But it was ok, because it was understood. And, just maybe, Candelli was not adverse to the idea of having a son, especially one who could argue with him on points, or women, if there was a difference.

Now Candelli was dead too and Jacob was left feeling lost inside himself.

The earth grows cold over the corpses of men, over their Fathers and over the dreams they had just yesterday been dreaming.

Jacob's dreams had returned to him though. Just like the fields around his father's home that would return to good health under the care of a new farmer. His life was full again. He had Love and adventure once more. Oh, and he being paid twice, which was good two.

***

Jacob's bus, comfortable seats, but no air-con, stopped at a large junction and Jacob was told that he must get off there, as the bus would continue along the main road to Takoradi. This was news to Jacob but he alighted with the other passengers and climbed up the small ladder to retrieve his bag from the roof of the bus, much to the delight of a huge fat woman who smiled happily at him and clapped when he returned to the ground. He pointedly ignored the Taxi drivers refusing their help and settled instead on a bench to smoke a cigarette and look thoughtful.

With all that done, Jacob approached the group. They looked more than a little chastened by his ungrateful behaviour, so he took out a 50,000 note. He hopped into the car of the most responsive taxi driver, a tough choice, and off they went with the exhaust scraping along the ground all the way to Cape Coast.

'I want to stay somewhere cheap' Jacob told the driver.

'How much would you like to pay?' he was asked, '100,000?'

'More cheap than that,' He replied 'And open too,' Jacob added remembering Accra.

'Ha ha, open, what is this?'

'Yes, In Accra a driver took me to a hotel that was closed'

'He he he, we are not like this in Cape Coast ha ha,' the driver told him secretly deciding not to rip off this Obroni as he would normally have done, just to prove the point.

Jacob's model taxi driver took him to three hotels free of charge before taking him to a Red Cross Hostel that didn't appear in the guidebook. It was cheap, unbelievably so and Jacob felt wary as he walked towards the rooms. He expected the worst and was very pleasantly surprised. The room was large and clean and had a bathroom with shower. On top of this there were three beds, so it would have been even cheaper for three people. Jacob was in miserly heaven.

Jacob confirmed that the room would be fine and took the key. And as he walked across the yard he received a friendly wave from the taxi driver, racism being obviously weaker than localism. As soon as he entered his room Jacob showered and rolled around on all three beds to get his money's worth before going out for a drink. He brought some notes to read and a sweaty wad of Cedis to fritter away. He was happier than he'd been for days. A new place, a new beginning, and maybe he was safer here than in the big city. Jacob felt refreshed by the possibility and headed out to the beach. The sound of the ocean rose above the chatter of the oversized gulls and cleared away the rest of his accumulated despair. He looked down past the town and out into the blue expanse. He wondered why he was so attached to the sea. Why did it always relax him so? After all, he couldn't even swim.

Acceptance, death, betrayal and rebirth

If you remember from before the man who thought that he was much the same as god? Well, it's time you knew his name. The first one he had any anyway. He was called Michael de Rhy for most of his life and he was a French millionaire, which is of no real matter except to point out that he was very rich and privileged. He had money to burn. And, as was alluded to earlier, Michael was obsessed with his own demise, what with it being so close and all.

Long before Jacob's story began, four years as a matter of record, Michael de Rhy had a visitor to his chateau near Nantes. The visitor was an old man too, but more notably he was a priest.
    'I can help you live past your lifetime,' said the priest, who was very much into getting right to the point, when in fact he was about to wriggle around in a little parable for a minute or twelve. 'Jesus,' said the man winding-up, 'was a mortal before he became a god. Like you Michael,' he told de Rhy, 'Jesus had acceptance and success and like you he wanted more from his life. So he went in search of the next stage of his existence. He

went looking for the sacred words that would set him free from mortality. Again, like you Michael,' the priest added, 'he had the will to achieve what he wished and the circumstances afforded him the opportunity. There are always three stages. You have achieved acceptance by your success, surely you have?' to which of course de Rhy agreed, 'The second stage is death, to which we are all drawing closer and there is no need to achieve that, as it is achieved by all.

And finally, there is rebirth. Only possible if you know how it is done, if you know whom to ask, and if you know where to look. You can have all three if you can find out, what he knew. What did Jesus find out?'

Now, to say that Michael de Rhy was not sceptical would be like saying that you, the reader, can't read. But you can, can't you. Well you're doing a pretty good job of pretending. Anyway, the key here is that besides his scepticism, Michael was obsessed, desperate and he wanted to believe so badly that he was willing to let the idea grow on him. And, that was enough.

Oh it grew all right. It tunnelled into him in a cancerous manner, its roots becoming imbedded in his vital organs. Oh for the chance to have another life, to feel again the strength of youth in your bones. It was worth everything to Michael De Rhy and he needed very little convincing.

Yet, there is always however, and De Rhy, being a businessman, demanded proof of the priest, hiding his excitement and his instant belief. So, the priest returned some weeks later with a scroll that he had obtained at great risk to his person and position. This writing was alleged of the lord himself and Michael De Rhy wasted no time in believing in its authenticity and the two began to scheme.

Through the priest, still unnamed and purposefully so, Michael De Rhy commissioned the retention of all such scrolls and between them they devised a method for doing so. It would allow them access to the information they needed without any need for high profile robbery and with very few casualties, just one as a matter of fact. But actually, in De Rhy's mind the number was really two, as he expected the priests company to become a lot more troublesome after he'd gotten what he wanted.

The plan was set in motion and was, for the most part, a very successful one. The number of casualties had now risen, but the number was negligible. What really mattered was how close Michael was to obtaining the information that he needed. The answer? Close, dangerously close. He had enough information now to begin the ritual, and transform himself into his final reincarnation. And, with one more piece of the puzzle, he would be able to remain on earth for all eternity.

But the key was in Africa, and Jacob was a lot closer to finding it than De Rhy. So the old man decided to act.

As for the priest, he had told De Rhy about the three stages that he must achieve to obtain rebirth. But he only spoke of acceptance, death, and rebirth and he never mentioned betrayal.

Recollections 9

Calling

A grey mouse sniffed at the remains of dinner on the polished hard wood table in the grand dining room of monsieur Michael L. De Rhy. It was a feast and the mouse began to gnaw at the left over beef with great vigour. It was in a red wine sauce that was congealing and had a jelly like consistency. The mouse always ate there on the table and with a guaranteed feed like this available the mouse would always come back, as long as she remembered her way.

Across the room in an ancient high backed armchair with an oversized glass of brandy slipping slowly from his slumbering hand, snored eighty two year old Michael L. De Rhy. It was habitual for him to sit there brooding in the evenings after he half ate his dinner and once more gave up hoping. Earlier than this he'd sat at the table where the mouse now nibbled and hoped a great many things. He hoped that he would see the cook who always managed to serve his dinner and ring the evening bell before he arrived in the dining room. He hoped he would receive a phone call from one of his acquaintances, but the antique phone on the table by the door hadn't heralded a friendly voice for a dozen years. Secretly though, and most of all, he hoped for the end. Yet he submitted to failure, as he had every evening for a very long time and stood instead to pour himself a glass of brandy and sit in his most comfortable chair where he could stare into the flames of the roaring fire, lit earlier by a houseboy who also managed unfailingly to evade detection.

Just then two things happened simultaneously, three actually. The brandy glass dropped from Michael's drooping fingers landing on the thick red carpet by the leg of his chair and a stone flew from the fire accompanied by a loud crack and a shower of sparks to land on the carpet before him, and, the mouse scarpered from her eating place.

Michael awoke confused from his dozing and waited as his aging mind and eyes focused on the few feet of floor between him and the fire. A few moments later he saw that there was something different about the expensive carpet and anything different was worth his attention. A ring of black was smouldering in the burgundy pile and in its centre was a black stone glowing slightly from the heat of the flames. Michael rose and went to the fireside to retrieve the shovel and brush so that he might pick up the ember, at least he thought that's what it was, and throw it back into the fire. But the smell of it stopped him.

It was like nothing he could describe. It couldn't be just the burning carpet he knew. Unless the carpet had been woven from something's flesh or had at the very least been rotting under his nose for many years.

And why not? Hadn't he been rotting under his own nose and all for years now? Fading away, loveless at the centre of his useless empire, always afraid to look people in the eye for too long when he talked to them. He heard them whisper in the halls of his office building in Nante. He's a horrible rude man, they said, but they were wrong. Oh yes he was horrid and he was rude but these were not the reasons he looked away. He was afraid they would see him. He felt, knew, that if one of them was fixed too long with his gaze, they would know what he was and run away screaming. He shook himself from this oldest moan and focused again on the ember.

It was now three days since the last package had arrived and he'd made the final decision. He was going to do that which he had only dreamed of until now. Now he had the means and the knowledge to carry on with his plan, it was no time for baulking, he needed to be firm of mind or else he would fail in the half measure.

So he'd gathered everything that was needed together, using the Italians notebook and the other writings. He formed the correct frame of mind for the task and spoke the words while his own blood boiled in a crucible. At the time he had retched at the stink of it, but now that the smell had returned and it was sweet and filled with promise.

But what did it mean? Had the ritual worked?

In the centre of the darkened circle of charred carpet sat the small black stone, smoking and emitting foetid waves. The smell rose from the stone and poisoned the air in the room. Michael enjoyed its filthiness. It seemed to him a real thing in his fake and manufactured life. The stone must have gotten mixed with the coals and lay in the hearth getting hotter and hotter among the flames until it was shot out in a gassy jet to land there on the carpet.

Little wisps of smoke that had been rising from the patch ceased suddenly as if the ember had been doused by invisible water but without any steam or hissing. Michael felt disappointment. For a moment he had thought to leave the stone there to smoulder while he retired to bed. During the night flames may have appeared and spread throughout the room until the whole floor took light. It could have spread to the rooms above where he was sleeping and consumed him where he lay.

Alas it would seem that this was not going to happen, so he sat back down to doze in his chair and dream about petrol. There was still time for it to work, but time was not unlimited.

At the age of eighty-two monsieur De Rhy was a rich and bitterly lonely man. These were words that had often been used to describe him. There was one word in particular though that was much more accurate.

The word evil has been used to describe many people but it is rarely precise. In movies, books and bedtime stories there are always evil ones with pointy hats or wicked laughs. But a truly evil person is hard to find, even in this world with all the evils it has to offer. There are many evil things, but very few truly evil people.

Michael L. De Rhy was definitely evil. Every day of his life he knew it to be true. Yet he acted with courtesy, wit and charm. He tried to smile correctly at those who should be smiled upon and he gave thanks to those he felt merited thanking. Still, he was rich, bitterly lonely, and most definitely evil.

It was the evil in Michael's soul that was the problem. Not in the same way that you or I have wickedness in our souls, no. Michael L. De Rhy had been born with a festering hate behind his eyes. For most of his eighty-two years he attempted to cover his malicious and loathsome nature.

Even as a child not bigger than a poodle Michael's powerful malevolence had shone through and he'd scared numerous minders to madness long after his parents had despaired and abandoned the very sight of him. He unsettled the hearts of Nana Jean, Nana Colette and ten others. They had all lost heart, battered by his obnoxious behaviour their gentle minds twisted by his cruelty.

He'd been a boy whose aura could pollute the very atmosphere until he'd learned to hide it, as if hiding it had done him any good.

Now Michael was finally ready to drop his kindly mask. He grew too tired to conceal his true purpose. Through all these long years the spark of humanity that strove to deliver him to God and not to himself had dimmed, and finally burned out. He could even remember the exact day it had happened.

Precisely one year before, as Michael sat in this very same room his mood frantic and desperate, he'd spoken to the flames as they devoured the coals in the hearth and felt the wretchedness of his own gaze reflected by the fire. They were like a picture of his heart or a portrait of his own damnation. He'd been thinking about the offer made him by an old priest and looking to himself for answers.

'What do you want me to do? He's asked but the answer hadn't come to him, not then.

From that point in his miserable life onwards he'd wandered in Hopkins fashion through the corridors and gardens of his highly prized home. He began to leer and sneer and hate everything made of brick and earth, and bone.

He built a storm around his person, not allowing a single soul to bring him to the door or call him from the phone, not unless it had something to do with the plan. The world he'd been hiding in was gone. Michael De Rhy had freed himself from it. He was not of this earth any more but born of hell, where he belonged. He knew that he'd wasted his life and there was nothing he could do about it. Unless? Unless the priest was right, if it could really be done.

His first thoughts told him that he was mad to even consider it, but the idea would not leave him and his second thoughts were much firm and more easily swayed.

'If *he* could do it, so can I,' Michael convinced himself. Why not? If it was possible, had he not the money and the resources to do it?

Yes was the answer, yes, yes, yes.

So he had carried out the plan with only a faint hope that he would succeed. Until finally, after a whole year spent waiting in

119

agony for this night to come, the spirit of the world had finally spoken to him, had given him a sign. Here it was

He looked down at the stone again and noticed markings upon it. At first he made to pick it up, but then he realised that he could not. Not yet. Now he must to go sleep; that was all. He had followed his instructions to the letter and he must not stop now.

"Then the misbeliever will sleep, and draw his final breath. And in the new day he will arise and take on the form that will carry for all eternity, his new self. So the third stage begins"

In dreamless sleep his aged body stirred only slightly at the sound of the screaming earth as it battled to reach him. But the earth soul lost the fight and her mourning echoed through Michael L. De Rhy's hateful home. There was not enough left in him that wanted to be reached. He was too far gone.

The next morning Michael De Rhy rose for the last time and almost skipped to his dining room in expectation. When he got there he discovered the stone lying on the floor where it had landed the night before. The fire was out for good now, the houseboy would never return. This was it, the sign of things to come. The tiny voice of his remaining humanity screeched at him to stop, but it was too small for Michael to hear above the rush of ecstatic devilry in his soul.

'Don't,' it pleaded with him, 'Leave it where it lies.'

The outcome was moot. Michael picked up the stone and held it to his breast, and there inside and out of the old man, began a transformation. He did not morph or shift in shape as would be expected from science fiction and fantasy.

Michael De Rhy was merely there one moment, an old man, nothing but a dead and rotting thing.

Then he was there in agony, a human shell giving in to his soul's desire, crying out for the change to be complete.

For a moment he was there again in liquid corruption, a demon of fire, a devil.

And finally, he was Leavon.

Michael Leavon De Rhy stood in the centre of the room with the stone still clasped against his breast. He was a blonde young man of no more than thirty years. He felt strong and healthy, but more than that, he felt powerful. A soft smile grew among his handsome features as he held the stone up and read the markings. There were three lines across it. One was a straight line, the second was undulated, and the third was long deep furrow much larger than the others.

It spoke to him: 'Man is alone,' it said, 'his nature weak, but his sins are great.'

Leavon knew then what he must do to deserve this second chance. He must pay the price for his rebirth and he was glad to do it. Leavon was alive now and had a task to revel in. For too long he'd been only middle name, given to him by his mother in painful delirium on the day of his birth. Well today was a day of re-birth and there was one last piece of the ritual to perform. It lay far away from where he now stood, and there was nothing as good as the present.

Leavon looked around his Chateau. He was rich, young and evilly inclined; all big pluses. This time around there would be no half measures. This time everything would burn.

He left the great big house with the door swinging open, left it to the mice and rats and the servants if they could bear to live in it, and entered the world to share vengeance with his new enemy. His purpose was written on the stone now hanging round his muscled neck. He would not waste this second chance. Leavon was here to stay and the message was clear:

Man is alone, his nature weak, but his sins are great.

Recollections 10

Lost Lines

At that moment of triumphant rebirth for Leavon, Becky was feeling alone. Eight countries were now between her and her true love and he was fading into hazy memory. From Israel she had travelled to Greece a long time target of hers, a dream of a place with a history she'd always loved and respected. Her expectations had been lofty indeed but surely the land formerly of highest civilisation would not disappoint her. It wouldn't have, before Jacob.

Before meeting him she had been ready to drown in the culture she once referred to as, the old world. The crumbling remnants of astounding architecture and the home of the ancient world's freest thinkers, Greece was to be one of the high points of her trip to Europe, but perspective is a changeable and slippery ally in the most normal of times. She had not counted on Israel, not counted on Jacob, not allowed for the possibility of love. Now her perspective had altered and her journey had become a chore.

Oh yes, Greece was a fascinating place to behold. She saw the debris of its once rich culture in every city and fenced-in site. Two euro to view the Parthenon, four for a tour of what later turned out to be a group of eight hundred year old pillars with worn writings her guide swore were the etchings of philosophers long dead. They were long dead all right, but not long enough. More likely they said, "Billy Popolopagus is a homosexual" or "Plato had no mates" maybe they were just the tired old, "Soandso was ere" graffiti's answer to practicing your signature.

It was magnificent though, the dryness of the earth the searing heat causing waves in her vision as she looked down from the heights upon the archipelago below. These were sights that could make a body think big thoughts and Becky was no different from any body and thought them too as she stood there looking out as the philosopher's had done. They all led the same way however, every bad experience made her wish that Jacob was there and every moment that took her breath away saw her turning to him to say,

'Wow isn't it…?' Well he wasn't there to share it and that was that. What was the point in torturing herself, she felt desperate and not like her self at all.

One day, after Greece, after Italy and two Onia's. After crossing Hungary, a Burg, and two countries ending in land, Becky was walking lonely in the black forest when she came to a decision.

Fuck it, she thought, and got the first plane to London. Not very much she'd had great plans for this year away from home and she wasn't going to let anyone, even Jacob, ruin it. She was going to London to get pissed and have a laugh. The guided tours and the fluctuating entrance fees could piss right off.

So here she was, in England and as lonely as ever. Carrying a backpack around the busy London streets would have been hard enough in the summer time, but in autumn it was a real pain in the ass.

Around the same time as Jacob was drinking in Cape Coast, Becky was standing in the lobby of the fifth place she'd been to today. It was called the Capital hotel and now she had finally taken with the blasted backpack off her aching shoulders, she was preparing to kill a little hairy man who had was taking a million years to finally tell her that: No there were no rooms left dear, and yes, he could have told her that half an hour ago.

'Are you sure?' she asked, desperate for a lucky break. Perhaps the man was just a moron relative of the hotel owner who was about to arrive from the back office and save her from committing murder most foul upon his person.

'Well em…' said the hairy little bastard, 'I could check again,' He seemed unsure. 'Maybe there's…' he looked down at the register again and up at Becky examining her, 'no, definitely not. You cannot stay here' Behind him there were plenty of keys hanging on little hooks. Six actually, that Becky could see having counted them for the forth time.

'But the Keys,' she gestured towards them, 'why are there so many keys still hanging on the wall?' The little prick turned and started at them, surprised by their presence.

'Mmm?' he mused. The canine receptionist shared a glazed exchange with the silver and plastic key rings. 'Keys, yes!' he said finally, reaching out to touch them where they hung. 'These keys are for, room number…' The man felt them for a moment, 'numbers sixteen and forty two,' and with that he turned back to Becky falling silent.

'And?' she asked, grinding her teeth, Becky was very good at not screaming.

'And?' he asked.

'CAN!' Becky took a breath and calmed herself, starting again. 'Can,' she asked, 'I,' she condescended, 'have one of them?'

'You want a key?'

'Well, yeah!' She answered in misbelief. The old man smiled enormously at her.

'Ah!' he exclaimed. 'Now, you can stay here,' She could have kissed him. 'Number Forty two it is,' He said handing her two sets keys.

'What about…?'

'No, no one can ever stay in number sixteen,' the man said waggling his finger.

Becky looked in her hand with a perplexed expression. She almost took the keys and ran, but couldn't help herself. She had to know why he'd given her two.

'Why?' she asked holding the two bunches tightly just in case, 'Why are there two sets?' The old man practically exploded with mirth, laughing deep and loudly his voice echoing around the wooden foyer. Becky waited until finally she had to clear her throat to get his attention.

'Oh,' said Mr. Marcus Capital, 'it's simple really. One set is to get into the room and the other, should you wish to use them, is to get back out,' He grinned with many large teeth and suddenly he wore a very different face. He looked younger, more mischievous and a little scarier too. Becky felt good about him though, he was a pleasant man after all, she was sure of it. -A remark could be made here about girls and their ability to see the best in people who give them things. But it won't, not directly anyway.

'You are welcome to the Capital Hotel,' he told her, 'my name is Marcus. Marcus Capital. Enjoy your stay,' and he gave her a wink as he spoke.

Becky felt that this was quite enough weird for one day, grabbed her bag and headed for the stairs. She was going to get herself cleaned up, dolled up and out as soon as was humanly possible. So she practically flew out of the Mr. Capital's presence.

'Yes,' he said, smiling long after she's gone, 'indeed.'

***

In Jacob's room there was stillness. That is not to say that all was quiet, stillness never alludes to silence. There are always noises. A person can never escape them. Sure, you could sit in a bank vault behind three feet of steel and claim complete quiet but then there would be the sound of your own movements or the thump of your heart as it its grows louder and louder. And, if you didn't hear these, then you're probably dead, or deaf, in which case the argument is a bit stupid to begin with.

No, the stillness in Jacob's room in the Red Cross hostel in Cape Coast did not involve the absence of noise or movement. This was an expectant stillness, the sound of a living thing lying in wait. There was a collection of little breaths that accompanied the filling and collapsing of the tiny lungs belonging to Sunburst the agama lizard whose head was currently poking out of Jacob's rucksack. Sunburst's co-ordinated swivelling eye turrets were taking in his surroundings, he was hungry and waiting for prey.

Scrambling the rest of his way out of the rucksack, he cast around again, noticing a movement in the air above him, Sunburst scurry-shimmied up the bedclothes and onto the bed where he lay still again as a large fly buzzed a lazy loop only an inch or two over his head. It was a Tsetse fly. Sunburst didn't know this of course but that made little difference. It wasn't as if the fly knew what it was either. Instead of worrying about his failings as an insectologist, Sunburst lay still once more and waited for his chance.

Insectology and dinner, finding one without the other

Earlier that day twelve Tsetse flies just like the one that was buzzing around Jacob's room had floated down from the trees attracted by the sounds and smells of a group of people pissing at the roadside. They were passengers of a bus travelling on the Accra road to Cape Coast. The bus was massively over loaded. The pile of cargo on its roof was easily the height of the vehicle itself, creating something the size of a double-decker bus, suspension creaking and bumpers scraping the broken highway. Once the people were all aboard, luckily unharmed by the lethal insects, the bus whooshed off carrying the flies in its wake. By the time it reached the Cape coast junction there were only seven flies left aimlessly buzzing around the government bus stop and STC station and after ten minutes there were only three left, the others had flown after other large moving objects, a bus, a car and a couple of Trotros.

When Jacob caught his taxi and headed into town, these three oblivious predators followed. And, by the time he reached the Red Cross hostel there was only one of them still in tow. From twelve to one, by luck and circumstance the last Tsetse Fly was now in Jacob's hostel room.

The Tsetse fly, which was about twice the size of a housefly, was looping around with its telltale scissors-like wings showing it apart from its harmless cousin. This random Tsetse was a testament to blind and powerful bad luck. Out of the twelve Tsetse's, and before those, hundreds, this was the only one carrying Tryponosomiasis, meaning that should Jacob be bitten by it he would certainly fall ill and within a couple of weeks, without treatment, he would die.

As the days passed Jacob would slow down, feeling tired, lethargic and wasted in general. He would begin to loose interest in everything and become listless before finally dropping off for good.

Unfortunately the chances were that Jacob would become weak and lazy before he noticed that anything was wrong with him. If it weren't caught he would succumb to the fatal "sleeping sickness" not realising that his tiredness was not a result of being overworked. He would in fact be checking out, expiring. One-way down, no ways back.

This possibly fatal insectly future finished its long journey and came to rest on Jacob's bed where it sat in the stillness resting after the long flight. It began sucking water and dirt from the fabric of Jacob's towel, flitting between the folds as if it were a helicopter stuttering over the desert.

The Tsetse paused. Could it sense something? How do Flies think, if they do at all? The hairs on the fly's body picked up a stir in the air and it launched itself upwards to safety, finding darkness instead in the Sunburst lizard's mouth. Crunch, crunch, a slight lizardly throat manoeuvre and the Tsetse Fly was gone for good.

Whip, whip, whip, went the ceiling fan, the cool air whipping Sunburst's scaly moustache. He seemed to relish the large insect, although it can't be said that the fulfilling of the basic instinct could be called relish. The Agama alpha male - hence the sunburst markings - began to treat the room to some territorial push-ups before scampering to the floor and under the bed to look for cockroaches. He'd already eaten them all, but he didn't know that.

*

Later that day when the evening began to fall Jacob returned. He showered and lay semi naked on the bed for a snooze, tired after the heat of the sun. That night, while he began again to write about Joshua, Jacob was bitten four times, by mosquitoes, but there were no flies.

Jacob wouldn't have noticed the difference anyway. He was in such a dark mood. The Syrian Jesus was supposed a sombre fellow, a righteous man and the Son of God. Not for the first time Jacob wondered whether the information he had received in Jerusalem was correct. Was this the same man? The man who had suffered the Passion, turning his cheek to receive every blow? It was impossible to think so.

Could the man in his papers have fed the five thousand? Walked on water or, brought dead men back to the living? It didn't seem likely. This man was human and maybe that's why he had never been allowed out in front of his people.

Jacob felt a bout of writer's block fogging his brain. Never did he need to write more than now. Two "employers" were paying him and millions of people, who didn't know it yet, were waiting to read his work. It was a great thing he was preparing to do. These were great lies he was preparing to weave.

Ok just start, Jacob told the sunburned face in a warped mirror over the deep sink in the hostel toilet. He spent a long time looking into mirrors these days, in fact he always had. He remembered little spots of rust and dirt on mirrors in hostels and houses all over the world. A large oval mirror he'd stared into in a town he could barely remember and a tiny square of tin that refracted his image in a village he'd never seen by the light of day. Did the Lord have mirrors? No. Well, maybe polished steel then? But Jacob couldn't imagine Joshua flicking at his hair or wondering should he get it cut shorter like Paul's. Perhaps he had?

　　　Jacob turned his head and walked back to his room and his bed, under which the Sunburst Lizard lay, and began to bang away at his laptop. This was how he normally wrote, his feet tapping and his disposition anxious. His leg bounced as he wrote.

POSSIBLE INTRODUCTION

Man and God, he walked upon the earth, the son of a virgin and a carpenter. Joshua is the name of the Lord.

As a child Joshua questioned the society into which he had been born. As a man he gave himself for us so that we could become again God's own true people. So that we could remember our beginnings and our destiny, coming as they did from God our most heavenly father.

　　　The in-between time of Jesus' life, the teenage years and his young manhood have never been given adequate reference by the Catholic Church. Joshua gave us certain lessons to learn and the Holy bible, the interpretation of his words concentrates on these lessons. This of course, is bound to leave certain parts of Joshua's life unknown. To transcribe every minute of the Lord's life would have only served to describe the unworthy hands that hold the Holy Grail of Jesus, the days spent in thought and realisation as he grew to understand his father's message and how it could best be transferred into our simple misbelieving souls. Knowledge of all these seemingly inconsequential days would only serve to crowd the holy book and distract his flock from the true message. The meaning he must give to all our lives.

Since the Bible was first compiled the world had changed a great deal. The world however is only the environment for the instruments of these changes, Mankind, and it is us that have changed it so. Certainly we have done great things in the time we have been given, but we have also committed great evil with our misinterpretations of the words of the Lord.

Mankind: This animal has grown so complex under God's watchful eye and with our free will we have taken many positive forward steps. We have also however, taken a great many negative steps. Two thousand years of life after Christ has divided and disfigured our world resulting in what we know of as Modern Earth.

Religion has had the largest part to play in this disfigurement.

There are too many voices crying out in the wilderness now, the truth is muffled, and unclear, a sick dove trapped in a cage filled with crows and ravens, gulls and vultures ripping at its juiciest portions.

No longer can this go on. The modern human being demands more in-depth and complete data from which we can device the truth. Too many religions depend upon vague characters delivering unclear messages meant for the minds of simpler beings two centuries ago.

The Proverbs and Parables of the past are not the signposts they once were. Numerous cult-like religions have followed suit and used the Bible's ways to create their own vague characters.

And yet, there is one God and he has one son in Joshua. Joshua is our most powerful link to the creator of the universe, but Joshua has become nothing more than another character, in another religion. This is why God's Church has been asked to fill the world with the entire life, from birth to death, of Joshua Christ our Lord. It is time we learned of the experiences in which our Lord found himself and the truth of the world

Jesus is the one true Lord and all, not just those of us who claim to be Christians, will now be able to rejoice in the reality of his existence.

Joshua is man and God. We have all heard enough of the God in him, now we will see the man.

- Note -
Insert a suitable prayer here. Rejoice in the truth, blah-blah-blah.

Amen.

Jacob looked down at ten minutes work. It always came fairly easy if he didn't let himself get sidetracked. This was the perfect gist for his introduction it was a pity he couldn't remember writing it. He knew that one of the Church's main aims was to tidy the clutter of earlier writings. Sheer volume of words could not astound Man as they once had, so content would be all-important. This passage would be re-written, probably a dozen times, but it outlined the style in which Jacob's "The Creation of Jesus" would be written.

'Good,' He said aloud and rose from the bed, saving the pages before he did. The Floppy disk quaked and katchinked its way through the save function as Jacob rose to look for a shirt. Backing up your work was very important; although Jacob never managed to loose any of his own work he'd watched Michael Douglas loose his in a movie once. And, it didn't look like fun. Pages fluttering in the air, lost forever, it gave him the shivers.

As he rummaged through his backpack, which smelled slightly of something unfamiliar, an ache in his stomach began and another in his head followed swiftly after. One moment he was standing there, fit and healthy, and the next he was folded over on the ground moaning for help in that sheepish voice reserved for spoiled children and patients. Something had definitely come over him.

'Ooooooh fuck!' Jacob felt the pinch. He struggled to stand up feeling what a doctor may have called a sharp pain down one leg. It certainly was sharp, maybe even searing. So he lay down on the floor again to wait until it passed.

Jacob tried to figure out what was happening. His leg had fallen asleep and his lunch had probably been cooked in dirty water, or it was a cramp or something. In a brief respite, Jacob decided wrongly that the moment had passed. He should go out, get some air and have a walk that would surely help, but he intended on showering before heading out. He was approaching the bathroom, tottering on his dead leg, Jacob felt really ill. Then the nausea became a dreadful fit of retching where nothing would come from his mouth but saliva mixed with blood. He fell to his knees and stayed there until this second wave of sickness passed. Well one thing was for sure he wasn't going to walk this off.

Jacob felt wretched but rose and grabbed his keys and wallet all the same. He had to go to a doctor, now, so he left.

On the screen of Jacob's laptop an error message appeared "File not saved" and on the computers desktop the accursed message "illegal operation" also appeared.

On his way across the yard to the Red Cross Clinic building, Jacob began to feel a little better. What a time to get malaria, he thought, entering the reception building to find out where he could get hold of a doctor.

The Sunburst Lizard finished cowering under the pillow and ventured out to investigate the now humanless room. He scampered highhanded over to the laptop but found it uninteresting. He climbed onto it, standing with one claw pressed on the enter key and the program that had refused to save now revealed the "illegal operation" to the undiscerning reptile. Sunburst's weight quickly agreed with the computers intention and the program was exited. No pages fluttered in the air, but the words were lost all the same, forever.

***

Becky gave up trying to slide her hand down the inside of her backpack and stood up on the bed beside it, grabbed the heavy luggage and upended it on the large double bed. Where the hell were her red tops? She searched through the pile of clothes and there they were; she was sorted now. All she needed to do was pick one and match a pair of jeans with it; and maybe a belt.

The hotel room had turned out to be a gem of a place. There was the massive bed, huge window and a large shower room and toilet. But especially, there was a dresser with three mirrors and a comfortable chair to sit in while she made herself up. This was more like it. Sometimes all the wondrous sites in the world couldn't compare to a bit of comfort. There was even a long Hookah for smoking tobacco in the corner. It was shaping up to be a fantastic place to let her hair down, have a few drinks and make some friends. It was positive and it felt good.

Red top on, Becky sat down at the dresser and looked at herself. She was pretty enough she knew, and she'd gotten a really good tan over the last couple of months, but her eyes glazed at her appearance as she wondered about Jacob. How did he see her? What did any guy think when they saw her face?

'Yeah yeah you're gorgeous!' shouted a voice from behind her. She jumped, shocked and spun around, stumbling from and over the chair in one clumsy and embarrassingly graceless move.

'Ah! What the fuck? Who?' she shouted at the young man that stood before her. She felt frightened and angry. How did he get in, she'd locked the door! She was blushing too, fuck! Becky struggled to her feet.

'Who the fuck are you?' she demanded. He was blonde she noticed during her rage, and cute too.

'Ha!' he dismissed her. 'I'm sorry if I frightened you, I just hopped in the window!' He was incredulous. What right did he have to be incredulous?

'You haven't stayed here before, have you?' he asked, amused. Becky could feel the redness in her cheeks.

'Who fucking cares if I've stayed here before?' she said. 'This is my fucking room you weirdo, get out!'

'Oh come on now. Language, language, chicken sandwich,' he said, 'it's a free hotel! You can't expect to own a room in a free hotel,' the young man exaggerated the "own" as though it was a joke word.

'What?' A free hotel, could it be? She hadn't paid the mad old man downstairs it was true, but you usually paid for a hotel when you were leaving didn't you?

'Come on,' the young man tried, 'come out for a pint?' It didn't matter to Becky. She had to make a quick decision. Run him out, or run out her self. Fuck him, she thought again.

She picked up her separating comb. It looked sharp even if it was made of plastic and ran at the man screaming.

'Get out, get out, get out!' she screamed. The intruder looked stunned for a moment and then ran for the window and leapt out. Becky gave chase as far as the ledge and poked her head out shouting as loudly as she could in the hope of scaring him further off, but he was gone.

She wasted no time slamming the window shut and turning the clasp. For some reason she pulled the curtains too, it made her feel safer. Then she stood there, weak from the excitement and relieved that she'd escaped from whatever it was that might have happened. Regaining her breath she ran to the door, which she must have locked. She sought frantically for the keys, either of them would do. She found them on the bedside table and ran back to the door. She tried the first, which didn't work. What sort of a lock needed a different key for each side? She tried the other and it turned. The door swung open and Becky was face to face with the young man again. She yelped in panic and fell back into the room.

'No no, no,' said a woman's voice, 'don't be afraid dear. Don't fret,' a middle-aged Indian woman pushed past the young man and knelt beside Becky, taking her hand and patting it in a comforting way.

'Please diary,' she said, 'please, do not be frightened of Julian. He's just a stupid boy!'

'Pooja!' exclaimed the young man stepping forward.

'Don't come in here,' Becky warned, regaining some of her lost composure and brandishing the comb in front of her. The Indian woman rose quickly and shooed the man out. 'Out out, you foolish boy,' She ordered closing the door and turning the key.

'See?' she said as she did so. 'You're safe now pet,' her accent was strangely English and Indian at the same time. The woman had a gentle look but Becky was wary all the same.

'Who are you?' she asked. The Indian woman sat down on the floor beside her and spoke softly, taking Becky's hand in a reassuring manner.

'My name is Pooja,' she said, 'I live in this hotel,' Becky felt herself relaxing. The woman's presence was calming.

'Who is he?' Becky asked about the man, 'what was he doing in my room?' The old woman sighed before she spoke.

'Julian is very simple. He would never harm you. He just doesn't understand the rules.'

'Rules?'

'The rules,' Pooja said, 'everybody knows the rules. You know the rules,' she explained.

'I do?' asked Becky, sceptical.

'Sure you do!' exclaimed Pooja helping Becky onto her feet. 'Here, sit down,' She said gesturing at the bed. They sat themselves down and the Indian woman continued.

'You can't just climb in through people's windows without invitation. That's a rule. But nobody ever wrote it down. That's the sort of thing that Julian doesn't understand. You have to tell him…' Now Pooja had her hands held out, palms up, and was moving them up and down like a schoolteacher.

'I have to tell him all these things because he has no sense. He is very simple, like a clean white sheet that needs to me to fold it. It will sit folded forever if you do it but it can't fold itself. You understand?' Becky did.

The woman Pooja made perfect sense to Becky. The two began talking and the minutes passed into hours. The next day she would find it strange that she had spent the night in conversation with a strange woman on the bed in her hotel room. Even stranger that she could fall asleep with Pooja stroking her hair without a care in her heart. But at the time it seemed completely natural and she drifted off listening to the woman speak of her many children, of whom Julian was one. It never occurred to her that Julian was not an Indian man and couldn't be Pooja's son.

Becky just fell fast asleep picturing the woman's children all running around together in the street, laughing and running free and happy. They seemed filled with joy when they noticed she was watching them and they called to her. Pooja was there too. The Indian woman beckoned to her.

'Come Becky,' she said, 'look at what is most important. Come look,' suddenly they were at the edge of a cliff with just the two of them peering over.

'What's down there?' Becky asked Pooja who was pointing.

'Look harder,' said the woman, 'and you will see it!' Becky squinted downwards and began to see what it was. It was a city. She didn't recognise it but then again, she was sure she had never seen a city from this angle before. She stared ever closer and soon she was able to make out tiny people. She focused on a couple of them. They were holding hands, a man and a woman. The woman was she. The city was Tel-Aviv.

***

On their last day together in Tel-Aviv Jacob and Becky wandered around hand in hand. It was like they were sixteen-year-olds freshly escaped from parental supervision in a strange town. They walked around with innocent love, or at least it was fairly innocent lust, in their hearts. Big smiles were being enjoyed.

The sun was beaming down on them in a similar fashion, it was around lunchtime and they wandered along the beach watching the swimmers risk their skins in the dirty Mediterranean where the waters chemical breakdown was H2Oil. They were headed for, as sad as it may seem, the Hard Rock Café. In some countries it actually is a cool place to go, honest.

Outside under and umbrella they ate shish kebabs, neither being a vegetarian, and drank Star beer until there was none left. Becky remembered that it was manky stuff but it had been all right that day, company being the real stimulus.

The meal had passed in complete and perfect comfort. They had been so happy. At one point there was even entertainment provided by the Israeli Armed forces. From their seats they watched the destruction of a bather's innocent underwear from fifty yards, proving that you never ever leave bags unattended in Israel, unless you want to return to find holes in your slinkies.

Becky and Pooja watched from the cliff top as a particular conversation began. It was after the meal and the two chitchatted a blue ring around the city and back to Dizengoff Square.

'When are you going?' Becky asked finally, 'Tomorrow?'

'Yeah,' Jacob answered, 'I'm off to Jerusalem to meet someone to do with work.'

'I could join you?' Becky asked. 'My Visa isn't up for another week' Jacob paused. He seemed about to say something, but he didn't. They sat down outside the hostel and Becky wondered whether Jacob had lied to her about Jerusalem, she hoped he hadn't. The idea was there though, Becky found that guys lied to her often, not to be nasty, but to impress her, but Jacob seemed different.

'It's going to be a week of solid meetings and research,' He told her. 'My clients are serious chaps and I've promised to give them all my time until the book is finished.'

'Soon I hope,' he added, looking into her eyes to let her read his intentions. He was telling the truth, she was sure. There was something else there too. He seemed afraid of the "serious chaps" that were supposed to be his clients. Becky wondered why she hadn't noticed this the first time she had lived this moment.

'Oh yeah, Mr. Writer,' Becky exclaimed, deciding not to take it any differently, 'I must pick up one of your books,' She beamed at him, 'fancy me meeting a famous writer?'

Jacob smiled back. He had caught a glimpse of the lie there. Becky had heard of him all right but she was only hiding it so he wouldn't think she was a groupie and not because she was a groupie.

Let's go to my room,' Jacob suggested, 'those Korean guys are probably out working on the sites until this evening. And you never know, I may even have a bed left to sleep in.'

'OK,' Becky answered, 'but then you're taking me to dinner in a real restaurant, yeah?'

'Definitely,' he said, and they went up the stairs to his empty room. Becky felt both excited and sad as she watched herself being led up the stairs. She had loved everything about that day, but it had ended like every other.

'There it is,' said Pooja, 'the most important thing to you at the moment,' they were back on the cliff again and Becky felt the loss of that day for that second time.

'I don't understand,' She asked the woman. 'What am I supposed to do?' Pooja didn't answer. Becky remembered Jacob's face when he spoke about his clients. There had definitely been fear there.

'It is worse now,' Pooja told her. 'He will really die.'

'Why?' Becky asked. The idea made a sudden pain grip her heart and shot up her spine. She needed an answer, but Pooja was gone. Becky spun around and called out to the Indian woman.

'Why?' She asked again. She stood for a long while on the cliff top saying it again and again until she began to forget what it was she was asking. She looked down at her dream of Tel-Aviv from her vantage point and had the notion that Jacob was standing in front of her arms outstretched and smiling wondrously upon her. She felt herself swept up under the light of his appearance. His form came into existence there on the cliff and she moved to embrace him, but something was amiss, she felt the urge to run from, rather than to him. Her steps faltered and she paused. Jacob noticed this and smiled even more widely attempting to coax her to him. Becky would not go however. She knew now that this was not what it seemed, he was not who he seemed to be. She recoiled from him and tremors began underfoot, she could feel them growing in strength as they began to rattle her bones.

The form of Jacob sneered at her and began to change its appearance. Instead of Jacob's sandy hair there was blonde. The eyes were light intensive blue instead of Grey-blue. This man was taller, more typically handsome and looked practically vicious when compared to Jacob. He roared at her in words that she couldn't understand. The words carried a wind with them, which built up and pummelled her, knocking her backwards towards the cliff edge. The Man came after her, first he walked, then he began to trot until he was sprinting towards her, obviously bent on barrelling her over the cliff. Becky knew this yet she could not move. He reached her and in the split second when they were face to face
Becky saw deep into the Man's eyes. It was horrifying. The man seemed both powerful and inevitable. She could feel her resistance falter as his hands finally came in contact with her body and pushed through, casting her out over the cliffs edge. She conceded to it, he was much too powerful for her to resist. She was finished.

Only, she wasn't finished at all. A cloud of bright colour clawed her away from the Man's grasp, bore far out across the air, and down at great speed to the ground below she was in a forest and the danger was gone but she still felt the heat of the encounter. There glade in the woods with a pool of clear water and suddenly she was swimming in the fresh water. Her mind began to slip from image to image as Becky was released into normal sleep and harmless dreams, random and disjointed, as they should be.

*

Back in Becky's room Pooja stood from the young woman's bedside. She felt disturbed and a little frightened by her experience with Becky. When the Indian had sought to calm the girl earlier after that silliness with Julian, she noticed that Becky was out of line with her true nature, stifled. So Pooja had decided to help the girl to sleep or at least face her discordance in a dream sequence. It was a simple meditation technique, which seemed to have been working perfectly until a shadow had been cast over this Jacob boy.

He was the Key, Pooja was sure. He was incarnated with a very specific purpose and he had encountered Becky because she was vital to his fulfilling that purpose. Jacob was obviously a long way from England. The great cliff in Becky's vision signified that, the girl should be by his side and her presence would help him should he allow it.

Pooja was feeling guilty too. She had not actually seen Jacob's death, only the possibility of it and then only if Becky was not with him in the end. If they were together he may survive what was to come. And, what of he who was to come? It made Pooja shiver to even acknowledge that he existed.

That creature, that thing! Its very presence in Becky's dream was impossible but whatever he was supposed to be he was strong and he had not been interested in killing Becky there and then, for Pooja felt that he could have. No, he was there to welcome the girl. Call her into the fray as it were. This thing was not just the unleashed fury of some demon. He was a human soul, twisted with evil. He wanted to play as well as destroy. He even whispered his name as Pooja tore Becky from his grasp. It was Leavon.

142

Pooja didn't know what to do. It was not her business, she knew. But could she aid Becky at all? Not likely. Becky must make her own choices. The Indian woman made a sign above the sleeping girl's body, blessing her with reviving repose and left the room. Fading into a wraith she locked the door behind her with Becky's first key and slipped it under the door before losing her power to effect the physical.

Before disappearing completely, Pooja stood at the top of the stairs and looked down to where she knew her misguided knight was sleeping. Capital, or whatever he was calling himself these days, was not a bad man, but he didn't understand that love couldn't be controlled, that it must be treated like a delicate thing, with care and patience. Someday he would understand, someday soon perhaps this could be why Becky had been able to see them, her and Julian.

***

The next morning Becky awoke with an ashtray quite literally in her mouth. She'd gone to sleep with bowl of ash and chewing gum beside her head and when she awoke she found that there were butts in her mouth and soot on her face. She sprung from the bed fully alert. Urge! What a disgusting way to wake up. She ran straight directly to the bathroom and washed her face thoroughly, brushing her teeth as she did so. And, when that wasn't enough she hopped into the shower for good measure.

As she scrubbed herself with vigour Becky began to recall the previous evening oddness and the strange dreams she'd had, but was already forgetting. That weird boy Julian, the Indian woman Pooja and that other thing, it all had to have been a delusion, as it could never really have happened. If all that had really taken place then she would have to believe that Jacob

143

could be in danger of being murdered by some unknown devil. It was too ridiculous!

In this way, Becky managed to believe that it had indeed been some mad dream and that maybe she'd only just arrived at the hotel and was still enjoying her first shower. She laughed then, reminded of Dallas, a Soap Opera she'd watched growing up. After a character had been murdered the ratings had plummeted, so much so that a year later the studio wrote the character back into the show and pretended the entire last season was just a dream. The really crazy thing was, people actually bought into it, amazing, no?

So maybe this was her rewrite? It amused her to think it was. That she could just step out of the shower and find herself back home in Australia before all of this Jacob nonsense and the confusion he was causing her. She had a strong feeling that she would be much better off, had she never met him, and for the duration of the shower at least, she pretended it was so.

Unfortunately when she exited the shower Becky found her hotel room in the same state, place and position, both geographically and spatially, as it had been twenty minutes before. There were clothes everywhere and there were cigarette butts and black stains at the head of the bed where her head had been. Yuk! The thought of it sickened her and she moved to clean it up noticing as she refilled the ashtray that some of the Fag ends were covered in red lipstick.

This proved of course that Pooja did exist and that Becky was going to have to take all of the rest of it on board too. She pulled the sheet from the bed not wanting to look at the outline that her face had left in the ash.

She was going to have to deal with everything as it stood. The nosey freak that climbed in through her window, the increasingly horrible loneliness she felt the longer she was separated from Jacob, and that thing in her dream, the one who was going to harm her love. She would have to warn him when he called her, if he called her. Becky hoped that he would.

***

Jacob watched the fog obscure the sunlight as it fell across Elmina beach. He often tried to describe scenes to himself in a scholarly manner and so he tried this time to forget his aching stomach and solidify the picture he saw before him. It was as though a perfectly sunny day had been spoiled by one's own eyesight, the fog seemed so impossible and out of place. How to describe it?

'The dimmed yellow sun hung behind a haze caused by mists from the sea, the blowing sand, or both. Lines of light escaped the cataract sheen and stripped the treetops of their pallor. Widening down to the beach where figures advance towards the spot I now sit upon,' awful! So false and pretentious, even the word pretentious was pretentious. Jacob was sat a few metres elevated above the approaching Africans on the rocks. A few more moments and they would be within shouting distance. Fifty feet more and they would be upon him.

Jacob stopped narrating as the figures came closer but it was not Mr Marshall, nor the dangerous Arab Rajette, just two young boys emerging from the face of the dipping sun to where he could make them out. They passed without incident.

'Obroni, how are you?' 'I'm fine. Bye, bye!' They said together as they moved on. Jacob understood by now that he was not expected to answer, so he just smiled and gave them a wave.

As Jacob feared, the dangerous Rajette was indeed watching him. From the Parapet of the nearby slaving Fort, bored and restless he was imagining his favourite ways to kill a man and which one he would, hopefully sooner rather than later, use on Jacob. He was favouring strangulation at the moment.

'I'm getting far too jumpy,' Jacob said to himself. The project had set out to be mysterious enough without strange men luring him into spooky buildings paying him at gunpoint to further complicate matters. He closed his notebook and stood up. The doctor's office should be open now. And, although he was feeling much better now, he decided not to risk it. He'd better get a Malaria test. It would probably cost him nothing or half nothing anyway.

    Jacob took out his wallet. There was thousands of Cedis in there, which could be any amount of money and the small envelope he'd received in Jerusalem from the Americans. It was unopened.

Recollections 11

A stomach ache, the last supper, and the sky-blue soul

For the second time since his arrival in Jerusalem Jacob was at the foot of the Western Wall. His hands traced the blocks scored and dimpled by billions of fingers attached to the hands of the sorrowful and curious alike. In the grooves there were little shreds of paper presumably with prayers and wishes written on them. Jacob was wondering how many of them had been answered and was itching to read one when a hand came to rest on his shoulder.

'You are Jacob,' said a voice, 'I have seen your picture,' Jacob put on a nonchalant face and turned to see who it was that could pick it out from a crowd, especially when it was wall adjacent.

'Yeah, hi,' said Jacob to Richeloe's bright blue eyes, 'I'm Jacob.'

After the initial impression Jacob would have said that his Israeli contact was aged and poorly, with liver spots and grey patches of skin around his face and robes that were brown and frankly, a bit tatty. But what he saw first and immediately was the sharpness in the scribe's blue eyes. They were fucking scary actually. Jacob likened them to eyes one would see only in a horror movie. There was far too much life in those eyes for such an old body.

'You appraise me openly,' said Richeloe, it didn't please him. It was true though, Jacob had a rude habit of letting himself give people an obvious once over, or an old up and down as his uncle Diamond had called it. He'd tried to stop doing it but only managed to if he reminded himself beforehand and life was too short for all the instructions he felt that he needed to give himself. He would spend his entire time saying; Smile - nod - then make sure you look at the friendship triangle - don't stare - chin up - shoulders back. If he was too careful he would always be trying and never living. It wasn't worth it.

'Yeah!' he said, 'I always do that,' Jacob held out his hand to the man, 'Jacob,' he said, 'and you are?'

'My name is Bishop Alexander Richeloe and I am very pleased to meet you. Now, if you'll follow me I think it would be a very good idea if we took a little walk to my offices,' He gestured to the back of the square and as he followed Jacob was transfixed by the hundreds of eyes that were focused on the Western Wall. Eyes that looked over and through him, all beseeching the wall to fulfil its duty of objectivity, a thing main purpose was to be a reminder of great sorrow, but doing so by being simply what it was, a wall. In the indifference of rationality, Jacob saw what was really happening. There were hundreds of people staring at a wall. It was sad symbolism and nothing more.

Cold

Jacob had to skip lively to catch up with Richeloe, through the crowd of people and up the ramp out of the male section of the wall. Richeloe began speaking as they went without bothering to check if Jacob was attending him.

'It is truly a wondrous thing to behold young man,' he began, 'all this belief and acceptance of words and events thousands of years ago. And yet they publicly turn a blind eye to events much more recent, not recognising the Lord as the Son of God,' With this Richeloe began to climb a set of steps, which would lead them out of the square and away from the Wall.

'Only publicly?' asked Jacob.

'Of course young man, privately the Jewish believe much differently from what they would admit,' Jacob wasn't sure that he was willing to believe that every Jewish person in the world was lying about their beliefs, but he was willing to listen to someone that did.

'Take this city for instance,' continued the Scribe, 'Jerusalem is built on a paper-thin alliance between denial and acceptance. Secretly the religions know that their counterparts exist. These counterparts all have their believers and their holy books of knowledge and history. Each of us knows that there are at least as many valid reasons to follow one of the prominent beliefs as there are to accept another. And, secretly we accept that. But publicly we deny it. Jerusalem is divided into quarters that believe in themselves and their God. They know there is no other God but their own and that those who do not share their views are heretics, misbelievers of incorrect messages. They see sacrilege everywhere they look; it is a wonder that there is not Chaos.'

Richeloe stopped on a landing overlooking the square. There was a little wooden door, bound with steel, set into the granite wall. Jacob watched as Richeloe fished for a key in his robes. If you have ever see this or can imagine what it looks like when an old man hitches up his robes to rummage in his underclothes for something, yes, it is funny.

'But they do fight all the time, don't they?' Jacob asked, 'I mean on the news, in the past. These people are violent. This whole region is one big war zone, isn't it?' Richeloe gave Jacob a sceptical look.

'Young man, think about, if these were violent peoples then there would have been much more bloodshed in the past. There would not even be any Palestinians or Israelites to kill anymore would there? These people want to live with their gods, not die. And, this is where acceptance comes into play. While

149

officially they must denounce one another, in their private lives it is vital, that they accept one another. Or there would indeed be chaos.'

Jacob had the feeling that Richeloe had spoken those words, in that exact order on a number of occasions, and it caused him to wonder why someone of this Richeloe's ilk was not writing this book himself. Thinking about the old mans theory of acceptance and denunciation Jacob followed him up another set of stairs, inside this time and came to the conclusion that Richeloe was attempting to sway him in his attitude to religious beliefs.

The Scribe led Jacob into an office and sat him in a comfortable leather chair. Richeloe took a seat of his own on the other side of the dark hardwood table, rubbed his hands together and spoke again.

'Now, we are here at last,' said Richeloe, 'Are you ready to begin your quest?'

Quest? Jacob thought, he hadn't considered that any of his previous writing projects were worthy such a title.

Quest

Writing was a pain in the arse sometimes, an escape, usually. He'd even thought of it as the greatest job on earth… once, but he'd never, ever, called it a quest. But this, he realised would be very different from all his other projects, so why not?

A quest, sure!

'Absolutely,' Jacob answered, thinking momentarily of last night's ambush by Rajette and Marshall. If things like that were going to keep happening he'd better be ready. Trials, he could call them, now that he was questing. The whole idea was giving his mood a touch of whimsy. When Jacob finished this thought he noticed that Richeloe had risen again and was rummaging through a stack of papers on a high shelf and Jacob was treated to a pair of knotted calf muscles on the thin ropes of the Bishop's ankles, as the old man stretched on his tippy-toes.

The entire room was stacked with books and papers. There was years of information here and Jacob felt a sinking feeling in his stomach. Oh, he was getting paid very well, twice, for doing this job but it wouldn't be worth it if it took his whole life. Although the powers in Rome had promised him that he would only need to refer to a minimum of source documents, Jacob felt that he would probably need to read a mountain of paper just to understand them.

Richeloe noticed Jacobs now paler face and wide eyes taking in the volume of information surrounding him.

'Don't worry my boy,' Richeloe said, 'this is not all for you'.

'Good,' Jacob said, obviously sounding too relieved for the Richeloe's liking and causing him to scowl.

'I was about to think that I would die writing this book,' Jacob said laughing falsely, trying to break the tension. He gave Richeloe a weak smile but the scribe quickly glanced away as if he felt that this had not yet been avoided. Jacob could see the edges of the room in his fear. His vision always went funny when he was frightened. Everything became bold and stark, and made him wince.

'Well,' said Richeloe, walking to a filing cabinet on the south wall, 'these are yours,' He repeated his skirt-lifting manoeuvre and took out a key to unlock the top drawer in side of which he began to rummage. A moment or two passed before Richeloe retrieved, not a file but another key that he brandished in front of him as he crossed the room. He brought it to a picture of the sacred heart on the apposite wall. Jacob was intrigued and, of course, there was a safe behind the picture, which required a combination as well as the key that Richeloe inserted and but did not turn.

'Securitastic,' said Jacob failing again to lighten the mood. Richeloe's hand paused in mid air. The comment was obviously a little flippant for the Bishop's taste but he didn't turn around, he just breathed deeply and continued, saying, 'only a boy,' quietly as he exhaled.

Shuffling to the left-hand side of the safe, Richeloe began with the combination. It was a long combination, like a special move in Tekken the video game, but Jacob was a killer in Tekken. He noticed Richeloe covering the window with his body so no one could look through. There were no buildings overlooking this one so a spy would have to be in a helicopter with a telescopic lens or something to be able to see the safe, let alone read the combination. How valuable were these documents? The mounting security was making Jacob uncomfortable. The papers or scroll or whatever they were could be worth millions if they were the true original accounts of Jesus that the Roman set had claimed.

It struck Jacob again that he had been given a huge responsibility. This could be the most important book of this generation or any, oh god, what if he made a haimes of it?

Don't think about it, he told himself. It's just a book. And these documents are just research.

Millions of people, millions! His inner coward bellowed. Shut up, he told it, and he went back to memorising the combination.

11 – 56 – 32 – 24 – 17 – missed that one – 19 – 59 – 37 – 87, and 35. An eleven number combination! Jacob knew that this was uselessly complicated; a cracker could as easily find a way to get

the safe open if it had been a three number combination, or a twelve number one for that matter.

Richeloe turned the key and opened the safe. He reached down searching the bottom and then Jacob heard a 'click'.

'Let's go' said the Bishop leaving the room after he'd locked the safe and replaced the key. Richeloe had a grave look upon his face as he left. It was obvious that the old man did not see how ridiculous these security precautions were so Jacob decided to try and hide his incredulity a bit better and hurried after the scribe, not convinced he was going to succeed in either.

The two men walked a long way down a deceptively lengthy corridor and entered a circular room. They exited the room via a stairway at the back and descended three levels before stopping on a landing with three doors. Jacob grew more and more sceptical as they went. Was there any need for this subterfuge, he thought? But this, as it turns out, was not the half of it.

'Sorry about this,' Richeloe said, holding a scarf up for Jacob to see.

'Oh you must be joking,' Jacob said, 'you don't expect me to…' But it was quite obvious that Richeloe did, so Jacob allowed himself to be blind folded.

He knew he was facing the middle door but was surprised at being turned around two and a half times and was surely now facing the back wall where the stairs came down. Jacob remembered a fire extinguisher and wondered if it wasn't a handle to a secret door. A secret door! What was this, Get Smart?

There were a couple more clicks and Richeloe led him through a doorway and down a stairs into another room.

'Here we are' sad Richeloe, removing the blindfold.

'Finally,' said Jacob, tutting, if it had gone on much longer he may have forgotten the way, as it was Jacob was positive that he could find the room again.

Richeloe responded badly to this, 'Listen boy,' he said, 'I've had enough of your flippancy!' Richeloe blustered. Then he calmed himself suddenly and with a great show of self-control he continued. 'Let us just go on, shall we?' The scribe turned away making Jacob feel more than a mite ashamed.

In front of them was a small open wooden door. It had a handle but no keyhole. This Jacob noted, was obviously the lock opened by the switch in Richeloe's office safe. The old scribe pushed the door wide and shoved Jacob ahead of him. Slamming the door shut behind them. It was metal on the inside.

This room was large and airy. It was decorated in a way that Jacob found typical of a chapel as opposed to a Church, with an altar on the far wall and no sacristy door at the back. Instead of pews though, there were desks and there were large wooden cabinets lining the walls. Jacob noticed the lack of candles too, which made perfect sense in a room that housed valuable combustibles.

'It is said,' Richeloe began, having seemingly regained his normal pomp and composure, 'that you can visit a certain site during a walking tour of Jerusalem,' He turned to Jacob who waited for a moment and then said

'Yes?' hoping he'd been queued to do so.

'The site of the Last Supper?' asked the scribe.

'Yes,' said Jacob, 'I saw it yesterday,' Richeloe smiled and Jacob knew what was coming next.

'The Last Supper; the meal over which Jesus made his ultimate sacrifice known to the apostles? This sacred room is not traipsed through by a hundred tourists a day young Jacob. The church would never let that happen,' Jacob was beginning to hate being called young and boy every two minutes. He felt he was growing older just listening to Richeloe, which ought to account for something.

'It happened here in this very room,' finished Richeloe, pausing for dramatic effect.

'Wow,' said Jacob in appreciation.

'The location the tourists visit has never been argued,' Richeloe stated, 'isn't that strange?'

'It is?' asked Jacob in return.

'Everything is argued,' said the Deacon, 'Nothing has ever been taken for granted when it comes to religion my boy, not in this part of the world. Remember,' The Bishop walked to the altar and genuflected, speaking as he went.

'They said it was there and we agreed. It was a small piece of history actually,' He gave Jacob the curly finger, obviously wishing him to approach the Altar. The last time Jacob had seen one of those he'd been about to speak at his father's funeral. He began to shake at the memory and his hands grew sweaty.

'They?' Asked Jacob, he copied Richeloe's genuflection badly and followed him to the Tabernacle. It was two feet high and made of marble with an unadorned golden door.

'Yes Jacob, they,' Richeloe gestured widely, 'everyone else.'

'And we are, the Catholic Church?' Jacob guessed.

'Very good, boy, your intellect is a staggering spectacle,' The Bishop took out another key and opened the Tabernacle. It held no Eucharist as it may once have, instead it contained sealed bags of parchment, six of them, and a red notebook.

'These,' said Richeloe, placing them on the Altar, 'are your concern,' Jacob actually gulped. 'They are copies by, but very, very old copies.

'Nice,' said Jacob, not knowing what else to say.

***

In Cape Coast, Jacob was proving to be suspiciously healthy. The Ghanaian Dr Yeboah was staring at Jacob in his Ghanaian way and asking again;

'So, why did you come Mr. Jacob?' Yeboah looked vaguely annoyed. His elderly black face was screwed up in a format of disapproval.

'We did a lot of tests on you and you are fine?' he added. Jacob squinted, a little embarrassed, and he felt fine too. The only outcome of today's sudden attack of stomach pain was guilt, not Malaria. People needed this Doctor's time for much more serious conditions than a bout of Phantom illness and it seemed that this was all it had been.

'In fact,' said Doctor Yeboah, 'you will live long,' the doctor made it sound like a threat.

Five minutes before, Jacob had been in a daze reliving his first meeting with Bishop Richeloe and waiting for the news that he had contracted a wicked dose of malaria. Although he felt fine at the time, he had assumed that another wave of sickness was immanent. Or, perhaps the bastion of safety that was the hospital had relieved his mind of worry and given him momentary respite from the tiny mosquito shaped organisms in his bloodstream.

It was strange he supposed that he always pictured Malaria so. He could see them now using their legs like skating flies on the surface of a forest pond, skating around inside him. In his imagination the Malarias multiplied by bumping into each other as they quickly took over his blood stream. Either way, after the vomiting and the stomach spasms he'd been experiencing in his hostel room, he didn't think for a second that he was in fact perfectly healthy.

Dr. Yeboah began to read out a list of tests and their results. And, as usually happened when anyone other than he began to speak, Jacob lost interest.

On the wall of the waiting room a sign said:

What the hell was that about? He was sure that it wasn't really true anyway. Jacob always felt that women, without exception, liked a bit of the dirty. Kindness and sensitivity were just the official party line designed to separate the real Jim Morrison's from the Cliff Richards.

Which one would she choose, the softy saving the kitten? Or, the Van Dam type, smashing through the bedroom window guns blazing, kindness be-damned? The sensitivity speech was laid on to confuse guys with another female standard impossible to reach.

This wasn't entirely true, he knew but it was better than having no theory at all. The sign was probably there to promote equality, and Jacob could understand that, even if it wasn't funny.

There were three or four more signs tacked to the white clinical walls. God said this, God said that, and the director for medical health and endemic diseases said the other.

Considering his current assignment Jacob thought he should have some interest in what was written there, but what some guy wrote about what he felt God was thinking had never really seemed worth listening to, especially now that he realised it could have been written by someone like him. Anyway, the presence of bible quotations on the walls of a hospital caused a packet of worry to be emptied into the previously calm waters of Jacob's nervous system. It didn't fill him with confidence to see the word of God splashed around in a place a medicine. This was a place for solid scientific talk. Religion and hospitals just didn't go. It was defeatist.

Dr. Yeboah was summing up by reminding Jacob without actually saying so, that: Yes he was white, but no, this did not give him the right to walk in here and waste the hospitals time with imaginary afflictions.

'But I vomited blood,' Jacob tried to convince the doctor, 'I saw it!'

'I'm sure you did Mr. Jacob,' Dr. Yeboah said, soothing the anxious white man, 'but maybe the problem is not in your physical body eh?' Jacob looked at the doctor's worn face. There was no spite there.

'You think I'm mental, don't you?' J'accuse, Jacob thought.

'Mental? No,' said the grey haired physician, not fully understanding the term, 'I think you may be mad,' he said.

Jacob waited for more. There was none. Ghanaian doctors obviously felt that some people were just mad and that was that.

'Oh,' said Jacob, what would he do now? He had been puking blood less than an hour ago and yet he was perfectly fine now. It was a mystery. Or maybe he was mad. Either way he was loath to leave the hospital, but realising that he was not going to get any mental help here and feeling desperate; Jacob rose and walked to the door with the intent of leaving the hospital.

'Mr. Jacob,' Dr. Yeboah called. Jacob turned quickly hoping the doctor had some suggestion for him. Anything at all would do. He could go to a fetish priest and have his demons exorcised. Anything but the cold helpless feeling he now experienced. Go on Doctor, move me, he thought.

'You must pay 20,000 Cedis,' the doctor said, 'for the tests,' he added, not leaving anything to chance with the mad white-man.

'Oh' Jacob said for the second time, 'of course.'

Leaving the hospital feeling confused and vulnerable Jacob made an important decision.

Once when he was a child Jacob had witnessed an old man dropping an Irish five-pound note as he crossed a busy road. Jacob had been four or five years old at the time, and like most boys of this age Jacob didn't even think about drawing the man's attention to the loss of his money. Instead Jacob froze in position, hoping that the other would continue to cross the road and leave the fiver there for him to pick up and make his own. There would be loads of Cola bottles and Wham bars and maybe a big bar or two like a Mars or a Marathon (remember?). Who knew what you could get with five pounds?

For a brief moment, untouched by time, the old man did continue to walk away and leave his money behind. Jacob felt pure elation rising in his chest. The moment passed however and the old man, the money dropper, realised his mistake and spun around quickly to retrieve his fiver.

Seeing this Jacob's elation disappeared, but in a random twist, so did the old man, under the wheels of an articulated lorry. There were bananas printed on its side. There was a lot of screeching and a glass shattering thump as the driver tried to turn back time by driving through the window of a butcher's shop twenty yards down the road. But it was two late, the old man was a goner. Jacob didn't see the truck go through though as he was busy watching something else.

For a wonderful moment all noise disappeared and Jacob's eyes followed the fluttery passage of the five-pound note through the air. It twisted this way and that before gliding down to land a foot in front of the four or five year old Jacob Terry.

Jacob looked at it and made his decision. He'd found a fiver and that was all. He gave a quick look each way and then reached down to pick up the note. As far as he was concerned the rest had not occurred and he went to buy sweets, although, he did choose to go to a shop that lay in the exact opposite direction from the butcher. No harm in being sure.

And then, outside Cape Coast's Red Cross hospital, Jacob made a similar decision. He chose to forget. As far as he was concerned the rest had not occurred, The Stomach pains, the vomit, the feelings of agony and wretchedness were unimaginable now.

There was no sudden bloody vomiting in his Cape Coast bedroom and that was all there was to it, there was too much going on that he couldn't explain, far too much.

How could he just forget what had definitely happened? Simple, Jacob had forgotten a dozen other similar things in his life before this.

It's a very human defence mechanism, to forget. We've all done it, probably more than once. You've done it, haven't you? Go on, try and deny it.

***

Back at the hostel Jacob even managed to check out of his room, without looking at the sick upon the floor. He packed his bag and went to the office where he paid cheerfully. The repression was complete, fool.

As he walked through the gate he paused standing there awhile at the top of the hill ignoring the Ghanaians who asked after him. He gazed long and lustfully downwards towards where the shore melted into the Gulf of Guinea. Before he left he wanted to get a last long look at his great blue impersonal friend, the ocean.

It was really was the most beautiful thing, the sea. More beautiful then any of the words Jacob could imagine, more astounding than any wisdoms God had been accredited with over the centuries. Could it be that it was more beautiful than God? Jacob thought that it must be. He felt that if it was true that God created all things. Then surely God must have tried to create the most wondrous things he could imagine. Otherwise God was an asshole, which, Jacob reflected, could easily be the truth.

Jacob turned away from the ocean and flagged down a convenient taxi that had been crawling slowly by hoping for his custom. He asked the driver to take him to the bus depot and climbed aboard. In the background a typical robust African radio DJ blathered from an unseen tuner. Jacob remembered finding this intrusion unsettling, even confusing when he'd first arrived. Now it was automatically ignored by his sense of hearing. He was adapting.

In Jacob's bag the Sunburst Lizard had managed again to survive Jacob's packing. He felt full and satisfied. He could feel the world around him moving but he paid no heed and dropped into a peaceful repose inside one of Jacob's stinking runners. The Taxi sped up the road to the depot and Jacob lifted the rucksack containing his passenger out of the boot and carried across the hot concrete to the office.

  Above Jacob the canopy of the bus-ticketing booth was ruffled by the warm sea breeze. Ah, the sweet shade! Getting here early had proven to be a waste of time. The teller could not sell him a ticket until the bus left its origin – Takoradi. Only then would they know if there were seats available to be bought. Jacob thought it funny that this did not surprise him. Africans seemed so lackadaisical in their travelling; late arrivals would be a certainty. He watched as a bus for Accra picked up stragglers for a couple of hundred metres after leaving the station. With at least twenty minutes to wait Jacob settled back and thought about what was waiting for him in Kumasi. Richeloe had not been very clear on the details and all he knew was that he would be given more information to hand over to the Arab Rajette -who was watching from a nearby car park. Well, this time he was going to go through it all before they took what they wanted.

That was he could find out what Marshal was really after and why the scrolls were being kept apart for so long.

***

'It will be important for you to include the material you find in Ghana,' said Richeloe, wringing his hands as they coffee on the morning of Jacob's departure.

'Why so?' Jacob asked sipping coffee, which was heavy with chicory, and looking up at Jerusalem's Damascus Gate. There was a soldier on the parapet pointing his gun in Jacob's direction. He knew that he was being paranoid, so he pretended not to notice

'Phaa!' Jacob spat the coffee back into the brown stained glass. 'This stuff is cat,' he informed the priest.

'It is coffee,' Richeloe replied, a glower crossing his ambiguously soft features, 'and so it is not as important as what I am trying to impart to you is very important,' He seemed upset by Jacob's indifferent manner. I shouldn't wind him up so I know, Jacob chided inwardly, wondering whether he'd feel a bullet through the head if it came at him. Or would it all just be there and then not.

'Shoot then,' he told the scribe, 'I'm listening,' Richeloe shook his head, sighed and continued. This poor boy was as good as dead. A younger Richeloe would have done something.

May have

***

A blinding low sun caused the few cars driving east into the city to slow to a very un-French twenty kilometres an hour as dawn and Leavon arrived in Nantes. The city was a brilliant gold and to someone who had never been there before it would seem that this was a beautiful city, but Nantes by day was very a different place, uglier certainly a many cornered cloud of industry. If Leavon had known this he probably would not have been so annoyed. As it was though, he was growing angry.

The earlier morning beauty of the place irritated him and the slow movement of the traffic was infuriating. The world in which Leavon found himself was already pissing him off.

However he did draw some pleasure from the blinding light of the sun, it was a welcome sight in this dull world and the stench of decay from the back seat gave him cause to smile. He'd acquired a Peugeot 607 outside the De Rhy mansion yesterday and had taken great pleasure in torturing its well-meaning driver before ending his life.

Unlike the other drivers, the glare was comforting for Leavon, even if it slowed the pace of his journey. Had he not just arrived from the bright and fiery depths of hell? He wasn't sure, but he was sure that his spirit welcomed the lucid brightness and his eyes were easily able to penetrate it to navigate his route as though it were midday.

Leavon gave up being annoyed and instead let his mind drift off in search of his target, the reason he was free now. He knew that Michael De Rhy owned a plane in Nantes and from here he could go wherever necessary to complete his payment. Leavon needed more information but was having trouble organising Michael De Rhy's memories.

At the moment he knew only three things:

Une – He was to find a man named Jacob who had the key to his continued existence and destroy him. This he would gladly do; avec pleasure.

Deux – The man was not in France, he was a great distance to the south.

Et, trios – he was in a hurry.

Leavon marked the man in his vision that morning. Of all the different colours and shades this Jacob had a sky-blue soul, which was unusual to the others around him. Leavon knew that his own soul was bright red, and this reflected his purpose. It made him proud. It was strange then that his target's soul was merely sky-blue and not directly the opposite of his own. It meant that Jacob was nothing either way, that he had no purpose. Even the poor passengers in Jacob's Trotro had stronger hues than he.

Leavon shook it off. What did he care? He had marked his target and that was that. Everyone has a specific colouring and now Jacob would be easy to find. So now Leavon was heading for the airport.

The only question now was, where in the south? Leavon released his own spirit and began to project.

Jacob saw, Leavon saw rose out from himself and his spirit flew south. Far off in the distance he could see a blue beacon, the spirit of his victim. Leavon found it easily amongst the energies of the world. Now he had to work backwards and pin the spirit to the physical world. He closed in. And, careful not to be detected, took a quick look outwards from his victims eyes.

He saw red earth, vast greenery. There were long broken highways that had pieces missing unfixed, where cars and vans needed to slow suddenly to crawl along subsiding dirt tracks.

They looked around in the Trotro that held the physical vessel for the sky-blue soul. It was filled with black people. Not surprising, he had guessed Africa already, but where? The language would be the key. Beside the sky-blue Soul an old black man was tapping the head of his walking stick against the seat in front and looking directly at them and in doing so was looking at both the hunter and his unsuspecting victim.

Leavon waited.

'Obroni?' the old black person addressed the sky-blue Soul 'Wofiri he?'

'Bain?' asked the Sky-blue Soul.

'Where are you from?' asked the black man.

'Oh, I'm from Ireland ... Irlandais.'

'Hollandaise?'

'Irlandais… Irish!'

'Ireland-oh,' said the man with the dog's-head walking stick and the conversation ended there. The old man, now happy to have spoken to the white man, turned his attention once more to the Rainy Forest.

It wasn't much of a conversation, but it was enough.

Leavon didn't know how he knew the language and didn't care. He knew though that it was called Twi, a dialect spoken in Ghana. He also spotted the license plate and the computer system on his private plane would provide the details. Leavon left the sky-blue Soul's as quickly as he could whilst remaining unnoticed.

As he drifted back from the Trotro Leavon noticed something else. There was a Yellow soul, not as bright a yellow as Leavon's own, travelling on that road too. In a black Mercedes car racing along only a mile or so behind the Trotro, Rajette was trying to keep up with the African van driver and having difficulty doing so.

Maybe there was another Leavon thought, sent to kill the sky-blue one? Leavon doubted that. This was his destiny, and no one else's he needed to find out the sky-blue's secret before he was killed. If this yellow soul interfered he would finish him, but it was obvious that he must be quick.

'Africa then,' he said, turning his attention back to the roads of Nante and driving. The traffic was speeding up now that the sun was rising above eye level. He would be in the airport soon.

Leavon looked at his head in the rear-view mirror. He was blond haired with symmetrical features. He tried a grin and thought it was winning, he pouted and became sullenly attractive. Leavon was glad to have such a usable visage. When he had first seen the old man's body through the firelight he had been disappointed. This was perfect, however. He was a handsome devil.

Recollections 12

A Job well done

Asamwa Ajakuma was an old man. His life had been long and fruitful with many healthy children and plentiful harvests. The years, like walking stones across a precious stream, were placed firmly behind him and he was proud to have laid each one. Asamwa was a thin man, not weakly, but wiry strong. He could swing his machete in the field for hours in the high sun without tiring and still return to help his neighbours shorten the grass in front of their homes.

Asamwa had the respect of his friends and his children, and though his woman was now three years dead, he had not died with her as a lot of lonely old men do. He mourned her but continued on. For Asamwa Ajakuma was a bright soul with a happy heart, and his woman Diane would be waiting for him with holy God when his time finally came. For now though he was also enjoying a little piece and quiet without her.

On this particular day Asamwa was a child once more. For the first time in his life he was in the city with the strange people he had never understood. Most of them had no land to grow on and seemed to have no position or obligation to their community, the oversized community that was the city of Kumasi. Men and women living only for themselves and their children and barely capable of doing so, it was mysterious and disappointing in ways but the novelty of it still effected greatly the little man's attitude.

Asamwa knew he would never come back to this place, he had never had a reason to come here and it would be unlikely that he would find one again. He was in Kumasi only, for the purpose of giving blessing to his son who wished to marry a woman whom he was sure he loved and Asamwa was proud to hear it. Yaw swore to him that he would move out of the city and back to the village once he had accumulated enough money to buy a large compound for his new family. After this Asamwa knew that he could move into this new compound and stop working, if he wished.

'Come see the city father, while you have the chance,' his son had said to him during his last visit. 'It is very different but contains great wonders too.'

After spending the entire morning in Kumasi, Asamwa wasn't convinced there were too many "Great Wonders" in the big city. The place looked dirty and there were white people walking around. True signs that the city was completely different from the village. Asamwa had no problem with the white people, hadn't he spoken to one in the Trotro that very morning? It only seemed to him that white people meant "business" and "business" meant the loss of the old ways, the loss of a man's obligation to his people. Business, was working indoors, making nothing, sitting in the same chair all day long and never leaving your computer machine. It wasn't natural, all this chasing imaginary money. It wasn't real.

So where are the wonders of the big city? He had intended asking his son when they met at midday beside the Lorry Park, but there was no need for that now. Asamwa had found one such wonder, he had been gawking at it for the last half-hour, and it really was great. More than that, it was unbelievable.

Towering above the old man on the main Kejetia junction stood a massive billboard. To the people of Kumasi it was merely an advertisement, but to Asamwa it was a wondrous sight. Every couple of minutes the sign came to life and with a swift rattle and clank; it changed.

First it was an advertisement for Mosquito Coils, then for Tomato Paste and finally for Hair Straightener, all appearing in the same space, three entirely different images with words too.

Mosquito Coils ~*Catchink*~ Tomato Paste ~*Catchink*~ Hair Straightener

How could it change like that? Did it know he was watching?

Mosquito Coils ~
Amazed, Asamwa, the old man from the village marvelled at the sign, while across the road he was being marked.

Tomato Paste ~
Kwaku Asawaa approached the old man with a slow measured stride like one he imagined a famous actor would use in this situation. His target was still staring dumbfoundedly upwards at the sign when Kwaku excused himself and took out his book of cloakroom tickets.

Hair Straightener ~
        'Good morning sir,' Kwaku began, 'how are you feeling today?' Asamwa started and turned around to face the young man addressing him.
        'Oh, hello,' he answered, 'I am very fine thank you,' He noticed that the young man had a pencil and a small book in his hand.
        'Do you want something?'

Mosquito Coils ~
The two men looked up as the sign changed.
        'It is wonderful is it not?' asked Kwaku, feeling it all click into place like the clockwork in the sign above.
        'Oh yes!' exclaimed Asamwa, 'what is it?'

169

'Sir this is the only one of its kind in all of Ghana,' Kwaku told him. 'It is an Electrified Communication Station.'

'An Eloc…'

'That's right my friend. When you stop to look at the Electrified Communication Station, the machinery inside looks at you and shows you three pictures of things you may need to buy in the city.'

'Wha!' Asamwa was re-amazed. What a fantastically new thing this really was.

Tomato Paste ~
The sign rattled again. The two men marvelled once more at its regularity.

'I like Tomato Paste,' murmured Asamwa, noticing also that the sun was almost directly above him. 'I must go now to meet my son, thank you sir for telling me of this modern machine,' He made to leave but was blocked by the young man who grinned regretfully and held up his notebook.

'Sir, I'm sure you understand that this machine is very expensive to run.'

'Oh yes, oh yes, it must be,' agreed Asamwa

'So you understand also sir that I will have to collect a fee from you for each time you watched the Communication Station?'

'Oh,' said Asamwa, understanding. Kwaku leafed through his book of tickets until he reached the next fresh one.

'Now, it is 2,000 Cedis for each viewing. How many times did you watch it?'

'Six,' answered Asamwa reaching for his pocket with a worried expression.

Hair Straightener ~
Catchink; clanked the sigh again. Asamwa did not look up. Kwaku leaned towards the old man and with a quick glance

about in case imaginary superiors were watching him, he whispered in Asamwa's ear.

'Let's just say you watched it five times old man,' He gave Asamwa his best conspiratorial wink and scribbled out a bill for 10,000 Cedis. Asamwa thanked him for his generosity and paid the 10,000 slowly out of his moneybag.

Mosquito Coils ~

Being careful not to look up again, Asamwa wished the young man well and headed for his meeting in the Lorry Park. Kwaku watched the old man go with an open smile. Ten thousand Cedis for watching the sign change five times. It always surprised him that there were still people who knew so little of the world.

A job well done, he thought to himself and crossed the road to wait for the next gormless villager.

Tomato Paste ~

Down the hill towards the Lorry Park Asamwa's bright old face also broke into an open smile.

10,000 Cedis to watch the sign five times, that poor fool of a young man was so easily tricked. He obviously knew little of the world.

If you could think quickly enough, you could save yourself in any situation. Yes Asamwa was very pleased with his presence of mind, as he was sure that he'd watched the sign at least twelve times.

Half price!

Asamwa walked happily on, highly amused. A job well done, he thought to himself, a job well done.

Jacob watched the whole episode from ten feet away and swore that he would remember it later and try and work out what had happened.

He turned away to view the Kejetia Market below as the smiling old Ghanaian man passed him. It was the largest market in West Africa, or so the Lonely Planet told him. It looked chaotic; there must be sixty or seventy thousand people in there. He had to see it close up.

He downed his warm Fanta in a gassy second and, after returning the bottle to the stall owner, headed down the hill for a closer look.

***

Landing in Accra proved to be a total bore. Leavon hated these idiotic procedures. Wait here, taxi there, the plane was on the ground and he wanted out immediately. It was stupid nonsense, drying up his non-existent patience. Finally he was forced to stop the plane and walk to the terminal. The sign did cheer him up though.

Airport Terminal

Yes it was wasn't it? For the crew of his plane it certainly was at any rate.

He'd consumed the hostess lovingly for two hours in the air. She was a dead shell now, as empty as the nine bottles of champagne he'd drunk during the flight. On his growing list of human pursuits Leavon felt alcohol was definitely one of his favourites so far. The pilot and co. were also Couchez avec les peché, dangling over their dials and levers, their headsets lodged in imaginative areas. Leavon wasn't thinking about the return leg of this trip and hence there was no need for there to be any crew to await his return. This was a one-way full-on hunt and he needed all the energy that he could swallow. It seemed that human food could not sustain him. That he was weakening already in this larval stage. He needed to find the sky-blue Soul if he was going to survive.

Had to

Leavon stalked through customs not receiving even a raised eyebrow. A normal person can just block out a fearful image when it is presented to them, their automatic defences activate. And, with a little help from chance Leavon passed completely ignored by most of the guards that clogged the corridors. The other airport staff never so much as held his gaze. This disappointed him greatly, and the lesser workers he didn't bother with, conserving his energy. A confident white man who strutted through the security lines must be very important; they stayed well out of his way, some falling backwards over the buckets and bags in doing so.

In Kotoka Airport's car park the practice was similar. He strolled through the lines of people until he came upon a row of taxis. The people here looked different from those he'd just left in France. They were a dark brown colour, bulkier and not as tall and their mouths yammered noisily in the same annoying manner, although the pitch was a little different.

He sat into the first car with a motor running and headed out of the car park. He was really on the trail now. Somewhere five or so hours away lay his target. It didn't matter that Jacob was still many miles ahead, it didn't even matter that in this heat the dead brown man in the back of his taxi would soon putrefy the air he breathed. The hunt was filling him with power, the power of expectation. He felt his jowls bulge with saliva at the thought, his only aim, finding and destroying the sky-blue soul. Finally he would be free to exist after all these years of frustrating humanity. He would be liberated to live and kill at will, never dying and eternally strong.

Leavon would always owe his new life to the flames of hell, if there were indeed flames there. But he would soon be immortal and beyond even those powers that would try to out class him.

Leavon smiled. Class was not a problem. The only problem here was when, not how, he would succeed. The brown and yellow taxi he'd stolen sped from the city of Accra and onto the forested highway. Soon, he thought, very soon.

***

The streets of London were wet and grey wherever Becky walked. It could have been her outlook that made them seem so bleak, but it was more likely the weather. Baffled by the events of the night before and ill at ease after an ambiguous conversation with Mr Capital on her way from the hotel, Becky was reduced once more, to sightseeing.

The buildings of London seemed chunky and overgrown to her. The new office blocks were as robust as the older more historic Abbey and Parliament were fat no, hulking, was the right word. Was this how she would see everything now that she and Jacob were apart? Would it be better if she called him? She'd tried to ask Mr Capital about making a long distance phone call earlier whilst complaining about Julian and his rude self-admittance to her room.

'Mr eh, Capital?' She had asked nervously of the man whose attention had been focused quite unstintingly on what looked like the beginnings of a Clockwork Chicken. Becky had already passed through the three stages of polite engagement and was now addressing the Hotelier quite loudly. The man's tongue was sticking out of the corner of his mouth as he turned a tiny screwdriver and mumbled along with the music of an unseen radio. The Brittany Spears song "Toxic" was playing. It sounded strange to hear the man talk and sing and coax simultaneously, the mechanism looked both tiny and complicated.

'Mmmla taste of ya -Come on don't ya just get in the- Toxic. Shit!' He yelped as a spring sprung from the palm-sized contraption and struck one of the lenses of his thick glasses.

'Mr Capital!' she repeated growing impatient and the old man started suddenly noticing her finally. Unfortunately her sudden appearance to him made Capital let go of the bauble, causing it to actually explode from his hands, spreading pieces of itself all over the narrow foyer counter.

'Damn it no!' Capital exclaimed, scrabbling frantically around him in a vain attempt at stopping the cogs, washers as they fell to the floor on their way to crevasses and nooks unknown. 'No no no no no no no no no no no no no!' he said flustered, 'hours of work. Hours!' So although Becky had managed to gain Mr. Capital's attention she had lost it immediately to the clockwork catastrophe.

'Excuse me?' Becky said firmly, not wanting to let the invasion of her room go without complaint. 'Can you help me please?'

'I'm trying, I'm trying,' said Mr Capital, 'can't you see that I'm trying?' He fussed for a few more moments over the pieces of his project before submitting with a large drawn out sign and turning his attention to Becky. He had a pained and beset upon expression and Becky felt almost sorry for him. But didn't.

'Yes?' he said. 'You bothered me?' He asked.

'Well excuse me,' Becky was incensed, 'I want to make a complaint.'

'And?'

'And what?'

'And, what,' asked Capital, eyes rolling, 'is your complaint?' Becky was only momentarily put off by his attitude.

'Last night,' she said,

'Yes.'

'Last night a man came into my room while I was in the shower,' she told him.

Mr Capital tutted and began to gather his pieces together again.

'Young lady, I hardly think it is any of my business what you get up to in the privacy of your own room,' Capital said, adding to Becky's aggravation.

'Listen!' she shouted, bringing the man to attention, 'Last night a man came into my room, without my ambition… I mean, without my permission, while I was taking a shower. I chased him back out the window and then I was going to come down here and complain when I met him again at my door with an Indian woman who told me his name was Julian and he didn't know the rules and that was why he came into my room, which doesn't make any difference to me, he had no right to be in there in the first place. And, I want to know what sort of mad hotel has people living in it that come into your room, uninvited might I add, and two keys for the door and then I fall asleep, which is not like me and I have terrible nightmares about… well that's nothing to do with it. And I come down here to complain to you and you're messing with a weird fucking…' Becky paused, not only for breath. Through here ranting anger she'd begun to notice something else. Mr Capital was crying.

At some point in Becky's speech he had begun to weep. He looked at her and his movement took her aback, a beseeching look on his face. At once she felt regretful for chastising with such vigour so pitiful he looked. Tears were streaming uninterrupted down his cheeks as he asked her.

'Pooja? You met Pooja in your room?'

'Yes,' Becky answered, 'that was her name.'

'Are you sure,' he asked, 'did she have big beautiful brown eyes? Did she speak to you? Did she mention me?

Ohhhhhh my darling Pooja, why won't you see me,' Capital wept mournfully, dropping his head to his arms shuddering and moaning loudly.

*

Becky had tried for another few minutes to speak to Mr Capital, but it was useless. She had tried asking him where the cheapest place to make an international phone call was, but that was twice as useless. So she'd gone out, sightseeing. Now she was sure, she had never been in such a bad mood in her entire life. The emerald city would have looked shit to her today and all the wishes in the wishes in the world could be granted on a day like this.

'Get your grief rambling!' shouted someone behind Becky as she walked, making her pause. Did she just hear someone say?

'Get yer grief ramblings!' hawked the female voice again. Becky turned to see an old woman, who could best be described as pointy, or dirty, or perhaps a word that said both, jagged? Becky approached the woman who was leaning against the railings of the common. Becky wasn't sure which, with a basket at her feet. The woman stood in a jittery way that made her look as though she was being bumped and jostled about in the back of a truck. Her motions were random and alarming. Becky addressed her anyway.

'Excuse me?' she asked.

'Scused,' answered the woman who continued to gyrate whilst staring blindly about her and not paying Becky any more heed.

'Ahem,' Becky began again, 'Excuse me.'

'SCUSED! I said,' said the woman turning to Becky as if interrupted, 'ya deaf?'

'Oh sorry, I was just...'

'Sorry? Just? Jest sorry eh? You want yer ramblings then?'

'Did you...? What are you selling?'

'Grief ramblings,' said the woman motioning to the basket at her feet, 'nice and fresh just the way you want em,' Obviously, Becky was confused.

'What exactly...'

'Nothing exactly little missy, Nothing's exactly. You know that?'

'Yes,' Becky said. 'Can I see one... some of them, ramblings is it?' The woman shook and flopped on the spot as if she was tap-dancing on a waterbed; she studied Becky for a moment and then reached down with considerable ceremony and picked the basket up. She shoved it in Becky's face.

'Go on then,' She said. Becky peered into the basket not sure what to expect. What were grief ramblings? The top of the basket was covered with a tea towel that Becky moved aside to reveal dozens of little balls covered in what seemed to be breadcrumbs. There was steam rising from them.

'Go on,' said the woman, 'grab one while they're still hot!' so she did.

'How much do I owe you?' asked Becky.

'Aw, ya can have one fer free gel,' said the woman smiling a pointy smile as she vibrated away basket clutched in her dirty mitts, 'I sawr ya with yer sad little face passing me by and I says to meself. Rhianna, look at that poor little sewing so all heart-broken and all and I thought, she could do with a Bit of grief rambling she could.'

'Oh em, thank you Rhianna. Thank you very much, I really did,' Becky told her.

'Goodbye now,' said Rhianna. 'Look after yourself,' and the woman performed a staggering leggy walk away down the street leaving Becky on the edge of the common with here grief rambling in hand feeling much better for the encounter.

Leaning on the railings looking in over and enjoying the greens of the common, Becky noticed the brightness of the colours for the first time that day. Although it had been raining the view did not seem bleak but rather washed and new. It was a tonic for her and her natural good humour began to return.

In the centre of the common there was a group of young men and women gathered around a low hill. They were cheering and clapping on occasion at a young man and woman who were dancing around on top of the rise singing and talking and carrying on.

Becky was intrigued. She walked quickly to the nearest gate and noticed as she went through that a sign had been driven into the grass on the verge of the path. It read:

THE BIRD OF THE LOST – Thistlewaite Players

It must be some sort of show Becky realised and quickened her pace towards the gathering. She found a spot at the edge of the crowd and found that she could see and hear the players quite clearly. They circled around each other talking grandly, she dressed in a golden gown with a Sari and tiara, and he, was dressed as a knight.

KNIGHT: Oh darling ladylove of mine, please let me hold thine hand?

PRINCESS: Never foul creature from the west, you shall never have me. For I am beyond your most desperate dreams and I swear to you that on this day you above all others, will never posses me!

The Knight grabs the princes, who struggles briefly saying:

PRINCESS: You are a foolish knight indeed. You know
                     that I am blessed with the sight and will
                     curse you for all eternity.

The knight laughs at this

KNIGHT: Aha! How could you curse me, when the
                     most immense affliction I could behold,
                     would be that I could never have you.

PRINCESS: I warn you knight who has killed my kin,
                     though love me I know you do. And I in turn
                     have loved you until this day. Your betrayal
                     of my...

KNIGHT: Betrayal, ye gods! It was I who was betrayed,
                     by your brother on this night. He would
                     have had my head if I'd not freed him of
                     his....

The knight brandishes a sack that Becky is sure is supposed to
have a head in it. The knight grabs the princess again roughly
and shouts.

KNIGHT: To England!

The crowd cheer as the two players leave the hill. Amidst much
applause and cheering remove their cloaks, and returned to the
top of the mound slightly changed.

PRINCESS: You evil worshipper of money. How dare
                     you steal me to your land and take me as
                     you wife. I will not let you have me now or
                     ever.

KNIGHT: Quiet woman!

The audience cheers

KNIGHT: You are in my kingdom now and will do my
                 bidding. You will love me again I know and
                 we will be happy. Don't you see it?

PRINCESS: I do not! I will never see it.

The princess exclaims to herself as though she has had an idea.

PRINCESS: In fact my dolted knight, YOU will never see
                 it! You will be cursed from this day forth to
                 never see me again. Although you trap me
                 hear in this house, you will never set your
                 eyes upon me from this day forth! I am a
                 ghost to you now until the bird of the lost
                 sings to me and tells me I am free...

KNIGHT: Your tricks do not fool me my love. You will
                 never be released from here so you may as
                 well relent. Come out and stop this
                 foolishness, as I will never repent.

The knight peers around looking for the princess. He looks right
through her on more than one occasion. He grows angry.

KNIGHT: You will never be freed from this place!
                 Never! I will find you out, my dear! I will
                 find you out!

181

But the knight cannot see the princess, and soon tears replace his anger and he slumps to the ground. The princess watches him with regret.

PRINCESS: Oh poor sorrowful knight you have brought this on yourself. Your misery will be as endless as my own until you release me from this place. Until your pride is broken and the Bird of the lost is singing you will never see my face. Oh sorrow dearest knight oh sorrow for our plight.

At this the Princess sat down on the mound beside the knight and began to weep as well. A young woman with a top hat on her head stepped up beside the players clapping her hands and the audience, Becky included, joined her.

The woman took off her hat and asked every one to give generously as the two players bowed and laughed. Becky waited for the woman to get to her and dropped five pounds into the hat.

'Cheers,' said the collector, 'did you like the show?'

'Oh I loved it, what was it called again?'

'The bird of the lost, it's a true story about the curse of the Indian princess,' the young woman giggled and winked at Becky. She had beautiful long blonde hair.

'A true story?' asked Becky.

'Well apparently,' said the young woman, 'the knight was from this area. So the group always puts it on in autumn,' the woman gave Becky another smile and continued her rounds leaving her alone again with her thoughts. The play left her in a strange mood. She was unsure how she felt and decided to go back to the hotel for a snooze. Something inside her had changed while she watched the play. She had become immensely fretful for Jacob's Safety. The feeling had consumed her and she made a definite decision. Becky was going to Ghana.

***

Kejetia Market was astounding. Jacob had been wandering around in it now for the last hour and a half. It just seemed to go on and on. The funny thing was that it began to repeat itself as you went through it, making it impossible to get your bearings or make any locations. There were in actuality, hundreds of stalls selling the same thing, it was obvious that the people who had to sell and buy in this huge crowded market had very few choices available to them.

The food stuffs were limited to chillies, rice, cans of tomato paste, actual tomatoes, and something called Cassava, which Jacob gathered was responsible for the slop he's tasted in Accra. Everything else on sale seemed to involve either second-rate electrical odds and ends or cloths which all looked second hand. The standard of merchandise was fairly poor, although there were a lot of spices and things that Jacob knew nothing about and therefore was not qualified to judge. The maze of muddy alleys wound around and round in a disconcerting manner until the press of bodies and the disorientation began to have an effect on Jacob. He decided then that it was time to leave, but he had no idea how he was going to achieve this so lost was he among the vegetable and starches.

Clutching his camera tightly, aware of the amount of eyes upon him, Jacob picked a direction and began to walk purposefully in it, depending on the idea that there had to be edges to the market.

Now, everyone who has spent any time in markets, especially a huge one like the Kejetia Market in Kumasi Ghana will tell you that markets do not work that way. They are alive.

183

The only way to move around such an enormous bustle is to realise this and act accordingly.

1) Never struggle against the market. If you try to beat it you will find yourself with sore feet and empty pockets.
2) Always know what you want before you go near a market of this size.

And,

3) Always ask for directions. You are a fool if you don't.

Many a big man has had his spirit crushed by the living bazaar, spending hours when a quick enquiry could have solved his problem in minutes or even seconds. In a market people always help you, if only to show off their knowledge of the place in which they have been raised. They understand that anyone, even themselves can get lost in the vastness of it. So how can a feckless westerner expect to muscle his way through with only his pride to guide him? It was foolish indeed and at that moment Jacob was playing the fool.

He could have sworn that the sun was directly behind him when he headed into the melee an hour and a half ago. So, thinking logically, all he had to do was walk directly into the sun to get back out. Thinking logically that was, but of course, for anyone who has been to West Africa, logic is as useful as the metric system in America. Africans can think logically if they want, it's just that usually they don't want. Jacob found that after making his squinting way sunwards he was led into new parts of the market rather than familiar ones. He seemed now to be in a cloth or fabric section or quarter of whatever you called a group of similar stalls together. A similar, he thought he'd call it.

This similar was focussed on garishly coloured lengths of fabric of the check-like Kente designs that "Master Weaver's' had toiled to string together. Unfortunately, the master weaving in a hot climate is usually comparable to the minor darnings of another more wool dependant one.

It was in front of one of these stalls that Jacob first came into contact with Leavon and Nana Adjua, a spiritual meeting followed by a physical one. Nana worked most of her days in the Kejetia market. Although, working is a term that only loosely applies to this particular market woman. If an accurate term were to be used it would have been, running. Nana Adjua was running one of the stalls, actually, five of the stalls in this similar. She also had a managing hand in four other stalls that were "owned" by sons of hers, both in-law and step.

    Nana was one of those women who really knew everything. She didn't just know things. She "knew" them, and not just the facts, or the wherefores and whatevers; no! Nana Adjua knew the way of things, how they worked and how they should work. A great many people think they know how things work, but believe this, they don't. If this were a show, Nana would be running it. If this were an orchestra Nan would be conducting it. If this were an army she would be leading both sides, scrubbing the dirt off a squirming child's face as she did so. If this were a mission to Mars Nana Adjua would be coordinating it. But seeing as this was a market, Nana was selling it.

    Nana Adjua was an all rounder and in Ghana, or more specifically in the great Kejetia market, there was no one more successful. The trick to Nana's success was the cunning and vital use of small boys.

Up and down the narrow paths they ran. Over to this man with a bag of onions they skipped and across to the woman with a load of fresh-ish fish, they sprinted. Their little dirty fists clutching money gravely entrusted with their bright looks and eager faces, bobbing and panting as they went. The faces were much brighter than the dirty rags they wore or the torn shoes on there swollen feet and if you stood long enough you would hear her say, 'Small Boy,' this and, 'Small Boy,' that.

'Ay, small boy,' Nana would shout proffering money, 'Take this to Alvin and tell him I want him to bring two boxes down to Leticia with the rice. And tell Leticia I want a half a bag sent to the compound and another bag given to Kofi. Tell Kofi that I thank him for the shirts he left at the house on Tuesday,' then she would press the money into the small boy's hand and send him off with a wagging finger. Orders like these were sent out constantly. Often small boys would be seen hanging around like bicycle couriers for their next job. It was a network, and it worked.

Nana had just sent Diane's youngest off to the fish stalls to indirectly deliver a box of canned tomatoes to the communication centre when a white man stopped in front of her stall, the one she operated from, and looked directly at her with a glazed expression.

*

The road was annoying Leavon. As soon as he was able to get up any speed, he was forced to slow down again and drive around or into, an unpaved section of the road. It wasn't any fun.

Leavon wanted action, and quickly. He kept thinking about the other yellow soul following Jacob. The soul, belonging to someone who, although they weren't as powerful as he, was much closer to his target. He wondered if he was close enough to try taking over the sky-blue's body to keep him safe. He must ensure that the sky blue escaped that one.

No, he was probably still too far.

The car screeched to a halt less than a foot from a deep hole in the road. Damnit! Leavon backed the car up and drove

186

slowly to a point where the road sloped into the hole and made his way down into it. The car scraped and juddered of outcroppings and because of smaller less significant holes, while Leavon strained unsuccessfully to keep a hold on his haste.

By the time he made it out of the fifty foot long pot-hole, Leavon had taken quite enough of this shit and was already sending his mind out in search of Jacob was his leaden foot set the car roaring through sixty.

Due to his earlier tracking of the sky-blue soul, Leavon found it relatively easy to locate Jacob. Through his eye Leavon saw that the sky-blue Soul was walking through a large crowd of people selling wares and bustling about. After a quick scout around himself Leavon ascertained that the other Yellow soul was nowhere near at present so for the time being at least, his target was safe from that particular harm. But Leavon was an arrogant greedy creature; he couldn't just leave it that way and wait for a clearer chance, when he was now able to effect the sky-blue physically as well as mentally. Oh he was far too zealous for that.

*

In the market Jacob felt a sharp pain in the middle of his head followed by a hazy out-of-it feeling. Everything was abruptly different. He was still in the market he knew because he could still see it, but it seemed further away. A man brushed by him and bumped him slightly and although he did feel it, it was as though it was happening to someone else. His body was moving without his volition and Jacob lolled back in his mind and let it take over. This disconnected feeling was more worthy of investigation he was sure.

A quick flick of his mind and Leavon was in two places at once. He drove the car as it powered down the highway on an

187

uncommonly smooth stretch and, as he steered, he also took over driving Jacob and soon was managing both with overconfident ease.

He looked out of Jacob's eyes and saw an old woman looking up at him concerned.

'What dza fuck are you looking at?' Leavon shouted at her from Jacob's mouth. Nana flinched at the harsh words. A moment ago the white man had only seemed bewildered but had had such soft large eyes.

'Well?' shouted Leavon through Jacob. Maybe she'd been mistaken. The face that looked down upon her now seemed cruel and hard. The man's top lip was curled upwards in a sneer.

'You staring at me, nigger woman?' Leavon jeered, 'eh? You want to get a punch in your face?' Leavon raised Jacob's fist and for a moment Nana Adjua thought that she was about to receive that fist, but the man changed again.

Inside, Jacob watched as the old woman looked up at him with concern, the sun seemed as though it was warm, but he couldn't feel it correctly. It was like being wrapped in something, a desensitising skin. A full body condom! He giggled to himself, his head airy from the experience. In wonderment he felt his lips move and his throat fired out the words.

'What the fuck are you looking at?' Jacob was stunned, what the fuck was that? He didn't say that. What was going on? He watched the woman's disbelief change to fear as he raised his fist. What? He wasn't raising his fist.

'You staring at me nigger woman, eh? You want to get a punch in your face?' Jacob struggled to take back control of his body. Stop! He shouted inside.

Leavon felt an immense tug and he was pulled backwards as if by the hair into the back of Jacob's mind.

'Get out!' said Jacob, 'get out, what are you?' he shouted.

'You fucking shout at me?' Leavon answered. 'I do what I want,' He said, but he was worried. The sky-blue should not have been able to budge him once he'd taken over. He pushed again to gain dominance but was thwarted by a solid wall as Jacob screamed.

'Out!'

Nana watched as the man jerked and shuddered before falling to his knees. His eyes became big and soft again before he closed them to cry out in pain. Then he fell on his face in the mud. For only a few seconds the market fell silent then the man was surrounded by Ghanaians and lifted, under Nan's command, onto the bench behind her stall. Once this was done the market continued on as normal, although many looks were cast over shoulders and warding signs drawn in the muggy air.

Nana would tell them what was going on when she knew, so they left her relatively alone with the white man.

Back to nature

On the Kumasi road Leavon returned to his body in a rage of fear and fury. He was blinded by his defeat. The sky-blue had thrown him out like a troublesome ghost. It was unthinkable. It was embarrassing. Leavon fumed and fused at the indignity of it, but only for a brief moment.

Very quickly Leavon was distracted from his anger by the cars immediate confrontation with an eight-foot thick Yaw-Yaw tree. The car disintegrated on impact and Leavon was launched forward with such force, his seatbelt, had he worn it, would have snapped under the pressure or at the very least beheaded him. As it stood, Leavon's skull clipped off the wheel and he spun out through the window like though the glass was blown like bubbles of soapy water as he shot sideways into the tree trunk, the centre of his spine hitting first and his body bending easily around it in the wrong direction. The back of his head visiting

189

briefly the same space as his heels, amidst a shower of cracking and popping noises.

Not having time to form even one full thought in this brief time, Leavon was overcome by the humanity of his new body. He had not managed to keep it unbroken even for a single full day.

***

In her room in the Capital hotel Becky was stuffing cloths quickly into her Backpack. She had just gotten off the phone with British airways and she was due at Heathrow airport within the next two hours. She wondered whether she could make it. She felt that she would.

As soon as the players on the common had finished their acting Becky had been driven by the strongest urge to go to Jacob that had only just subsided with the booking of her ticket to Ghana. Now Becky was overcome by panic in that chaotic organised way that only a woman can panic. When panicking, a man will – usually – become completely useless, incoherent and uncoordinated. A panicking man will where his socks on his head, sign his toast and use his telephone bill to dry his hands and face. A man in a panic is as useless and stupid as a dog with a coat on.

A woman however is an entirely different sort of panicker. A woman will – usually– manage quite well in the midst of a mild panic and could easily invade a country, Rubix cube in hand whilst in the grip of a wild one. Becky was ready to go in five minutes and ran into the bathroom for a circumventor pee before leaving. As she walked back into the room, considerably relieved she was sure she heard a strange ticking noise. She looked around the room until her gaze came to rest on a curious curiosity.

On Becky's bedside table accompanied by ticking and also a faint whirring, a brass representation of a chicken, complete with a wing-nut winder was stepping automatically across the polished wood towards the table edge.

It's going to fall, Becky thought, but it didn't.

Just as it reached the edge of the table, the chicken's head, which had previously been nodding rhythmically back and forward, stopped its usual motion and turned to its left. Its tiny moulded face was now looking directly at Becky.

Then, in the minutest of mechanical processes, barely noticeable and probably originating entirely from Becky's imagination, a tiny brass eyelid above the chicken's left eye dropped into place over the bauble's sightless metal eyeball. Then the chicken stopped where it was, clock out of work, and Becky shook herself, hoping she was seeing things.

'Oh my god,' she said aloud, 'that clockwork chicken just winked at me.'

Not stopping too long to dwell on the oddity that was nothing more than another glaring irregularity in her increasingly complicated life, Becky closed the door behind her and hit the stairs. She also hit Mr. Capital who was that very moment ascending.

'Oh, dear girl, I am sorry!' said Mr Capital finding himself deep in Becky's bosom, 'I was just on my way up to, oh excuse me let me help you.'

With that Mr. Capital relieved Becky of her Backpack and headed down the stairs in front of her, flushed and rambling.

'You know, I am sorry about all the disturbances, I'm afraid that I wasn't too helpful today dear,' He continued as they reached the lobby. 'I do however hope you don't have too many misgivings about my little hotel?'

Becky wondered whether she should bother confronting the man about the bauble left on her bedside table and decided that 'yes' she was in a hurry but 'no' she was not about to let people start walking into her hotel rooms unfettered.

'Actually, there is something,' She told him. 'Mr. Capital, were you in my room today, while I was out?' She asked evenly but with as many no nonsense tones as she could. Capital seemed deflated. It was obvious that he'd hoped she hadn't noticed.

'Oh, you saw it then,' he asked.

'Why did you leave it in my room?'

'It's a bird,' Mr Capital said, 'I made it for her,' the man was helpless to explain himself. This young girl would never understand, would never believe it if she did. Becky looked closely at the man's face. It was sad and innocent.

'It was very nice,' she said.

'It's just you said you saw her there, in your room and I wanted her to see it. But I can never see her so I thought I'd leave it there with you and she might come back and then she'd know that she can go any time she wishes now that she has…' Capital trailed off and looked doubtfully at Becky who decided that enough was enough.

'How much do I owe you?' she asked proffering her purse.

'Oh dear nothing please, due to the…   incident. I couldn't possibly take any money from you,' Mr. Capital hoisted Becky's bag and helped her put it on her back, speaking all the while.

'Now on you go young lady. And please, next time your in town, please do think of us.'

No problem there, Becky thought. She would, certainly.

Rather than argue or investigate, Becky just left. She had plane to catch and another more pressing mystery to solve. All this weirdness, it was as though the world was pushing her to Jacob's side, and again now, it was time to go.

Mr Capital watched her go and even waved as she exited the building.
He turned back into the lobby and looked around. So very long he'd been waiting for something to change. Today he'd cried in front of a guest and made a fool of himself. But the bird was finished, every tiny spring and coil of it. So maybe Pooja would forgive him and choose to see it for what it was: A job well done.

Recollections 13

Islands (The Fetish Priest

& the Mother)

The sound of children's voices brought Jacob to his senses once more. He felt weak and his bones ached. Disjointed blurry faces peered down at him from the left. They came into focus and he found that there were at least a hundred sets of white teeth grinning at him from the mouths of a million children. There were only two in reality, but the shock was overloading Jacob's addled brain in such a way that it may as well been the former.

He yelped and clutched at the bedclothes, in what must have look like pantomime fear, to Nana Adjua's children. With great excitement they both laughed and leaped away from the white man who was proving to be a source of great amusement today. Tommy and Jeff moved tentatively forward hoping to poke the white man to see if he would he do anything else funny but were called away to the yard before they could.

'Children, Jeff, Tommy,' called a stern female voice from outside in such a commanding tone that Jacob started as much as the boys, who scurried to obey it. Tommy and Jeff laughed as they obeyed, which led Jacob to believe that the children had a happy home life. And, he reasoned, if the children are happy then the place where he now lay, wherever it was, couldn't be too bad. Not if the children there followed orders with smiles on their faces. After all…

After all, what? That was a real question. Jacob searched in his mind for a memory of how he'd gotten here, but there was nothing. He gave it a few moments, because he knew that sometimes when he was travelling he awoke to find that he couldn't identify his surroundings. It was more a symptom of staying home in Ireland too long than of travelling, too used to the same bed different day. But when even after a minute Jacob was still lost, he began to worry and sat up in the bed, finding that he was still wearing his clothes, but they smelled of food. He tried again to remember where he was by looking around the small room. It was poor but clean; not a hostel or a hotel; that was obvious.

'Ok,' he said aloud, 'I was in the market and…?' Jacob thought. His head really hurt. 'I was in the market and I saw an old woman…' Something had happened then, but what?

'Hello,' said a Nana Adjua from the door and Jacob shied. 'You saw an old woman and?'

'I don't remember,' Jacob told her with all honesty. It was clear that he did not.

Nana looked at the white and decided that he was a good man. His behaviour in the market was completely despicable and she could have had a few of the market men, whom were also children of hers to beat him for his lack of respect and his evil behaviour. But he wasn't the same man now, and Nana thought that he might have a brain sickness.

So Nana Adjua told him what happened. She left nothing out either. Jacob couldn't believe his ears, but he could certainly believe his stomach. It dropped and churned as Nana recounted his antics and he realised that even if he couldn't remember it in his mind right now, his body affirmed that it held the unforgettable shudder of the truth

'I'm so sorry,' he told her, 'really I know I did… say that, but I didn't want to…!'

There it was. One memory was clear as crystal.

'There was someone in my head!' Jacob realised, 'my god, someone was speaking…' he brought his hands to his face to touch his lips, '…through my mouth,' Jacob looked up at Nana.

'I think it is the truth,' said Nana. 'Please come outside?' She asked.

'You believe me?' Jacob asked rising quickly to follow her.

'You believe me?' he asked again after he caught up to her outside. They were in a compound. The door they'd just exited from was one of at least a dozen. And there was another dozen across the yard from them. It was like a schoolyard from his childhood, with similar chalk markings and the same well swept look.

'Where am I?' he asked, 'who are you?'

'You are at the orphanage child,' Nana told him, 'My name is Nana Adjua Osei…' she trailed off. 'My name is Nana,' it sounded like Naana. 'We brought you here after you fell in Kejetia,' she said.

Jacob was running the event through his mind. He'd called her… oh god!

'I am so sorry for what I said,' he said as they sat on a bench against a shaded wall, 'please believe me I had not control over myself, you know someone else was in charge,' He said. Nana was careful with her words.

'You will not apologise, I saw you changing. You were just walking and then you were, angry and shouting at me. Then you change again and you fall. I have seen this happen when a man is cursed. He is weakened by the curse and can be controlled by another.'

Jacob felt disorder on top of his fatigue. If he was cursed, then how had it been done? Who would want to control him? A week ago he would have thought that it was unlikely than anyone could have that much interest in him. But his situation had changed drastically since then and he was no longer sure of what he wanted, so he could hardly make judgements on anyone else's desires. The strangest thing here, Jacob supposed, was that the old woman seemed to believe him and was not, from what he could see, pissed off after he'd called her a nigger woman.

'You think I am weak?' he asked her. Nana laughed at this, clapping her hand on his knee and showing him her own teeth, much yellower than her children's.

'White man you are not weak,' she said. 'When a man is weak he needs the priest to help him, but you helped yourself. I think that you are very strong,' the smile left her face. 'But I don't not like this other one, the one that took you,' Nana exclaimed, 'Oooaaah no! He was very-very bad. Boy you hear me? You have to get away from him-o.'

Jacob could only agree.

'But I have no idea who it was?' he said realising that he was asking Nana for an answer that she couldn't provide.

'Oh you know boy. You will not believe it. Just rest here a while, don't worry-o. I will get you some food before you go.'

So Nana left Jacob there to think while she went to make him some food. He leaned back against the cool wall and left his tired mind alone for a while. For a brief spell he drifted away and enjoyed the warmth of the day and the coolness of the wall, no complications just the moment that was all. The bench was certainly in the right place and he felt comfortable there.

Tommy and Jeff began to quietly gather any stick and leaves they could find –but mostly just simulating the action, and placed them on Jacob's lap. But he only snored loudly and caused them to Laugh and run away whenever they got anywhere near.

Jacob's bumps and bruises were healing well and they hardly stung him as the sun dried them out and fed his body through the skin. The soft machine was working slowly to repair itself, whilst others were not so lucky.

***

Leavon certainly wasn't in the right place. He was, quite literally, mashed. In the last few hours he had only managed to unwrap himself from the tree and flop hopelessly on the remnants of the car's hood. He was feeling things, feelings that were indescribable. The parts of his human body that were not broken, torn or bleeding, were delivering such horribly painful convulsions, they were causing new swells of blood and excruciating ripping of tendons.

Was this what he had been waiting for? All this time he'd wanted to own a human body, now here he was being tortured by it. How could men survive at all with such weak vessels for their souls? Leavon's own soul was practically leaking out of his body. The rips in his flesh were glowing yellow and he could feel his spirit seep into the air around him. He stopped it. He could not fail so badly. He did not care any more that the sky-blue soul had managed to push him away. Now all Leavon cared about was getting face to face with this man and pulling him apart with his bare hands mystery or no. He was beginning to appreciate pain and relish, between spasms the hope of inflicting it on the sky-blue soul's body. He was going to make him feel like this. He was going to… pass out.

It was an hour before Leavon woke again and when he did it was in response to a huge black and white African crow pecking at his torso. Only one of his eyes would focus on the bird and he watched as its distorted visage picked at his exposed flesh. Leavon was disgusted at this. He would not be beaten, not like this.

His first attempt to dislodge the creature was so pathetic that the crow didn't even notice. The second attempt however was far more effective and driven solely by the power of Leavon's will. With a great effort both of his arms came up at speed and he grasped the unsuspecting bird tightly in his bloody grip.

And then he hated it. He griped as hard as he could and he hated. He detested the crow for judging him weak enough to feed off of. But mostly Leavon hated its life and he began to draw it out of the creature and into himself.

It didn't take long for the bird to stop struggling in his clutches. A few seconds and Leavon had reduced it to a limp hulk. He screamed in frustration as the supply of life petered out and he was left alone again with his pain. It seemed worse than before, now that the rush of being had ceased. It was almost unbearable. Yet Leavon would bear it, would bear anything, rather than go back to whence he came. Anything.

On the plus side, and today was proving to be remarkably low on pluses for Leavon, he found that he could move more easily than before. The bird's life had replaced his in a small way. At least now he had a goal, more life to consume. Eat and be well.

An hour later Leavon had revolutionised himself. First he crawled from the car into the jungle where a large rat like creature had been too stunned by his appearance to run away and so became Leavon's second victim, leading him into a stagger so he went in search of more. He made slow progress leaning against the trees as he passed them until he grew weak again and had to stop and wait for the Rainy Forest to provide.

A wild pig trotted right up to Leavon and sniffed at him becoming more fuel for the demon. Soon he was walking. Not with the same confident swagger he'd used earlier when his body was unbroken, no. This was a disjointed jerky movement, but there was still and abundance of cockiness. Every time he caught another creature Leavon's body was relieved of more pain. It was like a morphine drip to him and he surged forward in the hope of eradicating is pain altogether.

It was in this manner, with a crazed leering expression and a shambling amble that Leavon burst into the sacred clearing of Nana Adjakimpa the Fetish priest.

It wasn't really a sacred clearing. Nana Adjakimpa knew this. It simply served him better to have a place where he could commune with the ancestors in peace or have a quiet snooze in the afternoon without being disturbed. The villagers were afraid to come here without being summoned and he liked it that way. So in a way, it was sacred to him.

If his father were alive, the old spiritualist would have tutted his contempt.

'No place is any better than any other place,' he would have said. 'The world is the only place. You cannot be afraid of one place without being afraid of all of the places,' Nana knew this to be true, but unlike his father, he was no wandering priest. Nana Adjakimpa was the Fetish priest for the village of Bring-Salt and he had a responsibility to keep the people content in their belief in the spirit of the world. These days there were hundreds of religions that promised great salvation and lofty explanations for the lack of reason in the world. There was no point in telling people to be good. You had to give them something to be good for. And, if that meant a bit of piece and quite for Nana's weary old bones, then he was happy to snooze away for them into the late afternoon, or the villager's sake.

Today the sleep afforded by Nana Adjakimpa's sacred clearing was rudely interrupted when the battered shell of Leavon burst into it and tore him from his latest dream. There may have been a monkey in it.

Nana woke with a jerk and sat up stunned to see what looked like a bag of meat stumbling towards him from the other side of the ring of trees.

'Shitty,' He said, for obvious reasons.

***

Diner in the Orphanage with all of Nana Adjua's children around him was a tonic for Jacob. Watching them as they pretended to eat with their spoons in front of her and then grabbing handfuls when her back was turned, gave Jacob a warm and contented feeling. This was the simplest form of existing. The children ate, played and were sent on jobs all the while surrounded by a protective communal mood, overlooked by the mother of the Kumasi orphans, Nana Adjua.

It was something that Jacob had never felt before. As a boy he'd always been too confused and fearful to enjoy his childhood. He worried and dreamt of the future much more, it seemed to him, than anyone else. He was sure that he'd never smiled like these kids did. He'd never been allowed to frolic the way they did either.

Was it a western thing, or was it just his family? Did civilisation just breed fear? Jacob knew he was never going to answer that one correctly. He wasn't sure that he was ever going to do anything correctly again, not that he thought of it. His mind had been violated and he didn't know by whom or why and the Orphanage and its simple "needs and wants" lifestyle, was just what he needed at the moment. Perhaps he could ask Nana to let him stay? He could even pay her for his room and board. All he needed was a few days of peace and quiet and he would be able to figure out what was going on.

Being human, as Jacob was prone to be, the incident that took place in the market had unsettled him so that he was now clinging to the only thing that he felt comfortable with. It never occurred to him that it could happen again or it occurred so deeply in his subconscious that instinct was choosing to drown it out in favour of warmth and safety.

To belong to such a family, must be a hell of a feeling, Jacob thought. He watched Nana Adjua manage the children with an even hand. She showed them respect and encouraged them to make decisions. It was a style of mothering that was completely alien to him.

One of the boys who'd been at his beside earlier, Jacob thought his name was Jeff, was caught by Nana with an orange under his vest when he'd tried to sneak past Nana without getting caught. But, instead of beating him, shouting at him, or humiliating him in front of the others, Nana simply asked him.

'Where are you going with this orange?' She gave him the chance to fix what he had done, a chance to learn.

'I bring it here to share it,' Jeff replied wisely deciding to give in quickly. And, Jeff knew that an orange was an orange and if Dorcas who was selling the oranges outside the compound wall had not caught him already it was because she didn't mind. He knew all this in a second, because children are very good at spotting possible trouble. After all, your average child, this is especially the case with young boys, is in trouble ninety percent of the time, if not more.

'Jeff?' Nana Adjua asked, 'you are bringing it back to Dorcas.'

'No!' said Jeff, shaking his little smiling head, feigning cuteness with cuteness.

'Yes,' stated Nana.

'Yes,' Jeff agreed, 'I will-m… to Dorcas,' He smiled at Nana rushing through the sentence and missed out the middle, He made to leave, but she stopped him.

'Jeff, don't take any more oranges ok?' she asked. 'You ask, Ok?'

'Ok,' said Jeff, his face was innocent and perfectly believable.

'Good boy,' and Nana let him go. As soon as she did so the other children surrounded Jeff and began propositioning with him for the orange. A tricycle, a ball, and even another orange, were all offered the boy, but he shrugged them off and raised his chin. He was a good boy, and being such he strode pompously to the gate and out of the compound to return the stolen fruit humming and making 'Peown! Peown!' noises like a little soldier.

Nana laughed at this and Jacob was more set on staying than before. This was where he was meant to be.

'Mrs…?' he began.

'Nana boy, my name is Nana,' it sounded like Na-Anna. The woman grinned brown teeth at Jacob and returned her attention to overseeing the girls who were clearing the table.

'Nana,' said Jacob, 'I… I want to stay. Here. With you,' the old woman turned back to him. 'If it is ok with you?' he added. Nana's faced looked pained and Jacob was curious to know why.

'Jacob-o. You are a good boy, I see,' she began shaking here head. 'It is very difficult for me to say you no. But I have to,' Nana stopped Jacob as he began to interrupt and continued with an expression of real fear on her lined face. 'You are in very-very big trouble boy. If you are not Kwasia… crazy, you are cursed.'

'I'm not crazy,' Jacob told her his face dropping, 'I just need to rest, or something,' He looked up at her.

'You are not crazy?'

'No,' this did nothing to improve Nana's spirits.

'If you are not crazy, then somebody…' the word body sounded like buddy, 'then some buddy was in your head?' she asked him.

'I suppose,' said Jacob.

'If he comes back when you are here with my children?' Nana asked, 'If he comes to the door, a man who can go into your mind?' Jacob realised then what Nana Adjua was trying to tell him. She wanted to help, but the children here were her responsibility. And, he was not. If she had to choose between Jacob and her children it would be the children, easily. Jacob understood this completely and his own spirits were sunken low. He checked the sun, high in the west.

'Ok,' said Jacob, and remembering a couple of words from the all powerful guidebook said, 'Me Co,'

'It is six o'clock?' he said. And, remembering a couple of words from the biblical guidebook he added. 'Me Co,' Nana looked at the sky and corrected him, twice.

'It is four thirty,' said Nana who then corrected his Twi. 'Me Ko,' she said.

'Excuse me?'

'Me Ko, I go,' she instructed.

'Ah, Me Co,' Jacob repeated.

'Me Ko, Ko!' Nana laughed happily at his attempt and repeated herself.

'Me Co… Ko. Me Ko!' Jacob tried.

'Yes yes. That is much better. Medaasai Jacob, my children are very important,' Jacob looked around and could do nothing but agree. He had to leave, so he rose from the table and hugged Nana Adjua warmly, embarrassing her.

'Medaasai Nana,' said Jacob, 'Me Ko!' And he left the safety of the orphanage behind, never to return.

As the troubled white man left Jeff, the self-important black boy, was returning. Nana noticed that he had orange juice all over his face.

'Show me your hands?' she ordered and he opened them to her. There were bits of orange pulp all over them. Jeff grinned at her and Nana Adjua just tutted him and rubbed his hands dry with the hem of her skirt.

'Oh you boys,' she said, speaking of them all, 'you are very bad.'

***

A drop of bloody goo went hiss in the fire as Leavon attempted to get the jump on Nana Adjakimpa burning his arm in the fire as he did. The Fetish priest, although greatly surprised by Leavon sudden and wretched appearance has been quick enough to resist Leavon's first lunges and keep the fire between them. Now Leavon growled as the pain of his arm added to the plethora of agony he was already feeling. He wanted this human. If he managed to catch it and drain it he was sure he would rejuvenate sufficiently to allow his hunt to continue, animal were one thing but a human would have plenty of life. Unfortunately for Leavon, Nana Adjakimpa was not about to let, what looked like a walking corpse, come anywhere near him, let alone would he allow the thing to drain his life force.

And, let's face it; in this same situation not many of us would need reasons to recoil from such a revolting abomination. For most of us dare I say, all, a simple "What the Fuck?" would suffice, followed by scurrying and retching in no particular order.

Leavon fell back from the scorching fire and for a moment Nana Adjakimpa allowed several ragged breaths to occur in him. Although the Fetish Priest had variously claimed the sight of thousands in the past, this was his first real confrontation with a

206

demon, for he was positive that it was certainly one that he was facing. His father, the wandering priest had reported to his young student many tales of demons of all shapes and sizes. The old man had seen great watery spirals that tore into the earth. He's seen demons made out of the air itself and also from fire and earth. Always in these stories the spirit of the earth rose to aid him and vanquish the demon, but Nana had never encountered such a power and doubted that it existed beyond the power of creation.

Nana Adjakimpa had only recently used the tale of the Air-demon to strike fear in the hearts of the villagers. After a tropical storm had rattled and in some cases, ripped their homes from the ground, even after he'd warned the paramount chief that the huts by the river, the ones in question, were not built with sturdiness in mind. With minds full of demonic fear the villagers returned home that day and began immediately to strengthen the walls in their wooden huts. The Paramount chief order everyone to ensure that their homes were built on foundations that were at least four feet deep, which was at least, in Nana Adjakimpa's eyes, a start.

After his father's death Nana had grown to believe that there was very little he could take literally from the old man's stories. As Fetish priest in this region, Nana Adjakimpa felt that each story hid an important and logical message, which had been disguised by priests in the past to convince the weak-minded that they must listen to the wisdom of their ancestors or face the consequences.

But now a real demon had just come bursting into his sacred refuge, his island of solitude. This was no fable or tall tale not a column of air or a fiery figure. This was a real creature, tortured and bleeding pacing in front of him like a broken angry animal. Even Nana with his limited facility for earth magic could sense the power within the man-shaped creature. It terrified him, for he knew nothing of fighting a real demon, all Nana Adjakimpa knew were stories.

'Wo Dindi sen?' he tried, one tale spoke of the power of possessing a demon's name. Leavon growled deeply and answer.

'I want to destroy you!' Leavon tried to rise again and attack the little black man dressed in rages and adorned with bone jewellery. The growl turned into a wince. He could feel that he was rapidly fading.

'What is your name?' Nana tried again in English. This creature had a powerful spirit but its body was weak. If he could fool it for long enough Nana Adjakimpa was sure that it would die soon or swoon and give him a chance to escape. He must speak with confidence, although his heart faltered suddenly when the demon spoke again.

'I need your life human, give it to me now and there will be no pain for you, But Leavon felt uncertainty. He had not properly consumed a human before now, but was sure that he would gain much more than he had from devouring the animals of the Rainy Forest. He remembered the wasted lives on his private jet. Oh, he could do with that extra energy now.

Since his rebirth in the old French Chateau belonging to his former self, Leavon had seen many humans, none of whom seemed to be in control of their surroundings. They were unaware of their place in the streams of energy surrounding or suffusing them. Indeed, Leavon was positive that none of the humans he had seen to date could even see the forces of the planet.

Now there was this old man. The little black man *was* awake to the world. There was an abundance of life force in him and this made Leavon's jaws slippery with saliva. He hungered for it as he had only recently learned to hunger. The last few hours since the crash the demon had begun to cherish his human existence and he'd become desperate to extend it beyond its rapidly gaining event horizon. It must be the pain, he thought. The humanity of possessing a physical body had not been lost on him before, but now that that body was in danger of expiring, the reality of human existence was now painfully apparent.

The old man's self-awareness and confidence were off putting to Leavon in his weakened state. Doubt was now creeping through him like a predator would through this Rainy Forest. It told him that he'd been wrong before. It said, 'be careful Leavon, this man may be strong enough to finish you, be careful, be careful, be careful.'

'I am Leavon,' he told the old man. Nana Adjakimpa had to try hard not to show his surprise. As soon as he'd heard the demon's name being spoken he was sure he felt a stirring in the ground below him. Nana hoped that he was not imagining it, maybe his father's stories were true after all and the reason that he had never felt the spirit of the World rise to help him was because he had never encountered a demon before. A tiny blossom of hope opened in his heart and he knew that if he was to survive this he would have to act like his father had in the legends he must put on a show and hope that the creature would destroy itself.

'Welcome Leavon,' said Nana Adjakimpa, 'I have waited many days for you to arrive-o!' Leavon moved to the left and Nana matched the distance, putting the fire between them once more. 'Eh now,' said Nana, 'you should sit down and relax-o. Or we will not be able to start,' he motioned to a log-stool that lay behind the demon. 'Sit down-o,' He told Leavon.

Leavon felt that he had no choice so he sat and watched as the little black man sat on a similar log opposite him. He waited for his chance. Surely it would come?

'Start what?' he asked with a growl in the back of his throat.

'What?' The Fetish priest exclaimed. 'We must heal you-o, or you'll be dying here beside my fire, in my sacred circle,' he said motioning to the circle of trees. 'And nobody has ever died here without my say so, eh?'

'How can you heal me?' Leavon was blunt. At this point he was again holding his human form together by will power alone.

'Your spirit is spilling from your body yellow one,' said Nana Adjakimpa. 'You must release it and then allow me to heal the body. Then you can return-o,' Leavon tried to raise himself and barked angrily.

'How can I return to the body once I have left it?' Nana Adjakimpa interrupted him by standing tall and screaming back with gusto and great conviction.

'You stupid demon!' he raged, 'if I wanted you would have been destroyed as soon as you entered my sacred grove,' Nana could feel his heart bursting with fear, he felt like crying out in desperation, but he continued to mock Leavon as though he were a child.

'I have no time for your misbelief-o. You will listen to me and live or you may die here in my forest like a hartebeest wounded from badly throw spear. Or, if you are lucky, I will kill you myself and save you the pain and humiliation of it?' This was Nana Adjakimpa's biggest risk. The demon was certainly stronger than he, but it did not matter if the yellow one believed in the power of the Fetish priest. He must continue to act as he did with the villagers, haughty and knowledgeable. The fire was waning, as was his safety behind it.

'Do you here me… Leavon?' Nana asked boldly. 'Will you do as I say?' Leavon felt his fury fading as the energy he had so long conserved began to drain from his body. He had no choice but to trust this human.

'I hear you,' he answered, 'and I will do… as you say.'

Nana Adjakimpa took a deep breath and tried to hide his relief. Now he needed to lull the demon. He wasn't sure what he was supposed to say, he just needed time to escape. So he was going to have to be inventive.

'Concentrate on your wounds,' Nana instructed, 'feel deeply the shreds of muscle and the pieces of broken bone,' across the fire Leavon screamed in agony as all of his wounds protested at once. Since crashing the car he'd been forcing himself to ignore the pain, but now at the old mans instruction he was feeling it thoroughly. It was unbearable.

Nana Adjakimpa was himself experiencing great pain. The scream of the beast were drilling into his brain, turning his fear into tangible hurt and transforming his cowardly trembling into painful vibrations of terror. He felt that he could no longer hold his calm façade in the wake of such an outpouring of malicious energy. It was too much for a mortal man to tolerate. But he knew that if he did not continue the creature would surely be able to launch itself across the now flickering remnants of the fire and tear him to shreds. The thought strengthened him and he continued his instructions over the sounds of agony from both the demon and his own mind.

'Think deeply of the blood in your veins!' he shouted at Leavon, 'Push your mind down through your body and into the earth beneath!' The ground began to rumble under their feet and the Fetish priest cowered from the demon as it began to glow from yellow to red.

'Arrrrrrrrrrrr,' screamed Leavon, he could see into the earth beneath his feet, 'what is happening?' It seemed to him that he was looking into the earth. It was as though he was the head of a great earthworm burrowing directly downwards whilst all around him the earth shuddered and recoiled from him. He felt a mighty heat rise to meet him. Leavon realised then that he was not burrowing down into the earth. Something was surging up to meet him. Something that was repellent to him. The heat in his body grew as he helplessly awaited his doom. He had been

211

tricked he knew it now. He'd shown himself to the soul of the world and now it was coming to destroy him.

The vision

Everyone gets a chance to turn back, to do what is right. In the clearing of the fetish priest Leavon was given such a chance. He was given a vision of the future. And it went something like this.

There was water all around. It seemed that the vision took place in a swamp, or at least a place that was swamped. There was an old man in a long dark coat trudging through the water, he was making slow progress but he seemed to know where he was going.

The old man reached what looked like a tree that had been recently submerged, so that only its topmost branches reached above the waterline, but what the old man was walking on wasn't evident.

As Leavon's vision got closer to the tree he could see that there was something snagged amongst what was left of the foliage. It was the clothes of a man, and the man was still in them.

The old man went down on his knees and began cooing like a doting father.

'Oh look at you boy, look what a state you've got yourself?' There was a whimper from the bundle of rags. 'Shh now boy,' the old man told it as he lifted the large bundle easily into his arms. 'Shh, you're mine now,' said the old man to the wreck that held in his arms, 'Mine, all mine,' He said looking up at Leavon through his vision.

And Leavon was back in the clearing once more.

Nana Adjakimpa watched in horror as the demon raised his head and its eyes locked with his. There was boundless fury in them and he knew that he was finished. Leavon made to attack the little black man but was prevented from doing so by a burst of hot energy that erupted from the ground beneath his feet. A pure white fire that surrounded him making the pain he'd felt before that moment became miniscule in comparison. His yellow soul burst from his body and for a few moments he was free of his mortality and the pain stopped. He felt like the cork of a champagne bottle would feel if it could. He'd been expelled from the physical world and he was floating upwards yet to reach the peak of his flight. Leavon was at peace for that brief time before his descent began he floated upwards slings until, for a nothing, he was just suspended there in the air without consequence. Then he dropped like a crashing plane, only going down and never up again.

He began to beg for mercy to the powers that had allowed him to return again as a young man, his pleading growing increasingly pitiful as he hurtled closer to the earth. He wanted hopelessly to survive and he promised that should his soul be spared he would serve whoever wished to command him.

As his essence careered through the rushing air, he realised that he was being affected by the physical once more. His tattered body came into view for only a split second before he was in it and the agony of his survival was upon him.

In the centre of the clearing Leavon raised to his feet, all the muscles clenched tightly and opened his lungs with an all-rending cry that echoed long and loudly through the Rainy Forest and did not cease abruptly but faded out as he slipped into unconsciousness. The scream pushed the animals before it as it swept through the expanse of green aging and instilling fear into every living thing that heard it.

At the epicentre Nana Adjakimpa fled from the onslaught of this terrible hollering. His face was tight with maniacal glee as his feet propelled him away from the episode he had just survived. If he had known that the danger was over he could have simply ran to the village and rested there but Nana was beyond reason now. His mind, which he had always thought of as strong and stable, was nothing now but a broken stem at the base of his brain. He ran and ran in pure automatic dread, through the village and out the other side, much to the shock of his people who were still shaken by the noises they'd heard. To them explanation of occurrences such as these was the responsibility of the Fetish priest, and to see him running in horrible death-masked fear through their homes was not a welcome sight.

Yet on and on Nana ran. In the days and months that would pass by, the people of the Rainy Forest, from just west of Kumasi all the way south to the sea at Takoradi would talk in hushed tones of the little man that ran the length of Ghana to the ocean as if chased by the all the devils in hell. He ran until his heart exploded in his chest and even then, a few steps more. Some said that he was a crazed criminal running from the law and others a lunatic escaped from a Red Cross hospital. Only the villagers knew who he was and not one of them knew why he had run so fearfully, but in everyone who heard the stories it caused a shiver and a feeling of uneasiness. What could have caused a man to run himself to death? They didn't want to imagine.

*

In the clearing Leavon lay recuperating for the rest of that day and long into the next. When it became apparent to him that he was not going to die, he began to crawl on his belly through the

214

forest. He didn't choose any particular direction nor did he care which way he went. He'd been allowed to live and for now that was enough. Some force unknown to him had spared him to complete his task and it was only a matter of time before he would be given another sign and his journey could begin anew.

The childish glee he had felt at the time of his rebirth was gone for good now. He'd entertained the brainless belief that he had chosen the course his new existence would follow, actually assumed that once he destroyed the sky-blue soul he would be free to wander the earth, killing and taking pleasure as he saw fit. But now he knew that these were ridiculous notions.

Until he became fully human he was bound to be a mindless hound in the control of an omniscient master or masters, he did not know which, destined for nothing more than a slave's existence. Pushed and shoved around on this pathetic planet until his usefulness was deemed negligible until he was thrown back on to the pile with the rest of useless humanity. It was disgusting and he couldn't bear to think of it.

Instead, he concentrated on how he would get to the next tree, how he would catch the next animal that would boost his strength. He would go on. And, if he were to become nothing more than a sword in the hands of another then he would relish the taste of blood when it came.

Recollections 14

Escape

'*Hey Baby..,*' her voice high and soft and not at all piercing.

'Hey Baby! How… where are you?' He could touch her in his mind.

'W…'

'How are you? What's the story?'

'I'm cool honey, I'm in London.'

'London? Cool! Em… how is it, how, when did you get there?'

'I'm just leaving now…'

'Leaving, how long were you there?'

'Oh you should have seen it I was staying in this mad hotel with these two weirdos… three weirdos!'

'Wha…'

'It was really mad, but anyway I was just moping around, you know? In Greece and what was the point? When I just wanted to…'

'I can't believe you called me. You wouldn't believe what's been happening here. It's eh…'

'Kind of strange?'

'Strange, yeah! I miss you baby.'

'I miss you too Jacob.'

[Silence - Last call boarding flight 154LH…]

'Ahem, it seems like… ages since I saw ya baby. I wish you were here you know. Everything would probably seem a lot more… normal if you were. Here, I mean.'

'You're still in Ghana aren't you?'

'Yep, I just got here to… actually yesterday. I'm loosing track of the days…'

'Good because I'm coming over to you…'

'You're what?'

'I'm in the Airport now. I have a ticket to… Accra isn't it. I'll be there in the morning. Are you in Accra?'

'No, Kumasi but, you're coming here? But I don't think it's safe for you here.'

'Not safe? I know, I think you need me though, really I do.'

[Silence – 'Hey Maggie, you have the boarding passes?']

'Why, what's been happening to you?'

'You wouldn't believe it. But I know you need me. I'm sure of it!'

'Listen, Becky, I'd love to see you but…'

'I love you Jacob.'

[Silence – 'Daddy I want to go to the toilet!']

'You do? Aw baby, I love you too but… things are getting real strange, I…'

'You do?'

'You know it.'

'I'm coming over and that's it.'

[Silence – 'Staff Call, Sarah Calotte please report to the information desk immediately…']

'Fuck it, you're right. Will you be able to get to Kumasi all right? Accra is a bit mad; I'm not sure how safe it'll be…'

'Jacob!'

'Sorry, what time are you getting in? It takes about five hours to get to Kumasi.'

'Cool, keep your phone on I'll call you when I get there. Let's see. I get in at five so, a couple of hours in Accra. So, let's say twelve-ish yeah?'

'Are you sure you want to do this? I have to be honest, there's something going on. Someone is… Well I think they're…'

'After you... I know. Listen, you need me. I'll see you tomorrow Ok?' I have to go time is running out. Love you, b… '

[Dial tone]

'Love you too baby,' said Jacob. He felt a sort of light-hearted happiness, a hangover from hearing the sound of her adoring and divine voice. She was like the sort of fresh summer breeze a romance writer might refer to. She cleaned up his thoughts and helped him to focus, for a brief period maybe. There was still the problem of all the mounting danger he could feel building inside of him.

~

Jacob was standing outside the central post office in Kumasi, the air was hot and wet and it seemed that this was always the way it was going to be inland in Ghana. The city was surrounded by forest for miles around and the moisture from the trees gave Kumasi a humid baked feeling. Kumasi was mainly perched atop two large hills. Atop the eastern hill lay the Palace of the Asante King, a building passed on to the people of the region by the English governors who had constantly perished in the prickly sweating grip of Malaria. These Governors of English rule were forced to live on the coast where the monster disease was caught less frequently.

It hadn't mattered. The white men died all the same. Jacob wondered what sorts of men were sent here to govern in the days towards the end of English rule; sent to their deaths, most of them leaving their families behind to spare them a feverish end in a foreign land. These men must have been out of favour back in Britain. Perhaps a governorship in Ghana was akin to punishment, a political as well as physical death sentence.

And, when they arrived here to die, what had they to loose? Why not use the locals like slaves, hadn't it been done for hundreds of years by the Dutch and the Portuguese?

They used the West Africans as they wished. With the men they formed the Frontline for the North African wars against the Germans and Italians whilst the women were used to fill the void left by the absence of kin. A governor would have a room full of black women for his personal use.

How could the faith of a people be entrusted to a Governor who felt their charge was nothing more than a punishment to him?

~

At least nature had helped the Ghanaians. A white population never flourished here and it was because of this that Jacob was at that very moment surrounded by small black boys with an assortment of wares draped over their arms. He was probably the only white man that had walked past all day. And if not, he was certainly the only one that had stood in the square outside the post office heedlessly talking on his mobile phone. When the phone rang he'd been walking across the top of Kumasi's western hill, Adum. He'd stopped in his tracks at the sound, he's forgotten that he had a phone in his pocket and he was doubly shocked to hear Becky's voice squeaking prettily out of it when he'd composed himself enough to answer.

'Obroni! How are you? I am fine, thank you?'

'Eh Hi,' said Jacob as Becky's recent presence wore slightly off. One boy was holding up a handful of belts.

'Obroni, you buy this,' Jacob was told as he looked around at the gaggle of boys he'd allowed to surround him and a sense of great paranoia cold-showered his brain. He was sure that he was in danger, Nana Adjua had helped him confirm the reality of it and now he was standing out in the open, dazed and lovesick. Anyone could be watching, he needed to get inside, or at least get his back to a wall. Maybe then the feelings of impending doom would diminish. How foolish.

'Small boy,' He said, remembering the way Nana used them to good effect, 'I want to drink coffee. Where do I go?' He held out a Five thousand Cedis note. 'Quickly,' He added feeling panic and desperation. Would he ever feel safe again now that his body had been invaded?

Becky was right.

The boy took Jacobs hand, the one with the note in it, and led him to an actual café called Baboo's, a little way down Adum hill. Jacob was surprised to see such a place but didn't spend a long time startling. Instead he entered quickly and found himself a seat with a concrete wall behind it and a full view of the door. The feeling of panic subsided considerably with this.

He needed her.

***

Across the road from Baboo's, Samuel, who ran the newspaper-and-book stand, lifted his head from the Stephen King Novel he was reading to watch a long black mud splattered Mercedes pull up alongside his stall. He waited to see if a customer was going to roll down the tinted window and ask for a paper, but nothing happened. After a few minutes he grew impatient. He wasn't about to let some rich man block his stand from view, Samuel had worked very hard for this spot close to the banks, where white people bought second hand books donated by the hostels and the black business men met to buy a paper an talk about the state of the country. He left Kofi behind the counter and went to knock on the car window.

'Hallo!' He yelled, 'you cannot stop here. Move your car (car sounding like Ka) immediately!' There was no answer. 'I said, move your Ka out of my way…' The electric window slid down and Rajette looked out smiling.

'Yes,' he asked Samuel, 'there is a problem?' He tapped the doorframe with his revolver and Samuel reacted with great presence of mind.

'Oh no mister,' said Samuel, 'there is a charge for parking here,' Rajette smiled. This was something that he approved of.

'Of course,' He said handing Samuel a wad of notes. It may have looked to the observer that he didn't care how much was in the bundle, but that was definitely not the case. Rajette was never casual with money. The wad held one hundred thousand Cedis, which was: twelve dollars, forty shekels or ten euro. He could translate into another dozens currencies but the most former and the later were the important ones. Plus, he had a soft spot for the shekels of his homeland. They helped place everything with a real value.

'Thank you sir,' said Samuel.

'No problem, black,' said Rajette and the rising car window left Samuel looking at his own nervous face as it was reflected in the glass, he looked frightened. He hurried back behind the counter with his money and turned to Kofi who was pointing at the car.

'It is a friend,' he said stuffing the wad into his pocket, 'he can park there ok?' The boy nodded and Samuel went back to his Novel. This King was a strange man. Samuel understood all of the words but could not make any sense of the stories. None of the characters ever went to a Juju priest for help. It always took them too long to believe what was happening to them. He should have more Africans in his stories and then maybe they would make some sense. King was good thought, and the fantastic story Samuel was reading was a fitting distraction from the upsetting reality of a man with a revolver, parked only six feet away from where he was reading. Samuel stopped with a thought. He found a pencil and wrote something down on a piece of paper, handed it to Kofi and off the boy ran. Then Samuel returned to his book make sure not to look suspicious and doing a terrible job.

It didn't matter because inside the black Mercedes Rajette had moved to the passenger seat to get a better view of the Café. Jacob was sitting in a good seat across the road in Baboo's Café. The boy looked nervous, almost as nervous as he had been the night they'd met in Jerusalem. How easy all this was going to be, all he needed was the word "Go" and the Palestinian knew that he could walk right up to his target and put a bullet between his eyes. The police wouldn't show for a long while, if they did at all. No, they probably would show.

Rajette had heard that the Ghanaian government had combated corruption with a novel ethos. The police were now very well paid, and a well-paid man has no economic need for bribes and kickbacks. Thus any police officer that took them was greedy and afforded no soft treatment if caught with more than his wages. Jail was what they got, unheard of for police but maybe here it worked, although Rajette wasn't convinced. He was sure at least that no matter how frank the local police were. They would be streetwise enough to wait until any extraordinary violence was long since finished before showing up to pick up the pieces in an honest and forthright manner.

The Palestinian was bored however, watching instead of acting. He lit a cigarette and savoured for a moment how it burned into his throat. Marshall paid well as did other interested

223

parties. Well enough for Rajette to stick to surveillance and overcome any violent urges for now. But they wouldn't allow him to have any fun with his quarry. No notes, no broken fingers, no slow blood poisoning even. It was so dull.

Inside the café Jacob was reading out of a Lonely Planet guidebook. He was such a tourist! Rajette couldn't help himself. He decided quickly what he was going to do and opened the door. Fuck Marshall and the righteous hypocrites, they wouldn't dare refuse him his money. He was too boundless for them to risk an attempt to bind him. In the end he would probably have to kill most of them anyway. It wasn't as though he intended to do so. Experience told him that something so big and profitable always ended with a lot of cleaning up to be done. So if the ones giving the orders were as good as dead, why would a carcass care if he had a little fun?

Rajette slammed the door closed and crossed the road throwing Samuel a glance as he did so.

'See you later,' he said.

'Later my friend,' Samuel answered peering only briefly over his book. The less contact with this one the better, the vender thought.

Jacob was regaining his composure as he sipped his coffee and read random facts about the region. Apparently Ghana's neighbour Togo was rife with Voodoo, or Juju as the natives called it, but Benin to the north and east was the birthplace of those particular religious mysteries. Jacob wondered how many beliefs there were in the world and could a man ever learn enough about them all to be able to compare or even explain them. A woman would probably be better equipped to do it. He'd heard that their minds were capable of dealing with a great many more things than a man could.

Jacob vowed that he would test Becky at the earliest opportunity. Already he was beginning to look forward to her arrival.

Jacob was staring right through Rajette as he entered the café. For a moment the Palestinian was taken aback to see there was on the white boys face, a definite lack of surprise. Then he realised that the fool was looking at nothing and continued to do so until Rajette was almost upon him. It would have been so easy for the little Arab to grab Jacob by the hair and twist his head around sharply -Crack! - But Rajette was forced to make do with the mental image instead.

A second later, as Rajette came to a stop in front of him, Jacob started doubly at the proximity of such an unwelcome sight. Rajette was a representation and a full reminder of the episodes to which he found he was loosing himself in these last few days and weeks.

Rajette took no little joy in seeing the horrific and undignified recognition that suddenly overtook the boy's face. His pride in the fear that he felt he would have projected on his past victims had they lived long enough to show it to him was undiminished. This was how they would all look if he'd given them a change to behold him. He sat down with careless graceless ingenuity. Rajette seldom put any stock in the look of the thing. It was the value that mattered to him.

Jacob watched as the little Arab, who had tricked him so easily in Jerusalem, picked up the menu and began to read it, apparently in no hurry to explain his presence or to put Jacob out of his misery, whatever that would entail. The tanned little man just sucked on his cigarette and read the menu.

Jacob couldn't believe he hadn't seen the malice that radiated from the hateful little thug on that first night. Was Rajette that good an actor, or had Jacob's own perceptions changed. He was inclined to think that both were equally probable.

What Jacob saw before him now was a taste of wickedness, but he took heart in the certainty that this was not the one who had invaded his mind in the market place. Compared to that one, Rajette was nothing more than a canapé. There was no solace to be taken from the fact that the main course was on its way and was, for all Jacob knew, inescapable.

'You've been following me,' Jacob began. Rajette never looked up from his perusal of the café fair. Jacob found the thug's nonchalance infuriating. 'Well?' he raised his voice slightly but lowered it again almost immediately when he realised he'd drawn the attention of the waiter and the other patrons, 'are you going to say anything?' Rajette closed the menu and looked back over his shoulder at the waiter.

'I'll have a milkshake,' he said, 'chocolate,' and he turned back to Jacob.

'Yes sir,' answered the young black boy who turned quickly to leave. He could tell when an argument was about to break out and the Black/White looked like a very dangerous man. Better to be behind the counter, where he could watch in safety.

Rajette gave Jacob another glance of appraisal and Jacob held his eyes trying to look strong. The boy was definitely harder than before and perhaps he thought that he was above Rajette? Well, he would have to change that.

'You think you are better than me, white?' Rajette even sneered as he said it. 'You would like me to kick the shit out of you?' What new found confidence Jacob had attained reducing the Arab to a secondary threat was quickly diminishing beneath Rajette's well-trained bluster.

'All I want to know,' Jacob said, 'why does Marshall need the scrolls? Don't worry I have no intention of breaking the

226

agreement with Mr. Marshall. He'll get everything before I give it to the Church. I'd just like to know what he wants with a load of boring historical documents.'

'Do you think I care about Marshall and his little papers?' The Palestinian laughed. 'I am here for money, boy. I am here to make sure you deliver, yes, but if you don't?' He smiled at this, 'I get paid anyway.'

'Actually,' Rajette added, leaning forward, 'if you fail?' Jacob couldn't stop himself leaning backwards away from the man, 'and I have t' Rajette blew smoke in Jacob's face from close proximity and then let the remains of the cigarette drop into the younger man's coffee.

-Tssk - It went when it hit the liquid. Rajette leaned back into his seat.

'You know, if I kill you, I get paid more,' The Palestinian smiled proudly at this, and why not?

Jacob didn't know what to say or what to do. He was no Hard Man who could just grab the little man by the collar and toss him out of the coffee shop. Even if this little bully wasn't the biggest of Jacob's worries, he was still a potentially terminal one. An Atom bomb may be on the way, but a bullet would kill him just as well.

'What do you want?' was all he could ask, 'you want money?' Rajette continued to smile, but the joy behind it faded.

'Oh Mr Writer want to pay me off, does he? You think that I am just an animal that you can distract with some nice smells, or some shiny gold, ha!' Rajette spat his contempt across the table, although he was hugely curious about the money.

'I just…'

'You just assume that you're better than me? Richer than me, do you? Well let me tell you, boy. You know what assume does?'

Oh my god, Jacob thought. He's going to say it!

'Do you?' asked Rajette noticing that he had somehow lost Jacob's attention.

'No,' Jacob answered, surely Rajette was not about to…?

'Assume, makes an ass out of you and me!' The little man said and sat back in his chair, no doubt filled with self-importance at his clever phraseology. Jacob couldn't believe what he'd heard. Real life couldn't be this stupid, could it? He looked at the man, who was quite probably going to kill him for it, but he couldn't help himself and he started to laugh.

Jacob laughed loudly and happily in Rajette's face and it felt good to do it. All at once the pointless nature of his greedy self-serving life had leaped out from wherever it had been hiding and was now hopping around in front of him, cavorting and gyrating outrageously. So much so that all he could do was laugh.

'An Ass out of you and me, ha ha! How stupid can you get? Ha ha!'

Rajette however was not even close to having his funny bone tickled. What was happening? The boy was laughing at him. Him! Rajette!

He was the man who had clawed his way through childhood, grasping his measly pathetic life in a murderous hold and twisting it, until its very bones dripped bloody success for him. Still this boy was laughing at him.

Rajette was a success. Hadn't he made money? More money than anyone he'd ever met, and not killed. He slept at times with a wad of it in each hand. Sometimes, when he was nervous, he even drew blood from squeezing the change in his pockets. Money was his God and it had rewarded him greatly for his worship. It drew him on, gave him nightmares and scarred his soul.

But the boy was still laughing.

'You little fucking bastard,' Rajette screamed at Jacob as he sprung forward arms swinging, 'you fucking fuck! You bastard! You fucking bastard!' Rajette landed on Jacob and began swinging wildly punching hard and fast, not caring where the blows were landing. –Thump. Wallop –

'I'm a rich man,' the little Arab screamed as he pounded and punched, 'I'm a rich man,' He continued to shout as the police dragged him out. He struggled and kicked but the African men were simply stronger than he and managed to get him out by the police car with minimal trouble.

Unfortunately, one of the officers, Peter, was very inexperienced. Rajette realised it when he heard the useless words that Peter was saying.

'Calm down now sir, calm down! Please sir, please. If you would...' An experienced copper wouldn't have wasted his breath. He would have paid more attention to the man in hand. You're never sure until the keys have been turned. When Rajette realised this and knew that he was overpowered, he gave up his struggling immediately. Peter thought that the man's rage had finally left him and relaxed his grasp. This is, as any experienced policeman or bouncer will tell you, a child's mistake and because of it Rajette was quickly free of Peter's grip and had skulled the other officer with a lazy punch on the crown of his head. In a moment he was across the street and into his car and was careering down the road in three. Peter got his act together.

Jacob lay on the floor of Baboo's Bazaar bloody, aching and unsure if he was whole. There were bruises on his face and arms that rose out of his body like miniature streaming volcanoes. The waiter came forward with a damp cloth and helped him to his feet handing him something, probably a tooth, which he put in his pocket as he rose.

Thankfully Jacob was still able to stand because outside there was an awful commotion. It became apparent that he should leave. And, although Jacob couldn't see very well with blood clogging his eyes, after he clearly heard a car screeching away down the street, obviously contained the liberated Rajette, he somehow managed to clear his head, wipe his eyes and pick himself up off the milk-shaken floor.

He looked around the restaurant. The coast was, for the moment, clear. He was going to have to hobble for it so he refused a cloth offered by the waiter and headed out the door. As he staggered away Jacob replayed the moment that had just passed.

'An ass out of you and me,' he said laughing quietly his breath growing quickly ragged under the exertion.

It was amazing. There was something really fucking weird about life that Jacob was at a loss to describe. And, in the immediate future, he had no intention in trying.

***

Whilst Jacob made his way up the road at a slow amble in Kumasi, Becky was taking to the air in London on a British Airways flight bound for Accra. She was wondering for the eight time at least, whether she made the right decision by racing to Jacob's side because of a collection of whims and daydreams? Or could they be signs and visions? Becky would never have claimed that there was a difference between the two. But she was hoping now that there was. Without the signs and visions she was just a silly girl who missed her man and had constructed elaborate fancies to allow her to run after him. That was stalker behaviour. She could be locked up. But, now that she was strapped in and in the air there really wasn't any other way to go but forward, so she let it go.

Finding Nomo was playing on the tiny screen that was set into the back of the seat in front of her. It was funny how nobody on an aeroplane ever called them chairs. Chairs moved, which would not be a welcome image for a person in a metal bullet flying through the air at 700kmph to visualise. It certainly gave Becky pause to doubt.

Well, doubts and all she would have to sit back and let the journey role out in front of her. When she hit the ground she was going to be in Africa. That was worth the trip in itself. Wasn't it?

***

Back in Kumasi, Jacob had reached his hotel without incident. He lay on his bed, sores stinging and reality paining him greatly. Even if he played the game and delivered to Marshall all the writings that he wanted, Jacob was not going to avoid harm. That little psycho was going to do him over no matter what and his earlier laughing was looking increasingly like a terminal straw that was going to saw through the camel's spine.

After making sure the door was locked and that there was a window in the bathroom through which he could escape, Jacob took out the book of short stories that Daniel had planned to give him for his birthday and looked again at the words that were hidden in Saki's – The image of the lost soul:

Demon folk pious and snug but the prisoner falling broken rang out the great bell.

231

It was still an inexplicable message, if it was one at all.

He leafed through the book and came to the fifth story written in stilted verse. *Hubal & Abel* it was called and it was even shorter that the Saki, but as he read it through, he could see that it meant a great deal.

Hubal & Abel – By Paulo Wanchope

Hubal and Abel rise up in the night, and with hopeless abandon they tried.
Where for and why for, the matter is trite, to dismember the other and render his hide.

With hopeless abandon they combated and injured, it seemed that forever their kingdoms would wait
New reasons were formed as the night bells rang, for a victor to mount his foes head on the gate.

Instead they'd march out onto newly raked sand, freshly cleaned and unbloodied by manservant's hand.

But one day raised Abel, in the suns orange light, and risking a lot, for they fought in the night, when so early a journey was risking his bite, yet knew that the stalemate was even and right.
So he lay on his belly and crawled in the damp, till with grinningly fiendish he spied Hubal's camp. Abel watched from the Cliffside as his smile broke to tears, when he saw that below held his deadliest fears.
Down in the valley was bold Hubal's tent; the fighter lay sleeping in front. And poking the fire and stocking the grain was his unmistakable runt.

So Hubal was father and Abel was none, and the spy he did fret for his soul. As he made his way back to his battleground tack, he felt bitter.

And daunted.

And cold.

When Hubal and Abel rose again in the night, by the great searchlight fires they started to fight. Though even once, they were even no more, which was clear to the viewer who'd seen them before.

From the start you could see that Abel was beat, and the normal sweet fleetness was gone from his feet.

Hubal dipped and then dodged and have at you, all normal, till his sword it was lodged inside Abel's old chest. Then Hubal he started, as shocked as the rest, as he maintained the knowledge he wasn't the best.

Abel went down, though he tried for his part, but the metal pierced deeper inside his soft heart.
Abel went down, and a huge cry rang out, from the darkness a he-child came scampering out.

'Oh father, oh father, you're dying!' He said, as Abel looked up at his boy's little head.

'I was fighting so long; I'd forgotten your face. I remember so little that death will replace.'

With his last tearful breath then, the beaten man sighed, and with no more than that, steadfast Abel had died.

He grew cold as a rock in that last battlefield, while the reason for all laid him out on his shield.

And for Hubal? No dancing, no laughing, no victory feast. There was mourning, and tears. There was guilt at the sight.

Of the things he had done, acted out like a beast. And the brother he'd fought for so long, in the night.

~

No sooner had the tale come to an end than Jacob was snoring loudly. He had enjoyed the story as Candelli had surely done before him. In his first dreams, Jacob imagined meeting the Old Italian once more, and discussing its meaning. Then he dropped more deeply into dreams that he couldn't control.

***

The Bus Station was a melee. There was no other way to describe it. All around in a city where strides were made to westernise and organise, in the Lorry Park, West Africa could not be transposed upon. The white world and the clockwork system of the civilised machine didn't just grind to a halt here. It couldn't exist at all.

Yet Becky was a marveller and for as long as possible she stood in the entrance to the Park, marvelling. It was nothing short of spectacular. She was sure that some sort of organisation was being practised there, although it seemed that organisation was as far away from here as her Sydney home. After all, hundreds of buses and Trotros came in and out of this Station every day so some rule must be enforcing itself through some hidden Lorry park Management system, invisible to the western eye.

Whatever is was, it was working, and buses and vans pushed there way in and out of the park, barely missing each other in their haste, while dozens of extras sold their wares, to future passengers, alighting home-comers, and boarded travellers alike. It was spectacular show of free commerce in action.

As her guidebook suggested Becky took a deep breath and plunged into the madness. The smell of frying chicken and the blandly spiced smell of sweat greeted her as she pushed her way through the different congregations that surrounded every vehicle.

After being shoved and pulled by various drivers eager to charge a white woman just a little bit extra for the journey north, Becky found herself on a small fifty-seat bus bound for Kumasi. She had a smile on her face a bag of ice cream in her hand and no idea what was about to happen to her. All she knew was that she would see Jacob soon. She could hardly wait.

The invisible workings of the Lorry Park ejected the Bus out into Accra thirty minutes later and they were on their way. Onto the highway they travelled, and out the black path would, into the Rainy Forest, where the heart of Ghana lay, and where other things too, were lying in wait.

***

At a bend in the road where the rains had worn the edges of the tarmac down, causing huge encroaching cracks to meet in the centre, a large male leopard drank from a pool of clear water, flicking his tongue and bobbing his powerful head. Habitually he raised his head to scan the trees and down along the road that clashed with the forest's shades of green and brown. It felt hard and unyielding under his padded paws, he was uncomfortable there, but he was thirsty. Always the Leopard returned to his drink, relishing the chance to rest and enjoying the silence. He was so thirsty that it was too late when he realised that there was far too much of it, the silence.

When he did notice the abnormal stillness of the surrounding forest, the Leopard's hackle rose immediately and his feline consideration was drawn off to his left where he realised in a particular spot, a certain lack of movement that could only mean one thing. He was being watched.

The Rainy Forest around him was now deathly still. The normal sounds of the trees, birds and insects, burrowing mammals and scampering reptiles, were missing. A predator was nearby and waiting.

The Leopard had no practice as a target. In the present Jungle chain of command, he was the predator not the prey. It didn't matter though. A hunt was a hunt and although the Leopard was usually doing the attacking, his instincts were sharp and tight enough to know when he was about to be attacked. He felt he was going to be on the receiving end of something.

Then a rumbling started.

It came from the surface of the Black path where the Leopard stood growing wary and increasingly more frightened. After a few moments it became a noise too. A growling that grew louder and louder the longer he waited. It was time to run he knew. And run he did, sprinting off the road the Leopard barely managed to scramble to a sudden halt at the forest's edge. He was trapped.

Lying in front of him was Leavon, or what was left of him. Leavon smiled when the Leopard appeared before him.

'Hello,' he rasped, 'you're a sight for sore eyes, my frightened little friend,' Leavon came slowly to his feet looming above the dread-filled feline.

Leopard could taste his own fear. The monster that now stared at him was like nothing he had ever smelled before. The head was torn in a grimace and its air was foul and filled with menace. He knew that he must flee but believed that he could not.

'Gwwwwrrrrwwwwwww!' he whimpered with his tail between his legs, backing further onto the black path. The sound from his own throat shocked the Leopard so much his hind legs buckled sitting him down in the centre of the road. Now he was the frightened one, he was feeling the emotions he had only ever seen in the countenance of prey.

There was a thud behind him that he didn't care to investigate. He just cowered there, waiting for the end, unable to take his eyes off the monster thing as it slid and creaked towards him ready to pounce on him at any moment.

'Gwwwwrrrrwwwwwww!' that sound escaped his throat again. It was the whine of a cornered victim; the shudder of dinner before it was brought to ground. The Leopard couldn't face Leavon's eyes any longer and turned away meekly submitting in fear. A large stag now lay directly in front of the Leopard's feet. It was not bleeding, nor was it lying still. The animal's carcass seemed bloated and swollen; the muscles were jammed with blood as it seized, jerking its nerves in shocked overload.

There was a growling from the monster as it stood over him. The Leopard tried not to look up but couldn't bear to see what had happened to the other tortured creature. Was the hartebeest dead? The Leopard smelled death from it but its blood was still running.

The growling grew louder and Leopard returned his attention to Leavon who moved by the roadside, ready to pounce. Leopard realised through his fear that the monster was not the source of the growling that grew louder and louder. It was something else something approaching along the black path. It vibrated and froze the leopard in place.

~

Becky's eye's were glazed and empty staring outward on the road ahead. For the last three hours her disposition had deteriorated from chirpy motivation, through tired impatience and into apathetic comatose. It was a long road ahead and the human mind somehow manages to tune itself out in these inescapably inactive moments. It replays dreams and memories in tandem and displays them behind the eyes like biological screensavers helping to pass the time.

How long she'd been staring through the weird scene ahead on the road, she did not know, but she awoke to it only at the last moment. And, judging by the way the driver slammed on the worn brakes, it was obvious that he had overlooked it too. The Trotro slid to an unsteady halt, its time worn brake pads stuttering once, twice and a third time, before locking the wheels and jerking the necks of the passengers. The Trotro bounced on its springs and a few banged their head off the seats in front.

After a brief stunned pause the passengers began jabbering in reaction to the sudden stop as the driver motioned wildly through his cracked and dusty windscreen, excusing himself from blame. In one movement all of the passengers looked out at the road immediately in front of them and caught sight of the Leopards last seconds in the land of the living.

Then there was a blur and a horrible crunching sound, a brief yelp and a long sigh. And everything was different. In fact, everything was the same except that there was no leopard on the road ahead. There was only a panting white man standing where the leopard had been. He was covered in blood and filth, but he stood squarely in front of them at ease in the oddity of his circumstances.

The Trotro fell still as he approached and opened the sliding door. They shrank back from him as he climbed up into the body of the vehicle, he smelt badly of something rotten and revolting. Becky tried not to wrinkle her nose as he moved down the centre aisle of the passenger van. It was sickening. Yet the Driver made no attempt to stop the man coming aboard, instead he stared straight-ahead not seeming to notice his newest charger. The engine started again and they were off in a cloud of smoke, leaving behind and forgetting instantly what had just occurred and the bodies of a hartebeest and a stately leopard, whose pride had lost him now for good.

Leavon approached the only available seat and paused before sitting down.

'Hello,' he said, smiling at Becky, 'may I sit here?'

Recollections 15

The futility of books

The wind was picking up out to sea. The cove was becoming the perfect spot for the accumulation of endless sets of perfect waves. The world was black and white.

Jacob could not remember ever being able to surf very well, but now he felt calm and confident. He would walk to the sea and stand with only his feet in the water, board in hand and allow the fingerless hands of the world most powerful and inevitable force stroke his feet. She would caress the tired and dried-out skin between his toes. No more walking in the hot sun with cruel humidity teasing him. He was at the shores of the ocean again and his horrors would soon be just a memory.

Just then Jacob felt someone else was with him as he walked towards the breaking waves across the fine grey sand. And, for a moment he was worried that the presence would ruin this delightful moment. Jacob turned to see and saw that it was Becky walking beside him and reaching out for his hand. She was smiling his favourite smile.

Then they were in the water, laughing and playing in the whites and greys of their colourless heaven. The scenes played out like snippets of film edited and taped together.

Highlights.

They swam after each other, first one then the other. They splashed and attempted to surf the waves using only their bodies, picking up speed as the largest wave in the set came looming in.

Jacob held Becky in the shallows and spun her around before happily stumbling and the two of them fell into the absence of blue.

The scenes changed then to snapshots of passion on the sand. Lovers, rolling around carelessly forgetting their laughter for the words of passion, they seized each other and delighted in their basic attraction. At times their seriousness caused them to laugh again and drew out the moments until they were finished making pictures and were lying again in real-time on the sand dozing in the warm white sun. They drifted off into contentment, almost.

As Jacob felt himself slipping into deep sleep listening to the sound of his heart beating rhythmically and enjoying the feel of Becky's hand as she softly ran her fingers over his face, he felt a note of uncertainly ringing out inside of him.

Was there something wrong? He thought, no. He could still feel the sun and Becky's fingers as they jointly caressed his face and wasn't his heart beating slowly and with comfortable regularity?

Jacob listened to his heart, because it was that that was the source of his anxiety. It *was* beating regularly, he was sure about that, but it wasn't the slow thud that the heart of a resting body would normally command. It was growing faster, and what was even more disconcerting, getting louder.

The sound of his heart became a raging thunder in his ears. It is the panic, he thought. If I relax myself my heart will subside, but it wouldn't. Even when Jacob drew as much calm into himself as he could, the beating of his panicking heart was causing enormous vibrations all through his body. It was a wrecking ball rhythmically thumping on the ground, with no hope of getting through but growing more insistent anyway. He felt that surely it would burst before he realised that there was a second beat, one quicker but not quite as loud. This was the sound of his heart, but what of that other noise; the earthshaking thunderous banging that was consuming everything?

Then he knew what he was hearing. He'd been stupid to think of it as the helpless pounding of his heart, it was obvious that there was much purpose in it. It was a giant's footfall, pounding, faster and louder as the monster grew closer to him. It was the approach of something powerful.

There were other sounds immersed in the beating, voices wailing and a rushing hum, but all of them kept rhythm together as the tempo grew. Jacob made a second mistake in thinking it was the creature from the market place that was causing the noise that continued to hammer at his mind, but it was not. The monster that had taken over his body for that brief moment was definitely present among the cumulative noises of the greater and more inevitable whole. The creature was getting closer with every moment and although he would have to face it before his nightmares were over. Now was not the time.

The beating grew from a low thudding into the high pitched droning of a giant humming bird, the tone rose again and the noise became a continuous screech that assailed Jacob's soul until he was sure that it would explode as it vibrated like a fine crystal that was being tested for flaws by a hundred thousand dog whistles.

Then it stopped.

Jacob waited for an explosion. He waited to be struck down. He waited for a conclusion. He opened his eyes again to the black and white world he'd been revelling in so recently, barely squinting at first and then wide open, startled and staring. Nothing happened. He could still feel the warmth of the sun on his skin and the weight of Becky on his arm. He turned to look at her and she was gone. He felt that he should have been horrified to see her replaced by a rotting corpse. But it seemed right to look upon her in such a state, after all, wasn't that what they all were headed for? He felt no interest in the remains of his lover and he turned back to the beach.

And, there it was, standing in the sand. It was the message that had been pounding at the door of his consciousness, attempting to wake Jacob from his contented dreams. Three large black letters standing typed in the air but also somehow sitting in the sand.

Run

Run, the letters read, and Jacob woke up.

**

Jacob lay stunned for a few moments, was covered in sweat and panting in his hostel room. His eyes were still closed but he knew that he was awake.

Run.

He could still feel the horrible pounding as if it were more than just a dream. He could still see the letters erected on the beach.

Run.

He fully intended to, but the insistence of the message was forgotten for a brief moment when Jacob felt something brushing his cheek and his right eyelid. He could still be dreaming. Could it be Becky's hand?

Slowly, dreading what he might see, Jacob opened his left eye. As he'd hoped the world was in colour and he could see the room fan turning on its lowest setting. He could also feel his bruises and the aches from his encounter with Rajette the day before.

The dream he'd just had was still lingering, Jacob could still feel something brushing his cheek, and for a moment he could have sworn that a finger had brushed against his chin. It gave him quite a start and with as much dread as before, Jacob slowly opened his right eye, only to see another eyeball looking into his with intimacy.

The Sunburst Lizard had become restless in early morning light and had climbed the bedspread for a look around coming to rest on Jacobs face. Jacob's skin was warm and the Lizard felt comfortable there where he'd fallen asleep again and had dreamed in his tiny way about a rough surface beneath his belly. And now his bed had come alive and the Sunburst Lizard was preparing to scamper away if there was even the slightest movement.

Jacob screamed in fright. The eyeball disappeared and he could feel something moving down his face and onto his chest and he almost jumped out of his skin. In a second he was crouched on top of the bed, scanning the room for some ghastly creature from hell or something else equally ridiculous. His nerves were still jangling from the vision he'd had in his sleep and the feel of the lizard crawling across his face made Jacob's skin do the same and for a few minutes he was afraid to budge.

Run.

And the urgency of his need to escape returned.

Human nature is a powerful and sometimes ghastly thing. But there are advantages to being a human being. Humans can cope. When there are dangers all around, the mind prioritises them for us. It makes us so horribly afraid of the most pressing menace and leaves us without enough alarm to spend on the lesser dangers. They are filed away somewhere. Possibly under the heading:

These things will not matter if you don't escape the other.

A lizard in his room was nothing compared to Rajette being on the loose and Rajette was a pussycat when compared to the thing in the market place. All of them were a speck of dust when measured against the hugeness of destiny and its enormous momentum.

So Jacob was able to rise from his bed as his fear of staying there and being caught by whatever it was that was stronger than all his other misgivings put together. He didn't catch sight of the Sunburst Lizard as he packed his bags in a hurry, but Sunburst managed to clamber into a briefly stationary shoe and was bundled away with the rest of Jacob's gear. The reptile felt comfortable to be once more amongst the now familiar surroundings amongst the luggage. Things seemed to be as they should be. In as far as a lizard can fathom the idea.

Jacob finished packing and rushed out the door. He was relieved to be outdoors once more. He felt like there were more places to run. He intended to flee Kumasi at once, probably to the north. Then he remembered Becky was arriving today; later today. There was something else too. What was it?

It was Thursday.

'Fuck,' said Jacob. He was due to meet the Kumasi scholar, wassisname? Bolin; living in the palace grounds. Was there any point in continuing with the book now? Jacob wasn't sure. He'd been reading for the last week that Joshua was a real man and not perfect. He was sure that if he had the time to study the writings more completely he'd be able to discern some sort of truth about the man, his personality, not just his actions. The small amount of study he had been allowed told him one thing at the very least. Even if Joshua wasn't perfect, he was strong but not without fear. He would fear danger but would be able to face it. Because he believed he knew something that very few people would ever know. He had faith. It was more than just faith in good too. Joshua knew something; the way a person knows he has eyes without checking.

Jacob felt as though he did not have the same faith, but he could grow to understand it at the very least. And, now with his life in danger, he was more alive than he'd ever been, if it was going to be over for him soon, then he was going to try and understand why, before he was finished. He was going to have to see what the Arab and the American were keeping from him. In the only place he had the chance.

The decision was made and Jacob stopped a car in the street and ordered the driver to go directly to the Manhyia palace. He would have to find time to pick up whatever was waiting for him there and give it a once over, twice over if possible, before he went to meet Becky.

At least they'd be together again. That would be something.

Run

Then they could get the fuck out of here.

***

Rajette watched Jacob leave the hostel. He was divided in thought. One part of him was embarrassed at his unprofessional behaviour in the café the day before. It told him to walk over there and finish the boy now, get him out of the way and hide his shame. The other part was pleading for caution. Jacob had broken through Rajette's strict code of conduct. Never do anything for nothing. It had nearly cost him a lot of money. And, that was inexcusable.

But there was another problem. The Irish had laughed in his face in an insulting but primarily confident manner. He was not turning out to be the easy prey that Rajette had first assumed. The Arab had not questioned his self-contrived belief system in a long time.

Rajette's mother had tried to turn him around when he was a young man.

'He married a monkey for its money. The money went, and the monkey stayed a monkey,' she had said, but Rajette had laughed at this.

'Ha, my mother! You tell me that I should think of my deeds in the future. But you do not understand me well enough,' He leaned across the table and leered at her, a great insult. 'I would have the monkey salted and save myself from spending the money,' His mother knew then the truth when she looked in his eyes and saw no way back for her Rajette, her sweet boy. None.

That was the day Rajette's mother gave up. She still let him stay in her house, eat her food, sleep for free in the back room, but from that day on she never complained or lectured him again. She watched him come and go with his hooligan friends and said nothing. She had withdrawn her guidance from his undeserving life and he'd missed it ever since.

Across the road Jacob was getting into a cab and Rajette had to curb his thoughts and concentrate once more on his transaction. All he really wanted to do was kill the little Irish bastard and forget about the documents. But Marshall had been both, most insistent, and generous, so the job was back on, Rajette could kill Jacob another time as he had the Italian. It pleased him to realise it while he put the black Mercedes in gear and pulled away from the side of the road. He did not bother to hide the fact that he was following Jacob. It seemed that he was going to need intimidation after all. Well, he was plenty good at that.

As the Mercedes and the taxi drove through the streets the two men passed within earshot of the Islamic call to prayer as it piped thinly from a speaker suspended over the pavement and it drew their attention to the gathering of men there. They were kneeling to begin their prayer and they were all facing Mecca, which lay roughly northeast as far as either Jacob or Rajette could tell.

Jacob, drawn as he was again to the sound of the call, was wondering if he could remember the five pillars of Islam.

There was one about Ramadan anyway, and another about giving alms to the poor, that was two. A true believer in Islam also had to visit Mecca one day, thus earning the name Hajj and number four had something to do with praying at the allotted times during the day. Jacob thought it was six times but wasn't sure. What was the fifth one? Oh, actually it was the first.

'There is none worthy of worship save Allah and Muhammad is the Messenger of Allah,' said Rajette to himself driving in the engineered silence of his expensive vehicle. He had learned this and great many other passages from the Quran when he was a boy. Later in life, laughing and joking with his thuggish friends, most of them too stupid to realise their blasphemy, Rajette had bastardised his own version of the pillars.

It made him smile to think of them now, as it often did. He'd felt so clever that day. And, what the others hadn't realised was that he had meant every word. Sometimes he liked to count them back in his head to pass the time. He did so now, but for a different reason.

5 – During Ramadan, fast only from chastity and abstinence.

    4 – During your life you must travel to the most craven district in the most loathsome cities of the world. Only then can you become a true believer.

    3 – Give Alms to no one.

    2 – Observe the prayers of others, for while they pray their businesses and homes, their wives and children, are left unattended.

& Number 1 - There is no god but Money and Rajette is its prophet.

First Jacob and then Rajette came to a halt in the square out front of the Manhyia Palace, the home of the Asantethene, the king of chiefs. Jacob got out of the car and watched as a peacock walked past him strutting and casting about, feather sheathed. He turned and saw the black Mercedes across the square. Rajette was leaning against the passenger door, watching, expressionless.

Jacob felt a prickling of fear along the back of his neck. If he was going to have this man follow him around, even beat him on occasion; then, Jacob was going to have to deal with it. Granted the beating had been a result of Jacob openly scorning the psycho but all that proved was that he could get to him. And,

250

if that annoyed the little lunatic, then there was plenty more to come.

Everyone has skills and one of Jacob's was the ability to be really and truly annoying. It was not always the most useful talent and it had never appeared on his CV, but he could drive you insane if you let him. Yesterday, Rajette had let him do it with nothing more than a laugh. So, starting with today and for as long as the little prick was going to shadow him Jacob was going to piss him off in any way he could. It was a good idea, if he was brave enough and Jacob felt that there was no time like the present. Start as you mean to go on, and all that.

So, before walking through the gates and into the palace grounds, Jacob smiled happily across the square, even waving a little to add to the insult. Then he turned and was gone, the smiling quickly leaving his face.

That may have been really stupid, he thought.

Across the square, fuming and impotent for now, Rajette was in full agreement.

***

Out on the Accra to Kumasi road in the back of a Trotro, which had been converted, incidentally, from a Nissan Hi-ace, twenty people bounced and rattled in silence towards their journeys end. Becky was staring out intent on the Rainy Forest surrounding them, her eyes frozen as she attempted to look casually out of the window like the others. Yet in reality, she was blind.

If you'd ever sat across from someone on a train as they actually look out at the scenery and chanced a quick look at their face, you may have noticed that their eyes are constantly flicking from side to side as they attempt to form a complete picture from the quickly renewing images. It is the kind of thing that you could never spot in yourself because, as soon as you attempt to do so, you find that you're looking at the window not through it.

Becky was doing neither. Her eyes were glazed in fear and she tried to avoid looking over her shoulder at the blurred wretched smelling creature sat next to her. There was no lush scenery in her perception. Instead, she looked out the window into her own white-hot panic. There was something very wrong with the man in the seat next to her.

Some of this wrongness was obvious. The blood and open sores all over his body, easily seen through the jagged rips in his clothing. The smell of rotting, a putrid odour she had only smelled once before after returning from a long trip to find she'd "left out" some chicken and forgotten it. But what was more wrong was the way the other passengers had decided to blatantly ignore his obvious abnormality.

Becky was sure that any one of these things would serve to alarm a person even only remotely in touch with reality. But it was something else that troubled her most.

She recognised him.

She recognised him, and it frightened her so much she wanted to scream and shout and cry. But she was trapped and all she could do was hope that he remained the way he was now and didn't recognise her too.

As soon as Leavon had taken his seat beside her he was overcome by an astounding weariness. He wished he could stay awake for long enough to feed off some of the passengers on the bus but, Mon Dieu! He was tired. Leavon had smiled and relaxed, his human side needed rest and he was finally able to give in to it, only because this time, it didn't mean giving up. Leavon was back on track again. His purpose had been restored.

Let the weak human side of him rest. He supposed that he deserved it.

Not for the first or second time since beginning his journey, Leavon faced something that that he'd never experienced before. It was a very human and gratifying thing to understand the joy of respite after undergoing uncontrollable events such as he had done. He was relieved.

Ah! Wonderful and sweet relief swept over him. Suddenly he was jaded, but that was ok, he was heading again in the right direction and he felt that he could rest a while and still ensure that the other passengers didn't notice him. Leavon could remember the shape of their minds from the airport and he felt he could fool them with a blurred image of him using only the tiniest bit of consciousness whilst the rest of him slept. Leavon rested his arms on the seat in front of him and leaned his head forward onto them. Who knew that tiredness could effect such contentment? He was fast asleep and snoring in seconds.

So Becky was trapped there, waiting and wondering when he would awaken, or if he would wake at all? This was definitely the creature from her vision. When she was standing with Pooja on the top of the cliff, she'd seen him and he had attempted to take her life. *He* was the very thing that Becky had sought to save Jacob from, the original reason she had come to Ghana.

There had to be something she could do? But Becky was petrified. To make it worse she had trouble seeing him. One moment he was there and the next she felt as though she had just woken from a bad dream and that there was nothing beside her. Becky realised that this was probably why the Trotro hadn't turned into a panicked fracas already. The other passengers couldn't see him properly, or maybe they could but their minds were trying not to realise it. He was disgusting, all bloody and sores, but only out of the corner of your eye. Directly he was blurred into the others.

253

Camouflaged, something was making him difficult to comprehend, but she was able to see him in a sort of shifting patchy way. Two nights ago in the Capital Hotel when she'd seen him in a vision, Becky had been scared to death, but not for herself, for Jacob. Now she was sitting beside the "thing" and although it was very selfish and unlike her, Becky regretted coming to Africa. Was she stupid? What did she think she could do against a creature that was able to warp the minds of a whole van full of people, and in such a wretched state too? Nothing, she guessed.

Another miracle of human nature is curiosity and from curiosity comes boredom. If the human mind, especially one as sharp as Becky's is not presented with anything new or different after a certain period of time then it will begin to loose interest. Some people, like Jacob, will disappear off into a fantasy world, and others, like Becky, will become restless.

The phrase "face your fears" is born from this simple human trait. Even when a person has a deadly fear of something, it can be diminished in potency by merely facing up to it. In simple terms, we bore ourselves with it. Change it from a deadly thing into an ordinary thing, or as far towards ordinary as it can get. There are millions of exceptions of course and bearing in mind that you are of reasonable intelligence there is no need for a list. Lion juggling would be close to the top of it though, and self-mutilating blindfolded surgery. Neither of these would be very easy to get used to but there is always someone somewhere who will give it a go.

It was according to this theory that Becky's panic and dread began to fade. Though nothing had changed, she was still registering the same horrors as before; there was some sort of vicious demon sitting in the chair beside her, but after a couple of hours of fear without recourse, Becky restless nature began to take control. So what if she'd made a mistake by coming here? She was here now and about to die; so why not try something? She weighed her options.

A) She could stay put, wait until they got to Kumasi and attempt to get out of the Trotro before the "thing" beside her woke up. It was a risky option and one that would leave her helpless, should anything wake him.

B) The toilet/ Sick option. She could ask the driver to stop so she could go for a whiz, or puke. Puke would be better because she could ask for a seat beside the door when she came back and would stand a better chance of surviving if the demon... Leavon woke up before they reached Kumasi.

B-2) same as option B but she could take her chances on the road and not get back into the bus. That way... Leavon could wake up whenever he wanted and she wouldn't be there.

Or

C) She could kill Leavon while he slept. This was doubtful as Becky was unsure how to kill a human, so killing... Leavon, whatever he was, was probably well outside her capabilities.

Becky continued to look out the window as she examined these three and a half options and it was obvious which one would... Leavon! That was his name; but where had she heard it? A few minutes ago she's been thinking of him as an "it" or the "thing".

Becky felt a movement behind her and at once she felt sick to her stomach. She turned slowly eyes closed to see if it was true. When she was finally facing him her bottom lip was already quivering with future tears. She didn't want to look but she had to. She had never been so frightened in all her life.

'Hello,' said Leavon, his face cracked open in a bloodied semi-toothed smile, 'I know you,' A hand caked in dried blood touched her hair and he smiled again in realisation. 'You know him, don't you?' Becky was shivering under his touch. When his hand moved suddenly she yelped in shock and burst into tears, wailing as she did so. Becky wasn't the type of girl to break down so easily, but it was too much for her. His eyes seemed to glow yellow as his maniac smile dripped blood and broken tooth on her kakied lap. One of the other passengers managed to shake the blurring effect of Leavon long enough to notice Becky and get some idea of what was going on. His name was Paul and the reason he could see reality was that he was in terrible pain, and had been for months.

Paul Osauwo was a farmer on his way to the hospital in Kumasi. He heard the white-girl's crying and looked at her over the shoulder of the non-descript man, obviously the cause of her plight.

'Ssss!' said Paul, tapping the man on the shoulder with his infected hand, 'Adɛn?' he exclaimed, why? But the man didn't turn around. Instead Paul felt a cold soothing sensation suffuse his bad hand, giving him his first relief from its ache in such a very long time.

It was two months since Paul had been helping a neighbour in the village move a large tree trunk to the roadside. It had been a muddy day and he'd slipped before they got the tree clear of the road. Struggling under the weight Paul had barely managed to not fall under the trunk, but the weighty block of timber had come down heavily on his hand. It hurt horribly at the time, but the neighbour helped him retrieve his hand and the fingers, although they were bleeding and had begun to swell immediately, seemed to be surprisingly intact. There were no broken bones and the pain was that a large dosage of Palm Wine would not cure.

Unfortunately the trees were plagued with hardwood termites. And, though it can't be said that the termite eggs had managed to hatch and prosper under the skin of Paul's healed fingers, it *is* true that they attempted to do so, but died in their effort, and began to rot.

So now, two months later, Paul's thumb and forefinger were huge. The thumb was like a large Passion Fruit with nail, and the figure was like a bratwurst sausage with knuckles. Paul told his son Kwasi that he'd stolen two fingers from a giant and stuck them on his hand and Kwasi had been proud as a chief ever since.

Over time the pain became really excruciating and Paul was plagued by a throbbing soreness that never went away. It had been driving him mad until he'd decided to go to the big city to have it fixed

So there he was, on the wrong Trotro.

Paul felt a cold soothing sensation suffuse his bad hand spreading from the strange man's shoulder and into his body. Oh it was blissful! Paul forgot immediately what was happening and just sat there with his hand on Leavon's shoulder the life seeping out of him and the hellish throbbing completely gone. Paul looked at his massive fingers again and grinned sleepily.

Like a giant's fingers, he thought and then he was gone.

Just like the Hartebeest, the Leopard, a French car owner, and indirectly, a Ghanaian Fetish priest. Leavon's total was rising.

Leavon was feeling in charge and refreshed. He'd heard the girls mind, had seen himself pictured in it. She was the one who'd been in his dream two days before. She was the one that would lead him to the sky-blue soul. Lead him to... Jacob that was his name. Aside from his confidence Leavon did wonder whether he was being tested. After all, he'd experienced so much pain in the last twenty-four hours. He knew now how pathetic and uncertain it was to be human and though he had been taking his newfound freedom for granted he would change that from now on and take care of what is left of his body.

From Becky's mind Leavon as learning the truth of the chase. His thoughts had attached the phrase "writer" to the sky-blue soul, Jacob. And, Leavon had remembered. There was a ritual. A ritual that wasn't complete. What was missing, Leavon wasn't sure, but he was sure that Jacob knew. This was why the sky-blue was in Kumasi, and why Leavon was going there. He was more determined now than before to catch the man. He would catch him all right.

Even the earth was trying to stop him, he would. He was being toyed with, pushed around, and punished all over again. Well it wasn't going to happen like that. He was going to have to play the game as it was set down in front of him. But he was going to find a way to cheat. He would work out what this was all leading to and *he* was going to be the one to benefit, not some foolish blue-souled human who obviously had no idea why he'd been marked, walking around with knowledge in his head that Leavon vitally craved.

For now Leavon was still remembering what it was Michael De Rhy had been after, but he was going to take charge at some point and Becky was a step towards that point. She'd happened along at the perfect time and even if it was contrived and extremely human, he was going to use her. She was going to be his bait.

He looked at her quivering tear-stained face. She was afraid of him, but he was sure he could see some hardness there too. He would have to watch that. He looked into her shocked wet eyes and he spoke to her.

'So, you've been looking for me haven't you,' he said, 'where is the ghost?' Becky forgot her fear for a second.

'Ghost?' she asked.

'The one who helped you, you thought she was alive, didn't you?' Ah!' Leavon found this very amusing. The Indian woman was nothing more than a memory of a person, kept alive by a curse. It was strange that the creatures on earth were given the gift of true life, but they couldn't spot those with an obvious lack of it.

'Where are you going?' Leavon asked, and spotting a stubborn intention in her he added, 'exactly.'

'Kumasi,' she said.

'To meet him?'

'Wh…'

'To meet him?'

'Yes.'

'Is he meeting you at the end of this car's journey?'

'Yes?'

'Yes? Good. At the station?'

'What does he look like?' Becky wanted so much to put Leavon off, to give Jacob a chance to escape. But all she had to do was to think of him, for the creature to know, and she couldn't stop herself.

'Merci,' said Leavon. And, reaching forward he placed his hand on her forehead. Feelings of horror flooded through her, consciousness without form, chaos and stomach churning loneliness. Becky couldn't deal with it. She wretched and felt the sick rise up inside her and into her mouth but as quick as the convulsion was, Leavon was fast enough to grab her head with one hand and cover her mouth with the other.

'Swallow it,' he said and watched her do it. It was mildly entertaining to watch her expression but the real joy came in feeling her shame and embarrassment when finally, she decided to give in rather than choke. Her pride would help him to, he was sure. Leavon removed his hand from her mouth.

'Now you will tell me everything you know about…?' He waited patiently as she caught his meaning and her breath.

'Jacob,' she said, subdued, now ashamed.

'Jacob, yes,' Leavon smiled sure she was telling the truth, a string of flesh hung from his top lip. Becky had two urges, one to pull on the string as though it were melted cheese and the other urged her to forget it and tell him everything. She opened her mouth and spilled her guts. It was eleven forty-five.

***

Betrayal and the futility of books

After a brief meeting with the Kumasi scribe, a man who seemed to be more hurry that person, Jacob found himself alone in a dusty reading room at the back of an immense library. He began to sweat. It was eleven forty-five. He had only just been left and already he felt uncomfortable in the presence of so many books. They cheapened him and scorning his contribution to their numbers. The weight of the sweat and pretension that filled their pages told him no, you are in no way special, others have written and died writing, and most are never read, fewer respected, less remembered.

Futility

This is the real reason that he could never have refused the project, even though it had now turned into an horrific undertaking. Jacob never entered large libraries and even preferred to buy his books online. On one occasion he'd been escorted from Eason's bookshop on O'Connell Street in Dublin, dizzy and tearstained, unable to accept that he could never read them all or that he couldn't even understand half of them.

But this was his only chance to see what he'd been surrendering to Marshall and Rajette, so he would have to abide the hulking presence of so many seldom-read pages. He knew that what he was looking for would have something to do with

260

Joshua, and knew also that it had little to do with the Lord as a soldier or even his escapades as a young man. It was becoming obvious that the writings that Jacob had been allowed access to were nothing but a load and a smokescreen only. But hidden amongst these papers were other documents. Pieces of writing that people were prepared to kill for, that an unearthly creature would also be after. Jacob had to see them for himself, even with Rajette outside, waiting for him with obvious intentions, he must at least find out what he was up against. Although he suspected that there was little he could do by way of stopping it, stopping it, stopping it.

The creature that had held his mind in the market place was still more than a memory. It was impossible that it could be anything else. There was no time for that now. He had to read fast.

Jacob sat down and physically shook out his trepidation, or the eeps, as he usually called them. The eeps were when you not only had the hair on the back of your neck thing, but the squirmy spine thing too, and the urge to hunch you shoulders up and down, like the creeps but more physical.

Jacob leafed through the sheaf of papers. He was in a hurry and almost, actually really, expected Rajette to burst in the door at any moment. He had to get through it all, find something out. All of this needed reason, didn't it?

As he went down through, he was immediately frustrated. It all seemed the same…

Except

This had to be it. It was in the form of a folded scroll, not too tattered and not really new, but it stuck out from the others and had surprisingly little writing on it. It said

There is no way back, all that there is, is this life.
First we are nothing, and then we are potential life.
We are born then and for a brief and wondrous period we
become human and die.
And with our full potential realised we become part of the
physical earth.
The Earth spends us also as we spent the life we once had.
Then we are free of the physical.
We become the sun, and with the sun we become the stars.
And, with that, we are the Universe.

This is what you have cheapened your humanity for. There is no
way back.

Jacob read it over and over. More riddles! But in it there was a
load crystal chime of truth, it made sense to him, somehow. It
made him feel, something. The words burned into him. This is
what they were looking for, but why? What question could
possibly have such an answer? Something like… What happens
after I die? Or, can I come back to life? He didn't know, or expect
to find out any time soon. But he would have to sometime.

Right now, Becky was on her way and he had to meet her. If he
could find no reason in anything that was happening to him, at
least he could always find reason in her. So he left.

***

At twelve o'clock Jacob was back in convoy with Rajette and
heading for the Lorry Park at the southern end of Kumasi. After

leaving the palace and a singularly strange old librarian named Kwasi, Jacob was keen to get a move on. Becky had said twelve-ish and that's what it was. As the two cars pulled up to the lorry park Jacob wondered how he'd be able to meet Becky. If she had her mobile on it would make things easier but he'd tried it and, it wasn't.

~

For that last ten minutes Becky had been alternating between relief and dread. The rainforest had changed into scattered farmland and settlements, rows of houses, billboards, other traffic, pedestrians, and finally shops. There would be no more waiting, very soon the Trotro would come to a halt and it would be over. She didn't feel brave anymore. Contemplating escape was no longer a realistic option. Leavon's raw anger and negative destructive presence had scraped her heart clean of hope. Becky could see the crowded Lorry park straight ahead and was thankful at least that she would be dead soon and hopefully without too much pain.

~

Jacob paid the taxi driver and got out, hefting his rucksack. The Lorry Park was packed with people, but as he neared Jacob saw that there was always room for one more, especially a white one. Before he'd even crossed the road he was being hailed by various hangers on.

'Obroni, where are you going?'

'Where does the Accra bus come?' he asked the nearest. A man grabbed him and tried to drag him away saying.

'You want to go to Accra I show you!' But Jacob had learned from Nana Adjua and called a young boy to him.

'Small boy, come here!' The boy did so and Jacob showed him 5,000 Cedis, which was far too much but was worth it to see the child beam. 'You take me to where the bus from Accra stops, yes? I don't want to go to Accra. I want to meet a friend coming from Accra. Ok?' The boy seemed to understand. After all Jacob had furnished the request with expansive gestures. The boy answered. 'You friend come from Accra?'

'Yes!' Said Jacob, 'Where?' he asked. And the boy took him by the hand and led him toward the other end of the Park. As they took off, Jacob noticed that Rajette was only a few feet behind him, watching and following. Jacob supposed that now, with any semblance of stealth completely dispelled, there was no point in the Arab taking the risk of loosing his charge for the sake of being inconspicuous. As he moved off, Rajette moved off too always a few feet behind, brushing off the clinging fainéants without a side-wards glance.

As they approached the receiving end of the Lorry Park, the blue Trotro pulled in and drove by Jacob, who just then looked up to see Becky, her face haggard and her eyes looking beyond him as the van drove by. Jacob felt the hairs stand up on the back of his neck. It could have been nerves but Jacob was almost positive that he'd sensed something wrong when he'd seen his lover's face, just then. He stopped for a moment picturing again how Becky had been looking forlornly out the window, ignoring the small boy tugging at his sleeve. Automatically Jacob freed himself from the boy and held out the 5,000 Cedis, both disappeared.

Jacob was sure he'd seen someone else looking out of the window beside Becky, which wasn't strange. But something else was; he recognised the other but hadn't seen his face, damn, he couldn't place it.

It took Becky more than a few seconds to realise that she'd just been looking directly at Jacob, fortune scorned and Leavon had no such trouble. As soon as the Trotro pulled into the lorry park he'd spotted the sky blue soul and rose to his feet. He began to go wild. Mad to be let of the van, he screeched in rage and started to climb over the other passengers to get to the door. The Trotro was packed with people and Leavon's outburst only served to more firmly block the exit with their panicky bodies.

Realising this, Leavon started to beat the side window in anger and frustration, landing blows on Becky and several other helpless witnesses the frame weakening as he battered the glass.

All Becky could do was scream; surely he would kill them all in this blind panic, but it was not blind. He was beating the window for a reason, which became clear to her when she felt the large pane she'd been pressed against begin to give way as Leavon pummelled.

Jacob watched with fearful curiosity as the blue van rocked back and forward. No doubt something horrible was happening inside the Trotro, but it looked momentarily like a comedy skit, where a couple are having sex in a car or van, and from the outside all the viewer sees is an exaggerated rocking. Jacob would have laughed, had it not been for the screeching and the desperate cries of the passengers.

Oh no, he though, Becky's in there. Then it came to him. The face he'd seen staring out the window over Becky's shoulder. It was somehow familiar all right. It was he, the one from the market place, the terror that Jacob was running from, only a few yards away. He'd come to kill him, or worse. The panic was almost too much, and tasted of copper.

Jacob was torn. He had to escape. But Becky, she was still in there yet despite himself Jacob cowered away from the Trotro. Each step he took in the opposite direction made it more difficult to reverse. He tottered at his cowardice and stumbled over someone behind him in his haste to get away. It was Rajette.

Rajette had been following the boy through the crowd and had seen the blue van pull up. He saw Jacob stop and had then been distracted by the commotion in the Trotro; until of course, Jacob back peddled into him and the two of them were eye-to-eye. It didn't last long though. There was a collective gasp from the assembled crowd as the side window of the Trotro came free and smashed on the ground. A moment later a white girl was thrown out followed by a horribly injured man who bellowed.

For a moment Rajette thought that the man was a victim of whatever had been going on inside the Trotro but it didn't take long for him to realise that the man-shaped bloody mass *was* what was going on. When the bloodied man got to his feet he grabbed the girl by the scruff of the neck and looked around quickly, stopping at Rajette. The Arab nearly pissed himself in shock. It was looking right at him, stalking towards him, roaring with fury, at him!

'Run Jacob, Run!' screamed the girl as she was propelled along. Rajette turned to see Jacob's back disappearing away with the rest of the crowd.

'Coward!' He screamed after the boy and turned around, right into the embodiment of anger that Leavon had become.

Rajette knew in that moment that he'd been mistaken. The girl's screams and the creatures not seeming to see him as it closed-in, made it obvious that it was after Jacob and not he. All Rajette needed to do was get out of the way and he would be safe.

But Rajette had never been one to get out of someone's way so he squared himself up to Leavon, and took the furious creature by surprise. Leavon had been so intent on Jacob that he hadn't even noticed the little man until he had already ran into him and was falling backwards, shocked.

Leavon quickly refocused his anger and howled at the brazen human who had dared to bar his way, but not for long.

Rajette wasn't only brazen he was impetuous. The little man saw his chance, reached into his jacket, and took out his gun. In a heartbeat he'd pressed the trigger twice. Leavon couldn't believe he was actually being attacked.

The impact of the bullets barely even stuttered his movement and he regained his feet quickly. Rising quickly Leavon grabbed Rajette by the neck. He was about to free the Arab from his neurosis for good when he noticed that Becky had disappeared from his side. Not only that, but he couldn't see Jacob any more either. There was a huge body of people moving together away from the lorry park and the sky-blue soul could be anywhere among them.

No! He couldn't be allowed to escape.

What happened next is difficult to describe. In simple terms Leavon threw Rajette to one side and let out a hideous roar, which stunned the crowd into temporary silence and inaction. That description lacks weight however. Whatever images the words "hideous roar" form in your mind, scrap them. Forget immediately whatever it was you thought of first and picture instead a bomb going off in a crowded area. Watch the people hit the ground for cover and let out little cowardly yelps of fear as the sound reverberates, not off the walls of the buildings, but instead, of the barriers in their minds. A protective barricade that is learned as a normal person grows into adulthood. This was something that they were not equipped to hear, to cope with, or to understand. Leavon's scream was unnatural and left them, as would the detonation of a bomb, stunned, bewildered, traumatised, and staggering.

The shell-shocked multitude began to crawl around as if stricken by invisible shrapnel. The victims of the blast were unsure which way they were going or even, what they were doing before they heard the scream. Now they just wobbled around, sat down in the street or just looked at each other confusion. All were rendered inactive.

All, but two.

Neither Jacob nor Becky was shocked to hear Leavon leashed that unearthly holler. Yet another thing that should fill them with fear, but they were already bursting. They knew what was behind them and it didn't make any difference what sound it made. They only knew that they should escape. Becky caught up with Jacob when he turned to see if he was being followed. He hardly acknowledged her at all. He did wait though, or pause to be more accurate. As soon as she got within two yards of him he began to sprint again. He was terrified, chivalry be damned.

Becky hardly noticed anyway, she'd been given the tiniest grain of a dot of hope and she didn't care who was running with her. She was running and that was all that mattered.

They ran out of the lorry park and up towards the railway bridge. On, over, and up to Adum hill they went, leaving increasingly less startled gawkers in their wake.

As he ran Jacob thought how surprising it was that something monumental can happen in one place and be completely missed and inconsequential only minutes away. People stared at the two running whites but simply because of their colour and nothing to do with the incident they had only recently escaped. A few of the onlookers smiled, poked each other and pointed. It was as though Jacob and Becky was a couple of Zebras, trotting up the hill, such was the Ghanaians reaction.

Well they won't be so amused in a minute when *he* comes by, Becky thought. They'd better stay out of *his* way. Jacob was having similar thoughts. Leavon was behind them. How close? Jacob couldn't tell. He was willing to go on running until he felt the monsters hand upon his shoulder and even then he wouldn't look back.

***

Men and women walk and run. They jog and trot, limp and shuffle. Children frolic and skip and men and women can do that to, if they are so inclined. These are ways a human gets around. There are plenty of other words for moving around on our feet, some of them quite fancy and others dull. Amble is both. In many stories a character has stepped out for a jaunt or a bit of legwork. Saunter has always been a caddish favourite and strutting denotes a certain confidence. But to march, pace, parade or stride, these involve the inclusion of something else.

Purpose.

Leavon was marching, striding quickly and with dreadful purpose. Imagine a machine of metal teeth and sharp edges, filled with grit, grinding mechanically with increasing speed. He was a horrific sight, powering out of the lorry park and up the hill sweeping anyone unlucky enough out of his way. The incline only necessitated an increase in power, resulting in a quicker pace. This was what the word stalking really means. There is a control, focus and intent. Leavon stalked on.

~

Rajette was in awe of it. He'd named money his god on several occasions, never truly in jest. An entity of human form had never held any reverence for him. No universal harmony came from being human, there was nothing blessed about it. The flesh was weak and unworthy of devotion. Rajette had always felt this way, even before he learned how weak it really was in his own strong and merciless grasp.

269

The man… thing, he'd just seen was certainly not weak. He/It was powerful and uncompromising. Divine.

Rajette suffered a delusion then. Like a drunken fool being lured into the marshes by impious sirens, he saw something that wasn't there and followed Leavon. He looked at the demon and saw perfection. Its flesh was destroyed but his purpose and will were strong enough to ignore the fact and ruthless enough to drive him forward. Rajette wanted the creature to be his god. He wanted to have this power and to worship a being that could make this possible. This was the real key to the Arab's existence.

Rajette was Rajette because he despised weakness in others, but mostly he was afraid of his own. He punished in others what he knew to be part of himself. Weak, weak, weak, weak, oh how he longed to be able to overcome his fragile humanity. It was a dread that haunted him always, that his flesh would fail him, that he would be too… human.

And, now there was Leavon. The closest thing to a god, he was sure that he would ever see.

'Malik!' (Master, angel, king), Rajette whispered after Leavon, 'I am Abdul-Matin from this day on. Lead me,' and the disillusioned thug began to jog after the already disappearing figure of his newly taken master. Rajette: A big bag of fools.

***

At the top of Adum hill Jacob and Becky found that their strength was beginning to flag. It had been a very long day for Becky, and, to be truthful, Jacob was out of shape. Whatever the shape was supposed to be he definitely wasn't in it.

He had run a marathon once and remembered quite clearly how he'd broken through the pain barrier and found that

270

he had some hidden source of fuel on which he could rely to drive him onwards. But now he could only run for ten minutes before something like a seizure was induced. Even with the extra impetus of Leavon closing behind, Jacob wanted to stop by the roadside, take off his backpack, and maybe have a Fanta. But afraid of any delay this would cause, he managed to stumble on, lagging behind Becky whose own engine was running low.

When Becky made to take a right turn, Jacob continued on for a moment before his weary brain stopped him and turned him around. He could see all the ways back down the steep hill. Where the hell was it?

Jacob had to squint a bit, but once he caught sight of him, Leavon became impossible to miss. The demon was eating up the distance between them with long powerful strides, his broken body glowing yellow in the evening sun.

Jacob remembered a horror movie with the living dead groaning and moving slowly after their prey. It was a pity that Leavon wasn't moving like a Zombie and the effect of such firmness and decrepitude was not so terrifying.

It was mesmerising. Jacob couldn't turn away and resume his flight. Leavon seemed too inevitable for that. Jacob felt that it would be much wiser just to wait until the creature reached him and them it would be over.

It came to the point where Jacob could almost see clearly into Leavon's eyes, so close he had become. It was only then that Jacob realised what was happening to him.

'Oh shit,' he said. I'm finished, he thought. Leavon was too close now, a hundred metres at most down the hill. Jacob could hear Becky screaming his name, but he couldn't look away. Leavon's gaze held him fast. He was rooted; frozen, stuck… you get it.

**

271

Kwame Adamfo was exactly one hour late leaving the STC bus station on Adum hill. This was a regular occurrence. Actually the last three times he'd left for Tamale, Kwame had been at least two hours late in departing. The tourists, whites mostly, were always raging and fussing over this, but they should know better.

'Hey,' he used to say, 'this is Africa. Nobody is in such a big hurry here. Let all the people with tickets get on the bus before we leave, aha!' For his bus you needed to buy the tickets in advance, so when it was leaving all the seats were sold and Kwame felt that it was only right that he wait for his passengers to arrive.

This STC government-funded bus was always full of people, because although it was often late in departing, it nearly always reached its destination, which was good enough for most Ghanaians. Plus, the long distance bus had a TV-Video system that a lot of its passengers didn't even have in their homes. If he had known the phrase, Kwame could have called it "Classy" and he was exactly the type of man who would.

So, only one hour late, driving a bus with only a couple of seats free and a new movie from America called "Tremors" about to start, Kwame turned the corner of station road and headed up the hill. At least he would have, if he'd been able. As it was Kwame was forced to slam on the breaks to avoid running over a white man and woman who were standing in the middle of the road.

Kwame was of course unsurprised by this and opened the doors to let his last two passengers on. The other passengers settled quickly after a minimum of complaining, as most of them knew also that late arrivals were a regular occurrence of the well travelled of them it was a relief to see the bus filled completely as this promised that there would be no opportunity for the driver to pick someone up at the roadside once they got out of town, just to make himself a little extra. Thankfully, the bus would now barrel along at full speed all the way to Tamale.

***

As soon as the bus blocked his view Jacob dropped out of Leavon's eyes and back into his own mind, which became quite close geographically to the pumping and firing of an eight-litre bus engine. There was a high-pitched screech and a moment later he found that his nose was only a breath away from the window of the thing. Becky who had been pulling at his arm was as bewildered as he when the driver beckoned them to come aboard. And, with zero fuss, they did.

Kwame closed the door and continued down the road. For a moment there he thought that the white man was going to put his hand on the windscreen for protection; thankfully he hadn't. The driver was very proud of his spotless windows and mirrors and he would have had to get out and clean any handprints off. Otherwise they would have annoyed him all the way north. His two mirrors were also beautifully shined and polished. Kwame was checking them again when he noticed another man running along behind them. This man however was obviously not a passenger, as he was too dirty and tattered looking to afford a ticket.

Kwame put his foot to the floor and put a little more distance between them but the man kept running. The driver also thought that he heard screaming or shouting, but the movie had started and he couldn't be sure. The bus arrived at the Kejetia roundabout, found it strangely free of traffic, drove right through to the main road beyond and accelerated steadily north. For another few minutes Kwame divided his attention between the road and the crazy street-man running behind them.

'Kwasia!' The driver said to himself as the bus finally left the madman behind.

There were all sorts of lunatics in the world.

Recollections 16

With all that we have forgotten

It was not long before Nana Adjua heard about the strange occurrences in the lorry park. One of her boys, Jeff, came running to her with a message from her nephew, who owned three Trotros that drove to Cape Coast and back again. Her nephews name was called John after the prophet and he had told Jeff to tell Nana that a demon had attacked the people in the lorry park, hurting many.

As soon as she heard it Nana was sure that this demon was the one that was chasing Jacob, the one she had met in the Market Place for a brief moment when he took control of the poor boys body. She felt a shiver of fear and shamefully, a wave of relief that she had asked Jacob to leave her home. She realised that he must be out there now facing that creature and she knew that she must do something to help.

'Jeff!' Nana turned to Jeff who was running after a lizard as it scurried across the yard, laughing and recoiling in excited fear whenever the creature changed direction. Such a simple and happy child, neither he nor his brothers deserved to have to face such a thing as the devil she had encountered through Jacob.

'Ɛna?' he responded, not taking his eyes off the lizard and then gasping in delight as it ran up the wall and stopped there out of his reach doing fierce push-ups.

'Go inside and help Dorcas with the food,' Nana ordered.

'Daabi' (No) Jeff replied.

'Go,' she warned, playfully wagging her finger.

'Daabi,' said Jeff, smiling through mock stubbornness.

'Jeff?' Nana asked and moved towards him suddenly and the boy took off like a light, into the kitchen. Nana laughed at his excited yelping. She had to do this job herself. She could not risk any of her children being caught in this.

Nana left the compound in the direction of the lorry park hoping to find some sign of Jacob's demon pursuer. It wasn't going to be hard.

***

Rajette was tired and sweating copiously. For the last hour he'd been walking along the road after the god-man who was still nowhere in sight. He couldn't decide whether he should go back and get the car or continue on down the deserted road.

Notions were beginning to enter his head. Notions like, 'What in hell are you doing?' and, 'If you catch up with him, then what?' 'Shut up,' he told himself. 'Do you think that you will ever discover something in your life with more meaning than this? These things don't happen.'

Not, *don't happen to people like me*! They just don't happen, to anyone.

Rajette was able to speak these words inwards because he finally felt something happening inside of him. Meanings and explanations were arriving like the gathering of a great crowd to a stall in a busy market place. A new product was on sale now and it seemed to have to be able to cater of all ones existential needs. He had to find out what was going to happen next.

Like Jacob Rajette was feeling that the whole world was a swamp and that sometimes a great flooding would occur. The flood caused fast flowing channels through the marshlands, which in turn produce eddies and offshoots that cause the entire swamp

276

to change its shape and depth. On the outer reaches away from the speed of the flowing river, the effects were always more subtle but nonetheless profound. Amidst the rapids there was nothing but impermanence and change.

The Palestinian felt that he was now at the edge of the great change. He could turn around and walk away, or he could hold onto his nose and jump in. There was never really any doubt as to what Rajette would do.

He picked up the pace.

~

Three miles ahead of Rajette, Leavon had finally lost his battle with biology. The bus carrying Jacob and Becky was long since a shadow and his chances of catching it on foot were atomic, as in the opposite of enormous.

Sheer willpower can account for a lot in this world and had already supplied far more power than a common man could Marshall. Leavon was once again a victim of his lack of training as a human. Women and men are born with a sense of their own humanity. Possibly some are less aware of it than others of course but it is there nonetheless, and it is responsible for all of our flinches and our fretting. Leavon wasn't in possession of this faculty and it had run him truly into the ground.

For the third time Leavon had hit the bottom.

First the Car Crash, where his back had been shattered and his flesh almost torn from his body. Then after meeting the Fetish priest in the jungle, Leavon had crawled away with only his determination and the foreboding vision of a flooded valley and a mysterious priest, to push him onward. And now, after the most recent incident in the lorry park, Leavon was dilapidated and empty with even his will completely tapped out. Now he was dying by the roadside like a dog or a chicken freshly run over by a passing car, the only difference being that someone would have picked up the chicken by now.

Leavon's body was the hull of a sunken ship. Perfect once and then dashed against the rocks or an iceberg, or in this case a tree. He had hit the bottom and settled for a spell on the edge of a larger abyss before loosing his purchase and plummeting downwards onto the deceptive safety of an outcropping of rock. Now he had broken through and was sinking freely into the blackening void.

The once proud and haughty figure of human possession was now a crumpled scarecrow quickly accumulating dust at the side of the dry African road. There was nothing left of Leavon now to keep the broken soft machine alive and the spirit of vengeance had sunk completely.

It was then that, quite quietly and without struggle, the flickering spirit of an old man took over Leavon's features once again. The body's original owner was returned to witness the final expiration.

Monsieur Michael De Rhy looked up at the sun as it beat him down into the earth. It was inhumane and indifferent and it cared noting that he had failed now in two attempts at life. He'd tried so hard to be real and good, and found no comfort in that. Then given a chance to relive his past he took hold of it in his aging grasp. Who could blame him, he thought.

Yet alas, he had been deceived, and had merely allowed another to control his second chance. Now there would be no more time or wondering. No attempts left at staving off the years. He had not spent his second lifetime wisely. If only he had waited for his goons to deliver the final scroll. He could have avoided all of this. But he had been too impatient. An old man like him should have known that there was nothing to be gained from haste.

Michael looked up at the sky from his fading spirit and begged for an answer. Why had he been born into this evil soul? Could he not be saved?

The question lingered there above him in the clear blue sky. And for a moment he felt that it could be so, that he could indeed be saved. God had been testing him and now the trials would end. In what; redemption?

But even as he thought it he could feel the presence of Leavon inside of him, rising up against his own pleas. No, God would not spare him. So Michael continued to stare up at the blazing sun, not bothering to shield his eyes. His sight began to fade as though there were clouds floating across the sun. It grew darker and he felt the rest of his strength ebb into the earth below him.

'Fuck you,' he told god, as his heart was growing cold. There was a tear upon his cheek, which confused him in a far-off way, as he was not a man for tears. He felt another slide down and drop onto the ground.

Was he crying?

As the seconds passed he found that his was soaking wet, only then did he realise that it was raining.

That was it. Their last moment and Leavon and Michael looked out from the same body at the same time and enjoyed the feel of the huge raindrops on his face and the warmth of the sun as it made the storm clouds glow with its muffled light.

For a moment they were able to share the view without conflict before it was blocked altogether, but not by the Sun, and not by death. Michael/Leavon felt a hand touch his face and a voice said:

'Malik?' And Leavon reacted quickly.

***

Weather or Not

All over West Africa Storms were in full fury. In Guinea-Bissau the people were forced to run from their homes and into those more solid, or simply into the deep forest to take cover from a gigantic hurricane. In three days time the high-pressure ridge was set to push a massive cloudbank ahead of it inland rather than along the coast, causing one giant storm after another as it headed for southern Mali. It was unnatural for the weather to act this way. It was as though the rules had been changed by nature and she was test-driving a new car. One that was more powerful and much less human friendly than anything she had previously owned.

Maybe it was her turn to do some damage? Goodness knows she deserved it.

The strange weather caused wild speculation amongst the West African communities that lay in the path of the storms. The people felt that it was going to keep moving inland and their crops needed protecting, but that meteorologists shook their heads and told the people that it was merely a freak occurrence, a knock on effect due to a slight change in the Earth's position caused by the recent Tsunami and the series of earthquakes along the Pacific Rim.

'It will blow itself out,' they said.

'And what if it doesn't?' asked the people who were looking out of there windows.

All over West Africa clouds were quickly gathering, regardless of Science and weather or not they were allowed.

So the skies were practicing their scariest faces without the permission of the apes. Bless.

***

Nana Adjua reached the lorry park not long after it returned to normal. Once again the nature of humans had taken over, and people had resumed their touting, hawking and boarding, desperately trying to pretend nothing had happened focusing on what was normal in their lives and skipping by the abnormal. But Nana Adjua knew these people, almost all of them and most by name. They were hiding badly the turmoil that the creature had wrecked inside them. Thoughtfully she spent the next hour talking to them. A ticket-seller here, an ice-water girl there, she made her way through the crowd learning by indirect conversation what she needed to understand.

'Have you been busy today?' Nana asked one particular woman with a basket of assorted wares balancing on her head. The woman immediately flicked a glance up Adum hill before shaking her head and saying. 'Not busy, not busy.'

This confirmed what Nana had gleaned from a couple of other furtive glances. The evil spirit had climbed Adum hill most likely chasing Jacob. Nana gathered herself and began the climb, following in Becky, Jacob, and Leavon as quickly as she could but dreading what she might find. She grew more frightened with each step and was now sure that there would not be a satisfactory solution to her part in this story. The story of her life had so far taken many volumes to complete and perhaps it was now time for the end to finally come. The *why* of it was not clear as of yet, but it would be, soon.

281

***

At the side of the road that lead north out of Kumasi, Rajette was crouched over Leavon in a posture of great discomfort. When he had reached down to his master's aid he had been full of concern for the man-god that lay fading before him. But now Rajette was full of despair and gone were the allusions of before.

The Arab's hand touched Leavon's face only a brief moment before it would have been safe to do so and the demon had caught a hold of him. Only just, but caught him all the same. Now Leavon burrowed into Rajette's soul as deeply as he could, until his hand was around the other's heart and he held the Palestinian under his control. The demon's soul would not slip away now. He had life for as long as Rajette kept his. Leavon looked into the frightened little man's eyes and spoke.

'Who are you?'

'Rajette.'

'You think that I am a God.'

'No, I thought you were…' Rajette tried to pull away from the broken figure but it felt as though he was pulling his heart out of his chest. 'What are you doing to me?' he cried and tried again to pull away, but the pain worsened as Leavon squeezed a touch harder to make him understand.

'Pick me up, fool,' Leavon ordered. And Rajette, shaking from the strain of what could only be equated to a mild heart attack, hefted Leavon into the air. The body was heavy and it reeked of rotten flesh and blood causing Rajette to gag and stumble. 'Do not drop me,' He was warned as he felt the heat of Leavon's ethereal fingers grasped around his core.

The little Arab managed to straighten himself and turn around. He settled Leavon's weight against his chest, leaned back, and began to head towards Kumasi with a staggering gait that looked as shambolic as it must have felt. Rajette's mind was under a similar strain. These changes of direction were unnatural and had sharp effect on the man. Salvation had turned into damnation and degradation had resulted from epiphany.

***

While Nana Adjua climbed Adum hill from the Lorry Park she began to think about Jacob and wonder why he was chosen for such a dangerous trial. It could be that the young man was cursed. Surely that was the only explanation for his being pursued by such a powerful unearthly spirit? It was as a mystery as the feeling she had that she was about to die, but it was a fact nonetheless, a sad fact.

Nana came to the top of the hill where the children of Islam were performing their midday prayer whilst at the same as Rajette was rounding the corner ten feet away with the body of Leavon grasped tightly in his arms. Forgetting her troubles Nana rushed to his aid, seeing only a tired man carrying a victim of some ghastly accident.

'Here, let me help you,' she said to Rajette as he drew near.

'No,' said Rajette not wanting Leavon to tug on his heart again.

'Let her,' Leavon whispered and he released Rajette who immediately lay down his burden and backed away, slowly inching down the street. Nana noticed this as she leaned over Leavon's body and inquired.

'Where are you going?' she asked growing suspicious. 'What happened to this man?' She could see the fear in the little man's eyes and imagined all sorts of reasons for it. Maybe he had caused the accident? Or, maybe it was such thing. Accidents can be such terribly sudden things, Nana thought. When a person, or a child is one moment be walking or playing in the street, happily laughing with his friends and strutting about as small boys do, she always thought of children with regard to her beautiful boys. They were such a joy to behold when they were playing happily and it always made Nana smile to see it.

Faintly, Nana Adjua became aware that her thoughts had drifted away from what she was supposed to doing, although she couldn't remember what that was. She looked down at the face of the man that was lying in her lap and realised weakly that he was not an accident victim at all. This man was some sort of devil. His eyes gleamed in delight as he drank from her. She knew that it was a horrible thing but she couldn't feel it. This was the creature that she'd spoken to before, in the market place, through Jacob, but Nana was powerless to escape him now. All that she could do was stare in passive horror as it gleefully took her life.

'You were staring at me nigger woman?' Leavon leered experiencing a surge of life force that, up to now, he had thought impossible. This old one was filled with the energy of a thousand lives. She was joined to so many others and had enriched them the same. A small piece of Leavon, the part that was Michael De Rhy's, felt guilty at depriving the world of such a powerful and needed individual. Leavon quickly suppressed the weak old man's thoughts. *You are not a part of me anymore*, Leavon told himself, *I am beyond guilt*.

This seemed to work and Leavon continued to feed himself off the old woman, but there was still a tiny remnant of him that was unsure, that needed to be ignored. He felt his body being restored to levels that he had not contained since leaving France. He was revitalised, whole again, renewed.

~

Nana Adjua looked up into the ecstatic eyes of her killer as her senses dimmed to nil and her mind began to shut down. As she

284

faded she found that she could see the demon for who he was, for the part he played in the ultimate story.

The creature had begun as an opposite of humanity, had scorned its weaknesses, but now he was being restored he would value his life so much more. Leavon would be unable to deny his soul. And, when he and Jacob finally met, something very important and crucial to the existence of the world would occur and reality would be reset.

This new reality would include a lot more harmony and children and happiness and no more beings like Leavon, Nana hoped. All she could see for him was failure, but there was a potent possibility he could succeed and Nana's last wish was that Leavon would not.

God bless him, she prayed as the colours started to fade, bless him, but let him burn. Burn forever.

***

Along the road from the spot where Leavon was just finishing with Nana Adjua, eleven Children of Islam were prostrate, facing eastwards towards Mecca, chanting and recounting their vows to Mohammad and Allah with nothing but piece in their hearts and pious joy on their faces.

Abdul-Hakim (servant of the wise one) always felt a sense of excitement when he heard the call to prayer. Usually he was expecting it, as it was, in many ways, an ingrained routine, but sometimes he was surprised by it and it warmed his heart like an unanticipated gift. Today Abdul-Hakim had almost been late. Firstly, a woman had come in and begun to order a huge selection of foreign foods for a birthday party and she did not seem to mind their expensive nature. This alone would have kept many of Abdul-Hakim's less devoted colleagues from attending public prayers with their brothers and maybe even stop them praying altogether. Abdul-Hakim however was careful not to mind what other people were doing. He wanted to worship with his brothers and he did not care who saw him or who didn't.

Abdul-Hakim was not a pompous man. He was a good man.

There were ten other such men praying speaking to Allah when Leavon caught up with Rajette and stopped directly opposite of their grouping of prayer mats. Not all ten of the men were as honest-and-true as Abdul-Hakim, but out of them only Boulos could have been described as "bad", and then only by someone who knew his inner thoughts. Even then, Boulos badness only stretched as far as petty thievery and large amounts of spite towards his contemporaries.

These eleven men, like a growing number of others, didn't deserve what was about to happen to them. Events occur, time passes, and everything changes but change itself.

***

Rajette came to a sullen hopeless stop when he felt Leavon's hand take a firm grasp of his shoulder. He had only walked away in the vain hope that the nightmare might disappear if he turned from it, or perhaps it would forget him and pursue someone else, but when he felt Leavon's presence a couple of yards behind him, was sure that that he could very easily just lie down and give up and let the demon have his way.

Leavon spun Rajette around and addressed him with a vigour he had not been able to summon for days.

'You,' he shouted, 'where are you going?' He threw his head back and mocked the little Arab. 'I thought that I was your God eh? I thought you had chosen to call me… Malik wasn't it?' Leavon shook him and Rajette let him do it.

'Just take me as well and end this,' Rajette asked him flatly, 'you don't need me any more.'

'No I don't,' said Leavon lifting Rajette of his feet and bringing them face to face, 'goodbye,' Leavon was about to do with Rajette as he had done with Nana Adjua when he realised something. It was a new idea, to him.

The last few days he had done nothing but force himself on this world. It was time he used his consciousness for something more than trying to kill himself. He lowered Rajette and said.

'Where is the sky-blue soul?' Rajette thought about pretending he didn't know but decided against it.

'He left on an STC bus. I could check at the station but I think, by the size of it that it was a long distance bus, headed out of the country. The buses go through customs much quicker than private cars. If we do not catch them in Ghana they will escape into Burkina Faso and it will be difficult to track them,' Rajette's words made Leavon grow increasingly angry as they reared up against him. He had made so many mistakes and wasted so much time that it infuriated him to think of his shortcomings. He had such power at his command and yet a simple human had nearly brought about his downfall. Actually, it was he, Leavon, who had almost destroyed his self. The other was only a man, a mere human who had escaped him easily.

'It has been many hours since they left,' said Rajette. 'We will not catch him in Ghana,' This was the final shovel of coal for Leavon, and now that he had the power to do so, the flames of his anger rose high and towered infernally over them both and he reacted badly.

In short, he lost it.

Lost it

The phrase is often used when describing a loss of temper in a person who has, up to now, managed to keep calm and unphased. Mostly, in the experience of an average man or woman going about their daily affairs and engaging in the usual amount of banter and gossip, solicited and unsolicited alike, "lost it" is normally the term of choice for someone who is looking for a way to, either excuse their own irrational behaviour, or ridicule the behaviour of another. The term *lost it* is hardly used with pure honesty and depending on your frame of reference, almost never accurately.

Examples of "lost it's" include:
      'He handed me the parking ticket and I just lost it!'
      'You wouldn't believe what happened; she just lost it, over nothing!'
And sometimes,
      'If you do that one more time, I'm gonna loose it,' See note:

Note: "Gonna loose it" being "lost it" with futuristic implications.

 The point being that "lost it" would not normally include any of the actions with which Leavon managed to redefine the phrase.

This is how you really loose it!

~

Leaving Rajette to drop to the ground, Leavon crossed the road in a rage and walked directly into the midst of the praying Islamic men. Their worshipping was an insult to Leavon's ears and, at that moment in time and he felt that if there was a god in heaven controlling or watching everything happening on earth, then it must be laughing at the blundering idiot it was seeing right now. Impotent in the face of minimal adversity, with power to spare he was too stupid to defeat one human target, too thick-headed to adapt to his surroundings and win out in he end.

At that time more than any other, Leavon hated humans. Their stupid civilisations, their imbecilic rules designed to give the less capable a chance to co-exist with their betters. He felt disgusted that he had to live inside a human body, feeling human emotions and subject to their irrational beliefs.

Only one of the worshippers saw when Leavon first came amongst them. Boulos, who hadn't really being praying anyway, looked up from greedily eying Abdul-Hakim's wristwatch to see the figure of a terrifying man looming over the prayers. He only managed a stifled squeal before Leavon seized him by the throat and easily separated the man's surprised head from his dangling body. And, that was just the beginning.

It only took Leavon five minutes to kill and dismember the group of men. An account of each would be gratuitous and unnecessary.

But.

Abdul-Hakim looked up into the face of his attacker. A moment ago he'd felt the warm touch of Allah upon his face whilst he was praying. Often Abdul-Hakim had longed for this feeling to arrive, never doubting its existence, always waiting and praying, but now when finally he'd felt the tender presence of god upon his soul, it had given him great sorrow.

As the noise caused by Leavon's frenzy awoke Abdul-Hakim from his reverence, he had felt saddened and confused by the experience, until he opened his eyes to see Leavon stalking towards him. God was saddened by what would surely be the end of Abdul-Hakim's life. Abdul knew this instinctively. The world would be robbed of a truly noble soul, at a time when every noble Arab was needed to show those of other faiths that the worshiping of Allah is not beholden only unto the crazed, but enjoyed and rejoiced in by many such as Abdul-Hakim.

Abdul-Hakim saw all of this and felt once more the same great sorrow, but like Nana Adjua he believed enough in the larger battle to trust in God and believe in the ultimate victory of good.

Leavon reached the eleventh man with a tightened desperate grimace still stretched over his face. He reached down to tear the man's head off his shoulders and found cause to hesitate momentarily.

Abdul-Hakim looked up into the face of his attacker and smiled.

'It is not every time that the clay pot survives,' he said, hoping to impart his resignation to the one that was about to destroy him. Leavon was confused not only by the man's words but also by the peaceful countenance in someone who knew his life was about to end. It made him feel uncomfortable and unsophisticated, Out of his dept once more amongst these complicated animals. Leavon's anger, briefly forgotten, returned with added fury.

'After this life,' he said to Abdul-Hakim with spite in his heart and raising his hand to strike the final blow, 'there is nothing,' And Leavon brought his hand down across the Muslim's face with great force, breaking his neck and killing him dead.

Leavon watched as the body slumped to the ground, empty, and he felt a mixture of shame and triumph. Just before the killing blow landed, he had witnessed the uncertainty his words had caused the human, and the dread it fuelled.

Abdul-Hakim's last moments were not peaceful and filled with hope as such a man deserved. His life ended in doubt. Perhaps there was nothing else, maybe this was it? Some believe that instead of heaven or hell, the final emotion that a person feels, their final thought becomes the summation of their life, which they go on feeling and thinking for all eternity. Forever caught in the final passion, a broken record skipping perpetually in its last groove.

It is a disturbing theory when the last thoughts of a torture victim or a suicide are taken into account. How horrible. On the plus side though, it is darkly humorous when you picture the last thoughts of the woman who was bitten on the ass by a poisonous spider while using the toilet, or the old man who died in the throws of passion with his teenage wife. Tee hee, very nice for him, the face of her. Ha-ha.

From the other side of the road Rajette was experiencing, from a theological point of view, a certain amount of cognitive dissonance. Or, from a layman's point of view, he didn't know what to do with himself. He just watched as Leavon vented his frustration on the group of men who had done nothing but pray peacefully. Even he, the dealer of many a deathblow or shot, had always had a reason for doing so. It was never such a random and meaningless display as the one that had just occurred.

Maybe all violence was random and meaningless? Rajette wasn't comfortable with the thought. It just seemed fairer for all concerned when there was money involved. After all, to have someone pay for your death meant that your demise, though costly, was more favourable than your continued existence. So, what? If somebody wanted you dead, you were worth killing?

It sounded stupid now that Rajette thought about it. A moment ago he'd been ready to die, actually hoping to. But now in the face of superior maliciousness, Rajette was forced to question his life's work and was suddenly not overly eager to finish this life for fear of what may be made of him in the next.

~

What next? Sated and more composed than he had been for many days, Leavon walked from amongst the bodies of the eleven children of Islam. In the distance he could hear the sound of police sirens coming from the vans filled with less than eager officers. They seemed to be just around the corner but would only arrive at the scene just after the slaughter had ceased and the instigator had barely slipped through their fingers.

Unfortunate.

They would be on time to show off their new machine guns and roughly question a couple of shady looking bystanders in the hope of being led in the wrong direction. Away from a man who was efficient enough to destroy nearly a dozen men in minutes, cruel enough to kill a harmless old woman, although her boys would tell you different. Powerful enough to cause havoc amongst thousands in the Lorry Park and all this before strolling off down the road and sitting into a black Mercedes with driver at the ready.

No, the police knew that this was a man that should not be confronted. This sort of thing smelled of the Secret Service and the Secret Service, though it had been officially "disbanded" four years before, were people that the citizens of Ghana would not forget quickly, no sir. So it was best to forget that the car had sped out of Kumasi headed north, best to overlook the fact that the registration number had been taken in connection with a disturbance in Vic Baboo's café earlier.

The Car, its driver and its murderous passenger were long gone now. The police would pick up the pieces as they always did. The people of Kumasi, like all Ghanaians, like all Africans, would have to move on and deal once more with the unfairness of their society. It was not the first time Africans had died at the hands of the white man, although it had been a long time since his methods were so crude.

292

***

At eight o'clock that night after paying a suspicious fee and suffering the tedium and inefficiency of the baggage search, Jacob and Becky were finally permitted, along with their fellow passengers, to cross the border out of Ghana and into Burkina Faso. Behind them the border was closing and the night guards were arriving, Jacob felt as he looked back at the barricades and fencing, felt that their presence should probably make him feel better in his mind, but addled and existing somewhere beyond fright, he remembered enough of the events of the last week to ensure that he wouldn't allow any measly construction of wood and wire to fool him into thinking that he was anyway safer than before.

Tall walls, small measures.

The impending nature of Leavon's pursuit wore upon the couple. They had not spoken since boarding the bus although they had often tried. Once, when it became obvious that Leavon was not going to catch them on foot, the two turned to each other, both of them trying to say something but not knowing what; and Becky felt that she was still too shaken to risk saying anything for fear of bursting into tears. Jacob, though he would not admit it, was as close to precipitation as she. Becky was as tough as he was and they both knew it and was now at her bravest, travelling around the world, experiencing everything and shying away from nothing. Jacob on the other hand, had grown soft in the years following his original success and was a word away from giving up his pretension of it.

Yet there were ghosts in his head that buoyed him. Nana Adjua, Joshua, his father and Daniel Candelli, all of their faces were clear in his mind. They would not let him give up and smoke to him in memory.

'You will miss your adventurous side Jacob,' Daniel Candelli, the dead old writer had said when he saw Jacob spend great sums of money on items of comfort. 'You will get soft and fat,' and here the Italian would grab a hold of his own belly with both hands and say. 'Then, like me, you will find that you are carrying the bastard child of Don Spaghetti Carbonara!' But Jacob would just laugh and say something clever like:

'I see, and if he finds out you ate it, he will be most upset… Aha-ha.'

The truth was that Jacob would have gladly given up everything to be half the writer Candelli was, would have taken the stomach as a fitting price too, if it allowed him to be much more like the Italian.

Look where it has led me, Jacob said to himself. Who was he to re-present the teachings of the Bible to a new generation? It was a Job that Daniel Candelli couldn't do… and this thought led to another, much secreted one. Maria had almost whispered her suspicions into Jacob's unheeding ear. He had suspected since the beginning, when all of this cloak and dagger began in Rome that there was something bigger happening that he was far too obtuse to realise. He hadn't believed it possible at first, but now?

What did he believe now? What did he know now?

Daniel Candelli had attempted to write, to re-write what many believed was the greatest story known to man. He had failed. It was so obvious, the flowers at his hotel, the phone call that fell upon stoned ears. The Saki story about the sweet voiced bird, Jacob realised that it had always been obvious.

Demon folk pious and snug, but the prisoner falling broken, rang out the great bell.

Jacob had already edited the sentence

Even now, sitting in the back of an overnight coach from Kumasi to Ouagadougou, a demon of some sort surely following close behind, Jacob found it hard to admit. Be a man! He told himself.

You knew, and you wanted to try anyway. You wanted to succeed where he had failed. It didn't matter why he had failed, what he had found out, or what he had been trying to say to you with the clues he had left behind. You wanted to be like him, be better than him. Well look at you now. Soon you'll be as dead as he is, killed by that thing, or the little assassin Rajette who was probably the one who took the shot that ended your only friend's life.

And what will happen then? Nothing; that's what you've always thought. But that passage about the universe. It smacks so clearly of the truth. No religion, just biology and physics, but beautiful and poetic, like real reasons.

Jacob had never before believed in God or religious doctrine. Too many exalted humans. And now, because of that he was in a unique position of hope. Before there had been nothing, now there was reason.

To be alive, that was the thing, the miracle in itself.

And what about an afterlife, beyond eternity in the universe?

How greedy.

Recollections 17

Accumulator

Ouagadougou (Wagga-doo-goo) was a city that lay in wait. Jacob and Becky observed that on the streets the people lacked the high energy and positive spirit that had sometimes tried their patience in Ghana but would usually be associated with any West African city.

The two distressed lovers walked along Les Rue of the French styled capital unmolested and un-hawked at, for the first time since their separate arrivals in the region. But instead of causing relief, the lethargic nature of Burkina's capital unsettled them both. They felt that the city knew they were on the run and was waiting to see would happen to them. It was something that they had in common.

At this time of year and at this time of day, most Burkinabes were indoors. Out of the sun and away from the Sahara wind they stayed, if they could, the heat being the second excuse to that searing air. The wind is called the Harmattan, and it scorches everything in its path as it transports tiny particles of heated sand across Burkina Faso, through the streets of towns or cities like Ouagadougou, into the back of a person's throat and even into their stomachs. Sometimes, when the mistake is made, of drinking water that has not been properly treated, it is joked that afterwards the Harmattan goes on a little further that that.

It was here that Jacob and Becky finally broke their silence and spoke their first words to each other in almost two days. They walked from the Bus Station to stretch their legs and wondered whether to stay in town or to continue onwards.

'Well?' Jacob said looking expectantly at Becky, 'do we keep going?'

'Do we have a choice?'

'Yes,' Jacob answered. 'We can go to Bobo-Djulasso, or Ouahigouya, or we can go to Mali... Or, we can go straight to the airport and get the fuck out of here!' Jacob tried a smile but the face he made would have driven a child to nightmares. He could feel the tightness in his face and Becky could see the lack of humour behind it but was proud of him for the attempt. Then she remembered.

'I have no passport,' she said, 'it was in my bag, on the roof of...' There was no need to continue.

'I'm tired,' Jacob told Becky, he felt it in his bones. Nervous energy had been bleeding his body dry for two days now; he could hardly keep his eyes open.

'Can we afford to rest?' Becky asked. Jacob nodded, fearfully understanding what she meant. He remembered the dream he'd had in Kumasi before Leavon's arrival and his possession in the market.

'I think that I'll know when he's near,' he told Becky. 'The night before you came to Kumasi, I knew he was coming. Except, I didn't know what it meant. Now I do,' they both did.

'Is he nearby now?' asked Becky and Jacob shook his head; 'I'm tired too.'

'I don't feel anything,'

'Then let's go into town and find somewhere to sleep and then a phone. We can call the embassy and get out of here as soon as possible.'

'Ok,' said Jacob, 'Perfect,' it was about as good a plan as any he'd thought of. Actually, he hadn't thought of any.

Decided, Jacob and Becky walked towards a grouping of green and white Peugeot taxis across the Rue Naba Tanga. Before they came to the cars they stopped and regarded each other. Becky reached out her hand for his and Jacob took it.

'I love you, you know?' He said to reassure her. Becky was as relieved as he was that he had spoken the words. It was difficult to think how they could ever just exist together without constantly reminding each other of what they were going through.

'I know,' said Becky, 'I love you too,' and that was enough for the moment. With some of their usual spirit restored they hopped into the nearest taxi and asked for a hostel that was clean and popular with tourists. This wasn't a time for "off the beaten track" travelling. It was time for bed and time for dreams. The only problem with dreams is that they can quickly become nightmares.

***

Inside the black Mercedes, Rajette had begun to fear for his life. It was not that he hadn't feared for his life before this. It was simply that each time he feared for his life and he felt that his nerves would shatter the normality of driving and the sheer impossibility of continuing the emotion indefinitely lulled him for a while into stupor. Until, he realised where he was and before he remembered whom he was with. Then Rajette would begin to freak out and fear once more for his life.

This most recent of times had been triggered by their arrival at the border crossing just north of the town of Bolgatanga and, more importantly for the Leavon fuming in the back seat, still far behind Jacob and on Ghanaian soil.

'What do you mean we can not go further?' Leavon demanded, his lips just touching Rajette's ear he was so close. 'You will go,' he added, his hand gripping the little Palestinians neck, 'where I tell you to go!' Leavon tightened his grasp and

Rajette struggled to emit a word that would stop his head being separated from his body.

'ChkLook!' he exclaimed pointing to the gates where a group of guards were forming, eyeballing the expensive car, wondering whether they should approach the vehicle. Luckily for Rajette, they waited.

Leavon released the pressure on Rajette's windpipe and tried to think differently. So far just killing everything in his way had not turned out to be a beneficial means to completing his task. He must think more clearly and use the humans against themselves, only then would he be able to catch up with the sky-blue soul. Once he did that, he would be free to do as he pleased.

'If we try and drive through they will shoot,' tried the little man who was once again beginning to fear for his life, this time at the hands of some trigger-happy guards, 'We should wait until the morning; get some rest. When the boarder opens we'll just pass through, no problems,' Rajette added.

Leavon thought about this. The little weasel-slave had a point, he could feel that he was tired and after the suffering he had endured from mistreating his body previously, Leavon was inclined to submit to Rajette's wishes. As well as this, the half-man had just had an idea. It was, he felt, time to approach matters using his mind rather than abusing his body.

'Ok,' he told Rajette, 'drive back down the road. Pull over. Then we will sleep.'

Rajette did as he was told and ten minutes later the two had settled down to sleep in the black Mercedes. The Palestinian would spend the night starting awake at every imagined sound, with many waves of fright and dread filled glances cast over his worried shoulders Whereas Leavon would sleep quite soundly, as he had work to do, people to meet, nightmares to visit.

From the north, being carried by the enraged Harmattan, like a convoy of salt being shipped in the most unusual manner, a blanket sandstorm came rolling southwards across the Sahara. In an eerily tidy line the waves of billowing sand surged towards Timbuktu where the already empty streets were deathly still and calm. There was so little movement in the air that the inhabitants of this once prosperous city became concerned and began to squint out into the desert looking for the coming storm and questioning any Touareg that came into the city from the north.

Unfortunately there was little news. Everyone to the north of the city was either trapped by the storm or cut off by it. Either way, in ten hours time the advancing tide of sand and air would engulf Timbuktu. Then they would know all about it.

***

Becky lay awake in the darkness drinking from a tin camping mug and watching Jacob dream fitfully beside her. What had changed between them, she didn't know. Two days ago she'd left London to be at his side. She had felt that he would need her, and the woman Pooja, who had shown her a method of esoteric meditation that had seemed so real, it had been as if she had stepped backwards in time and into her memory of her and Jacob's first days. It was there in that meditation that Becky had first met Leavon and he had immediately tried to kill her, there and then, inside her own mind and memory.

But Becky had come to Ghana anyway, to help Jacob. To help him do what? Die? So far she had not been any use to him, or herself. She'd led the demon directly to her lover's doorstep and now the two of them were on the run and most likely going to find out what it had felt like when Leavon took all those other people and creatures and sucked the life out of them. What did it feel like to just slip away like that? Becky was in no hurry to find out.

Maybe she wasn't meant to be here, she was almost certain that if she left now, crept out into the night, found somewhere to stay, and hid there that Jacob would not come looking for her. She would be free of the ordeal for good with no further part to play. She could probably have an emergency passport sent to her within a couple of days and then she could be off. And Jacob, a man she had only known for two weeks? He would be left on his own, to fend. She didn't owe him anything. He would understand. She could leave. It was completely possible.

Yes…

But she did have a part to play, she was positive of that. Jacob wasn't as strong as he thought. She knew it and he would never give up. She knew that too. There was something that he needed to do, face this Leavon. And, without her he would not be able to do it. Maybe she was supposed to bring trouble down upon him; he needed a kick in the arse anyway. Perhaps she was just that. A kick in the behind to drive him on; a reason to keep going; because he loved her and she loved him and she knew that he had something important to accomplish. It must have something to do with the book he was writing. He was meant to find something out. Maybe he already had. Becky looked again at the single sheet of paper that Jacob had told her was certainly the key to all that was happening to them. It was important, a deep statement about existence that scared Becky when she read it. She had always believed in heaven and hell, not some universal dumping ground. Or maybe she'd misunderstood. That could be why Jacob was the one, because he *did* understand it. Or, had the ability to at least.

Becky reached over and stroked Jacob's cheek. It was important, the opposition alone proved that. She was going to help Jacob do what he had to do and now Becky felt a moment of guilty sadness come over her, even if it was dying.

Like her dad would say. You're here now, so you may as well make the tea!
She put out the light and settled into sleep. She wasn't going anywhere.

***

The second trial of the Sunburst lizard

Quietly in the night tongue flicking fiercely, the bruised and weakened body of the Sunburst Lizard flopped, pushed and scrambled his way out of Jacob's rucksack. It took Sunburst five rests to make it to the bumpy floor and when he did the worn creature endured almost an hour's silent suffering before he was able to move again.

The events of the last few days were not lost on Sunburst. Although he hadn't understood all the noises that he'd felt through the backpack the lizard had received an awful fright due to Leavon's unearthly bellow in the Lorry Park. Like the humans around him, the Sunburst Lizard along with all the rats and beetles and every other living thing in the area were shaken to their little cores by the foul and unnatural sound. So great was the poor lizards fright that he, involuntarily of course, ejected something quite foul but most assuredly natural into the toe of Jacob's hiking boot. Little surprise then that after the jostling of Jacob's flight from Leavon up the Adum hill in Kumasi, the Sunburst Lizard found himself a lot less brightly coloured than usual.

Battered and covered in his droppings, or in this case squirtings, the Sunburst Lizard crawled across the floor searching for food. He was hundreds of miles from his birthplace in Accra, half beaten to death and involved in the adventures of humanity.

Also, he was completely heedless to the giant brown spider that was watching him from below the bed on which Jacob and Becky were sleeping. It is strange to think that such a simple creature was, if he were conscious of them, the only witness to all of Jacob's African trials. As strange as anything else really, and what can you do? At the present time the lizard was only worried about one thing and there was nothing strange or mysterious about it. He was starving.

Sunburst scanned around for the nearest and quickest source of food. His tiny stomach was barren and empty, and the sheer biological fact was that the lizard was close to starvation. He cast his scaly head around to see what he could see, he soon zeroed in on some tasty sustenance. Upon their tiny turrets the lizard's eyes were performing their vigilant task. In a couple of minutes these two actions combined with some strategic and economical shuffling the Sunburst Lizard had located what he was after.

Just beside the leg of the stool Sunburst caught sight of a fluttering movement. A flutter meant life and movement had potential. It was the only vaguely promising sight his desperate searching had managed to uncover, so Sunburst scampered over to investigate.

In wary stages the Sunburst Agama lizard came closer to the moth, which is what it was, that fluttered helpless in the web of the so far hidden baboon-spider. The spider was dark in colour and had just portrayed a something that could easily be mistaken for intelligence. Before now she had been approaching her well-caught prey walking extremely slowly upon her long hairy legs with what could have been described as a haughty bearing. This of course is ridiculous, humans have long studied creatures of all shapes and sizes and they know exactly what goes on in their tiny brains.

So, with a tremendously fortuitous show of instinct, Brown, as that was her colour, ceased her intuitive advancing and waited, watching as a certain Sunburst Lizard came into view intent upon the moth that had quickly changed from quarry to bait.

Brown seemed to gauge the Sunburst Lizard. Was it small enough to attack? It would be close, as the Sunburst Lizard was slightly longer, minus tail, but much skinnier that the massive, arachnidly speaking, brown Baboon spider. Obviously obeying some instinctive programming, the spider circled slowly, weaving as she went, with her thickest thread, a net strong enough to catch a lizard.

Sunburst darted forward with little care. He was too hungry to be cautious any more. The information that was being passed to his brain involved only the moth, how it could be eaten and how it seemed not to be flying away. Eating it would definitely be the right thing to do. He reached the leg of the stool and didn't dawdle. With a rummage and a minimum of scrabbling he was soon chomping into the moth with what could have been described as great relish, but probably wasn't.

At this point Brown had semi-circumnavigated the Sunburst Agama lizard and was scuttling quickly towards him, in a merciless but no doubt emotion-free hurry.

Sunburst was almost finished his meal and Brown was almost on top of him before the lizard noticed the presence of anything but him and his much needed food. By then it was almost too late.

Sunburst jerked his head sideways quickly and beheld the Brown, bearing down on him from behind and to the left. Sunburst then made the forgivable mistake of turning in the other direction and scampering away running directly into Brown's web, which and for a moment it seemed as though he would break through it. But didn't. Instead the thread stretched magnificently, depending on your point of view, as it was made from her richest most elastic of the browns inner materials. Sunburst was then only pulling against the spider, and Brown was a big girl; big enough to take on a lizard in the first place and heavy enough to keep him on.

The future was suddenly bleak for the lizard, who decided to approach the problem with very simple, very male tactics. He ran as fast as he could with all of his might against the clingy resilience of the web and kept on doing it, without any clear idea of what he would do when he finally ran out of energy.

Brown took the strain for as long as she could and then, in a marvellous show of instinct she scampered round a second leg of the stool and attached herself to the web that featured earlier in the catching of much smaller prey. The Sunburst Lizard was a goner. Well at least you would have thought so. But he kept soldiering away straining at his restraints, so vehemently in fact, that the stool began to rock on the uneven surface of the bedroom floor. The little lizard kept going for as long as he was able, but his strength was failing him. The food he had only just eaten had not yet given him any nutrition and he was running out of his last source, sheer nervous energy.

Brown, on the other hand, or, on the other hairy mandible, was quite well rested and ready for the second stage of her well-rehearsed hunting routine. The prey was obviously tiring now, so she would approach it and spin more threads around it to ensure that he was securely ensnared. And once this was done, she would drag the be-webbed Sunburst under the bed where dozens of similar, if smaller, parcels were awaiting her attention. There was far more food there than she would ever eat, but it was in her nature to hunt, the eating was merely a side effect.

Sunburst had ceased his struggling now and from a bystanders point of view, it looked as though he had given up the ghost, packed it in, settled for the night train etc. But he hadn't.

Above the miniature battle the stool had not stopped moving. Slowly rocked back and forwards, the motion prolonged by dip in the floor underneath two of the legs. It tottered and it swayed and looked for the world as though it may topple over. If only it received another shove.

One last time the Sunburst Agama Lizard raised his little orange head, which was now covered in webbing and had a moths wing stuck to it. He raised it up high and gave everything he had, which wasn't much, into one last push. And, although it certainly wasn't much, it was easily enough.

What happened next could be described in slow motion, but it won't be.

The stool on which the last scroll and Becky's tin camping mug rested, toppled forwards and the two rolled respectively out over the edge and onto the floor.

Meanwhile Brown the spider that had probably just been advancing menacingly, we can't be sure, was narrowly missed by the sheet of parchment, but neatly imprisoned by the camping mug, which landed upside down on top of her. This left the Sunburst Lizard free from a compost-like end to his mysteriously effective little life. It was almost perfect, but was ruined slightly by his continued and embarrassingly weak attempts, to escape the spider's web.

~

Above that minor, but no less essential battleground, Jacob Terry was stirring in his sleep. This did not mean that he was about to wake, as no amount of tin rattling the Sunburst Lizard got up to tonight would be able to manage that. Jacob stirred because something had just happened to him in his dreams. A connection had just been made between his and another's mind.

In a black Mercedes on the Ghanaian border that other mind was pleased with its newfound subtlety. This was indeed a different approach for Leavon and he would have to surrender complete control to connect with Jacob in such an unnoticeable manner. He would join the Irish in his dreams and find a way to bring Jacob to him, rather than chasing blindly after and getting broken up against trees and the like.

Leavon settled; eyes closed to watch as Jacob settled in to another dream.

***

'Erfois! Erfois!' called Gregory Pilkington Arcright, 'Erfois, you really must come here and talk to my new friend. Oh do!' Jacob looked towards the door, which was made of figs and nothing more. A mango with a dozen feet entered through the door, it laughed and danced and skipped about, calling on its way:

'Oh Gregory!' it cried, 'he looks so darling, wherever did you find him?' Lord Gregory Pilkington Arcright simply burst into flames at the very idea and Jacob was given cause to worry.

'Erfois, what shall I do?' he asked the talking mango.

'Put his flames out with a story, that's the only thing to do!' said Erfois, whose legs had somehow disappeared leaving the cheerful fruit rolling on the ground and tittering.

A friend of Jacob's had worked in the hospital once. Well, in all actuality it wasn't only once, it was many times. As a matter of fact it became apparent to all of those in town that Emily, Jacob's friend and one-time sexual partner, had made quite a habit of going into the hospital. Some of them, hairless or no, wig makers and wigged alike, had even been known to call it her job…

'Oh you do go on. Oh he does go on!' wailed Erfois to the enflamed Gregory Pilkington Arcright.
'Get to the core of the story boy, the core of the story,' called the mango, 'please?'

The core of the story, the middle of it, where was it? Jacob asked himself.

The mirror.

'Oh, very clever,' said Gregory Pilkington Arcright his flames already subsiding, 'that's it boy you've caught the parrot now.'

Emily did work in the hospital, St Jerome's hospital. She cleaned the rooms and sometimes the people, if they couldn't do it themselves.

Up the stairs on the second floor, past the nurse's station, there was a room named "The Second" by the ones who knew it well and the ones that feared it most.

Inside the room, there was a bed and a dresser with a mirror leaning on it. And, past the bed there was a window that allowed plenty of light and air to enter the room, giving it a positively cheerful feel.

But they did hate it, those who knew it well. Not for the look of it and not for the feel. They hated its purpose.

You see "The Second" didn't mean, the second room on the corridor, nor did it have anything to do with the room being on the second floor. It simply meant the second last room. "The Last" being the morgue. "The Second" was the coma patient room. The second last place to go before the fridge downstairs, where the bodies weren't in polished silver drawers like in American movies, they were in bags pilled up on each other in a cold room like that of a busy bar. Diarmuid the "Corpse Guy" kept his lunch in there and sometimes a twenty-gallon drum of homemade white wine that he sold to the nurses. So it was, almost exactly like a cold room in a pub…

'Ahhhhhhhhh!' Screamed Erfois, 'Tell tell, tell, tell, tell, tell!' For some reason the giant mango was now on fire.

'Yes,' said Gregory Pilkington Arcright who was now quite un-singed, 'do continue.'

In the bed sleeping peacefully lay a woman and there was nothing strange about that. But this woman had been in a coma for her entire life. She had grown to adolescence and on into adulthood and not once had had she shown any sign of life outside a random twitch of a muscle or the escaping of bodily fluids.

When Emily asked, the doctors told her that when the baby had come out into the world she'd looked just like any other. The doctor who slapped her was rewarded by a lone tiny scream, just one, and then the baby slept.

It was because of this, of course, that the girl and then woman grew increasingly malformed. An inactive body cannot grow correctly no matter how often the muscles are massaged or exercised. So although she was lucky in a way to have rich benefactors, she still grew into something that could only be described as, well, hideous. On Wednesday it was Emily's task to wash the woman, if she was on that day and for some reason she didn't mind it one bit. There was something peaceful about the way you could sponge the woman down. Oh sure, Emily was first to admit that the strange lumpy growths on her face and body were disturbing at first, but she likened it to washing a life-size doll.

The woman, Sheryl Dempsey or Sherri… No definitely Sheryl. The woman Sheryl Dempsey rejoined the waking world one day whilst receiving her weekly wash from a distracted Emily. Emily didn't notice straight away that Sheryl's eyes had finally opened, the position she was in at that moment prevented her from seeing anything but the patients back, as she propped Sheryl up into a sitting position and reached around her body, sponge in hand.

When Emily finished cleaning the back she lay Sheryl back down on the bed and it was only then she was treated to Sheryl Dempsey's horrified grimace. The woman seemed completely awake and for a moment Emily was frozen, petrified in shock.

After getting over the worst of that shock Emily noticed that Sheryl was not looking straight up at her but over her right shoulder at something behind her.

Emily couldn't resist the urge, and spun around to have a look herself but she could find nothing strange or amiss in the room. There was a closed door, a table and a mirror. When Emily turned back around to look at Sheryl she was just in time to witness Sheryl's horrified mask return to normal. The woman who had slept her entire life until that day closed her eyes once more and finally died.

It turned out that a heart attack had been the cause of her death. And, though it was true that the poor ever-sleeping Ms Dempsey was not in prime physical condition, the doctors were curious as to what had set off the woman's weakened heart.

Nobody knew. Was it the shock of waking up that had killed her?
Or maybe the face she'd seen in the mirror, an unexplainable thing to someone who had never before seen anything.

Sheryl had slept a lifetime away. What had she been doing all that time, had she been dreaming?

Had she even known that she was human?

Did she even know what a mirror was?

When she saw herself, did she think? 'Oh no, that isn't me. I am not a thing like that. I am made of light, aren't I?'

But the mirror is reflected light, and you are what you are, even in the darkness.

The End

'Bravo, bravo!' cheered the man and the mango, back in the vestibule of Jacob's dream.
'Yes Bravo,' said another voice the source of which Jacob could not see, 'that was a wonderful story.'

Jacob turned and found he was standing on giant spoon bouncing up and down over a calm circle of water.
'Da da da da da da da dada!' said the voice almost happily. 'Ladies and gentlemen!'
'Don't jump!' exclaimed the figure of Erfois the many-legged talking mango on the other side of what was now a large leaf shaped swimming pool. 'Spend your money on the stock

311

exchange!' added Gregory Pilkington Arcright appearing behind his friend.

'Away with you,' said the announcer's voice and the man and mango lost their balance and fell into the pool, which extinguished their pleadings. Jacob felt only a tiny stab of worry before returning to his enjoyment of the springy spoon.

'Ladies and Gentlemen,' said the voice again, 'You have not seen me before!' This seemed an unusual announcement to make but Jacob wasn't sure.

Down on the surface of the pool a face was forming and as Jacob sprang up and down happily on his oversized piece of cutlery, the eyes appeared, then the nose and eyebrows, and so on. By the time the face was fully formed on the surface of the pool, Jacob was positively giddy from the thrill of springing.

It was Leavon's face. Jacob knew it was Leavon's face but couldn't remember if that was a good thing or a bad thing.

'You have not seen me before,' said the face again.

'Em?' Jacob enquired, 'Weeeee?' he tried

~

'You have not seen me before,' in the black Mercedes Leavon's lips moved as he spoke the words, and Rajette cowered at the sound.

~

'I have not seen you before,' Jacob copied laughing out loud as he lay in his bed. In his dream he was still springing on a spoon over a happy faced pond

'Now jump,' Leavon ordered, 'Aide-toi, le ciel t'aidera.'

And Jacob was quite happy to jump. He flew high in the air, revelling in the freedom that a dreamer always feels before the

312

fall. Once he reached the pinnacle of his dive, Jacob became concerned. He was beginning to fall. And not only was he going to fall from such a great height, he realised; he was going to fall right into Leavon's gaping maw.

Jacob hurtled downwards, reaching terminal velocity and plummeting onwards towards his doom.

It is at this stage that a dreamer would usually wake up.

Back in his bed in Ouagadougou Jacob caught his breath sharply as his dream self was swallowed by the mocking waters of Leavon's pool, but he didn't awaken.

~

In the black Mercedes by the roadside on the Ghanaian border, Leavon's eyes had just opened and he was smiling. Rajette was wide-awake too, woken by his captor's incomprehensible sleep talking. Leavon turned and laughed at the Palestinian man's frightened face.

'Help yourself, and heaven will help you,' He translated and settled back to see if he could find the dreams of another. And this time, if he could manage it, they wouldn't contain any talking fruit.

***

The next morning Becky was the first to wake. She felt different somehow, more relaxed. Than when? She wondered. More relaxed than yesterday, but she couldn't remember why.

Beside and below her the other occupants of the room were still sleeping soundly.

The Sunburst Lizard had built a little nest for himself in Jacob's hiking boot (the other one), and was now nestled amongst the scraps of paper and shreds of Becky's underwear that he had chosen for the purpose. He'd had a busy night after his brush with Brown the spider and had eaten far too many crawling insects in his ravenous state. Now he was stupid with fullness and wouldn't be able to move for a long time.

Curled up in a ball on the wall side of the tiny bed Jacob was snoring deeply and mumbling to himself. Becky could remember a similar scene in her hostel bed in Tel-Aviv, which seemed a long time ago. It was crazy to think that it was now just over two weeks since the two had met outside a kebab shop in Dizengoff Square. She had fallen in love with him then, he was so full of ideas and himself, but still a good man who also seemed sad beneath it all, far beneath. She knew his friend had recently died and that he had been Jacob's father long after his real father had gone. The sadness he cherished went much deeper than that, though Jacob had some other reason to be sad and no amount of bravado would ever change that. He was never happy, could never settle.

This morning however, Jacob seemed to be sleeping quite peacefully, his face alight in a smile as though the last two weeks hadn't happened at all.

The last two weeks.

What had happened? Becky tried to take stock. She had landed in Israel and travelled around for a couple of days. She'd been surprised by how tiny the country was. You could drive from Tel-Aviv to Jerusalem in a couple of hours and from there you were basically on the shore of the Dead Sea. It was amazing to think that there could be so much trouble over a country that would fit in Sydney Harbour, if its shape were only slightly changed.

Where was she?

Oh yes, then she'd met Jacob and everything had changed. After their week together and they had separated, Becky could still remember the sorrow that she'd tried so desperately to hide. Then there was Greece, Italy, Estonia and up along to Holland where she caught ferry to England. In London she had intended on doing a bit of partying and maybe try to forget her heartbreak. But what happened after that? She couldn't remember. She knew, and only just, that there was something to remember.

Actually it wasn't that she couldn't remember, more like she wasn't able to remember, which sounds the same but it isn't. The memories were there ready to be recalled. Becky could see the shape of them, but every time she tried to enter them, to picture the hotel she'd stayed in, or the funny man who worked there, she just wasn't able to keep her mind focused on the single specific memory.

Things had been happening; this she was sure of. She knew what these things were, but for some reason, and now she half snickered in disbelief, it was like she wasn't arsed remembering them. It was mad.

Oh well, she thought, they'll come back to me. I must be tired. She could have left it at that but there was one other thing too…

'Honey?' asked Jacob. Who after waking and waiting for consciousness to dawn, on him had realised that for the first time in his life. It wasn't going to. 'Where are we?'

Becky smiled down at her lover her eyes glazed with happy confusion. 'I don't know,' she said, laughing softly, 'I really don't know.'

Rajette knew exactly where he was, down to the millimetre. He was in hell. He'd been unable to sleep last night, horrified by the sounds that were emanating from the front of the car. What was happening to Leavon? He hadn't been able to understand, but if this was how creatures like Leavon slept? Rajette wanted to be very far away from him when night fell once again.

Once they had cleared the border Rajette had driven the black Mercedes as fast as he dared on such treacherous roads. But Leavon, to his surprise, had asked him to slow down.

'I thought you wanted to catch them?' Rajette had enquired, a cheeky question, but he just wanted to get this ordeal over with as soon as he possibly could. Leavon hadn't answered the question directly.

'Pull over,' he'd ordered and Rajette of course had complied. Leavon then reached forward and gripped Rajette's head in his hands pulling the little man back into the luxury headrest. Rajette then immediately felt a link forming between them and it had almost made him vomit to be subject to the clemency of such an odious mind.

'Feel,' Leavon said, and Rajette did. He felt himself being thrown through the window of a car, not this one and it caused him to gasp in pain. The stabbing torturous but bearable pain of passing through the glass, replaced quickly by a disgusting crunching agony as Rajette's body was smashed against the tree. It was as if a giant had scooped him up and done just that. Swung him mightily like a weak branch against the rock hard trunk of some anvilous oak. It was what a horrible death feels like and Rajette had faded away, dead.

But of course he wasn't dead. He had merely been re-experiencing Leavon crash, and when he had realised it, rather than feel relieved it made him more afraid of his tormentor than ever. How had the demon survived such a fatal collision? The impossibility of it robbed Rajette of any hope of killing the Leavon himself. He knew then that he was never going to escape. He knew then he was finished.

~

So now Rajette was driving at Leavon's pace, hot and sweating freely through his suit whilst cursing and muttering under his breath. At his best Rajette was a crazy bastard. Now, he had completely lost his marbles, gone mad, hoped off his rocker, he'd been disconnected from the normal train the screws had altogether been removed. In short, he was fucked up.

From the back seat Leavon watched as Rajette began to talk to himself in a whiney mocking voice. He had no idea that this was another way in which humans were weak.

Folie, Leavon remembered from his life a repressed française, now he new what it meant. A person's mind could be broken too. Leavon found it deliciously interesting and leaned forward to hear the little man's madness more clearly.

'You don't even have a licence to drive.'
'Of course I have a license to drive.'
'You wanted to be like the big rich American man.'
'People can come back after you kill them. That's what the Italian said.'
'Like a mobster in a movie.'
'They come back the Italian said so.'
'He was trying to confuse you. Not difficult'
'But he was right. They all came back.
'You thought you could kill them all and take over.'
'But they come back.'

317

'I know.'
'They came back after me.'
'Yes.'
'He is they, them, whatever.'
'Yes. Yes, yes, yes!'
'Where did they come from?'

Leavon thought that all of this was quite amusing, but he tired of Rajette's drivel, leaned back, looked out the window, and tried to redeem more of Michael De Rhy's memories.

The Italian

Yes, there was more to the little man's babbling then what first seemed evident. In Leavon's mind recollections from a different life were connecting themselves. Leavon had recently become interested in memory, especially other people's; so he was shocked to realise that he was having trouble controlling his own.

Last night he'd managed to effectively mess around with the minds of others sufficiently, to defect their memories and now he found that he was unable to un-mess his own. All he could figure out was that it had something to do with "the Italian" He'd know an Italian once or at least Michael De Rhy had, but the constant concentration that he needed to allot to Becky and Jacob was clouding his mind. He couldn't risk a lapse or Jacob would remember everything and…

'Merde!' he said aloud, it was so close he could almost say the Italians name. 'Candle… Candelli!'

'Oh my god, what's he doing now!' Rajette worried inside his own head; in his most pitiful voice.

'That means shit in French, why is he saying shit in French?'

'Why does he speak in French?'

'Oh my god he's looking at you, he's watching!'

'He's them. He's all of the ones you killed.'

'Because they come back?'

'Yes.'

'From where?'

'The Italian told you where.'

'No he didn't finish.'

'Why?'

'Because I killed him.'

'Destroyed his nice suit you did.'

'It was a beautiful suit.'

'You used to wear a nice suit.'

'Your nice suit had a gun in it.'

'Yes?'

'This suit has a gun in it!'

'Yes!'

'I could kill him.'

'No, wouldn't work, he's too strong.'

'You could…'

'I could…' Rajette's prattle ceased here and he hunched over the steering wheel, to whisper one last thing.

'Yes, you will.'

'What will you do?' Demanded Leavon reaching out to read Rajette mind, but the little man was ready and he swerved the car dangerously off the road, dumping Leavon back into the back seat.

'Aha!' he screamed happily as the black Mercedes bounced and vaulted across the humped cracked dirt of the parched Savannah, 'Big man-demon with the strong powers, afraid of some dangerous driving!' Leavon regained his seat only

319

to have it wrenched from under him again as the little Palestinian swerved back again towards the road. Mounds of earth were loosing their caps to the underside of the careering vehicle. Leavon continued to try and keep his balance but found it impossible.

Rajette brought the car back on to the road with a roar of delight. He felt alive because now he had a plan. With his foot all the way down on the accelerator Rajette watched in the Mirror as Leavon came at him. In the space of a second, Leavon lunged, Rajette Jerked open the door, and the little Arab was gone.

Inside the car, Leavon panicked. All he could think about was the pain of his previous crash. He feared so much a repeat of this pain and his return to the state he had been in only two days ago that he was frozen in place, leaning over the back of the driver's seat staring out of the open door.

Fear was something that Leavon had a lot of trouble coping with, he hadn't experienced enough of it to realise that it was an emotion and could be mastered, but he would have to learn quickly. The car swerved of its own accord and traced an arc towards a solitary tree in a field of clay. The sight of the tree wrenched Leavon from his panic and he grabbed the steering wheel and began to climb into the front seat as the car straightened out.

Leavon slammed on the breaks as soon as he could and received a crack in the forehead as a side effect to his lack of foresight, but the car was stopped and he felt again that most wonderful of sensations, relief.

Then there was the loud report of a gun being fired.

Bang, it said. Fuck you.

'That little bastard,' Leavon said, his eyes flaming yellow with anger as he started the engine and reversed the car back towards the road with dust and sunlight dying in his blazing yellow eyes.

Rajette hit the ground laughing as the car continued on, the cruise control set to 160kmph.

'Fuck you,' he shouted back at Leavon as the stones of the roadside tore at his skin and the violence of his escape bruised his body and cracked three of his ribs. None of it mattered though, there wasn't going to be any need for them now.

He rolled to a stop at the foot of a boulder, which he quickly scrambled round and sat against. There in the lee of that boulder, Rajette felt a serenity that he could never have imagined, and all it had taken was a couple of high-class murders and an encounter with some sort of hell possessed monster. This made him smile. What had he been doing all this time? Nothing good anyway. If it took a situation like this to make him realise what sort of man he'd been, then he mustn't have had much of a chance at realising it on his own. He just wasn't a good man. And, even if Allah, or God, or Shiva, or even Spiderman intervened at this stage to save him from that thing in the car, it wouldn't matter. Rajette would go back to doing what he was made to do.

Hurting people.

So now it was time to take it to the next level, to see if the Italian had been right. Recently Rajette had feared his death, but in the car jabbering to himself he'd remembered the words of Daniel Candelli as he pleaded for his life.

'Please,' the old man had implored of him, 'please don't kill me. There isn't anything else. After this, there isn't anything else,' Candelli had wailed with the sorrow of his discoveries, but Rajette found that, to him it meant something else. It calmed him and let his soul rest easily. There would be no punishment for the wrongs he had committed. There would be nothing.

Rajette reached inside his coat and took out his revolver. It was the same gun he'd used to put four bullets in Candelli. The gun was shiny and struck a cord of fear in Rajette. This was what it was like to look down barrel of it from the wrong end. It was frightening to be sure, but he was decided and he shook away his last doubts and raised the gun to his head, deciding quickly to hold it straight up to his right eye.

Straight into the brain, that was the way. He clenched the stock if the revolver and took a deep breath.

As he pulled the trigger, Rajette thought about a lot of things. He though of the wrongs he so regularly committed, he thought about his horrible bitch wife and how he would never again see her face but mostly he thought of Leavon and he wished that he could be there to see the demon robbed of his slave when he found Rajette's body. The gun went off.

Bang, it said to Leavon. Fuck you.

Recollections 18

Crawling out from under

'*Ahhhhhhhhhhhhhhhh!*' Becky screamed jumping up onto the bed in a split second of catlike agility. She stood there tensed and grimacing with Jacob looking up at her from where he lay still a bit sleepy and completely confused. 'Oh, shit, oh shit, baby, oh baby, oh baby!'

'What what, what the fuck is it?' Jacob responded, alarmed by Becky's panic so suddenly after such a tranquil and, quite frankly pornographic morning. 'What, tell me?' he insisted. Becky calmed herself a little and leaned forward with dread peering over the edged of the bed and then recoiled in horror, once more cursing and shouting, 'Oh shit, oh shit, oh shit,' After a moment or two Jacob thought he'd figured out what was wrong with the woman.

'Oh, a cockroach or something,' he sighed tutting the poor scared girly. He turned away from her and moved to the side of the bed where he laughed and stuck his head out over the floor on which stood a very confused, very, very large Brown spider. Jacob yelped and jumped back at a remarkable speed. Any faster, he remarked later on over lunch, and he would have been travelling back in time.

Brown, the spider, was bewildered and angry; vicious even. She'd spent the entire night underneath the metal cup, frightened into a ball, not understanding what had happened. At one stage she'd been about to make a huge kill, and then suddenly she'd been thrown into darkness. Now, she wanted to bite something. To kill it and wrap it up all saved. To see it rot and someday eat it… yum.

323

The spider observed that there was movement on the bed, sprung high onto the blanket, which was well within her reach and scurried the rest of the way up on the bed, sending Jacob and Becky into the air and out the door with fright.

Tenneh Turay was darning Oni's other dress when the whites burst into the main room, both of them naked and smelling of sex. The poor girl was instantly ashamed for them and covered her eyes so as to avoid any unnecessary sin that may result from catching sight of their pale bodies. She wasn't sure what sort of sin it was to see two people naked but she felt that if the pastor were here he would be condemning their ludeness and her for witnessing it. So it was better to play it safe and not to look, though she did glance quickly at the young man's member and was surprised that he did not have a twig between his legs like all the African boys said that the white man had; pleasantly surprised.

Jacob and Becky realised only a moment later that they were probably showing off more white flesh than this or any Burkinabé in the area had seen outside of a chicken run, though the embarrassment of it was quickly forgotten when the brown spider followed them out of their room and the two of them leaped out of its way with little regard for Tenneh's immortal soul. The poor girl was forced to bless herself repeatedly as she watched Jacob swinging past her to the laundry room, with Becky wobbling after. The spider stopped in the middle of the main room, apparently deciding what to do next. Tenneh watched it and smiled. It was no wonder there hadn't been any cockroaches around lately.

Moments later two heads peered out of the laundry room. Jacob and Becky both gave Tenneh a wane smile of apology whilst eyeing the brown spider with wary and distrustful glances.

Tenneh was disappointed, no, relieved to see that the whites had wrapped themselves in yesterday's sheets and she was able look at them without risking damnation.

'You fraid of spider?' Tenneh asked in broken English. Jacob straightened up at this and was about to say something like, well actually I'm more surprised than afraid, when the spider moved again and his attempt at bravado was circumvented.

'Yes!' They echoed cowering into the laundry room. Tenneh laughed and clucked her tongue.
'Oni!' she called for her daughter who came rushing into the room from outside the hostel. 'L'araignée,' Tenneh said pointing to the large brown and immediately going back to her darning. Apart from the one the little girl was wearing it was Oni's only other semi decent piece of clothing and was basically a collection of darned areas darned together anyway, so Tenneh had to be careful not to upset the delicate balance and unravel the entire dress.

Jacob and Becky watched enraptured by Oni's movements from the relative safety of the laundry room door. The little girl seemed to be well used to spiders of such size and was moving from side to side humming as she swayed. Bending as she moved, her upper half drew slowly closer to the brown spider.

Then, fast as a cat, Oni's hand snaked out and picked up the brown spider by the body. To the white's surprise the spider did noting but curl itself up and didn't' struggle at all, and that was that. Crisis averted.

~

After, Jacob and Becky packed their bags, paid and got out of there as quickly as possible, embarrassed but for all the right reasons.

325

Tenneh thanked them and waved as they walked away. A strong cool wind whipped up the sand from the dusty street and threw it into the air. It felt strange, she thought. The doctor-wind was never that gusty and always hot to the taste. Yet this wind seemed colder to her. There must be a storm on the way, she thought, she must remember to hang the clothes inside tonight. Laughing to herself Tenneh pictured again the sight of the two whites jumping naked across the room. She must remember to remember that too.

~

After breakfast Jacob and Becky were faced with a decision. They had intended on leaving that morning but couldn't remember why they'd been in such a mad hurry. They stared at Becky's notebook for a long while trying to remember. It had the flight numbers and prices written in it as well as a number for the French embassy. Why? The earliest and most expensive flights were circled. And aside from all this, both of them were positive that they hadn't travelled around this part of West Africa at all, so why should they leave without seeing the place? To say it was odd would be a definite understatement. They contacted the embassy and they were told that an emergency passport could be issued but it would take at least three days for it to arrive from the Australian Embassy in Nigeria. They both avoided the obvious fugacious confusion by not asking:
     'What the…!'

So their choices were: Stay in Ouagadougou for three more days or go somewhere and do something. It was an easy decision to make.
     While they packed Jacob noticed that something else was missing, this time a physical thing, but he couldn't think what the hell it could be. If he could have seen the Sunburst lizards

nest inside his hiking boot it would have caused him real mystification and the scraps of aging script inside them would have waved in his face the pathetic blindness that was forced upon them.

At eleven o'clock they left the city in a rented car headed for Bobo Djulasso where they planned on having lunch and then on to Banfora where there was all sorts of wildlife that needed spotting.

 As the rental car ate up the miles between them and their destination both Becky and Jacob pretended not to be bothered by their puzzling lack of recall. Becky was now convinced that they'd been bitten in the night by the spider that had been in their room and Jacob was sure that the two of them had been out the night before and ingested something. Something that would definitely be illegal at home, but had probably fallen of a tree, grown on a bush, or could be wiped off the back of a frog here.

 Either way they were on their way now and neither of them was ready to admit that, though they felt quite healthy apart from Jacobs unexplainable bruising, they were frightened and paranoid and didn't know what to do. Partly because they didn't want to ruin the simple joy of being together again after whatever it was that had happened to them, but mostly because they felt that with every moment they were drawing closer to some unrecognisable danger, something sinister but inevitable, something close behind, or just in front. They shook it off though and headed onwards, because it felt right to get on the move.

Sometimes people aren't paranoid enough.

***

Weathering well
Only thirty or so miles to the north the raging sand storm having

originated in the desert was blowing southwards across the savannah, warm and powerful, steady and strong. From the south and west came the tropical storm, moving more slowly bearing clouds that were actually bursting with rain but with a cold draft that kept them vaporous.

The two storm fronts like waves in the perfect surfing cove would collide later that day and form a typhoon front that stretched from south-eastern Mali to central Burkina Faso. The winds would do some damage but not as much as the meteorological community, having finally put down their instruments and looked out the window, expected it to.

But the winds were going to be the least of everyone's problems. When this storm did finally break it was going to be all about something else.

It was going to rain.

It was really, really going to rain.

A lot.

The sky was going to open up and all those massive sponge-like clouds that had somehow managed to hold onto there heavy burdens were going to let rip on the countryside below. It was going to come down hard, fast, big and plentiful.

After the initial stage of precipitation a downpour would begin. After the downpour had come to an end, it was going to lash whole torrents of rain, down on the parched ground. The torrents would then become deluges and, as soon as they finished soaking the earth, the monsoon would begin.

A weather girl on CNN would coin the phrase "Fasoing down" before the end of the week and for seventeen straight hours this part of West Africa was going to experience rain that was not only driving down from the sky, it was giving all of its friends a lift, in a juggernaut.

The pools of the area would become lakes, the streams would become rivers, the rivers would become more rivers, which would feed into the many colours of the great Volta River that would swell and roar as it crisscrossed the region.

Flooding was going to seriously affect the whole area but with few deaths connected to it and, for the most part, people would just wait for the rain to die down and ground to absorb the waters, which it did, hungrily. The majority of the water, finding nothing in its way, just kept on running until it was swallowed up by sand, found a dip in the earth, flowed into an old riverbed, or ended up collecting in a hole, like the abandoned quarry not ten miles north of Banfora.

From three newly made rivers the quarry began to fill and continued to do so long after the rain ceased to pour. For three hundred years the Burkinabé had been plundering this particular piece of land until it became obvious that anything the deep pit had left to offer wasn't going to be worth the expense of its extraction. A half a kilometre wide from east to west the quarry was a man-made bucket shaped valley that, up until today, held a reasonably sized watering hole and was home to a family of wildcats and several varieties of bird.

Now of course, the valley was filling up. The southern wall, though lower than the others, was at least ninety metres high, it would take a lot of water to fill it, but after tonight, water would not be an element lacking in the area. That southern blocking the previous flow of the river headed for the Cascades was indeed well made, but it was newly built. And new walls are always fresh and soft and expected pressure can cause understandable movements.

So it can.

***

Only hours after Jacob and Becky passed through for lunch, a black Mercedes came powering through Bobo-Djulasso, stopping only on Boulevard de la Revolution to fill up on petrol. The fuel belonged to a recently sheepish Adamo, who didn't seem to mind giving it away for nothing after he caught a glimpse of the man he would have to approach for payment.

Then the car took off again into the late evening. It too was headed for Banfora. Leavon and Jacob, like the storms, were rushing towards their breaking point.

If a lesson can be taken from the weather, it would seem likely that the two of them would blow themselves out.

Recollections 19

A lesson observed

Hippos kill. Well "kill" would perhaps be the wrong word to use. "Eat" would be better. But, Hippos eat, is just not as descriptive a statement. What do they eat? They eat all sorts of things, presumably. Hippos Kill, now that's a more accurate description of what they do, even if the killing is really only eating anyway. It's *what* they eat that changes the term to "kill".

Hippos kill people. They do it all the time. Perhaps you knew? Every year the cherubic monsters kill more people than any other animal in Africa. They eat bits of people too. Legs arms, arses, the small of their backs, a hand, whatever, they eat it. Why? It isn't a theological question. Hippos are big and they have big mouths. If you get too close to them, they open their big mouths and, if you're lucky they bite a chunk out of you.

In Banfora, or rather nearby, there is a lake with hippos in it. You can tell that it's hippo country because even on the hottest days, people don't just jump in the water for a swim, no. People are very careful to only swim on the opposite side of the lake from wherever the hippos are currently swimming, or wallowing, whatever it is they do. Eating people from out of town would be a good guess.

Another way to avoid hippos or hippo interaction is to run quickly away if you see them coming towards you at a thunderous trot, like many people from Banfora and its surrounding villages had to do on the night of the storm. A certain type of person would maybe say, 'Wow, what a sight that would be!' or 'I'd give anything to be that close to nature.' Does that sound like anyone you know? The sort of person that doesn't realise that being close to some sorts of nature is far too close. If you are one of these people, sorry, it's not too late to get a refund, 'It was a present for my cousin,' you can say, 'and I forgot he couldn't read,' Goodbye.

For the rest of us it would be beneficial to imagine how that particular day was going for in the inhabitants of the lakeside area. Patrice the boatman for instance, was not having his most profitable day, nor was it a happy day, or a pleasant one. In fact, if Patrice spoke English, he may have said that it was a fucker of a day, pardon my French.

Around midday it began to rain.

Patrice looked up at the sky and thought, here is that storm that Rocu was talking about last night, and he was right. Taking shelter underneath his lean-to, a small frame with some tarp stretched over it, Patrice wondered whether the structure, really only used for shade, would be able to withstand the rain that was expected.

An hour later as he ran for the village through the forest, the lake having already encroached on his normal pathway home, Patrice laughed at that. What a joke, nothing could withstand this for long. The rain poured down.

Aside from the obvious inconvenience, Patrice was feeling exhilarated by the storm. He had never seen, felt, or smelled anything like it. It was alarming how quickly the lake had begun to broaden its circumference. The phrase, burst its banks, would usually be used to describe this process but the whole area was a basin and the lake was merely the lowest level of it. So the torrential rain raised the level of the lake in a gradual way, as there were no banks to burst.

From Patrice's point of view, what was far more surprising than the rain, were the colours of the forest.

The different shades of green were brighter than he'd ever seen them and the redness of the earth had ripened in the weather, growing more swollen and full. Patrice was positive that he could smell the ripeness of the forest as it burst into life; its dormant seedlings growing almost before his eyes. He wanted to stop and enjoy the sight but worried about the effect that the risen lake was having on his family home. So Patrice hurried on, his t-shirt pulled up over his head in an attempt at shielding his eyes from the driving rain. He smiled as he did so and thought about how wonderful the rain really was, so nurturing and beneficial for both the plants and the animals.

Patrice knew that he was a simple man, but he was sure that he had just witnessed one of nature's treasures. He would remember this for as long as he lived. Which was about twenty-five more seconds and after that, he was hippo food.

***

'Fucking rain, Jesus!' Jacob was complaining, as he looked out of the hostel window at the sheets of water exploding all around. 'I can't believe we came all the way down here and then it starts to piss down. What crap luck.'

'Oh come on,' Becky teased, 'there are plenty of other things we could be doing,' She came up behind Jacob and hugged him around the shoulders. 'If ya know what I mean?' Becky purred. Jacob turned around and kissed her. She was so playful and sexy and he was so happy to have her at his side. But there was something wrong and they both knew it. What had happened in the last few days, what had been happening since he arrived in Africa? Jacob looked into Becky's eyes and there the same worried confusion. She didn't know either and was trying very hard not to show it. But, whatever it was, it was maddening. It was like spending eternity looking for your keys.

'I'm sure I don't know what you mean,' said Jacob and quickly he grabbed her and threw her on the bed. 'Actually, perhaps I've misjudged the situation altogether. You and me, inside all day, while outside the rain pours down? Normally I'd feel guilty going somewhere and not seeing the sights but here,' he gestured to the wall of raindrops just outside their window, 'we can't really do anything else can we? We're practically forced too,' he laughed and tried to give her a sexy look, 'to stay indoors,' And, with that, he jumped onto the bed with a little too much force and was rewarded by a loud crack as one of the bed boards broke loudly.

'Shit,' said Becky.

'God,' Jacob explained sitting up on the, 'what terrible luck I have,' Becky put her arms around his neck and pulled him back down to her.

'Oh yeah baby, you have such bad luck.'

'Well, maybe it's not that bad,' said Jacob and he moved into her arms.

Not as bad as, getting eaten by a hippo, for instance.

~

For the rest of the evening Jacob and Becky lay together talking, and joking, and having sex. For the two of them it was their first week together revisited. It was almost as though the interim, which they worked out was fourteen days, had never happened. Almost.

After five or six happy hours, the feeling of wrongness began to return. The two of them found that it was impossible to lie there and ignore it any longer. It was time to face up to it or just run from it again. So they decided to go out.

Across the road that was more like a river Jacob and Becky found that a large number of locals had gathered to the sound of the drums, to dance and laugh the storm away together rather than be alone in the cold wet night. From the second Jacob and Becky walked into the Barn-like area they were accosted by the owner, a barman, they weren't sure who he was, and the two of them were led towards the bar.

'Ca va mon amis. Hello hello. Je suis Sami, Comment va tu? Alemaigne? Anglataire?'

'Iralanda,' Jacob tried struggling to remember the correct term, 'Irlandais?' Sammy's eyes brightened.

'Ah! Hollandais, I will speak English to you,' Jesus Christ, thought Jacob, again? Someone had said the same thing to him recently. Where though?

'Ghana,' he said aloud and turned, looking for Becky who had already been whisked off by Sami, who obviously intended to sell them some of the imported drinks that none of the locals could afford. All around him people, the people of Banfora, were showing him their happy white smiles and talking to him all at once. Two children ran past with an older woman in pursuit, wagging her figure and remonstrating with them in words that were easily understandable, even if they were spoken in unintelligible French.

'You two come back here,' she was surely saying, 'do what you are told,' this too was familiar to Jacob. It reminded him of two little boys looking down at him as he awoke. Then he remembered them, a whole gang of children running around the yard of a school, or something like it. He remembered a woman called… Na, something, what was it? Jacob swallowed his frustration, tried to smile as openly as he could and began to follow Becky to the bar. Damn his stupid memory! He had to be able to remember something?

At the bar Becky was holding up a large bottle and saying something that was lost amongst the sounds of chatter, the banga-banga and the bap-bap-badap of the drums.

'Beer,' said Jacob, his smile authenticating itself, now there was something that he did remember.

For the rest of the evening the two of them managed to put aside the disconcerting knowledge that they did not know why they were where they were or how they'd managed to get there and get completely hammered; with alcohol becoming what it is and always has been for humankind; a replacement for life.

Drink, how it passes the spare time that the rise to civilisation that has given us. Too many years without fear for survival and constant physical struggle have bored humanity biologically, until we invented it. The body and the mind are incredibly advanced pieces of machinery with very little work to do and alcohol whittles away the potential of both until they are microwavable, five-day-working-week engines, running on half power. It re-introduces challenge into minds that are far above any test that modern life can initiate.

In short, it's brilliant, and we should thank (insert deity) for it!

The reason being that there are only a few places at the table of filled potentiality and without alcohol there would be a bitch of a queue. And, the ones amongst us, the specials with that something extra, the ones who should be inside running the show, would be stuck outside with the rest of us, like teenaged girls waiting for the unattainable "second issue" of tickets. They would probably be making a fortune selling scarves or places ahead in the queue or course, but they'd be outside all the same. And then the whole planet would be under the rule of those who managed to get there first, or their nephews and then we'd be clogged up. It makes a body want a drink just to think about it, doesn't it?

Alcohol makes everything a little easier to take, makes life more… believable or something. So Jacob and Becky got themselves in a horrible state that night. They drank beer until they were too full to go on, they drank vodka and fruit juice until there wasn't any left. They drank until there weren't any people left, and then they drank some more.

As the night went on the villagers had all begun to leave the barn/bar. This was partly because the rain had long since stopped and the ground had begun its thirsty work, but it was mainly down to how obnoxiously drunk Jacob and Becky had become.

At about five o'clock in the morning, after discovering the cheap and plentiful local gin, Jacob was composing/reciting a song that he was almost sure he'd just made up in his head. He was sure that he'd made it up, but he wasn't sure in whose head. It went something like this.

'Am Aram Aram a Na Na, to the roater very birds and the balance of the weekend is hang-ing in the, the, the… balance! Ah ha haha ha ha he!'

'Yeay!' Becky applauded, 'Baby that was amazing!'

'I know,' agreed Jacob picking up his glass and clinking it with hers, 'We should have been drinking this stuff all night!'

'I know,' Becky agreed giggling. 'Hello Sami,' she exclaimed as Sami the owner approached with a *tortured look* that he only used in extreme cases, like when he wanted drunken tourists to go home. It came along after, *looking at his watch pointedly* and *extremely politeness*, had completely failed, as they had done tonight. 'Sami! Sami!' Becky chanted putting her arm around the Burkinabé, 'how are ya going Sami? Can we get another gin off of you? Or are you boring?'

'I'm sorry but…' Sami began, trying a new, *so very tired* look.

'Oh he's boring,' Becky interrupted, turning to Jacob and putting her arm around him instead.

'He's boring, he's boring, he's boring!' the two of them sang as they were ushered out of the bar. It was black dark outside and Becky and Jacob made the mistake, twice, of thinking that they were alone in the street. They actually ran into, and in one case, clothes-lined a couple of West African's to the ground.

'I'm really sorry,' they both apologised. 'They're just so black, I can't see them in the dark,' Jacob added in a drunken whisper that was as loud as his earlier recitation of the song that he now called, balancing the weak-end. Get it? Weak end, ah ha, and so on.

An hour later when Jacob and Becky finally reached the hostel, it being directly across the road and drunkards being allergic to straight lines, the two of them fell in, or in Jacob's case, fell out with, the front door before diving into bed. A few moments, a ripped t-shirt and a half of an impossibly complicated ride later, the two of them were fast asleep.

In reality it is hard to cut the scenes up into manageable portions. How difficult it is to end each argument with a pithy remark or paint each goodbye with worthy words. In reality all they had was that last drunken embrace, and their ignorance. They had no idea that it was over for them. Jacob and Becky would never sleep together again.

***

338

During the night Leavon slept in the black Mercedes and turned his mind once more towards his prey. When he closed his eyes and began to dream. He found it easier this time to enter her mind and smiled broadly when he locked himself into the dreams of the one he wanted. He was pleased with himself and how much he'd grown. He was not struggling against the ways of the world anymore, now he was using them to his advantage. Jacob was a hard one to control. It was as though the Earth itself were aiding him. But Becky was a different matter. Once he had her, Jacob would follow. Then he would get from the sky-blue soul that for which he had destroyed himself. He would be able to complete the ritual and he would be able to succeed quite easily in this world now that he knew how it worked.

So Leavon, who had come unnaturally into this world, was now becoming accustomed to it. He only needed one more thing to make his transformation complete and, as he probed gently with his powerful mind, he felt that he had found the perfect way to get what he desired. Life, eternal and bountiful; how he longed to say those last words and feel himself freed from this fading existence.

He wondered what those words would be, something triumphant, no doubt. Well, when he had Jacob he would have them, and victory.

The black Mercedes stood at the foot of the Karfiguela falls whose water supply had been diverted two weeks prior, to feed the new manganese mine twenty miles east. The waterfall was, temporarily and in the smallest way, back in action as the run-off from the rains spilled over its crags and attempted to fill its crevasses. Although it had rained mightily this was a pitiful amount of water for such a significant falls. As the name suggested there should be tons of water cascading down amongst its sharpened shale and rounded boulders. The water had built it over hundreds of years, the natural constancy of the flow that had scraped and battered the landscape into the correct shape for a majestic falls had been taken away by man and the stream that ran along it now was an insult to it, a spit in the face of nature. It was vinegar, for the crucified.

Eight miles to the north there was plenty of water. It lay in wait, growing heavy with itself, and flexing its increasing mass. The quarry was a solid ball of rainfall, barely contained and stretching.

Above all of these scenes the light of the morning sun had begun. Firstly the darkness became grey and then the yellows appeared. It was only then that the effects of the previous day's rain became apparent. And, instead of its wrecked and washed out remains, the countryside was alive.

In the orange light the air was full of buzzing and fluttering, the brush full of hopping and trotting, and the earth full of slithering and burrowing. Flowers that long ago grew in this part of West Africa had returned and were opening their petals to the merciless sun that had forced them into dormancy.

The beauty of Africa, the land of plenty was being flaunted once more, refreshed and vibrating with energy. So rich was this land in all things that man could ever want, it had become valuable property to any who perceived its value. But they, all of her suitors, held her too tight and strangled her, until the continent was choked and began to die.

Below the sun and sky, amongst the life of the land, encased in the black metal of an automobile, a pair of matt brown eyes stared out at the colour and the nature around them. The eyes felt that everything they beheld outside the car was beautiful, natural, and good. And, that everything inside the car, the dead leather, the sleeping figure in the back seat and the eyes themselves were unnatural, horrid and despicably bad.

340

The eyes belonged to Rajette. There was a hole between them.

'You,' said Leavon, opening his own eyes from sleep without even a moment of recovery, 'go into the town and bring him,' the three eyes looked down the road towards the town. They saw a movement. She was coming as expected.

'Wha…' They began to ask but Leavon interrupted.

'Never mind that. Do as you are told and I may let you go,' Leavon opened the door for it and the three eyes that had been Rajette stepped out onto the road. 'Bring him,' Leavon repeated, 'and I'll let you go.'

The eyes said nothing. There was nothing to say. They turned and headed for town with lacking the emotion to be depressed by the knowledge that they would probably never be free again. Ever.

***

A lesson observed

-What colour is this? This is colour r-e-d!

Eve moved closer to the classroom window. Inside she could hear the children repeating the words of the teacher, or at least trying to.

-What is red?

Eve knew what red was. Tomatoes are red, she thought to herself.

-Tomatoes and chilli, and jam on bread!

341

As she drew closer she could see that the other children were in a circle all holding hands in the centre of the room, singing a song. On the table in the centre of the circle were a tomato, a chilli and a red shoe. They were all laughing as they sang and smiling as they danced around the table.

Jean her neighbour was there and he only had one shoe on. It made her cry to see them so happy. It always made her cry.

-What colour is Jean's shoe? Asked the teacher who was part of the circle.
-Red! The class all shouted together.

Eve felt very sad, looking in at them as she did, from the outside. Eve was a good girl and not prone to jealousy at all, so the feelings of resentment she felt towards the others did not please her one bit, they only made her feel more empty and sad.

With a sigh and an expression that had no place on the face of a child, Eve turned around and picked up her large metal bowl. Inside the bowl were the fist-sized bags of water that she was supposed to be selling. The bags were dirty and the water had never been cold. It was unlikely that she would sell them all. School may be free but she was not allowed to attend because her family needed her income to survive, and Eve could only go home when it was either too dark for her to stay out or all the water was sold, which ever came first. It was usually the former.

Leaving the sounds of merriment and learning behind her, the five-year-old Eve walked back across the road to the bus station to wait for the next bus into town. It was going to be a hot morning and if she was lucky she could sell most of the water to desperate travellers and come back across the road in time to watch the other children playing in the yard. She could imagine that she was amongst them, running and laughing, fighting over toys and eating their nourishing lunches.

As her mind wondered, the poor little girl tortured herself with visions of the basic life that everyone should have Eve stared fixedly into space. She was staring up the street watching for the bus to arrive and thinking thoughts too desperate to fully grasp when a figure came towards her along the main road from the east. The figure was that of a body that had eyes and mind, being kept alive by an unnatural force.

Rajette had not other emotions left, but he seemed to have been left with despair. Despair and anger were all he had left. Do as he was told, that was all that he could do. Keep trudging along and maybe…

'Wata?' Eve interrupted his self pity; Rajette had been so distracted that he almost walked into her, as it was all he could see of the little girl was a large battered metal bowl full of small leaking plastic bags. Rajette just stood there staring at them unable to decide what he should do.

'Wata?' asked Eve again, wondering if it had been a bad idea to offer this strange figure any refreshment at all. Slowly Rajette lowered himself down until he was sitting on his heels, he was the same height as Eve now and they stared into each other's eyes for a long drawn-out moment.

Rajette looked at the face of the little girl before him. Her face was screwed up in concentration and there were lines below her eyes. Deep lines on a face so young, how could it be so? But Rajette had seen it before. He knew how it could be.

Poverty.

The little girl was poor and it had aged her. Instead of a bright and open face that would sooner smile than anything else, this girl's features were closed, wary and sad. Rajette could tell that she'd recently been crying and that she cried often.

Eve peered into Rajette's face and saw what was left. There was hole between his eyes. And, at the angle he was standing, she could see a tiny speck of daylight coming through his head. He was empty.

The Empty Man looked very tired and Eve supposed that having a hole in your head must be very tiring indeed. Yes tired, tired and sad. Eve knew how that felt and she reached out and patted his cheek.

'Shhh!' she said comforting him as she'd seen mothers, never hers, comforting their children, 'shhh.'

It was almost too much for Rajette and on an impulse he grabbed her and held her to him. He hugged the poor little girl who would suffer for no reason throughout her life. He hugged the little West Bank boy who had forgotten how to show compassion for anyone in the way that this child who had nothing had just done for him. And then he let her go, stood up straight, and marched towards the hotel. There was nothing he could do now. He had lost his way and it was too late to go back. Forget her, forget them all.

Eve watched the Empty Man go. He seemed so weary. She hoped he would be able to rest soon. In the meantime the bus had arrived at the station and Eve had to rush over to it to catch the passengers alighting.

Please, she thought, let me sell them all. Please?

***

Jacob awoke in a haze of confusion and nausea.

'Oh fuck,' he mumbled into the pillow the words hurting his head as he spoke them. He heard the chinck! of a Zippo and after a few attempts he managed to turn his head to one side once more, but he was still unable to open his eyes. He smelled cigarette smoke, she must be smoking, he thought, trying to ease one eye open and dreading the presence of any light as he did so.

'Morning baby,' he said, but Becky didn't reply. Becky didn't smoke either. A shudder of trepidation rippled through him. Maybe, he thought. Maybe if he just kept his eyes closed it would all go away? But morbid curiosity and a dreadful urge to take a piss answered that question for him. He counted to ten as the smell of cigarette smoke filled the room making him queasy, and then he opened his eyes and sat up in one dizzying movement.

Rajette watched as Jacob awoke. It took a long time. And, finding a packet of cigarettes in his pocket he decided to try one and see what they tasted like now that they could no longer harm him. After puffing hard on the cigarette, he decided that they tasted and smelled like burning leaves. He couldn't remember if they'd always tasted that way.

'What are you doing here?' Jacob demanded, 'Where's Becky?' He jerked his head around the room filled with sudden fears. Everything seemed normal, apart from Rajette, at whom Jacob then launched. He landed on the dead Arab and began to pummel and pull at him. Rajette allowed himself to be borne to the floor and beaten. It didn't matter to him anymore what anyone did. He also recalled when he had done something similar to Jacob. Let him beat me then, he thought, he deserves it.

Jacob thumped and punched, fighting hard against his hangover and the sense of futility that was settling over him. After a couple of minutes his blows became slaps, he shook Rajette for as long as his strength would allow and then fell back against the bed, sobs shaking him instead. Jacob knew where Becky was, and he also knew that it didn't matter what he did to Rajette. He looked the Arab up and down through his tears and noticed finally the state of the little man.

'You…' Jacob began. Rajette raised his fingers to his head in a gun shape and mad the noise: phaoww!

'And you're still alive?' said Jacob and Rajette nodded, in a way, 'you'll take me to him?' Jacob asked and Rajette nodded again. The little man seemed to be about to say something, but he held back. Jacob rose and dressed himself automatically thinking how he had been tricked. There was no block on his memories now. He knew what had been happening and he also knew how Leavon had caught up to them. Why had he bothered to escape at all?

'Ok,' Jacob said to Rajette, 'I'm ready, let's go,' Again the little man seemed to be about to say something, but afraid to do so. Instead he opened the door for Jacob who was about to leave through it when Rajette spoke.

'Demon folk pious and snug but the prisoner falling broken rang out the great bell,' he said. Jacob stopped in the doorway his head pressed against the wooden frame listening. 'Your friend, the old man, the Italian, he said it. Do you know what it means?' Jacob shook his head and continued to listen, it was true then, Candelli had been murdered and it was something to do with all of this. 'Marshall said that very important people wanted the documents. The Italian passed them on, like you. He left them in his room, for me to take. Except the last time,' Here Rajette paused as he remembered the day he spoke of. It was then that he had begun to lose his conviction. Jacob turned around and faced him, new tears in his eyes.

'Tell me,' he said.

~

But the prisoner, falling broken, rang out the great bell

346

Everything had been going well. Rajette was revelling in this his first chance to work for an American. Although Marshall claimed to be from the government Rajette severely doubted it, the American government had had little use for someone of Rajette's calibre up until now. They owned the Israelis and so had no need for the services of a Palestinian thug, unless of course they were trying to spark retaliation, which again, he doubted. No, Rajette's guess was that the ultimate boss was a European, as he had overheard Marshall speaking French on two occasions. It didn't matter to him who was paying the bills. Marshall was American and definitely operated internationally, he was just the kind of employer Rajette had been hoping to find for a long time. He was finally branching out.

In his third week on the job Rajette had been followed the target, Candelli, from Rome to England and then to Germany. The Italian was collecting documents of great value for some sort of novel he was working on. It became apparent that the documents were long sought after by his ultimate employer and the Italian writer was one of the only people to whom they would be released.

The first three collections went like clockwork. Candelli was always on time and after some perfunctory note taking, he left the documents unguarded in his room and went out to dinner. Then Rajette would break in, take them and pass them on to Marshall. And that's the way it went, the first three times. It was neat and it was tidy, until the Italian reached Israel.

Immediately after Candelli arrived in Jerusalem the Italian began to act erratically. He missed his appointment with Richeloe, who was grudgingly organising the fourth and penultimate meeting. And, he went missing in the old city for days. Rajette was amazed how difficult it was to find the old writer, Jerusalem being after all, the Palestinian's own territory. But he did find Candelli eventually.

Candelli had secreted himself in a brothel in the Islamic quarter, he had bought a room and a girl, whom, from what Rajette was able to learn, merely cooked and cleaned and went out of doors for him and nothing more. Rajette had to admit, it was a good idea, but the old city was very small and he was only going to last so long.

After receiving his orders from Marshall: Find out what you can and then kill him! Rajette waited for his chance. Causing a disturbance in Jerusalem was never wise, especially if you wanted to kill somebody. So after two days waiting, the target, Candelli, left his room and went to make a phone call. One of Rajette's "friends" cut short the Italian's call as it became obvious that the man was going to spill his guts to someone and the trap was sprung. Then Candelli was chased back into hiding, whilst Rajette had already climbed down from the roof of the building and come in through the window of the writer's brothel room. He was waiting there when Candelli returned and struck him from behind as soon as he walked in.

'Please,' Candelli asked, 'let me explain,' Rajette allowed him a moment. Find out what you can…

'You don't understand,' the Italian continued, 'he wants to come back.'

'Who?' Rajette asked.

'Whoever is buying them. It doesn't matter,' the writer pleaded, 'don't you know what it means? Did you read them, did you work it out?' Now Rajette was curious.

'Work it out?'

'Yes yes,' the writer went on, scrambling through his bag and emptying out on the floor and going through his papers eventually settling on a notebook. He proffered it to Rajette and continued, 'he thinks that they'll tell him how to come back.'

'What?' Rajette was only going to put up with a tiny bit more of this before he moved on to the: then kill him, part of his orders. 'What do you mean?' he asked ignoring the fat man's offer.

'Animation! Rebirth! Whoever is collecting these wants to find out how he did it. Jesus. They want to find out how he came back. You see? Because they know the truth, now *I* know the truth!' The Italian was now on his knees in front of Rajette hands together making a prayerful pleading motion as the Palestinian pointed the gun to his head.

'Please don't kill me! No heaven! Please! Don't you see? We only get one chance, one! After this there is nothing. Please don't finish me, let me…'

'Shut up,' Rajette ordered. The man's words were beginning to get to him. Could it be true? He turned and paced up and down in an anxious way before returning to the prostrate Candelli and putting the gun to his head once more. The man's face was flat against the floor now and he was weeping.

'Please! Demon folk pious and snug,' Candelli whined without conviction, 'but the prisoner falling broken rang out the great bell,' He began to sob quietly and repeated the sentence again and again like a Mantra. Rajette didn't understand it and he smacked the writer to shut him up. 'This is all there is. Please we've been tricked,' Candelli tried to explain, but Rajette couldn't take any more.

'Nobody tricked me,' he said and pulled he trigger. The report made him flinch and filled him with loathing. It was as though this was the first man he'd ever killed. He kicked out at the dead man's head, angry with himself for such weakness, noticed the notebook on the floor, and picked it up. It was written in Italian and couldn't make any sense of it. He searched through the man's dirty suit for some proof of the hit. There was a pin on his lapel. It was a red sword. As he took it from the worn collar of the Italian suit, he realised his hands were shaking. He rose to his and spat on the Italian.

'Fuck you,' he said, and left the room.

~

'I gave the pin and the book to Marshall and he gave me the money,' Rajette finished, 'and that was it. Until you came along and I was told that you were going to finish the job,'

Jacob had nothing to say. He had known all along in his heart that there were things happening that he would never understand. But now hearing the facts, as Rajette knew them, he could only wonder at how much more he did not know. Had he just heard that his one true friend had discovered before he died that there was no after life, that there was no bounds for faith? Or, had he just heard that his friend was involved in stealing valuable documents for the type of man who hired a Hit Man?

If the later was true then surely he was as guilty as Candelli. It was so bloody difficult to understand. He was about to die at the hands of some spiritual madman, or demon, or something, and Becky was probably already dead, for what? If there was nothing after this, why did it matter?

Jacob remembered the passage that he hadn't seen for days. There is no way back… it made more sense now. Candelli had been way off. Only being alive once wasn't a bad thing, was it? Not to Jacob anyway, but to someone with real faith it was a disastrous realisation. Only one chance and they you become part of the universe. It made everything more worthwhile somehow. But it didn't help him right now.

'Let's go then,' He said to Rajette. The little man nodded and sat up from his chair. As he stood he pushed the chair backwards and bumped against Jacob's backpack causing it to slide from upright. From it Jacob's clothes spilled on to the ground. One of the items, a black sock, seemed to take its disturbance personally and began to move around in circles between them and the door.

Eyebrows were raised at the sight of such a random and odd occurrence.

Jacob reached down and plucked up the offended article only to realise that, thankfully, current events had not reduced him to madness just yet. Not quite anyway. There on the floor stood a startled looking lizard. It had orange-golden colourings around its scaly little head, which it seemed to be drawing attention to by doing press ups in Jacob's direction.

'Hello,' said Jacob, 'I know you,' He remembered the lizard he'd seen briefly in Kumasi. 'You slept on my face, didn't you?' he asked. Jacob put his hand on the floor and to his surprise the lizard scampered onto it. He raised the lizard up and addressed it head-to-head. 'Don't tell me that you were in my bag all this time, eh?' Jacob was amazed. How had it survived? Why not?

'Ok my little Sunburst friend,' Jacob said motioning Rajette to the door, 'you've come this far, let's see what happens next, will we?' Sunburst did some more press-ups before settling quietly in Jacobs's hand, relaxing. He felt safe.

Outside in the street Eve watched Jacob and Rajette walk out of town. They were a strange pair, one with a hole in his head and the other always talking to his hand. She was young and uneducated but she was not stupid. She'd never seen people like these. They were definitely not normal, even for whites. She wished that she knew what it all meant, why people acted so strangely sometimes.

Someday she would find a way to go the school. Then she would understand everything.

***

It took Jacob and Rajette two hours to reach the Cascades of Karfiguela and for the last two miles Leavon had been able to watch their slow progress. He was bursting with anticipation. In a few minutes he would have success. He was to be the first to succeed and complete the transformation, and then everything the earth had done to try and stop him will have failed.

'Oui!' he exclaimed, 'Jai chouette,' He was the coolest. Well saying that probably wasn't so cool but there was no one here to hear him and he was feeling positively giddy with expectation.

Leavon remembered to calm himself, he had been close before, and he had failed, so he needed to be careful. Gently does it, there was nothing to be gained from doing things à l'abandon and falling short again.

Jacob's slow approach was agonising though and he was beginning to feel the other's presence as a tangible thing. Leavon could see as well as feel the radiance of his yellow essence being fed by the closeness of the sky-blue soul. It was delicious.

Jacob on the other hand was not finding things so salubrious. As he trudged behind Rajette he watched the sodden landscape change before his eyes, the ground rising until they took a turnoff to the north and a large embankment came into view. It was heavy going. Usually in Jacob's novels the final confrontation was reached without everyday concern for distance and journey time. He couldn't remember any of his heroes ever need to sit down in the final chapter for a bit of a breather. And that's what this was he supposed, the final confrontation. But wasn't he supposed to have a plan?

As soon as he saw the high ridge Jacob knew that that's where Leavon would be. Up there on the highest point he was surely standing, looking down on him as he drew nearer. The bastard was probably enjoying himself, or was he doing something to

Becky. Oh no, he couldn't bear the thought of it, if that… *thing* hurt her. It didn't matter what it was, when he got there he was going to fuckin murder it. He would have to find away. Well, he was going to try at least.

The Cascades grew closer and the ground rose more steeply than before. It seemed to Jacob that Rajette was flagging; the poor little prick. How long had he been dead? How long could Leavon keep him alive? The acknowledgment of such power filled Jacob with dread. He didn't stand a chance against someone who could arrest such a blatantly final death. Not a chance.

Then, too soon and too late for Jacob and Rajette, they arrived at the black Mercedes. Having completed his allotted task the little Arab sat down on a stone and his head drooped. He just sat there dejected looking, waiting for his next set of orders. What was left of the Palestinian was destroyed with fatigue and he could barely move, but he was still alive and would be for as long as Leavon wanted.

Jacob felt sorry for the man but only for a moment. His compassion was soon overshadowed by fear for his own life, and for what had happened to Becky. Jacob took a deep breath and ascended the forest path to the top of the falls. Inside the breast pocket of his shirt the Sunburst lizard squirmed a little bit in response to Jacob's nervous energy. He could have been nervous too, if he knew, but nervousness is probably only equated to an instinct for a soulless creature like a lizard.

***

Eight miles north of the Cascades concentric circles were forming on the surface of the now filled to bursting Quarry Lake. At the base of the weaker southern wall the ground was getting muddy once more. This time however it was not the rain that was creating the moisture, instead the water seemed to be coming from beneath the ground.

It was neither odd nor sudden. Not really. The wildlife in the area didn't seem to think so anyway. They had come to a decision an hour ago and now it seemed that only the worms and the insects had been left behind. The quarry just sat there, being a quarry, a mile wide and a half a mile deep, straining. A couple of days later and the water would have been running down the soon to be excavated channel to the magnesium factory. But it wasn't.

And

There is one thing that happens consistently to something that is filled to bursting.

Recollections 20

The Cascades of Karfiguela

Pain and blindness, a blur of yellow and Jacob cried out.

'What happened to the sky?'
'You are here now and that's all.'
'But where is the colour gone, where is the ground?'
'You and I are the colour. You are blue. You are here to give me what I need.'
'I'm here now, but I don't know what you want.'
'You don't know, but you can guess.'
'What has happened to the sky?'

Two blows to the head. One from above and the other following from below, against… was it the ground?

'What has happened to her?'
'That, you can also guess. Now tell what I want to know.'
'There was a Passage.'
'Yes, yes.'
'In Kumasi. Is she dead?'
'You know she isn't. Give it to me!'
'Yes. I don't have it anymore. It is lost. Please don't hurt her.'
'But you remember it. Tell me.'
'I…. I don't know if I should.'

Pain again. This time repeated. All around Jacob was aglow with yellow harsh light. You should tell him, said a woman's voice, coming directly into his mind in the same manner that Leavon's had. There was a brief moment of blue calm and then Agony blossomed all over his body. First his stomach, his back, his groin, and then to his head again.

> 'Stop please.'
> 'Tell me.'
> 'Will you let her go?'
> 'No. Tell me, I offer nothing.'
> What are you?'

Jacob felt his head rebounded again off the ground. Tell him, whispered the woman's voice again.

> 'Stop please! Tell me how to save her. That is all I want.'
> 'I offer nothing. I'll take her, like all of the others. You are all the same to me. Once the ritual is complete I will not need her or you. I will not even need to take her, but I will. Now tell me.'

The pain returned but it overwhelmed him and his consciousness faded for a second. But the yellow light brought him back and fully awake once more. Jacob felt resignation.

> 'You are not going anywhere. Tell me now.'
> 'There is no way back.'
> 'I can suck you dry, like I did the others, like I did that old nigger woman. She was…'

Was it uncertainty that Jacob heard, felt from Leavon? He could see a chink of clear blue sky above him as the yellow faded.

> 'There is no way back!'
Pain again and the yellow encompassed everything again and turned red with anger.

'Tell me!'

'I am, listen! This is what it said. There is no way back…

~

We are born then and for a brief and wondrous period we become human.
And with our full potential realised we become part of the physical earth.
The Earth spends us also as we spent the life we once had.
Then we are free of the physical.
We become the sun, and with the sun we become the stars.
And, with that, we are the Universe.'

~

'This is what was written; the message to you from all of them.'

'No!'

Jacob's entire body exploded in agony.

'Tell me the truth. Now!'

'There is no way back, all that there is, is this life. First we are…'

'Arhhhhhhhhhhhhhhhh!'

Leavon screamed. It was an awesome and horrific sound. Then there was blue sky and Jacob felt the coldness of the water running around and over him. Leavon was standing above, having lost his control as tormentor, shouting up into the sky.

'A human being is the ultimate living thing. It should be rewarded not punished. It is too unfair, to be used up and turned away. Only given a short time to live and then nothing, no hope, just spent,' Standing astride of Jacob a frenetically proud look on his fine features, Leavon continued speaking to Jacob who could do nothing but stare in horror as the creatures voice grew louder and its expression more frenzied.

'I will be the first to succeed,' he said, 'you see Jacob. I worked it out. I died and then before I drifted away I took control of my soul and brought it to a place I had prepared in the ritual. Then I chose a form and returned. I will be the first, the first one to have broken the rules, to live twice and beyond the One Life to which we are all cursed. Jacob looked up at Leavon and shook his head.

'You are wrong,' said Jacob, 'to be alive once, that's the point. That's why it's so… important,' and Leavon knew that it was the truth.

Leavon was stunned. Could it be that he had been wrong? No! Surely this was a trick on the Jacob's part. But he looked down into the weak human's eyes, and there was no treachery there. He had given up his soul to chase after nothing but failure? The truth in it dawned on him and for a moment a huge sadness invaded Leavon. He had failed.

But sadness was an emotion that came from Michael De Rhy and Leavon had no time for it. He looked down at Jacob and hated him truly.

'One blow,' Leavon said aloud and clapped his hands with glee. The truth would die with the bearer, he thought, kill him kill him. He picked up a rock and grabbed Jacob by the collar with his free hand. 'Hold still now,' he said, 'this is going to be messy.'

'But what will happen to you now?' Jacob asked frantically vying for more time. To do what? He didn't know.

'Why, I'll come back again,' said Leavon, 'I'll find a way, no matter, no matter.'

'You won't survive, you're unnatural. You're not meant to be alive. Didn't you hear?' said Jacob. Leavon hardened and Jacob saw that he was truly mad.

'No more talk,' he said, and raised the rock above his head.

***

Rajette sat at the foot of the Cascade waiting for Leavon to come down and tell him what to do next. It was obvious that Jacob had not succeeded in killing the demon. Rajette's continued existence was proof enough of that. As he sat there the Palestinian thought about his life. He found that he was able to access his memories as if they were stored in well-organised filing cabinets. All he needed to do was reach in and pull them out. Obviously there were parts that were damaged by the passage of the bullets, but on the whole it seemed that everything that was not destroyed was easily recalled.

They shamed him, the memories. He would have thought that in the course of a whole lifetime he could have found something to be proud of. Yet there was nothing.

When he was a child the Israelis trundled into town one day with their tanks and rocket launchers, looking for a man that was high up in the Hezbollah. In true Israeli/American fashion the soldiers began to systematically destroy the town until someone told them where the man was hiding. Then they killed him and anyone standing within twenty feet of him and left. They killed Rajette's father that day, his uncle, and his two sisters; people trying to do what was right for their families, rather than protecting them from harm.

It was not this that caused the Palestinian's fall from the grace of Allah, not the actual random murdering. It was their faces, the faces of the Israeli soldiers as they carried out their

359

duty. They looked pious and smug, as though they *knew* that what they were doing was right, actually knew it. It was the same look he'd seen on the bastards faces his whole life. The Israeli people had suffered the holocaust and now they *knew* that they had the holy right to kill women and children, destroy families and communities because it had been done to them. And, did Rajette hate them for it? No. Did he say, fuck them, like many of his childhood friends? No again.

He wanted to be like them, wanted to feel like that. He wanted to kill, maim, and destroy with such pompous impunity.

'Oh God,' Rajette said aloud, 'why do I only see it now?'

It was too late for him to become a better person. He would need to be alive to do that. He was dead now, and not even properly dead. He was in between and would stay there until that *thing* up there on the waterfall allowed him to get on with dying, allowed him to go to hell, which was surely where he was bound, if it existed.

From the boot of the car there was a muffled scream and a banging sound. So she was alive and awake, he thought. Instantly Rajette felt something stir in him, some voice that whispered from the Earth. It told him that he could escape Leavon's clutches; that he would be repaid if he could do something in death that he would never have done in life.

If he could do something good, he would be set free, into the universe, just as the Italian feared.

~

There was darkness. Becky struggled and screamed with little effect, gagged and tied as she was. Through her hangover she tried to recall what had happened to her, how she'd ended up here. She remembered waking beside somebody, Jacob, and feeling nothing. She remembered getting out of bed and leaving the room in a sort of dream, except her mind had been completely clear. She must walk to the waterfall, that's what she had thought. Walk to the waterfall and bring a rope, and that was exactly what she'd done. Why? She didn't know.

Then she remembered meeting him and she began to feel even sicker. She'd gone to him and he'd been smiling.

'You are fixed,' she remembered saying, noticing distantly that he was no longer covered in wounds.

'Hello Becky on your own I see, Yes that's right, I've been feeding well,' Leavon had whispered, stroking her face and beginning to tie her up, 'thank you for noticing.'

Becky's skin writhed at the memory of his touch. She pulled at her restraints and cried out when she hit her head on something hard. Then she remembered climbing into the boot of the car without struggle and Leavon leaning in to tie her hands and feet together.

'He'll have to come now anyway, won't he?' Leavon had said, before closing the boot and letting out the darkness.

Jacob was going to come after her and then Leavon would have him. And, it would be her fault. How had she been drawn in so easily? How had Jacob escaped compulsion? He was obviously stronger than she had given him credit, if Leavon could just put her into a trance and bring her to him.

Then Becky feared the worst. How long had she been out? Were they finished already, was Jacob already dead? Leavon could right now be coming for her.

Suddenly everything was ablaze with light and Becky's eyes were burning. She felt her bonds being cut. Was this it? As her vision cleared Becky realised that, no it wasn't Leavon after all,

361

nor was it Jacob. It was a small-headed man with three eyes and he was holding something. What was it? No he wasn't holding anything. It was his fist.

Rajette punched Becky hard in the temple. Not hard enough to damage her badly, but just enough to put her out. When he was alive he would have enjoyed doing that, but he didn't any more. He did it only because it was the quickest way to do what he had to do. And so, bracing himself, he hoisted Becky over his shoulder, he knew that he would have to walk with her on his back, because Leavon would hear the car starting and the rescue would be cut short. Oh well, if that was the way it had to be done.

For the second time that day Rajette pointed himself towards town and began to hobble. He hoped that he could save her from the monster behind them. He also hoped that if he did he too would be saved, if not from an eternity in hell, then at least from this grey and minionistic existence.

He hoped.

***

Leavon brought the rock down on Jacob's head. He brought it down against reality, against all of his victims, in the vain hope that it would forge for him a new reality. One in which he was not a mere fool, tricked and betrayed. A reality where he could exist in this, his newest form, for all eternity.

The current reality however, felt that things were fine the way they were. The world didn't want the rules to change or to allow Leavon in and it was willing to do anything that it could to stop him.

Drastic measures had been called for. And, from the

powerful winds in the sky down to the tiniest creatures that skittered on the ground, those measures were being taken. It's amazing what an entire planet can do when it thinks ahead.

Pari Passu

At exactly the same time and exactly the same rate as the rock in Leavon's hand came down on Jacob's head, the Sunburst lizard made a break for freedom and darted from Jacob's breast pocket and onto the rock face between Leavon's feet.

The little creature stopped behind Leavon, confused for a second, and cast his darting glances about before deciding on a route and scampering away quickly upstream.

In the same moment as Leavon caught sight of the movement he jerked quickly around to smash the rock down on the lizard. He did this automatically because he was Leavon, and it was easier for him to kill the tiny creature than to let it run away. This was all he could ever be, a mindless killer.

So, he smashed the rock down on the Sunburst lizard with a powerful crack. But he missed and Sunburst avoided the mucky stone as it exploded on the spot that he had only briefly occupied. Leavon snarled and took another step after it raising his boot, this time attempting to anticipate his tiny prey's next turn. Down he stamped, but on the empty ground as Sunburst skittered up the riverbed.

And they were off. With a scurry-scurry here and a swift turn there, Leavon was always just out of reach of the lively reptile as he stamped down hard again and again too late to catch the Sunburst Lizard before he was off again, scampering upstream with Leavon in tow away from where Jacob lay, shocked at his sudden liberation.

Leavon roared with frustration, he hated the Sunburst

Lizard. Like so many other weak creatures on this earth it managed to survive against ominous odds. Insignificant animals were able to breed and prosper through adversity whereas as he, the powerful and intelligent hunter was forced to undergo such terrible hardships. It wasn't fair. The lizard would pay.

Leavon leaped after the reptile, Jacob now fully forgotten. All he wanted at that moment was to feel the wet squashing crack, as he crushed the lizard underfoot. He chased it up the riverbed, dashing staggering and stamping as he went, his yellow soul flaring orange in anger and glowing from his body.

Finally Leavon cornered the Sunburst lizard, as it turned back from a narrow crevasse in the stone and he was about to stamp down hard on the little creature's body when his scaly foe took refuge in the crevasse itself and ran down the vertical wall of it, with no respect for gravity. He was safe.

Leavon's fury grew to frenzy when he realised that such a vulnerable opponent had thwarted him, so he dropped to his knees and began to scrape at the rock with his bare hands. Why was this world so impossible to him? He was determined that it would not beat him. He was Leavon; he was supposed to be the first to return. He alone would be potent enough to make this world yield to him.

'I am in control!' he bellowed, 'do what I want!' This he shouted at the very earth itself before continuing to bang and scrape at the rock with every pound of strength. And, for a second he believed that the world had indeed begun to give way. The stone of the Cascades seemed to recoil from his bloodied hands and the ground began to shake.

'Aha!' he cried, his rage was so fierce that the earth itself was shaking beneath his might. He was the first one to return, Leavon, a new power. He could feel the thrill of it in his bones. The Earth was trembling beneath him, he felt truly great.

Until a voice, that of an old woman, piped up in the back of his mind.

The ground isn't trembling, she told him. It is shaking.

Jacob felt the vibrations too. After realising that his demise was not imminent Jacob watched in dopey amazement as Leavon chased the Sunburst lizard around the rocks atop the Cascades. Only when Leavon started to dig at the rocks screaming and shouting like a madman, the ground shaking beneath did Jacob realise what was happening.

Throughout the confrontation there had been a steady stream of water flowing thinly along the riverbed. It trickled down the bare Cascades and landed with large sporadic splashes on the uneven rocks below. This shallow flow had been soaking Jacob through as he lay there on his belly, waiting for his life to end. But now it had stopped completely. Why?

Jacob knew that this was odd. There had been too much rain for the flow to just stop so suddenly. And, coupled with the ground shaking, it made a connection in his brain.

He was reminded of a night drinking in his hotel room and how he'd watched the drops of whiskey join together the biggest drawing the smaller ones into it, because that was how liquid worked. The larger body attracted the smaller into itself. The stream of water had run dry. And, the ground was shaking. The two were linked.

The shaking had changed into a rumble, which is just a fancy way of saying that the vibrations were making noise. It was then that Jacob made the connection.

'Fuck!' Jacob exclaimed and scrambled to his feet making for the trees on the east bank of the former rapids. He knew that he had to get out of there quickly and in his haste he forgot about Leavon, but Leavon didn't forget about him.

As soon as he heard Jacob's exclamation Leavon abandoned his inane digging, recognising it for the folly that it was. He scrambled to his feet and cursed himself harshly for forgetting the sky-blue soul, the one who had brought him failure.

How could he? Had his desperation for any victory, clouded his judgement that badly? Valid questions, but Leavon wasn't asking any of them. He was focused once more on his target.

No more distractions. The sky-blue soul was going to die-die-die.

Jacob made slow progress over the rocks. He slipped and struggled whilst Leavon gained easily, bounding after him, oblivious to the shaking earth below. The would-be cheater of death was laughing and screaming while at the same time producing an intermittent screech that rattled Jacob's bones. But Jacob still was going to reach the trees first, whatever good it would do him.

Then the water arrived.

Two hundred yards upstream and closing fast, the wave of water approached at high speed. It was a giant ball of liquid, hurled from the Earth itself.

You are unnatural, it rumbled at Leavon as it bore down the riverbed towards him, loosing some of its ample load but the retaining its inevitable force. The very atoms of the wave were spurred on by gravity and the promise of more to come once they reached the waterfall.

The Cascades that would once more deserve the name.

Leavon paid no attention to the increasingly unstable ground or the huge body of water he would have easily been able to see if he had only looked to his left. He was only twenty yards from Jacob now who had just managed to climb from the empty riverbed and reach the trees on the bank.

He nearly had him. The sky-blue soul would again be at his mercy and he would prevail. Jacob had no chance. And, as Leavon ran on it seemed that his prey knew it too. Up on the bank it looked like the sky-blue soul had given up running and had wrapped himself around a tree in some final desperate plea for protection from his pitiful Earth. Well the chase was over now, thought Leavon.

The end had arrived.

Jacob watched; hanging on desperately, as the water smacked Leavon from his feet with immeasurable force. He didn't even see the demon/man's body go over the edge. There was no edge any more, there was only water, and it filled and overran the riverbed in a single heartbeat. Then almost with regret it reached and overran the trees where Jacob was clinging in vain.

In his last moments Jacob formed upon his face an expression of horrible despair. It was all he had time to do, before he too was plucked from his anchor and tossed out over the Cascades amidst the churning molecules of water as they hurried down to the hungry rocks below, flowing once more, to see what would happen next.

***

In Banfora, west of the rebirth of the Cascades, Eve was watching the Empty Man as he came down the street. He had a woman in his arms and he was staggering badly. Eve left the schoolyard fence and lifted her metal bowl, balancing it on her head with one hand and whipping a tear from her eye with the other. She ran over to them to see if she could help.

Coming to a halt, Rajette found his body had nothing left with which to propel it, so he did the only thing that he was able and he fell to the ground. Actually, it was more of a crumple than a fall because even with his last movements he tried to cushion Becky's fall with his own body. Then he just lay there with her on top of him, staring at the sky, hoping that now finally, he was going to die.

'Halo,' said Eve her little face appearing in his field of vision. Rajette recognised her as the girl who tried to sell him water earlier, the girl with the face of an old woman. What sort of life would she have, those intelligent eyes fading on the streets?

'Halo,' he said.

'Wata?' Eve offered, biting corner off one of her bag and holding it to his mouth. Rajette didn't stop her, he didn't need water but it felt good running down his dead throat. When the bag was finished he smiled at her and she smiled back. Such a beautiful and innocent child for a moment before the old woman returned. Rajette reached into his pocket and struggled to pull out his wallet. Eve had to help him, and he left it in her hands.

Although he was obviously giving it to her Eve didn't open the wallet until he told her to and even then she did it with slow nervous movements of her dry cracked fingers. The wallet was full of money, American money. It was enough to buy her a house if she wanted it.

'Take it,' Rajette told her, Eve shook her head frantically, she couldn't. 'Please?' he said, she looked hard into his dead face. He nodded, 'please, take it,' and she did.

~

Eve ran all the way home and gave the money to her mother, who praised god continuously and promised her that she could go to school any time she wanted, her father would regret the day he left them now…

Eve, being clever, kept some of the money hidden just in case the promise was forgotten. Because promises are forgotten often, and little girls like Eve deserve a future as much as anyone else.

~

After Eve left it took only a few more seconds for Rajette to die. Really die. And when he did, it was with one good memory to take with him. One good thing was probably not going to be enough to save him.

But it might be.

Recollections 21

The worst thing

Of all the horribleness that has befallen any man, I have experienced very little by the way of bone shattering cold or skin melting heat. I've never been so hungry that I was forced to eat another's flesh or been so overcome by anger that I struck out and killed a man. All the hurts in my life have been of the emotional kind. I have felt real sorrow at the loss of friends and even witnessing the hardships of other human beings.

On certain occasions I have been overcome by the desperation brought on by loving someone I could not see and been moved to hopeless internal screams and self-loathing by the inevitability of my own uselessness. But what follows this introduction is an account of my ultimate sorrow, the very worst thing that has ever happened to me.

And, as is normally the case, for I am nothing if not frustratingly normal, the worst has led me to my most profound and greatest discovery. I am no different from you or anyone else. As tired as it sounds, I am merely a human, but I feel also that I am an amazing thing and worth as much as everything in the universe and not a penny more.

The worst thing

By Jacob Terry

I was found lying on the roof of a black Mercedes a kilometre or so south of the Cascades of Karfiguela, my back broken and my brain suffering from lack of oxygen, a result of being drowned and re-drowned continuously until the waters had finally subsided and the car had become snagged on a fallen tree. It was painful and frightening, but it was not the worst thing that has ever happened to me.

What then, you may ask, could be worse than that?

To lie broken in a hospital bed, a smelly wretched thing, unable to control the organic contraption within which you still reside? It is terrible indeed to find that one side of your body lies unresponsive to the simplest command, and the other side, though responsive, only receives instructions that are random and humiliating.

Yes, this is an awful thing, but not the worst.

Is it then, to lie there twitching and soiling your sheets, as the relatives and friends are ushered in? To notice the quickly veiled disgust upon their faces when they realise that yes, this is the right room after all! This discoloured freak of thing is the one they have come to see.

Can it be worse to see that look replaced by grim determination? They will not turn away or cry out as you attempt to command your body, your face, and your lips. No, they look at you instead with miserable abhorrence in their eyes, with faces that would serve you better turned away. You try to thank them for coming, ask them to leave.

'I am still here inside this patient,' you shout, but it never comes out like that. Even when your mouth and tongue do answer your summons they disgrace you and never communicate. Now you feel the horror that comes with hearing the sound of a voice so unlike your own, but belonging to you nonetheless, jabbering and chanting forgotten snippets of muscle memory instead of voicing the real thoughts that are burning in your clear and perfectly conscious mind.

'Holy God holy God holy god put down put, put I, I, I, I, a left, a left ones so is blue, its blue, blue! A line tap, tap a line.

Teach! Teach!' The only thing you can make them understand is your desperation, as your wailing grows louder and less coherent.

'TYA THUSK OHN PHILLIP PETER SARAH, JOHNPHIPTERAH!' You are frightening them now, a sister bursts into tears, and so you stop and only stare.

You want to say: 'I am here. I am not finished yet. Please listen, please!' but there is nothing you can do. You are beyond yourself.

Can this be the worst thing that has happened in my life? Oh, very nearly, but not quite. There's more.

You can see your brother, his son, your friend and your enemy as they leave in disgusted hurry. Darting glances over their shoulders and asking under their breath. 'That's not him, that poor thing? That's not my friend, my son, my brother, surely? He's long gone. That's only a sick thing. Our Jacob is gone, that thing isn't him.'

Again you shout with the false words flooding out.

'I am here I am here! Oh Universe, help me please. If you think, kill me now, kill me and take away this despair. I am not broken; I see and hear them as they come and go. Can't you hear me? Haven't I hurt enough for one person?' Is there an answer? No, instead you feel the urine running down your 'good' leg and you go on pleading inside your imprisoned mind.

'You have to stop it. Was I bad, was I wicked? Did my soul hide sins so great from you that I deserve such punishment? Kill me! Kill me sister, kill me brother, kill me cousin. Friend, won't you do it? Strangle me before you go. Help me, I'm still in here, I can see you.'

But by now you know that you will not be released so easily. It will be slow. Oh so slow.

Surely *this* the worst thing, you can now justifiably ask? And, it was for a brief time, but you're not there yet. There is one more thing worse than all the rest. And, here it is…

Here she comes.

Becky, the love of your life has just walked through the door. You almost explode with anguish as she nears. You try again and again to wish yourself out of existence. You even try and close your eyes so that she might decide to leave this creature with its pain. Let it sleep. It isn't him. Let it rest.

But you are not granted even that small mercy. The eyelids, you see, they're not working right either. They flick up and down like those of a bashful cartoon dwarf. You can see perfectly, and she can see you, see what you have become. She bursts into tear.

Oh Becky, go away, you want to say, I can take the rest but this is too much. But you won't even try to speak, because you've heard how it will come out and you want to save her from that at least. Instead you lie there and you wait for her visit to end.

She was the one.

She was the one that used to speak to you with a waver of emotion in her voice, she loved you so. You used to find yourself regenerated in the beams of light you felt were coming from her adoring eyes. Yes, here she is, the one you loved, the one you still love, and her eyes are dead to you now; as dead as you are to her.

This is the worst thing. This has made your life forfeit.

'End it now,' you whimper as she mops your brow for duty, changes your sheet for memories, leaves you forever inside yourself, never to return.

'End it now,' you say, 'I am finished.'

But it does not end. You sink down away from them all, you've given up hope and your coma hugs you warmly, saving you from your thoughts.

And then, there is something else.

***

You see a boy in rags. He is running down a dusty road between ramshackle houses. He is jumping and skipping as he goes, humming under his breath and chatting to himself between verses of a made-up song. He is a happy child.

He has just finished working for the day, well, not really working. He spent the morning under his father's feet "helping", but now he's free to run around like only little boys can, recklessly and without worry.

All around the boy there are people moving slowly in the afternoon sun. This is a very hot place. The only way to get through the day in such a place is to move slowly and only when necessary. The merchants sit back and watch their wares shrivel even in the shade, and every purchase is accompanied by a long sigh and an appraising look that asks; 'do you really want to buy it? Because I'm not getting up if you don't.'

Carts that are far too empty move slowly down the road pulled my emaciated donkeys and led by the tired. This is a poor place.

But the boy doesn't notice any of this and remains happy. He is blind to the poverty he lives in and it will be another year or so before he notices that there is not enough food and that there is very little water. He has youthful energy that he will never have again in his lifetime. A power that in the future will only be replaced by the power of his will and the belief he will need to find in order to survive this barren climate.

For now, he is just running. He runs down the sandy road to the fences of the herdsmen, sometimes he stops in the middle of everything, panting and wide of eye, flushed from the heat and laughing loudly. He smiles at the weary women as they wash their sheets in dirty water, who forget themselves and their destitution for a moment to respond to the innocence and hope that this child emanates. They smile back at him and wave as he darts off again towards the corral at the other end of the village. He is going there to see the goats and camels because he loves them and because they always have time to play.

On arriving at the rickety enclosure the little boy climbs quickly over the bottom rung of the wooden fence that would collapse under the weight of any one else and runs up to his favourite white goat with the little brown head.

He has noticed something special about this goat in the last few weeks. Its belly is growing larger like that of his cousins before he disappeared, but unlike that sick young boy the goat is not lying motionless on the ground unable even to disturb the flies on her face. She is healthy and cantankerous, fighting a baaing at the other goats, knocking heads with the other females so much that Ramhel the herder has had to separate her more than once so she would not hurt herself. Ramhel always felt the she-goat's belly when he did this but the little boy wasn't sure why.

Today brown-head looks different to the boy. She is still prancing around among the other goats voicing her opinion in the goat's language, but her belly is a different shape. Reaching down the boy balances on the ground and rubs her stomach with his spare hand. There is something hard pressed up against her flank from the inside. The boy is surprised. The thing is round and hard and doesn't feel as though it belongs inside the brown-headed she-goat.

'What's this?' he asks her, 'did you eat a stone?' Brown-head answers him but he doesn't understand. Yet he is sure Ramhel will know.

So the boy rises and looks around for the herdsman and spots him outside his hut talking to another man. As the boy gets closer he realises that the men are not talking, they are shouting. He wonders why he didn't hear them before, but the thought is lost in his restless fleeting mind.

Ramhel the herder looks very angry. His face is red and he is spitting and jabbing his finger into the chest of the other man. The other man does not look like one of the villagers. He is wearing a small skirt made of leather and has a short sword tied to his belt, there's a metal hat on his head too. The boy remembers something.

'Soldiers!' he exclaims with delight.

The Roman soldier has a goat by the horns and is shouting too. His face is not red though and he looks haughty and confident.

'I can take what I want, herder!' he says and spits at Ramhel, 'and you should be careful not to anger me,' the soldier makes a move to leave and Ramhel stands in his way.

'You cannot take it,' he is pleading now, his anger gone, 'please I need that animal. At least buy it,' in one movement the Soldier draws his swords and sticks it in Ramhel's stomach. The herder slumps forward onto the soldier and their faces are nearly touching.

'I take what I want herder,' the soldier says and pushes Ramhel to the ground where he lies alive only momentarily, before dying with his eyes open.

The boy is frozen. He doesn't understand what has happened. He has played soldiers with his friends before so he waits for Ramhel to stand up again and attack the soldier who is walking away with the goat struggling in his grasp.

But Ramhel lies still and the boy decides to go to him. He shakes the herder and calls his name, but Ramhel doesn't answer. The boy finds that his hands are covered in blood and he moves Ramhel's head so he can see into to his eyes. They are dead. Ramhel the herder is dead.

The realisation of it stuns the boy. Most children would never be able to understand the enormity of what had just happened, but this boy, is not most children. He is special. This boy sees the emptiness ahead, the life that is now gone from the herdsman. There will be nothing more for this innocent man and the village will be robbed of his contributions. The endless swirling blackness of death tears into the boy and he breaks away from the body and runs screaming through the crowd of sad onlookers. For the first time in his life he feels that a ball of horrible desperation has formed in his stomach. He stops in the road and jumps up and down shouting as loud as he can for it to go away, but it doesn't. It never will.

Then he feels arms around him, his mother, comforting him, stroking him and whispering in his ear.

'Shh Joshua, it is alright, everything will be alright,' But he knows that it isn't. That it cannot be, alright ever again. But she continues all the same.

377

'Shh Jacob, it is alright, everything will be alright.'

***

You are back in your broken body and the air is filling your lungs in a giant gasp. This room is a different one, smaller than the last. You are in a room without a window, a place to store a body when it hasn't yet had the decency to die. They have given up on you and you suppose that this was the right thing to do. A death can be dealt with if not understood, but a living death is an unfinished book too difficult to read.

Something else has changed. You have been altered. You have grown to understand something that you could never have fathomed in your walking, talking, laughing, crying, living existence. You have relearned an important lesson. A lesson first given in an empty riverbed atop a giant waterfall, taught to you by the very Earth itself but forgotten in the pain that followed.

You will never forget it again.

Months later in your reawakened life and you feel yourself being lifted up by orderlies. You realise that you haven't been jerking and rambling like you were before, and that there are new thoughts, without desperation, stirring once more in your mind.

They bring you to a different room and put you in a chair. Every day for a week you sit in that chair trying to help them as they bend and manipulate your body. It doesn't seem to be working, but at least you are at peace.

Then one day it happens. As you sit in your chair watching other shadowy figures as they amble around on metal supports moaning and groaning with exertion, there is a flicker and a

378

sharp pain as the muscles of your arm are woken by a thought in your mind. This is movement and you did it on purpose.

You try and try but you can't make it happen again. You feel frustration instead of apathy, impatience instead of resignation. There is hope. The days pass painfully from then on as you try to wiggle a toe and then move a limb. Yesterday you said 'No' to an orderly as she tried to feed you the hateful vegetable that you've always despised. And, it had almost sounded like 'No' too.

A month later and you are struggling along a rubber path flanked by railings. Another two and you are home with your family. Every day people are smiling at you and chatting to you as though you are a real person again, and with each day your strength returns and you feel that, yes, you are a real person again.

A year from the time that you awoke from your coma you find yourself outside on your own, leaning on an old person's frame, out in the street, free at last. You feel great joy at being given the chance to control what is left of your body.

Young people hurry by, pretending not to notice, thinking, 'That will never happen to me,' and, 'I could not live like that,' some of them notice you are young too. These ones bless themselves or greet you sincerely. Others mock and laugh as you totter along. They are disgusted and frightened by you. You hear their taunts and you see it in their eyes, but it's all right, you don't care. Today your nephew sat on your lap and talked rapidly of Yu-gi-O or Captain something or other before running off to watch TV. You are part of the world again.

~

So finally, you have reached the end of my story.

Today I am outside shuffling along the footpath on my way to the park. It is a hot day and my brow is sweaty from exertion. The sun is touching the skin on my lop-sided face and I can feel it stroking me, wishing me well. It is a beautiful and wondrous thing, the sun.

Soon though I become tired and need to rest for a while. I choose a bench and drop my weary body onto it with a grateful sigh. From where I am sitting I look around at what there is to see. There is so much of it all around me, so much happening, so much meaning, it makes me gasp to realise it.

The world is still going on all around me and I am still a part of it.
I am still here. I am not finished.

The clouds of my despair have broken. I wanted to die once, but I did not. And now the world is here whispering to me as long as I remain, telling me over and over again to never forget the things that I have lost, the love that I once had. It tells me that everything has meaning and I find the pain and the joy of it to be inescapable.

Every second that I live on, is fresh, and perfect, and new. I know now why once is enough for anyone, that any more than that would diminish its meaning. I know it because I faced it that day atop the falls, and again when I was a broken thing. But most of all I understand it, because I am alive.

The Énd

For more information about
this author logon to:
www.eanna.eu

Printed in Great Britain
by Amazon

79674362R00222